Abby Wize: AWĀ

by Lisa Bradley

AuthorHouse™
1663 Liberty Drive
Bloomington, IN 47403
www.authorhouse.com
Phone: 1 (800) 839-8640

Published by AuthorHouse 08/27/2019

ISBN: 978-1-4520-2490-5 (sc)
ISBN: 978-1-4520-2491-2 (hc)
ISBN: 978-1-4670-4943-6 (e)

Library of Congress Control Number: 2010906941

Print information available on the last page.

Acknowledgments

This book is dedicated to Ahang Rabbani for planting the seed at Oklahoma Bahá'í School and to J.K. Rowling for causing the seed to sprout.

The author also wishes to thank God for all the prodding that made the plant bear fruit, her family for being part of the process, the Bahá'í Writers Group for encouragement; June Fritz for help with Esperanto; Justice St. Rain, founder of Special Ideas (www.BahaiResources.com), for support and assistance; Judy Selmer for the wonderfully childlike Appaloosa drawings; and Lucki Melander Wilder, founder of Earthstar Works (www.EarthstarWorks.com), my editor extraordinaire, smart-wallpaper programmer, and hard-question specialist.

Notes to my readers:

When I take you into one of Abby's dreams or daydreams, I show it in *italics* and set it apart with infinity signs: ∞

Songs are identified by a music symbol: ♫

The bold numbers in brackets – such as: **[1]** – refer you to notes near the end of the book. These *endnotes* contain information that may interest you…little extra somethings such as where an idea came from or the source of a quote. You can flip to each endnote while reading the story, or wait and read them all after you finish reading the story, or ignore them. Or ignore them the first time you read the book, and flip to each one the second time you read it (smile). Whatever way works best for you.

Most books, magazines, and websites in the story are detailed in "Resources"; some endnotes also refer to them. I can't guarantee how long the URLs listed in "Endnotes" and "Resources" will remain valid, nor the books in print. When typing a URL into your computer, be sure *not* to include the punctuation that follows it in the book.

Whenever a Yuter is whispering or speaking out loud, I show the words in a simpler style of printing that looks like this:

"Hello, Abby."

Lastly, when a person and a Yuter are *silently* conversing, I use dialogue dashes around their words instead of quotation marks, like this:

—Hello, Yuter.—

—Hello, Abby.—

Table of Contents

Chapter 1: Moony 1
Chapter 2: Riding... 7
Chapter 3: Home.. 11
Chapter 4: Church.. 19
Chapter 5: Packing... 27
Chapter 6: Driving 31
Chapter 7: Sofia 39
Chapter 8: Vacation 49
Chapter 9: Horseplay 55
Chapter 10: Bookstore 63
Chapter 11: News 73
Chapter 12: Flying.. 77
Chapter 13: Friend 81
Chapter 14: Town 89
Chapter 15: Library... 97
Chapter 16: Pollution.. 103
Chapter 17: Dream.. 111
Chapter 18: Service... 113
Chapter 19: Creation... 125
Chapter 20: Party 133
Chapter 21: Dragons 141
Chapter 22: Happiness... 155
Chapter 23: Deepening 167
Chapter 24: Animals 181
Chapter 25: School 195
Chapter 26: Lunch 211
Chapter 27: Return.. 213
Chapter 28: Phonecall... 221
Chapter 29: Reentry 233
Chapter 30: Sunday... 243
Author's Notes.. 251
Endnotes 253
Resources... 277
Counted Cross-Stitch Patterns 283

Chapter 1: Moony

Abby Wize had disliked her mother and loved horses for as long as she could remember. The two feelings fought for the turf of her heart, intertwined, interrupting each other. Her mother's random criticisms haunted even her peak equine times, and she often escaped Mother's tirades by floating into four-legged fantasies.

Abby could only conclude that Vivian Wize had hated her younger daughter right from the moment of her emergency Caesarian delivery. It explained all the attacks, arguments, and disapproval. Abby asked for a diary when she was eleven, so she could start documenting her childhood. Mother had apparently forgotten what it was like to be young and imperfect, and Abby didn't want to repeat her mother's mistake when she grew up and had kids.

Her father was no help, either. Paul was absent more than present – physically and also mentally. Whenever she tried to speak to him, he usually stared blankly at her. Occasionally he talked with her, really talked, which was very nice; but usually he arrived home just before the evening meal. If he'd had a bad day, he'd pick on the family at dinner. Really badly, if he'd had a drink or two first.

Yet this fog of unhappiness lifted when she went to The Ride Place for her weekly lessons. Abby loved it there. Lesson horses and private boarders' horses lived comfortably in pastures, paddocks, or pens, according to their owners' wishes. Tony, a high-school sophomore, was Abby's usual instructor. She admired his knowledge of horses.

Abby could now catch her assigned horse, groom it, put on the tack (Western saddle and metal hackamore), and lead the horse to the arena. Tony had hinted that Abby might next learn about feeding the horses. Abby was very interested in this, because the horses seemed to adore anyone who brought them food of any kind.

After her upcoming lesson, Abby would miss the next two, because her family would be vacationing with relatives in North Carolina, an entire day's drive from her home in central Tennessee. Abby already dreaded the thought of being confined in the car. At least she would have her older sister with her, as well as the new *Harry Potter and the Deathly Hallows*, which would be released just before their trip. She was counting on Harry to carry her through the dreaded drive. Mother had agreed to go buy the book, adding that Abby could only have it once they were in the car, not before. Abby accepted the arrangement, because she got only one dollar a week allowance – with half of that going for savings, college, or whatever Mrs. Wize decreed – and hadn't seen how she could possibly buy the book herself.

Mother had also told Abby to take a check to Tony at her next lesson. He'd phoned to say that the cash Abby had handed to one of the ranch workers had never reached him. He'd hinted that cash tended to disappear. Mother had strongly implied that it was all Abby's fault for giving the money to just anyone, and charged that "those no-good barn rats" were probably using her money to get drunk or high. Abby privately admitted Mother might be right, but was offended anyway. She also suspected some of them had spread rumors that she was stuck-up. Why else a few weeks ago would one of the newest, smallest riders have exclaimed, after Abby helped her with her horse, that *she* didn't think Abby was stuck up. No, Abby was just quiet, that's all.

On the Saturday before the family was to leave, Abby got up full of her usual anticipation for her riding lesson. She put on her underwear inside out so the seams didn't dig into her seat bones when she rode – she was sensitive that way. She dressed in her longest, most comfortable jeans, a belt, T-shirt, and her tall socks turned inside out so the seams didn't press into her toes, especially since her boots were getting too small. She'd been putting off telling her mother, as this was sure to cause a scene. She parted her hair down the middle, braided two pigtails straight down from behind her ears so they'd be out of her way, and then put on her combination sunscreen/bugspray. After eating her usual milky breakfast of Leprechaun Coins (sometimes it was Choco-Champs), she packed her water and sack lunch.

Barbara Curry and her daughter Chloë, who also took lessons at The Ride Place, arrived to drive her. Abby slid into the car and said hi to both. After riding in silence for a minute, Chloë asked her mother if she could listen to some music. When Ms. Curry said yes, Chloë turned the radio on. It played classical music. Chloë looked at her mother in a silent request to change the station.

"Hit the SEEK button," Ms. Curry said, looking over her left shoulder for a merge.

While unwrapping a crumbly Qwik Breakfast bar with all her other fingers, Chloë pushed the SEEK button with her left pinky. The radio spewed a man's voice singing seductively, "You're so hot, you make me want to do it all night, you make me want you…"

Ms. Curry squawked but was busy switching lanes. Chloë's fingers were now all occupied with her breakfast, and it took a moment to get her pinky freed up enough to hit SEEK again. So they all had to endure several more awkward moments of lustful lyrics, while Ms. Curry muttered darkly about the trash on the airwaves these days.

Chloë's second SEEK landed on a family pop station, which offered "Beautiful" by Christina Aguilera, "Unwritten" by Natasha Bedingfield, a Phil Collins song, an Avril Lavigne, a Jack Johnson, and an oldie by Journey. They hummed and sang parts of the songs, enjoying the last bit of cool before the summer morning heated up in Surely, Tennessee. Abby did not hum, though; her nose was usually all plugged up in the morning.

Ms. Curry pulled up at The Ride Place's office in the faded barn, Abby thanked Ms. Curry for the ride, and the girls got out. Tony and his helpers gathered all the riders, took their money, and began to name lesson horses. Whoever wanted to ride that horse spoke up. If two kids wanted the same horse, Tony flipped a coin. Informal; but it worked well and ensured that the kids rode a variety of horses.

Abby won Moony. Not her favorite but not the worst horse, either. He was fat and slow but didn't actually fight her like some of the other horses did. From a row of hooks inside the barn, she picked the halter with Moony's name markered in black on the wide, faded webbing. A short, bumpy, unraveling, cotton lead rope was attached to the old halter by a rusty bull clip.

Before going to find Moony, Abby went to the lounge to put her lunch in the refrigerator. The lounge was a crude addition onto the right side of the barn. Its doorless front was open to the elements, the floor was hard-packed dirt and, best of all, it featured a view of the horses in their yards. A ratty assortment of grungy old couches, chairs, buckets, boxes, and tack trunks provided places to sit.

One of the many things Abby loved about The Ride Place was that the lounge was always so very dirty. Of course, she probably ate as much dirt as food here, but it hadn't killed her yet.

No one else was in the lounge right now. Abby knew, though, that around midday people would take a break from the heat. She looked forward to that more than she dared admit to anyone; life with Mother had taught her that if she showed she liked something too much, it'd probably be taken away from her.

Abby left the lounge and, on her way to Moony's pasture, said hi to the riders she saw. She also saw two of the ranch's workers uncoiling garden hoses at one of the dry paddocks.

"Hi, Abby," they said without stopping their work. She thought she detected a slight "tone" to the boy's voice that might indicate he'd gossiped about her. Hard to tell. Nothing definite.

"Hi, Craig; hi, Liz," she answered, the halter and lead rope parked comfortably on her shoulder and tapping her leg as she walked. She had heard that those two were "an item" and wondered again if they'd kept her money after she'd handed it to Liz last week before lesson.

Tony passed her in a golf cart, pausing briefly.

"Got the right halter? Remember which horse you have?"

Abby proffered the halter that might once have been green but was now the color of sun, dirt, and rain. Tony peered at the fading letters on the halter and confirmed that it was the right one.

"Good job. Is everything okay?" He looked right into her eyes and she, suddenly feeling scrutinized, ducked her head.

"Yeah."

What a nice change to have a conversation without the verbal jabs her mother usually poked at her. Even though Tony was in a hurry, he was still friendly. She felt her chin and her spirits rise along with the sun and the thermometer.

Abby turned with an inner smile and headed for Moony's pasture. Passing Parker the Pony's dirt pen and two paddocks housing private boarders' horses, she slipped through the aged, wooden pasture boards and headed towards the blob she thought was Moony. Steadily ripping and chewing grass, he eyed her with no signs of pleasure or worry.

"Hi, Moony, ready for a ride today?" Abby asked.[1] She patted his roan hide heartily, put the lead rope around his neck, and hauled up on it. She held the halter open and slid it onto his nose, then flipped the longest strap over his neck behind his ears. She was understandably proud of how quickly she could let go of the crownpiece on his right side and grab it on his left side before it all slid off. A couple of years ago, when she had first tried to halter a horse, she had been totally un-coordinated and incompetent at it. The horses often got bored with the whole thing and tried to wander off before the job was done.

She was supposed to examine her horse for injuries before bringing it in. She looked at and felt Moony's mouse-brown nose, his face with black and brown and white hairs, then his thick speckled neck and wide flat back. His legs, black below his knees, seemed fine as well, as did his ample rump. His other side was also clear of bites and wounds. She headed towards the gate, holding the lead rope.

Moony didn't want to come. He didn't move.

Abby clucked and kissed and tugged on the rope but Moony just stretched out his neck and planted his feet. This was the part Abby was not so fond of. Horses were too big for her to force into obedience, but they often resisted. She wasn't sure what to do when they did this.

"Come on, Moony, we'll be late!" she said, frustrated. She pulled the lead rope way to his left, hoping to unbalance him. He took one step and then thrust his head down to eat again.

"Moony! Come *on!*" Abby cried out, then scanned the ground; but there were no sticks to hit him with. She did see a rock but was sure she would get in trouble for throwing it at him. And what if she cut him?

She circled around to the horse's right and pulled harder. Miraculously, this worked and he grudgingly relented, although he resisted the pull of the halter with every step.

Abby leaned as if into a strong wind, dragging Moony towards the rusty gate. She remembered to open it wide, but he still nearly knocked her over as he scurried through it. He did not like going through gates. Lots of horses at The Ride Place didn't. It was just how they were.

Still, her cheerfulness returned as she led him (on his left side, as she had been taught) to the barn; she had caught him all by herself and had the sweat popping out on her face to prove it. The humidity, always high in Tennessee in the summer, seemed especially bad today.

She spied a spot to tie Moony at the hitching rails on the left side of the barn, not too close to a red horse who was obviously upset from having stepped on its lead rope. Abby had seen it many times: horses panicked when they felt their heads were trapped. They flung up their heads and thrashed to get free. If they did this when they were tied, they could destroy the tie rail and hurt or even kill themselves. They were called "pullers"; Abby had heard that one of them had broken its neck, flailing like a trout on a line. They had shot it in the head right there at the tie rail, then buried it in the far pasture.[2]

Abby led Moony around the wide-eyed horse and unnerved student coaxing it back to the rail. She ducked low under the far end of the rail, careful not to knock off her white straw hat, and concentrated on tying the hitching knot correctly. She wasn't sure it was right but thought it would hold well enough.

She went through the big sliding doors with stapled flyers layered like badly done wallpaper, then turned left into the student tack room. There she found Moony's pad, saddle, hackamore, and bucket of grooming tools on the labeled post sticking out of the wall. She lugged the heavy leather equipment out of the tack room, trying not to trip on the dragging stirrups and straps. Just as she reached Moony, it all fell out of her hands and thudded to the ground in a pile.

Wiping her sweaty face with her T-shirt sleeve, she fished in the bucket and chose a round metal currycomb and an old grooming brush. She tried to do what she'd been told – curry in a circle and avoid the bony parts – but it was harder than it sounded and she earned a few glares from Moony as sharp metal teeth scraped the thin skin over his knees. She then plopped the saddle pad on his back, followed by the saddle, which was very hard to lift high and plunk on him. She looked at her handiwork and, deciding the saddle was too far back, pulled the pad and saddle forward. She was rather proud of getting the saddle on. If only Moony would stop swinging his head around, trying to bite her.

She knocked her hat askew reaching under Moony's belly to get the cinch, which was full of crud from the ground. She plucked off as much junk as she could, tied the cinch knot, unhooked the halter, rebuckled it around his neck as she had been taught, and slid the mechanical hackamore up onto his head.

There, Moony was ready for lesson, and she had done it all herself! "Ropes, straps, chaps, dopes," as Tony sometimes chanted. Though she hoped she was not a dope. And she didn't own any chaps, nor was she one...she wasn't sure which way it was meant. Cowboy sayings were like that.

After she led Moony a few steps towards the dirt track, he stopped, stretched his nose to his side, and seemed to be trying to chew through the faded, scratched leather fender of the saddle.

"What are you doing? You're going to hurt the saddle. Stop it!" she exclaimed and pushed his head forwards. He pinned his ears flat back against his head, and she slapped him for it. Never allow pinned ears or bad manners, that's what she'd been told. He paid her back by snapping his teeth at her hand, which she jerked away.

"Let's just get to lesson, huh?" she hissed. He chewed at the saddle once more and then walked on, ears only half-pinned.

Chapter 2: Riding

The lesson was very basic. Instructors checked student-placed tack, and saddled the newer riders' mounts as the awed kids watched. Tony said Abby had done everything right except that the cinch knot was twisted and backwards, but he decided it was close enough. Everyone then mounted from the left side of the horse.

"Everyone circle to the right, kick to walk, and a LOUD cluck!" Tony called from the middle of the dirt patch, where he stood with his two slightly younger helpers, Rana and Cory. The students, ranging from very small to very tall, did as they were told. The horses walked in a ragged circle. After a lap or two of walking to the right, Tony called out, "Ready to stop, everyone say 'HO!' and pull back on the reins!"

"HO!" rang out over the dirt track behind the barn. Horses in adjoining yards lifted their heads to watch. Several circling horses stopped and several did not.

"Shout louder and pull back harder!" Tony yelled to the students on the still-walking horses. Eventually all the horses were stopped.

"Everyone turn around and walk the other way! But wait until the horse in front of you is going, don't ride up on his butt!" Tony hollered. Some horses turned left, some right, and others not at all. "Make 'em go, show 'em who's boss!" he loudly chided.

After several circles at the walk, he yelled, "Everyone who's not ready to trot, come to the middle!" Three beginners steered their reluctant mounts to the middle; the remaining six kept on walking. "Ready to trot? Loud clucks, and kick! Kick! Kick!" he urged.

The six students obeyed, and the air filled with kissing and clucking sounds as hunched kids drummed their horses' sides. All the horses but one gave in to their riders' heels and trotted reluctantly. The lone holdout merely walked faster. He had not trotted in years; he was, however, an excellent confidence-builder for the beginners.

"Try turning while you're still trotting!" Tony hollered. Abby did her best to keep Moony trotting. He wanted to fall back into a walk at every other step, and she added whacking his shoulders with the ends of the reins to her heel action. She tried to turn while still trotting, but the horse felt this was unreasonable. Most of the other riders weren't having much better luck, Abby saw, so she didn't feel too bad.

"Make 'em trot; you gotta be boss!" Tony commanded. Abby tried again, in vain, wishing the reins were long enough to hit Moony's rump. But after a half-circle of futilely thumping him with her heels, she suddenly recalled pictures of cowgirls smacking horses' hind ends with their hats. So, despite Mother's "don't ruin your clothes" warnings in her head, she started to hit Moony's butt with her hat. That got him half-heartedly trotting for another quarter-circle. She was pleased at getting such good results and proud of thinking to use her hat. The instructors must've agreed, shouting, "Good job, Abby! Good job, everyone!"

Only one mare and her rider were up to cantering, so everyone else moved into the middle. At one cliffhanging point in its canter, the horse veered off track while the rider did not. But he clung to the saddle horn, managed to stay on, and eventually got control of the horse.

"Great start on your rodeo career!" Tony yelled out. "Calf roping or steer wrestling at the least, I'd say! Maybe bronc riding!" Ten-year-old Jimmy grinned, pleased to think he'd done something tough guys do.

Tony sent the group back onto the track to finish with two more circles of walking each way. Then everyone came back into the middle to have a friendly argument about which game they'd play. The candidates today were Duck Duck Goose, Rescue Race, and Keyhole. In two tosses, Tony's nickel chose Rescue Race. No matter what game they'd argued for, everyone cheered; they loved all the games they played.

Tony directed those with the slowest horses to go tie their mounts to the hitching rails again, sending Cory and Rana with the newbies.

"Put their halters on! Don't tie 'em by the reins! And tie 'em beside a friend! When you get back, stand in the partners line," he hollered after them. The remaining riders lined up their horses at the near end of the dirt patch, where Tony drew a line with his boot heel. then waited for the first couple returning kids to line up at the far end.

"First rider ready? First partner ready?" he hollered, looking at the first kids in line at both ends of the informal arena, then at his watch.

"*Yes!*" they both yelled back.

"Ready...*Go!*" Tony cried as the second hand hit the twelve.

The first rider whacked her horse into action, getting a trot fairly soon and heading towards the boy waiting on the far side. Everyone yelled, whistled, and cheered for the contestants. When the horse got to the line of partners, the rider – a girl of maybe fifteen – pulled hard on the reins, stopped the horse, and tried to figure out how to help the small boy up onto its high back. All the onlookers, even still-returning riders, laughed, hollered advice, and cheered as the kids struggled. At the end, the boy climbed up the rider's leg, holding onto her arm and the horn. He scrambled over her thigh to sit behind the saddle, holding its cantle. She turned her horse around and tried hard to kick him into a trot again. When this didn't work, she said something to the boy, who reached one hand behind him and spanked. They got a few steps of trot...and an enthusiastic reception back at the start/finish line.

"Three minutes and eight seconds! Awww-*rrriiiigghhttt!*" Tony pronounced grandly.

Abby was next.

"Ready...Set...*Go!*" Tony barked.

Abby set her heels into Moony's flanks and used her hat right away. Moony trotted well; she reached her partner, a tallish girl, in good time.

Abby had played this game before, so she told the inexperienced girl, "Here, Sarah, use my stirrup and grab my arm; get behind me."

On the third try, Sarah swung right up behind her! They were doing great! Abby turned Moony towards the finish line, then kicked him as hard as she could. Unfortunately, so did Sarah; and Moony broke into a canter.

Abby had never cantered on Moony, rarely cantered at all, and now found she was scared. If the horse obeyed at the canter as poorly as he did when being led, she was about to be run away with.

Well, at least he was heading towards the finish line; and if he didn't get pigheaded, they might even win.

Just then, she saw a funny shape near her right elbow. Sarah's face. The girl was leaning over and trying to see around Abby. There was a strange, slow, sliding sensation...a lot of yelling...the saddle slipping... no, no, it couldn't...yes, it *was* happening...they hit the dirt.

Abby hit face-first; her hat flew off when the brim hit the ground. She slowly got up, spitting dirt, testing what hurt the most. Time moved strangely, as if everyone were wading in syrup.

Sarah was not getting up...people were running over to where she lay...somebody caught Moony and shoved his saddle on top of him again...the girl was moaning...Abby spit more dirt and tested a tooth that felt funny...a crowd gathered around Sarah, who was lying twisted in the dirt...someone handed Abby her bent hat...Sarah got up slowly, still moaning...Abby assured people that nothing hurt too bad...everyone asked Sarah where did it hurt...the girl cried and held her left upper arm...someone shouted to call an ambulance or at least Sarah's mother ...Tony had the assistants make a human chair and carry her to the barn ...Sarah sobbed that as she fell, Moony's moving legs had kicked her, knocked her around, might have stepped on her...

Tony cancelled the game. He called to Abby to wait, however; and after giving instructions to several students, he said that her team had reached the finish line with a time of fifty-seven seconds before they fell. She had won a small first-place ribbon.

Abby took the ribbon and limped over to Moony. Tony asked her if she really was okay. He looked right at her again, and sounded truly concerned. She assured him she'd be all right. They followed the other horses, acknowledging the good parts of the lesson.

As she walked Moony back to his hitching spot, Abby discovered more aches in her right hip and leg from the fall, but felt pretty sure it would only be bumps and bruises. And a bent hat. Tony offered to have Rana take a look, but Abby thought it would probably be okay. Sarah seemed to have a broken arm at the least, maybe more. Tony dismissed it, saying riders broke bones, that's how it was.

At the hitching rail, they found that two horses had changed their minds about being friends, kicked at each other, pulled back, and one had stepped on and broken her reins. That was bad; she was wearing a bit and could've hurt her mouth. Tony grumbled about getting in trouble for the broken tack, and blamed the new students for not tying the horses' leads correctly. But Abby knew the lead ropes were stiff and hard to tie tightly.

Abby tied Moony and unsaddled him, looking at where Sarah had been sitting when she kicked Moony "from the back seat." How stupid! Like standing up in a canoe – one of the basic safety rules that you did not break. And then leaning over; that was doubly dumb. But it would be terrible if she were badly hurt. Didn't anyone tell the new kids how to do things? Someone should've. And what about the saddle knot that wasn't right? Tony had said it was okay, but the saddle had slipped. Gee, what else wasn't being taught right around here?

Abby walked Moony back to his pasture, lost in wondering if Tony had missed some important things with the kids, herself included. She snapped to awareness as Moony's heels barely missed her head when she turned him loose and he spun, kicked, and bolted back to his buddies. Two close calls today, she thought darkly.

The kids, gathered in the lounge, seemed intent on ignoring today's incident. They tried not to watch as Sarah's mother picked her up to take her to the hospital. Then they went out of their way to tell ridiculous jokes and play boisterous games with the barn cats.

Abby's back was hurting now, along with her leg; but she figured she should just tough it out, the cowboy – or cowgirl – way. Sitting on a dusty tack trunk, she ate her bologna-and-cheese sandwich and potato chips. Absentmindedly loosening her hat's tight hold on her head, she remembered the dent in the brim. It didn't bother Abby; after all, many hats were sold pre-distressed. But Mother always wanted things to be so tidy and fashionable. No, Abby had better hide the hat when she got home. If Mother saw it, she was sure to attack Abby for it. And what if she said it was ruined and threw it away?

Abby's silently swirling thoughts touched on other realizations she didn't feel she could share with the overly rowdy riders: that Sarah had caused her own injury, that all of them might likely get hurt and, wonderfully, that she'd won her first-ever riding ribbon!

Chapter 3: Home

The Currys dropped Abby off at her red brick house on the corner. Climbing the concrete front steps, she passed between black metal handrails sheltered by large pine trees on both sides. The basement garage's short concrete driveway led to a side street. Around back was a nice-sized yard with two young maple trees, but Mother didn't allow anyone to climb the slender trees or play near her flower beds.

Happy, hot, and hairy from the horses, Abby paused to prepare herself for what awaited her. She repeated the mental inventory she often took, looking at herself through Mother's critical eyes. Today, she did not pass inspection. Mother hated anything unpleasant. She didn't mind getting Abby out of the way, especially when someone else drove her, but she never liked the dirt her daughter brought back from the ranch.

Abby's only hope was to get inside quickly, hide the bent hat, clean up fast, bury her filthy clothes in her hamper, and hope to be presentable and blank-looking before dinner. She wiped her booted feet on the grass, and then again on the cement walkway to get any grass off, but they were still dirty and would smudge the carpet. She sat on the top step to take them off. Her socks were almost as dirty as her boots. She debated, then took them off as well.

Hat on, socks and boots in hand, she quietly opened the screen door and slowly pushed the front door open.

Her older sister, Jennifer, was watching TV in the large open living room to the left. If Abby was lucky, Daddy would be away working extra hours and her mother would be downstairs sewing or out in the back yard. Jenn looked up and Abby waved a small hi, crossed the flagstone-floored entryway, and tip-toed barefoot across the Berber carpet to see what Jenn was watching.

It was the old movie *Hook*. One of the Lost Boys was telling Robin Williams as Peter Pan that he needed to find a Happy Thought to fly. Abby touched Jenn on the shoulder. Jenn touched her hand in return, a small, silent gesture of affection.

Abby headed down the carpeted hallway that split the house. First she passed the doorway into the kitchen on her left, then walked cautiously between the doors leading left to the basement (always open), right to her sister's room (always closed), left to the big bathroom (open unless in use), another left to her door (usually open) and, opposite that, her parents' room (preferably closed). Today her parents' door was open and Mother looked up sharply as she passed. Abby saw the tallish, dark-haired woman bolt off the bed towards her. Only the fact that apparently Daddy was asleep made Mother hesitate and quietly close their door. Then she sprang to angry life again.

"You're filthy!"

Abby was busted. The fastest way out was straight through, as unpleasant as that was.

"I'll just take these off and get—"

"Not on my carpet, you won't!" Mother lashed out. "Go to the bathroom and take them off...no, it'll get the bathroom floor dirty and I'll have to clean that, as if I don't have enough to do! Stand in the tub to undress. Shake everything out in the back yard. What did you do to your socks? They'll never come clean! They're *ruined*, Abigail Clift Wize! You have to throw them away. What else did you ruin with those beasts today?" She jabbed at Abby's chest as she ranted.

They were not beasts, they were the one good thing in her life. And Abby didn't know why Mother complained about cleaning, since she made Abby clean everything. To be dramatic, probably. While Mother crabbed about Abby being a drama queen with her allergies and sensitivities, Abby privately thought Mother was the one who made such an overblown deal out of stuff. But she'd get her head chopped off if she ever hinted at having such a thought.

"Nothing, Mother, I'll get started now."

"Don't you lie to me, young lady. Look at your hat! What did you do, beat your horse with it? If you don't straighten out that hat *and your act*," she pontificated with sternly folded arms, sounding proud of her verbiage, "we may have to reconsider this horse-riding business."

Mother was really on a roll; best to get away as quickly as possible, before she guessed how close her accusation was...or made good on her threat right then and there. So Abby sidled away into the bathroom, not daring to turn her back on Mother in case that would escalate her wrath, but not willing to actually back away as that seemed too servile.

Mother had apparently gotten enough of Abby's hide, as she finally let her go.

After trying to straighten out her hat brim, then carefully wiping it with a damp washcloth and setting it on its crown on the sink counter, she undressed inside the tub. Mother had given her the ultimatums, but had not said exactly how to do them. Hmmm...somehow Abby had to keep the dirt off the floor as she took the dirty things outside. Wrap 'em in a towel? Then she'd get in trouble for the dirty towel. Turn 'em inside out? A hassle with the jeans. Turn one inside out and put the rest inside it? Best yet. She turned the T-shirt inside out and folded the jeans inside. Socks tucked on top of jeans. Boots perched on top of the pile.

Now to take a shower. Pull out a towel and place it by the tub so as not to drip on the floor. Turn on the water. Wait for it to reach the right temperature. Look around while waiting.

The house had been built in the '60s, when earth tones were "in." Vivian had redone it in more modern shades of mint green, pink, and peach. The large frameless mirror over the window reflected shoulder-length, slightly wavy, red-brown hair surrounding a lightly tanned face sparsely sprinkled with freckles; a somber mouth of good proportions; green eyes with bright yellow flecks and large black pupils; and average ears with one pierce each. No zits. Dirty face. Dirty neck, too.

Mother occasionally said things like: "You are such a pretty girl, Abby, why don't you do something with your hair?" Or: "Be grateful you have such a clear complexion; take care of it." Somehow it never felt like a compliment, and Abby distrusted that she was pretty. She leaned closer to look, really look, at the eyes that she doubted were as attractive as Mother claimed. Normally she avoided looking directly in peoples' eyes; it seemed to provoke the people she knew. She forced herself to keep looking past the point of comfort, and fell into the large black pools that grabbed and held her.

"The eyes are the window to the soul," she'd heard. Was that what now commanded her attention? Hesitantly, doubtfully, she looked and saw…something like the vacuum of black space, with Forces moving, plotting, fighting. She pulled herself back before she became truly terrified. She had to shake her head to get rid of the very disturbing feeling that such awful turmoil lived within her.

Stepping into the back of the out-of-fashion tan tub, she washed all the horse dirt and happiness down the drain.

Half an hour later, showered, redressed, and the bathroom cleaned, Abby headed toward the back yard with her dirty clothes, holding her boots just above them, but found her mother passing in the hallway.

"Come set the table, Abby," Mother said without preamble.

"Okay," Abby said, and followed her mother down the hallway, not too closely, eyes down.

"We are having cold tuna salad on a bed of lettuce," Mother dictated. "The red and white dishes should set things off."

Abby knew that she was referring to the pleasing colors of the foods against the plate, not to emotional outbursts.

"Which glasses?" Abby asked.

"The usual…no, set out the clear ones. There's a slight blue tint to the usual ones that would clash with the red in the dishes. It's past Fourth of July, after all." Mother turned into the kitchen. Out of the corner of her eye, Abby saw Vivian smiling at her own joke. As *if* it were all that funny. Abby set the clothes just outside the back door, out of sight…but not out of her mind, unless she wanted to incur some nasty punishment for leaving them there.

After quickly rinsing her hands, she reached above the sink and got down four dinner plates. She wondered how many other thirteen-year-olds in Tennessee knew the difference between dinner plates, luncheon plates, salad plates, and saucers. Not too many, she guessed, although it was actually pretty easy; each was smaller than the last. And the thing about which fork to use when they gave you more than one…usually just start from the outside and work inwards with each new dish. If in doubt, watch the hostess and copy her.

But deep down Abby often felt that, no matter what she did, she was going to get in trouble for breaking some rule. Mother seemed to expect her to know things without being told. And there were a *lot* of rules! Mother regularly reminded her that they came of High French Breeding and that People With Class *Knew* These Things. Abby simply knew that she wanted not to be yelled at so much.

But no one would know they were of Good European Ancestry if they looked at the faded orange metal cabinets around three sides of the kitchen. It had been the height of fashion in the 1960s, but now it was outdated. And since her dad was Scandinavian, Abby herself was only half French. She had been hoping lately that Mother's holier-than-thou attitude had not rubbed off on her. But if she *was* snobby, maybe she'd be the last to know it, wouldn't she? She despaired whenever her thinking took her down that kind of road, so she usually avoided it.

The fourth, far side of the kitchen used to open into the back yard through the back door, but that wall had been removed and a sunroom added. Mother claimed the low, east-facing counter for her work desk. Her papers spilled onto the breakfast bar. Too bad for Abby, who had thought it would be neat to sit on a high stool to eat. Instead, she often ate at a small round table placed in the middle of the sunroom. Still, it did allow the diner to enjoy the trees and flowers through the sliding glass doors opening into the back yard. And in winter, snow sometimes swirled like in a snow globe.

Abby shut the cabinet door, slowly turned around with her load, and walked carefully through the door opposite. She laid the place settings on the dining room table, where the family ate together.

Silverware, napkins, salt and pepper shakers, salad dressing cruet on its saucer, all had to be brought in trips. Then report to Mother, who was washing large leaves of head lettuce at the sink. Meanwhile, Jenn had been asked – meaning told – to make the tuna salad on the kitchen side of the breakfast bar, away from Mother's papers.

"Is there anything else?" Abby asked, eyes down, voice low enough not to be called impertinent but loud enough to avoid being labeled…

not loud enough.

"Yes, Abigail, please go tell your father that it's time to eat. He is in the bedroom resting."

"Okay," Abby replied obediently in the same monotone.

Daddy didn't normally sleep during the day. The bedroom door was still shut, and she wasn't sure what to expect. She tapped softly with the back of her hand. No answer. She tapped a little louder.

"Daddy?" she called.

A grunt answered her.

She didn't know whether to open the door then, as he always did with her door, or not. She decided that as the child she should not open it without permission.

"Mother says it's time to eat," she said in a voice she thought would reach him through the door.

She heard another grunt and his weight moving on the bed. She still hesitated, not knowing if she was supposed to wait or go, and decided to split the difference by watching from her room.

She wandered over to her windowsill, where several dusty model horses posed on the wide ledge. Daddy was still not coming out, so she cleaned the dustiest, a small flocked gray that came with its own plastic brush.

Daddy finally exited his bedroom wearing jeans and a polo shirt instead of his usual business suit. He looked normal: wavy brown hair combed to the side, large green eyes accented with bags and lines, and mouth formed carefully into a patient, neutral smile. He met her eyes and must have guessed what she was wondering, because he said, "I did not sleep well again last night and was tired today. So I took a nap."

She nodded and followed his medium frame down the hall, through the living room, and into the dining room. Jenn and Mother sat waiting at the dinner table, with the sunroom's sliding doors showing the fading daylight behind them.

The family sat and Daddy intoned, "Bless us, oh Lord, and these Thy gifts which we are about to receive. Amen." Sometimes Daddy said a different grace, from the Lord's Prayer: "Give us this day our daily bread, and forgive us our trespasses. Amen." But Abby liked one better that, ironically, she'd learned at church camp: "Rub-a-dub-dub, thanks for the grub, Good God, let's eat!" She recited it silently now and allowed herself to remember some of the good times there.

Her memories of camp sometimes supplemented her horse fantasies. Hiking, swimming, softball, Capture the Flag, crafts and, every year, an operetta performed for the parents. No horses at church camp, though. But Girl Scout camp had had them; she'd earned her Horse

Lover and Horse Rider badges there.

When she slipped into those memories at the table, though, Mother sometimes caught the vacant look on her face and told her to get her "head out of the clouds." She wondered if her spacey face looked any different when she recalled standing on the stage, terrified, her lines completely forgotten in stage fright; or nearly drowning in the church-camp lake; or the reports that some of the girls had kissed one of the guy counselors.

Mother's typical dinner conversation usually ran along the lines of: "Elbows off the table, Jennifer; it's bad manners." Or: "Abigail, only vulgar people chew with their mouths open." Abby usually anchored her left hand under her left thigh to keep it off the table. She kept her head down except when spoken to. Her right hand held her fork except when she was cutting food; then she held her turned-over fork in her left hand, tines angled downward, and cut with the knife in her right hand. Her mother had told her this was the European way and was thus superior to the crude American fashion of holding the fork straight up and down in the left hand. Abby knew how to pile the cut food onto the back of her fork and, still with her left hand, bring it to her mouth without spilling anything. Of course, when she had to use a knife at school lunches, she just did what her friends did; she did not want to be labeled "weird."

Near the end of dinner, Mother asked, "Paul, how was your nap?"

"It helped," he said. "It's been harder and harder to sleep right."

Abby regarded him for a moment, wondering what this would mean for the family. She couldn't tell. She cleared the table when dinner was over, and Jenn did the dishes; next week they would reverse the chores.

After dinner, Abby made a point of shaking out her clothes where Mother would see her do it. She banged her boots together to knock dirt and grass off. Was she supposed to take them back to her room? Or try to leave them outside? "The Nazi" had not said. If she guessed wrong, she'd get more venom. She thought the solution least likely to get her in trouble was to fold the clothes up and put them in her hamper, the boots on newspaper in her closet. Preferably keeping them out of Mother's awareness. Vivian seemed to forget about things she didn't see; Abby counted on that a lot.

Abby escaped into her reading nook, the little space between her bed and her bookcase. That kept her old-quilt-covered bed neat, as Mother wanted.

She was almost done rereading *Harry Potter and the Order of the Phoenix* – the one she'd least understood – in preparation for #7. She had especially enjoyed the part where Harry and his friends rode on the

flying thestrals. It must be a lot like galloping on a horse, as she sometimes dreamed about doing. When it was windy, she imagined that she
was going fast. With today's experience cantering on Moony, it would
be much easier to imagine, if only she erased the disastrous bit about
being scared and falling off.

Harry had no parents – just two close friends – and suffered at the
hands of the Dursleys. Abby had two parents, but often felt her treatment was just as unfair. She, too, had only a few friends: her sister Jenn;
Chloë Curry at riding; Grace, Kendra, and Maria up the street; and the
girls at church…who didn't really count because that's the only place
they saw each other. She, too, never had friends over; it was too hard to
make sure Mother wouldn't go off her rocker about some tiny thing.

Harry had adopted Dumbledore as a kind of grandfather figure, but
seemed to switch between being angry with him and adoring him. Abby
would have been delighted to meet Dumbledore, let alone have him as a
grandfather. She knew J.K. Rowling had just imagined him; surely no
one could be that funny in real life, that smart, that…*everything*. Still, it
was fun to pretend he was real.

Abby had never known either of her grandfathers, which made her
sad. Lois, Daddy's stepmother, lived in Florida, where they had visited
her several times. Granny, Mother's mother, lived in New York; and
having moved from there several years ago, they'd gone back last year
for her seventieth birthday. Between the two, Abby was much fonder of
Lois, who was much nicer and who bought one piece of Abby's silver
pattern every birthday and Christmas, as did Mother. By the time Abby
got married, she might have eight complete settings, something Mother
felt was essential.

At least Abby had her sister Jenn, while Harry only had that awful
Dudley. He was a Dud, all right. But Abby and Jenn got along pretty
well. They'd played with Barbies and other toys in the basement, back
when it was a playroom. They'd gone to neighborhood kids' houses
together, and to the closest swimming pool; and when Jenn got interested in boys, they compared notes. Abby was not nearly as interested
in boys as in horses, however; and at ages thirteen and sixteen, Abby
and Jenn weren't quite as tight as they had been.

Leaning against her bed, Abby finished her book. While sliding it
into the bottom drawer of her bureau, she saw her diary, pulled it out,
and wrote a quick entry about the riding accident. Then she started her
laundry in the basement. She'd dry and pack it tomorrow, ready for tomorrow night's car-loading so they could leave early Monday morning.
She went to bed at nine o'clock, after calling "goodnight" down the hall
and hearing the same words echoed back.

That night she dreamed that she called a Pegasus to her by raising a shining halter in the air...

∞   ∞   ∞   ∞   ∞   ∞   ∞   ∞

... it flies down to her, glowing gold in the sun ... bows for her to mount ... they rise up and fly over trees ... buildings ... lakes ... she senses the houses where other girls are in trouble ... shoots bolts of power to them from her hands, which turn warm ... the warmth spreads to her whole body ... the winged horse is one with her thoughts, turning as she looks, slowing when she wishes to slow ...

∞   ∞   ∞   ∞   ∞   ∞   ∞   ∞

She always loved the dreams where she mastered beauty and control and power...so unlike her real life.

Chapter 4: Church

Sunday morning brought church, heat, and humidity. Abby ate her usual breakfast cereal in her PJs, took care of her laundry, and took the suitcase her father handed her. Reaching into her closet, she pushed aside her favorite peach skort, knowing Mother would criticize it as being too casual for church. Instead, she took out a short-sleeved yellow summer dress with small flowers on it, matching sandals, and her biggest gold hoops for her pierced ears. It would be a sunny day, so why not wear sunny colors!

At least the dress covered the bruises on her legs from yesterday's fall. She definitely would not bring it up to her family, and would rather not give anyone a reason to find out. She located her prayer book and her yellow straw hat, and went to wait in the living room.

Jenn was just coming in, too. They gave each other the once-over.

"Nice dress, where'd you get it?" Jenn asked with a growing grin.

"Best place in town," was Abby's quick and practiced reply with an identical grin. It was a standard joke between them, as many of Abby's nice things were hand-me-downs from Jenn. Neither of them minded it. Mother prided herself on her sewing abilities, and she even made them matching or coordinating outfits on occasion. Abby's favorite was the matching super-fancy Easter dresses – from a Daisy Kingdom pattern – with coordinating shoes and hats.

Mother often drafted the girls to sew with her. Jenn enjoyed it even though she felt the same towards Mother as Abby did. Jenn must have thicker skin, Abby decided, as she seemed to feel sewing with Mother was worth the bad parts. Jenn wanted to learn more and to use the large stash of interesting fabrics in the former playroom, now the sewing and family room. Jenn had made cloth toys, bedding, dresses, even shirts; and she said that this winter she was going to learn how to make down-filled vests. Abby believed her. But Abby disliked how picky Mother was, and how hard the projects were. Pleats, interfacing, darts, ruffles, buttonholes…weren't there easier sewing projects?

Jenn wore her latest creation, a simple dress made from a baby blue T-shirt attached to a pieced skirt. It set off her blue eyes well. She had completed her outfit with Huarache sandals, a straw purse, dangly chain earrings, and a simple plastic barrette in the straight brown hair that fell to the middle of her back. She looked comfortable but stylish sitting in the reupholstered armless chair in the living room, leafing through the current issue of the *Keepsake Quilting* catalog.

"Look," she said.

Abby took the catalog and saw a quilt made of horse pictures.

"Neat," Abby replied, looking closely at the small photo. Horses of several breeds in various poses adorned the center of the quilt. Border panels depicted horse-related items such as saddles and bridles. The catalog said that directions came with the preprinted fabrics.[3]

"Wow!" was all she could add. She did not know whether or not her single-sized bed with the old, tattered, hand-me-down quilt was the right size for the 55-by-80-inch beauty pictured in the catalog. Still, she was sure she could find a place for the tan, green, and brown work of art in her room, whether Mother approved or not. But seventy dollars. That seemed like an awful lot of money to Abby.

She slowly handed the catalog back, imagining owning that quilt, maybe enjoying it in her reading nook. Her eyes followed the picture as it went into Jenn's waiting hands, so she did not see how closely Jenn watched her reaction.

"Thanks," Abby said, coming back to reality. Rather than to move Mother's current knitting project from under the brightest lamp, Abby chose an empty spot on the couch's far end. She surveyed all the neatly displayed magazines on the coffee table. Mother ordered them mainly for looks, but Abby did like a couple of them: *Muse*, a kids' science magazine, and *Reader's Digest* for the jokes. The *National Geographic* on top showed a scary-looking man with slightly bloodshot, scowling brown eyes, looking out over the big gray word "Pakistan." He gave Abby the shivers.[4]

Abby picked up the magazine to see what the man on the cover was so angry about. She flipped past the current downloadable screensavers and paused briefly at "Culture." This issue showed pictures of foods unique to different regions of the US. Nothing was listed for Tennessee but North Carolina enjoyed "Livermush – pig parts and cornmeal fried in a block." Abby wondered if she'd be expected to eat it during their vacation. She quickly turned to the cover article.

Pakistan was portrayed by poor people and war, but a horse caught Abby's attention. Slightly blurry, framed between a rifle, a dangling strand of bullets, and a soldier's arm, it was harnessed, probably to a cart. Was it an Arabian horse? What breeds did they have there?

Abby liked horse-breed books. She owned two, and checked others out of libraries. What was the name of the bony kind from the Middle East? This dirty-gray horse might be one of those. Its mouth was open; was its driver pulling hard on the reins? It looked like it was straining to trot; was the load too heavy and the driver forcing it?

Abby had once seen a "joke" photo that she didn't find funny at all – a small donkey suspended in midair by its harness, strapped to a cart piled ridiculously high and tipped up onto its back edge. Were so many animals in other countries overworked and underloved? Abby did not know if she could tolerate a working animal not being cared for right. She suspected she wouldn't make a very good Peace Corps volunteer.

Mother interrupted her thoughts, announcing that it was time to go. Abby and Jenn put down their reading, stood up, and straightened their clothes for Mother, who wore a loose, lavender-colored linen skirt with a short-sleeved, silk floral blouse and low brown heels.

"Change those ludicrous earrings, Abby! Do you want everyone to think you're uncultured?" It was just amazing how Mother could wrap so much venom into a mere sentence or two, Abby thought viciously as she went down the hall to put on her smaller gold hoops. Her cheerful earrings were ludicrous, she was uncultured, and "everyone" would think she was trash. Good morning to you *too*, Mother.

The two girls followed their parents downstairs, turned right at the bottom, and entered the cluttered indoor garage. All the outdated and unattractive things were gathered here: boxes of Daddy's old papers, dishes that Mother had tired of, chairs waiting to be refinished...there was no room for the family's two cars, which stayed in the driveway.

Jenn hoisted up the heavy garage door, and Daddy joined them at the silver four-door coupe in his white open-throated polo shirt, khaki-colored dress pants, and brown woven dress shoes. Mother had bought them for him. In her most resentful moments, Abby felt that the family was all Barbies and a Ken, with Mother playing house and dress-up on them. It made her feel like a thing instead of a person.

Abby headed for her customary spot, the back seat on the passenger side, behind her mother. As her seated mother carefully arranged her own skirt so that the crisp linen would not wrinkle too badly during the drive, Abby opened the back door, pressing her right hand on the door frame for leverage. Suddenly, Mother pulled shut the front passenger-side door faster than Abby could jerk her hand away. Her pinky finger was trapped between the front door and its frame.

"Ow! Ouch! Ooowww!" Abby began to howl in pain. She could not twist around far enough to open Mother's door with her left hand. But Mother merely stared at her daughter's unseemly outburst.

"The door! Open the door!" Abby cried through her pain, barely getting the words out. Her swelling finger felt like it was being cut off.

"What's the noise about?" Daddy demanded on Mother's behalf.

"My finger, my finger!" Abby would have sunk to the ground from the unlivable pain shooting up her arm and shrieking in her brain, but the door held her immobile.

Mother looked at Daddy. "Paul, would you see what's the matter?" she scowled, angry with the delay and the breach of social etiquette.

Jenn said loudly and calmly enough for the adults to hear, "Mother, her finger is caught in your door; she needs you to open it."

"Oh! Why didn't she say so?" Mother was irate at the commotion in general and at Abby in particular.

Vivian opened her door and released Abby's finger. Blinking and wiping her eyes, Abby could barely see her hand through her tears. Pain shot up her arm with every heartbeat. The pinky was swollen and growing purple, nearly black in a deep crease across the middle bone.

"Well, if it's not bleeding, get in and stop crying about it!" Mother ordered impatiently.

Abby resented her mother for not examining her possibly broken finger; but it wasn't bleeding, and no one seemed to consider changing the church-going plan. Abby would have to figure out during the drive whether or not any bones were broken. She did her best to stifle her sobs, even though her finger was hurting even worse...throbbing, continuing to swell, the purple spreading. She slid into her seat, took the tissue Jenn offered, and quietly sucked on her finger, not knowing what else to do. It hurt a lot, even worse when she tried to bend it. She knew she'd get an earful, though, if she said anything more about it.

The drive took twenty very long minutes. She suffered in silence. Jenn didn't dare say anything, but gave her sympathetic glances, once mouthing "You'll be okay, Abs!" When Abby finally leaned back into the seat, face wiped of tears, eyes closed, trying to manage the pain, Jenn held her good left hand. Once, when Abby tried resting her hand on her thigh, Jenn tapped Abby's arm, then held up her own right hand in front of herself to model the idea: "Hold it up, not down in your lap." She was right; it throbbed worse when it was down.

Daddy parked the car in one of the slots around the huge building of blond, rough-cut stone. Abby knew Mother required her to appear as normal as possible, so she quickly experimented with different poses to hide her smashed finger. The best answer seemed to be hiding it behind her prayer book at waist height. Jenn glanced stealthily at her as they followed their parents past the carved wooden doors that stood open, inviting them into the T-shaped old church.

St. Zosimo's was an Episcopal church, one of the oldest and most respected in Surely, Tennessee. Straight ahead glowed a huge rosette-shaped window of stained glass above the elaborate marble altar. Ranks of organ pipes flanked the altar. Under them, choir stalls faced each other, with the organ console to the right. Plain wooden pews held the congregation. Daddy led the family up the center aisle, found an empty pew, and slid in. Daddy bowed and the females curtseyed, all making the Sign Of The Cross on their chests.

At least the thick stone walls helped to keep the inside cool, Abby thought, still quietly nursing her finger. Sucking on it seemed to help it some, and it seemed to not be getting worse. As usual, her nose was stuffed up. She had to hold her breath to close her mouth around her finger, then open her mouth to take a breath – all while looking down, using her hair as a curtain, sucking noiselessly so her parents wouldn't notice and tell her to stop it. She glanced up once to see if the tall old trees outside shaded the stained glass windows high in the walls. Some of the ornate depictions of various saints and Biblical events did look darker in places, where leaves cast shadows.

Dr. Laird, the organist, played background music as the congregation sat quietly, scanning the program and the hymn numbers, adjusting their clothes, and scoping each other out. Abby spotted several other kids from her Sunday School class.

The music changed. The congregation stood up at the musical cue and began to sing the first hymn. Abby and Jenn shared one hymnal, Daddy and Mother another. Everyone glanced at the door they knew would now open to reveal the long-robed processional: the lead cross-bearer, minister, two assistant ministers, choir, and final cross-bearer.

As the parishioners sang all the verses of the hymn, the procession, also singing, walked the length of the far-left aisle, turned around behind the congregation, and progressed up the center aisle. As it reached the steps leading up to the front – excuse me, Mother, the *chancel* – the ministers continued on straight to the altar while the choir filed into its stalls, right and left, singing with the music. The stately procession was designed to be impressive and it usually succeeded.

Today's service was a regular one, without Holy Communion. Heat and summer vacations had lowered attendance. It was all so familiar to Abby. Her main challenge was to find something interesting, possibly even spiritual, to keep her awake.

Abby had taken catechism classes and received her first communion last year. At the small party at her house afterwards, she had been given her prayer book and a necklace she particularly liked from an expensive local jeweler. Its clear lucite front magnified a tiny mustard seed against a white background, and its back enlarged the Bible quote about having faith like a grain of mustard seed and being able to move mountains with it.[5] Although such allegories sounded nice, Abby did not really understand most of them.

Today's sermon covered Jesus returning to the earth.[6] Reverend Davison declared that the Second Coming is extremely important for Christians. He detailed some prophesies Jesus made about His return, explained how – one by one, over the centuries – they'd all happened:

the tearing down of the temple in Jerusalem seventy years after Jesus' crucifixion; enemies killing the believers, and love dying; the sun and the moon growing dark; earthquakes, floods, and other terrible natural disasters; the Gospel spreading all over the world just before the end, when He would return like a thief in the night to judge who had and who had not obeyed Him. The righteous would live eternally with the Lord, and the cursed would be cast into eternal fire with Satan.

The Reverend described Jesus' return on clouds of glory with angels blasting on trumpets. Some people would be taken up with him and some left behind. Imagining all this, Abby grew alarmed; but when he said he thought these were more like parables than actual mechanics, she relaxed a little.

The purpose was to keep us alert, he said, ever checking ourselves, always ready should Jesus return and see us. If we thought He wouldn't like something about us, we had better change, because no one knew when He would return.

This worried Abby, who *already* had to watch her behavior every second around Mother. Now Jesus could arrive any minute, looking at her like that stern Pakistani man, and throw her into Hell with eternal fire. That was too awful to think about.

She sucked quietly on her finger, trying to banish this newest threat from her mind, when the Reverend abruptly said, "Let us pray. O Lord God, we thank you for the promise of the return of Jesus Christ when there will be an end to all suffering, sin, and death. Grant us the grace to live so as to be happy at His appearing. In Jesus' name. Amen."

Dr. Laird played, the choir sang, and the collection plates passed from hand to hand around the congregation. Abby and Jenn put little church-issued envelopes containing their portion of allowance into the collection plates. Daddy put in a larger one.

All the while, Abby thought about how it would really be amazing to live in the time of Jesus' return. No suffering, sin, or death...wow! It sounded like everyone would be happy all the time!

Sadly, the rest of the service proved to be an exercise in boredom, broken only by the happy announcement that today was the church's one-hundred-thirtieth birthday and, instead of Sunday School, there'd be a celebration on the lawn.

The organ music for the closing processional stopped when Reverend Davison reached the little side door. He raised his first two fingers and gave the final benediction while slowly sketching the Sign Of The Cross in the air.

"May the Lord bless you and keep you. May the Lord make His face to shine upon you, and be gracious to you. May the Lord lift up his countenance upon you, and give you peace."[7]

Then he turned and went through the door, which quietly closed.

There were, after all, parts of church that Abby liked; and that little blessing at the end was one of them. She needed all the help and good-will she could get. She rose slowly in what she hoped was the graceful way her mother always prodded the girls to perfect.

Daddy – relaxed-looking and, for once, holding Mother's hand – led the way out toward the lawn. Abby wished he'd hold her hand as well, but there wasn't room for three abreast in the crowded aisle. She settled for pretending she was balancing a book on her head to help her walk gracefully, as Mother had instructed.

The Ladies' Auxiliary busily laid out the refreshments on a folding table. Yellow icing spelled "St. Zosimo's Church 130 Years" on the sheet cake. Small, sophisticated, yellow sugar roses bloomed brightly in two diagonal corners. Once the Reverend blessed the cake, the ladies sliced it and poured the punch. It was already getting hot at ten-thirty, driving the adults into shady spots under the large trees. The youngest children played tag and threw pine cones, and the preteens teased and shoved, while the teens dug out their cell phones and stood in groups.

Abby and Jenn headed to the group of teen girls.

"Hey," they said to Kat, Hope, Tiffany, Laurel, and Deirdre. Then another girl, Sissy, left her brother and also joined them.

"Hey, 'sup?" several replied.

"Not much." Abby decided a smashed finger didn't rank as news.

"Hey, did you hear about Reverend Gottle?" Kat breathed.

"No, what happened?" the Thomkins sisters immediately replied, Lauren leaning forward and Deirdre even stopping her compulsive text-messaging.

"They caught him having an affair last week, with Mrs. Talinda! They're deciding what to do with him."

This was astounding news indeed. Reverend Gottle, an unmarried assistant minister, with Mrs. Talinda? She was, well, *married*…to Mr. Talinda, with two kids just younger than Abby herself! Abby's mouth fell open in disbelief and shock, while Jenn managed to remain more composed.

"What, like send him away?" Deirdre breathed.

"Yeah, like to another church in another state maybe. Or pay a fine. Stuff like that," Kat said, relishing being the one to bring the news.

Abby thought a more fitting punishment would be jail or even stoning like they did in the Bible for sexual crimes. Yeah, if he followed the Bible, shouldn't he get a Biblical kind of punishment?

"That's all?" she blurted out.

"Well, I don't know, really," Kat said. "It's just what I heard. It's gonna be decided sometime pretty soon, I guess."

Abby wondered why he had appeared in the processional just like nothing had happened and, come to think of it, even passed right by the Talindas. How could he even be in the same room with her, knowing that others knew? She looked around, but couldn't see him on the lawn, even though all the other ministers were there conversing with church members. Well, maybe at least he had some sense of shame and didn't want to face people who might know about what he did. But maybe he should come out and face his music.

Whatever he should be doing now, Abby felt, he was doing it as a hypocrite. The nerve to even show his face in church wearing that robe and colored shawl, when he'd done something so very wrong. What had *he* thought of Reverend Davison's sermon today? Was it directed at him? It changed how she thought of everyone and everything at church today, it was so...so...unminister-like.

Her throbbing finger brought her attention back to the group of gossiping girls. She'd forgotten to hold it up.

Chapter 5: Packing

Finishing laundry and packing for their trip took the remainder of the family's afternoon. They would be going to see Mother's sister and family in North Carolina for six days: two for the round-trip drive and four for visiting. They'd be an hour and a half from the closest beach, and Abby hoped they could swim in the ocean.

To her great relief, her finger was better; but she did band-aid it to remind her not to bend it. The last joint hurt a lot when she forgot and tried to use it. Bruises from riding had also bloomed on her legs.

"Pack clean pajamas!" Mother dictated, standing in the doorway of Abby's room.

"Yes, I will," Abby said.

"Let me see what you have." Mother marched across the tan carpet to the suitcase and its future contents.

With a silent groan, Abby stood aside while her mother knelt over the project on the floor. She unpacked it all, scolding her for folding the clothes too much.

"You must fill the whole space with the clothes. The more folds, the more waste. And the biggest items on the bottom. Like this." She laid the windbreaker out flat at the bottom of the suitcase, folding only the sleeves in.

"How many shirts have you packed?"

"Six, plus I set aside one to wear on the trip."

Surprisingly, Mother did not find anything to criticize about that, and asked about bottoms.

"Three shorts, two capris, and one jeans. They coordinate with most all my shirts so I can fit the weather."

"Speak properly, Abigail. 'Dress for' the weather," Mother quickly corrected. "Leave the jeans out. It will be too hot for them. Pack one more pair of shorts instead, so you will need to do laundry only once while we're there. Shoes?"

Abby had not really decided on all her footwear but tried to sound firm as she said, "One sandals, one tennis shoes, one boots."

"Boots?" Mother raised an eyebrow. "There's no riding there, why do you need boots? Leave them here, they take up way too much room. Besides, you want to just stand around and *pet* the horses."

Abby didn't know why she wanted to take boots and jeans. "Just in case" didn't seem a defensible answer, so she said nothing. The petting comment stung, but she knew she would be punished for talking back if she tried to explain the boost, the thrill, of just standing next to a horse. Smelling one, seeing, touching, let alone riding it, made Abby's day.

Mother packed the bottoms next, in order of size, then shirts, biggest first, followed by swimwear and underwear.

"Where are your bras?" Mother asked, looking not at Abby but at the suitcase.

"Um..." Abby said.

"You need to take them and wear them, young lady. I have noticed you're not wearing a bra, and you are to the age where you should be."

Abby's heart sank further. She hated the so-called training bras her mother had left on her bed for her one day. They restricted her arms and cut into her sides. The hooks rested smack against her spine, and hard chair-backs made her squirm to get the hooks off her bones.

Mother still wasn't finished. "Also, Daddy says you need to shower more often and shave your arms and legs as well. He says that he has noticed a certain odor."

Mother left. Abby kept packing, dwelling on Mother's cruel words; her mother delivered intimate news with the tenderness of a butcher.

Mother returned, placed a travel-sized deodorant on top of the pile, and gave Abby the "I mean business" look. "Don't forget your toothbrush, either," she added, glowering at Abby.

Abby's humiliation grew. Her toothbrush? She wasn't *stupid*. She added Mother's items to her toilet kit, and tucked it into her suitcase, struggling not to sink in an ocean of embarrassment beneath Mother's critical gaze.

Why couldn't Daddy tell her himself; did she stink that bad? Did he not know how to talk to his younger daughter regarding anything more personal than...well, honestly, he didn't really talk to her much at all. A thought struck her: Daddy wanted her to shave her pits, but why didn't he shave his? Was this a double standard?

Mother must have ESP'd the nature of her thoughts.

"You must start shaving your underarms, Abigail. It is very unladylike to be hairy."

"European ladies don't shave, and they seem all right," Abby said, voicing her train of thought.

"Do not talk back to your elders!" Mother exploded. She seized her daughter's wrist and dragged her over to the bathroom sink. Abby knew what was coming and stiffened in loathing.

Mother grabbed a handful of Abby's hair, wrenched her head back, jammed the bar of soap into her daughter's mouth twice, then let her go. Abby thought it was over, now that she was gagging with the taste of soap. But then Mother grabbed Abby's T-shirt and pulled it upwards. Abby fought to hold it down, sure that whatever Mother planned could not be pleasant. Mother won the tussle, tugged off her child's shirt, and threw it down on the floor, her face a cold mask of fury. Abby bent down and grabbed it again to cover herself; but as she straightened back up, Mother slapped her face…hard.

"You will not defy me, young lady! You will *do as I say!*" Mother shouted, spit flying.

She grabbed one of Abby's arms, raised it high, and used the soap, moist with Abby's saliva, to lather Abby's armpit. Abby was frozen in fear, not daring to fight but unable to cooperate with this assault. Vivian got a pink disposable razor from a drawer and roughly swiped at the few pitiful hairs sprouting from Abby's underarm. The razor cut her, once, twice, before Mother seemed to feel that her point had been made and stopped.

She took a washcloth from the rack by the sink and wet it, used it to wipe Abby's armpit once, and tossed it down on the sink countertop in disgust when she saw the blood mingled with the soap lather and bits of hair.

"You bled on my good washcloth!" Mother spat. "Clean it all up! Now!" And she turned and stormed out of the bathroom.

Abby allowed herself to sink to the floor in pain and humiliation. This was a new low, even for Mother. Her finger had gotten wrenched again in the tussle, her armpit was cut and bleeding, her mouth was absolutely horrible from the taste of soap – she wondered if she'd soon be a connoisseur of the various tastes of soap; Mother would be pleased at her sophisticated palate, no doubt – and worst of all, even her father had turned against her. Too miserable even to cry, she just wished lightning would strike her now.

But no lightning visited her just then; and she knew she'd likely get another round of the same treatment if she did not clean up the mess, as unfair and galling as her mother's words had been.

Her throat was stuck shut; it was hard to breathe. Part of her listened for Jenn to rescue her or for Mother to return with more abuse. Tears would not come. But odd vicious thoughts did, filling her with a nightmarish daydream of suddenly being bigger than Vivian…

∞   ∞   ∞   ∞   ∞   ∞   ∞   ∞

… she washes out her mother's mouth with soap, just to see how she *likes it … screams What about love thine enemy children, huh? … slaps her mother … demands How is it my fault that I bled on your washcloth when* you *cut me? … growls Who started stupid shaving anyway? … sneers Oh, but we have to be sooo stylish and presentable … for you, you, all* **YOU!** *my mother the witch … spelled with a 'b' …*

∞   ∞   ∞   ∞   ∞   ∞   ∞   ∞

Abby's thoughts grew more and more bitter as she rinsed out her mouth, willing herself to breathe past the large rock stuck in her throat. (And how *did* one get that horrible taste out?) She lathered the washcloth with the hated soap to get the bloody streaks out, hung it back up – straight, so as not to be hauled into Mother Court for Crooked Washcloths – put away the razor that had been so painfully used against her, and squeegeed the counter clean of water and soap bubbles with the back of her good left hand.

She returned to her bedroom and closed the door quietly lest the sound provoke her mother – wherever she was – and leaned against the cream-colored wall. She'd have to get on with packing, or she'd probably get a strapping.

She surveyed the suitcase on the floor, mute testament to Mother's domination. Would Mother notice if she repacked how she preferred, with bottoms and tops already paired? Though she liked pulling out an entire outfit, ready to wear, it probably wasn't worth it in the current climate. She dug the bras, still in their boxes, out of her bureau drawer. Then came her shoes, each in a plastic bag as Mother wanted so that no filth from them could touch her clean clothes.

She was getting hungry, but heard no sounds from the kitchen. The entire house was quiet. Sometimes Mother just drove off when she was upset. It seemed that dinner was do-it-yourself tonight, so she looked cautiously into the refrigerator freezer for a TV dinner, microwaved it, wolfed it down standing over the sink, drank tap water quickly using her left hand as her cup, cleaned up fast, and scooted back to her room.

It had been a horrible day from start to finish. So bad it merited an entry in her diary: "M is a B. Shaving, bras." She didn't feel like adding Harry Potter's woes to her own, so she got ready for bed at eight-thirty, hoping tomorrow would be survivable.

Part of her doubted it would be; and she laid down evaluating the chances for lightning, thinking she would try to find a way to get out of the car if it looked like a storm. (She knew from *Muse* that rubber tires prevented lightning from harming people inside cars.) One possibility was to claim she had to go to the bathroom, but that excuse had to be used sparingly in case of real need. Another option was to point out any sewing stores that might tempt Mother to stop. Armed with all these desperate plans, she fell asleep wondering who was the more debased tonight: she or Reverend G.

Chapter 6: Driving

The next morning, the usually empty kitchen hummed with activity. Normally, Daddy had left for work by the time Abby got up, especially in the summer. Mother rarely got up before ten o'clock, and Jenn was also usually either gone or sleeping.

Abby ate a quick bowl of cereal at the sunroom breakfast table with Jenn, who glanced at Abby's pinky finger and then raised her eyebrows. Abby silently nodded that her finger was better, but added rolling eyes and a disgusted mouth to let her sister know that something else bad had happened. Jenn raised her eyebrows again, and Abby jerked her head slightly towards Mother, who was making coffee for herself and Daddy. Jenn gave Abby a sympathetic look and watched her for any other silent messages. But they had no signals for Abby to convey that: "Mother attacked me with soap and a razor last night." So they finished breakfast in the customary sympathetic silence, got up together, washed their bowls and spoons, and put them in the drainer. Abby went to her room; Jenn followed and quietly shut the door.

"What did she do?" Jenn whispered.

For a moment, Abby's throat closed and she could not speak. Tears threatened to spill down her face. Jenn's face twisted in shared pain and humiliation while she waited for Abby to do whatever she needed to do.

In a minute, Abby was able to whisper back, "She made me shave, and washed out my mouth with soap." Abby could not bring herself to say the absolute truth out loud.

Jennifer's eyes opened wide as she filled in the details herself. "Oh no! Abs!" she murmured, reaching out to squeeze Abby's arm. "Was it bad?"

Jennifer's sympathy brought it all back again. Abby couldn't stop the tears from running down her face, and her breathing threatened to become a wail squeezing past the rock in her throat.

"Shhhh," Jennifer said and brought her into a hug. Abby knew the shush was meant equally to comfort Abby and to quiet her lest Mother hear. The door was shut, but still…

A sob escaped her. Fortunately, it was muffled by Jenn's shoulder.

"Shhhhhh!" Jennifer hissed more loudly; and Abby knew she was very worried about what might happen to both of them if they were discovered like this. That fear stifled the crying. Abby got a tissue from her bureau top, blew her predictably stuffy nose, and wiped her eyes. Jennifer still looked at her, very worried.

"Are you gonna be okay?" she asked.

There was only one possible answer, so Abby gave it. "Yeah," she mumbled, not believing it.

Jenn interpreted the answer correctly. She stood there for another long moment looking at Abby, knowing she was not okay but unable to undo Mother's deed. Then Jenn gently patted Abby's face and quietly left, leaving the door open so as not to signal Mother to investigate.

But Abby did feel oddly better. It helped to know that somebody looked straight at her and cared how she was, what she went through. Bringing it all up again was no fun. Fortunately, she didn't have to explain every last detail. Jenn had plenty of her own run-ins with Mother and, while extracting the things she wanted from home, was counting down the seasons until she could leave for college.

Abby realized that she hadn't put on a bra...and she knew Mother would look. Could you see bras through shirts, or would Mother again rip off Abby's shirt to check? In front of Daddy in the car? Probably.

Abby peeled off her shirt and took one of the stupid training bras out of the box. Were you supposed to reach behind your back to hook it? Abby's arms didn't bend like that. She'd have to hook it first, then slide it over her head. And which line of hooks were you supposed to use? There were three sets. She picked the middle one.

Once she wrestled herself into it, the bra was tight. Uncomfortable. The hooks sat on her spine. She wiggled, trying to tweak it into a better position. The hooks did shift a little, and the shoulder straps seemed a tad looser. Probably the best she could hope for.

That done, she reached down and picked up her shirt, only to see the deodorant staring accusingly at her. But it was just too much to deal with right now, so she prayed Mother wouldn't sense – or scent – its absence.

She carried her suitcase through the house, out the front door, and down the cement steps to the street, where the car had been parked for loading. Mother directed, as usual. After all the items on both the paper and the mental checklists were completed and everyone else was in the car, Daddy locked the house door, slid into the driver's seat, and drove away.

Abby positioned her backpack at her feet and hoped for a mostly trouble-free trip with her saltines, orange drink, new book, and drawing supplies.

Mother handed her the treasured *HP #7* and – after carefully looking at its vibrant orange cover for clues about the upcoming story – she held it on her lap while they drove through Surely, past familiar neighborhoods containing friends, her school, and Daddy's medical software office. The silver sedan turned onto I-65 heading north. Once on the interstate, when all was quiet, Abby nudged the bra hooks over to one side, settled in, and lost herself in the magical worries of the world's most famous young wizard: Voldemort's evil, the Malfoys' resentful involvement, and Harry's pain...physical *and* emotional.

She looked up when they turned east onto I-40 in Nashville. The interstate was jammed with traffic, especially semitrailers. It was surely a lot different from sleepy Surely!

Daddy had tuned the radio to a classical music station. When the music grew loud, Daddy turned it down; and when a softer part started, he turned it back up.

After several changes, Mother said, "Paul, there are *supposed* to be louder and quieter parts!"

"Oh," Daddy said, sounding taken aback. He stopped changing the volume; although occasionally, when the music got very loud, his right hand would twitch an inch or two from the steering wheel.

Abby and Jenn began a game that they always played on long trips: finding cars from different states. For ages she gazed, amazed at the license plates. They counted fifteen states in a half-hour. Abby found the first North Carolina plate, evidence of their destination: "First in Flight," it boasted, with a drawing of an early plane.

When they hadn't seen any new states for quite a while, Jenn pulled out a book of Celebrity Sudoku puzzles. Abby, having never done one, asked Jenn to show her how. As Jenn demonstrated, Abby murmured a couple of suggestions and Jenn accepted them. They worked companionably for a while, finishing one and starting another.

Mother knit, occasionally making comments to Daddy about the radio talk show now coming from the front speakers. He set the car on cruise control, leaned back, and growled replies at the emcee. The program debated whether or not to impeach President Bush because the Iraq war was floundering. The host injected opinions like "It's time to *dump* the parties, register as Independents, and *protest* the politics in this nation!" Sounded like Mother on a tirade. Abby was glad the sound was low enough that she could ignore the haranguing.

As he often did while driving, Daddy took his small clippers from his shirt pocket, moved both hands to the top of the steering wheel, and began clipped his thumbnails. Mother had long ago given up on protesting about safe driving or nail clippings on the floor. Daddy stowed the clippers but held the top of the wheel with both hands, repeatedly stroking his thumbnails with his thumb pads as he drove.

Mother and Daddy chose a roadside rest stop for lunch. Stepping out of the air-conditioned car into the humid noontime heat was like stepping into the school gym showers. Mother handed bags and baskets out of the trunk, then led the way to a shady picnic table, which she covered with a plastic sheet. Jenn distributed paper plates and plastic utensils. The girls assembled bologna sandwiches and juice. The adults ate cold roasted chicken and various leftovers. Daddy had crackers; but Mother grumbled about the "styrofoam hockey pucks" she had to eat – though she daintily held out her pinky as she did – because the doctor had told Vivian that she needed to eliminate several foods she was allergic to, including wheat. Abby had been sensitive ever since she was a newborn (shortly after birth she'd been covered in a head-to-toe rash, Mother liked to bemoan) and also could not eat several things. It made eating together difficult.

Mother handed Abby a plastic box of green jello with pears. Abby could not stand the texture of jello and passed it on to Jenn but Mother said, "Abby, take some of the jello, you're not allergic to it and we need to use it up."

Abby took the smallest scoop she thought would pass her mother's scrutiny and put it at the side of her plate. Mother honed in on this possible flaunting of her authority, so Abby stirred it and put the spoon in her mouth with only the smallest bits clinging to it. Mother frowned. Abby wished to distract her and drop some of the jello on the ground, but could not throw it far without drawing Mother's attention. Dropping it right under the table would invite discovery and a flogging.

Mother hadn't spanked her with the hairbrush or had Daddy use the belt on her since fifth grade, but that didn't mean they wouldn't. Perhaps Mother would give her the same choice as with liver years ago: eat it or sit there all night. Abby had resigned herself to sitting in her dinner chair all night rather than eat the vile stuff. Mother had finally seen how it was going to be and let her go after two hours.

How would it be if they all drove off and left her there at the truck stop, returning in five days? Abby supposed she'd at least have a bathroom, a roof, water, and perhaps not-too-horrid scraps of food from the trash bin. Staying warm was not a problem with this heat. She was pondering sunburn prevention and heat exhaustion when Mother spoke to her again.

"Eat your jello, Abby," Mother commanded. "Waste not, want not. You should be grateful you have food in front of you; lots of children around the world don't."

Abby could see no options. She grimaced while she scooped up the smallest bit of jello that could pass for a bite. She scraped the top layer off with her teeth, trying to leave as much as she could on the spoon.

It was already impossibly mushy; how were you supposed to chew it? It was like trying to swallow raw eggs, like they did on the extreme reality shows. The thought nearly made Abby retch. It was only fear of being spanked – in front of everybody at the rest stop – that made her fight down the rising tide of her other lunch and try to swallow the jello without any other nauseating images making it all worse.

Mother watched Abby for signs that she needed to be pounced on. When Abby finally managed to swallow the one bite and thought it all might stay down, Mother said, "Eat it all, Abby. I don't want any left."

Abby sank on her bench. It was not possible to eat it all; there was no way. Jenn was looking at her own jello-free plate; Abby knew she was trying to think of a way to eat Abby's jello without Mother noticing. Abby could not see any way out of this one that Mother would not catch and punish, possibly by making her eat something else disgusting like the wilted leftover salad that Daddy liked and was just starting on.

A remnant of sandwich on Abby's plate suggested alternating bites of the jello and sandwich. She took another teeny bite of jello to mollify Mother and then a smallish bite of sandwich. Abby ate as slowly as she dared, hoping Mother would lose interest in her vigil so that Abby and Jenn could think of something else when Mother's back was turned. But Mother showed no signs of lowering her guard.

Each bit of jello threatened to evict all of the sandwich. The more she ate, the more queasy Abby felt; but there was nothing to do except continue to eat the slimy stuff. She managed to tip a bit onto the ground from her spoon while Mother was packing away the remaining snacks; but other than that, she had to eat the whole thing. She felt wretched.

At last lunch was over. Jenn jumped up to collect the disposables and throw them away. Abby wasn't sure what would happen if she got up to walk. She turned around slowly, with the contents of her stomach threatening to mutiny. She stood up gradually and felt the whole lot in her stomach rebel. Wildly searching for something to throw up in, she rushed after Jennifer, leaned over the trash can swarming with flies and bees, and threw up her lunch…as well as what was left of her breakfast. It burned her nose as it came back up; and she had to taste the jello yet again, which triggered more heaving. Her nose and mouth streamed with goo. When she finally opened her eyes, she saw Jenn standing beside her, methodically tapping the food off the paper plates, precisely folding each one, and tucking it just so into the trash barrel. Jenn was, Abby realized, blocking Mother's view with her body, taking the longest possible time. Jenn had also saved out several of the cleanest used paper napkins, which she handed to Abby. Abby took one at a time to swab her nose and mouth. She hoped it was over; she felt herself slowly coming right.

Jenn timed her folding and tucking so that when Abby straightened up, Jenn pushed the last utensil into the trash can. Jenn reached over to gather Abby's hair back and smooth the heat-induced frizzies in one quick but meaningful gesture of concern and care. Abby sent an appreciative glance her way, pushed a hoarse "thanks" through a sore throat, and glanced towards her parents. They were carrying the remains of lunch back to the car, apparently not noticing anything.

"We'll say we were watching the bees, Abs," Jennifer said quietly, twisting Abby's hair into a short rope so it would stay back.

"Yeah, good," Abby said. At least one person cared about her, she thought grimly. She would truly be sunk without Jenn.

"Next time, pretend that you have to go to the bathroom, and call to Mother when you're going; I'll switch plates with you."

It was a perfect plan. Too late to do her any good, but perfect. Abby only wished she could guess everything Mother was going to do and have plans for it all.

Jenn and Abby approached the picnic table, awaiting orders.

"Go to the bathroom; then we'll leave," Mother said, looking their clothes up and down but missing their faces, which they attempted to arrange into neutral masks. Abby's was still slightly pale, but she was right in guessing Mother wouldn't notice it.

As they left the cement-block bathroom, Mother saw an overweight couple walking their little wiener dog – dachshund – in the pet area.

"Girls, *never* let yourselves go like that," she hissed. "Stomachs hanging over their pants; they can hardly walk. It's revolting."

The girls knew better than to say anything. Abby thought it might be hard to do things, being that overweight. Walking did seem to be quite an effort for them. But they seemed far happier together and with their dog than she did at the moment, and she fantasized about trading places with them if it meant she could be happy. Perhaps if she gained a lot of weight, her mother would hate her enough to leave her alone? No, that would surely backfire, she quickly decided. Mother would hound Abby around the clock about anything that broke her tyrannical rules of acceptability.

In the car, Abby's bra was unbearable. She just wanted to escape it all. She took a pillow from its corner on the back window ledge and leaned against the side of the car for a nap. When she woke, they were nearly to Aunt Sofia's house on the outskirts of Little Lily, North Carolina. Abby's empty stomach clenched painfully. Mother repacked her knitting and books, looked for trash to throw away, and directed Daddy …who already knew the way. He turned the radio up while nodding vaguely at Mother.

Abby made sure her space was in order, then took a small notepad and pencil from her backpack and drew horses. She challenged herself to draw the Appaloosa horses from the quilt Jenn had shown her. She looked out the window and saw they were driving through gently rolling hills that were mostly tan from late-summer dryness. Abby always looked for horses in fields, but now saw only cows and crops.

At last they stopped in front of a large yard sloping gently up to a house surrounded by big oak trees and azalea bushes suffering in the August drought. The central section of the white wooden house was the oldest, with two stories. To the left was a long one-story addition that Abby knew was the large family room. To the right was another smaller one-story box: the kitchen.

The Wizes stepped from the car into the humid warmth of the North Carolina evening. Slanting sunshine glowed on Mother as she directed car unloading procedures.

"So-FIE-ah, they're HEE-er!" a muffled voice called. Suddenly, the house door swung open and a dozen people streamed out onto the lawn, smiling, calling hellos, and yelling at the last one to shut the door so the bugs didn't get in the house nor the air conditioning out.

Leopard
Appaloosa

Chapter 7: Sofia

Abby recognized several people in the crowd now streaming down the golden hill – its brown grass gilded by the last rays of sun. Mother's older sister, Sofia Holsworth, came down to the car to embrace her sister and take a bag.

As Mother embraced Sofia, Abby compared them. Mother's hair was shorter, carefully curled, and naturally dark. Sofia, the smaller and thinner of the two, had straight brown hair streaked with lighter strands; she wore it loose at shoulder length. Sofia's laugh emerged more easily than Vivian's, and she seemed generally more lighthearted. Both sisters were pale, dressed tastefully, and carried themselves with poise. Sofia was the divorced mother of three children, who were also standing on the lawn to welcome the visitors.

The oldest was Jonathan; almost eighteen, a senior this year, standing by a girl of color whom Abby didn't know. Next was Penelope – Penny for short – sixteen, with two girlfriends beside her. Then Ricky, twelve – Abby's favorite and the life of any party – with a couple of guy-friends in tow. Two dogs raced around barking at everyone. And assorted cats policed the occasion with their unwavering gaze.

"You're just in time to help us destroy the pantry!" Ricky called out. "Mom's cleaned it out, and we're all human garbage disposals!"

"Make it any more appetizing and they'll run you over to get to it," Sofia retorted with a wry smile. "But there might be something edible, actually. Kids, help your Aunt Vivi with her things. Many hands make light work!"

It only took one trip. Daddy locked the car and joined the procession into the house.

"Girls, you'll share the room all the way at the end of the upstairs hall," Sofia waved upwards as the Wize sisters filed into the blue-wallpapered entryway. "The grownups have the foldout couch in the family room. Meet in the kitchen, okay?"

Abby followed Jenn and Penny up the wooden stairs. Several bedroom doors led off the white upstairs hallway, some open, some closed. The last one was the smallest, a plain room with a single bed against the right-hand wall and a low trundle bed next to it.[8] An Oriental carpet peeked around the edges of the beds, leaving a narrow strip of wooden floor visible. The sisters parked their luggage next to the left wall and followed Penny back downstairs, turning left at the bottom of the stairs, and going straight on through the dining room to the kitchen addition. There, a line of family members had formed towards the left, each one picking a plate from a stack of mismatches, helping themselves from the many bowls of food on the counters along the right-hand wall, and sitting at the kitchen table or the one in the dining room.

Jon maneuvered around Abby's position in line while introducing Melissa, the girl with light-brown skin. Her hair looked like it was ordinarily fluffy but was currently straight. Abby looked closer and saw an intelligent, lively expression on Melissa's plain but welcoming features. Jon invited Mother over to sit with them, which Abby felt was either very gallant of him or very foolish.

Penny's two friends, Barb and Carol, stood in line ahead of Abby. Carol was quite tall and heavyset with straight, waist-length, auburn hair. She seemed quiet. Barb stood as tall as Penny, but she was slender as compared to Penny's average build. Barb's short, blonde, very curly hair was also markedly different from Penny's long brown hair pulled into a bun.

"Penny tells me you're into horses?" Barb said.

"Sure am," Abby replied, looking at Barb with new interest.

"So's my sister Angie," Barb said with a funny look at Penny and an equally strange little move of her hand.

"Oh?" Abby said, wondering what this was all about.

"Yeah, she does this horse whispering stuff. It's kind of…kooky, I think."

"What does she do?" Abby pictured a horse draped in silk scarves, surrounded by lighted candles, with a girl in bare feet and a long dress softly chanting strange words and showering the horse with handfuls of flower petals.

"She wiggles ropes at the horse, waves an orange stick at it, talks about its 'horse-enality'. Nutty stuff like that."

Abby didn't know what to think. She remembered seeing an orange stick hanging on one of the private boarders' tack racks, but she didn't even know who the boarder was, much less ever seen anyone use it. She could not imagine the managers at The Ride Place allowing anything kooky. But Barb obviously thought her sister was off her rocker.

They stood there regarding each other uncomfortably. Finally, curiosity overcoming her, Abby asked, "Will I get to meet her?"

Barb shrugged. "If you want to, I s'pose."

"Well, if it works out, it might be interesting. Good for some laughs if nothing else, I guess."

To Abby's relief, that seemed the right thing to say. Barb smiled, nodded, and said she'd check everyone's schedules. Abby smiled back and then, having reached the counter, tended to her aching insides. She was glad there was no livermush.

After cleaning up the meal, everyone went to the family room. Jenn chatted with Jon and his apparent girlfriend, the adults gossiped, and Ricky and his friends played *Magic: The Gathering* cards in a corner.

Penny and her girlfriends channel-surfed. *Oprah Winfrey* featured women who had unknowingly married wife-beaters. Abby thought their lives sounded even worse than hers.

"They're so stupid," Barb commented to Carol and Penny. Pointing to one woman, she added, "Anyone could see that guy was trash. Why did she marry him?"

The girls agreed that the men's drinking and low-paying jobs – if they were employed at all – should have been a good clue. Mother and Aunt Sofia nodded approvingly at these assessments.

The downtrodden wives suddenly gave way to Vanessa Anne Hudgens and Zac Efron being interviewed regarding the new *High School Musical 2*.

"They're going out together in real life, you know," Penny said to no one in particular. Her light-brown eyes sized them up on the screen. "He's kind of cute but not my type. She seems okay, nothing special," she decided.

"They lip-synched it all, you know," Barb said.

Abby felt very out of touch. She hadn't seen the sequel, and had not even paid much of attention to the original movie. She glanced at the shelves of DVDs next to the TV and saw dozens of new titles that she had only heard about: *Pirates of the Caribbean*, all three DVDs; all the *Shreks*; *Bridge to Tarabithia*; and several *Harry Potter* movies, the last of which she had not yet seen. Maybe, if she were lucky, she would see it while she was here.

She realized that she spent a lot of time hiding in her room reading. Her bookshelves contained mainly horse books: all the Walter Farley and Marguerite Henry books, several beginner riding books, and some comprehensive books like *Horses for Dummies*.[9] Most of them she'd gotten for birthdays and Christmases, having so little spending money herself.

"Let's go look at somebody who's really hot," Penny leered to her friends. Suddenly animated, they stood up and nodded to Abby in silent invitation to accompany them upstairs into Penny's room, just to the left of the sisters' guest room.

Good-quality antiques furnished the room styled in what Mother might have called "Early American Teen Disorder." Sofia, a realtor and antiques dealer, kept many of her best finds. Clothes were draped over most available surfaces, shoes were scattered around like land mines, jewelry spilled over the top of the dresser, childhood mementos hung from the walls, and trinkets escaped from baskets on the shelves and in corners. Mother would have pitched a fit.

Penny slid into a wooden chair in front of the computer table at the window, and the other three girls arranged themselves around her. Penny found the YouTube page in her Favorites and clicked on it. Daniel Radcliffe, the eighteen-year-old actor who played Harry Potter in the movies based on the books, appeared on the monitor. Apparently Penny had spent a lot of time searching the internet for photos and video clips of him, because a long list of sites popped up when she selected another picture.

Again Abby saw how behind she was. The sisters were not often allowed to use Mother's computer. Mother didn't want the girls visiting inappropriate sites or messing up her Crafters Circles party information.

Abby had never seen any interviews with Daniel Radcliffe and was completely captivated by his bubbling energy, his wicked humor, his infectious grin, even the way his lower lip wiggled when he was deciding what to say. She watched the new video avidly.

"I don't mind signing autographs, really," he said in his attractive British accent. "Except the professional autograph sellers, they really get to me. Like, when I know it's, sort of, about the twentieth time I've signed for the same guy, I might finally tell him I'm not going to give him another one to sell on eBay."

Wow, the issues famous people have to *deal* with, Abby thought.

Another site showed him in a snapshot with an Asian girl. She'd posted the photo; her friend was in a play he'd come to see and they'd met backstage. She said he was "very sweet." One of the comments under the picture called the girl a nasty name and screamed in rude all-capitals: "DON'T YOU KNOW WHAT I WOULD DO, WHAT I WOULD GIVE TO MEET HIM, LET ALONE GET A HUG FROM HIM?? I ADORE HIM!!!!!"

The girls called her a ranting lunatic. "Duh, we don't know, 'cuz we don't know you!" "What a groupie!" "Get a life, you slut!"

Larry King interviewed Daniel on CNN Live, in which he was quite serious. Martha Stewart hosted him, teasing him about shaving, which he handled gracefully. A Brit, Jonathan Ross, said shocking things to and about him, which he again handled very professionally.

The only time Dan did not answer at all was when Jonathan Ross asked him about a play he was acting in called *Equus*. Abby knew this meant horses and so was very curious, loving both *Harry Potter* and horses as she did. But it seemed the only live horse involved was the one Dan had been photographed nude with for the promotional photos; his on-stage horses were actors inside horse-shaped props.

Penny and her friends leaned closer for the next screens. Parts of the play apparently featured Dan in the nude. Actually naked. In front of a live audience. Abby was flabbergasted. He was so...normal!...in the *HP* movies. Wasn't he embarrassed? Why did he do this? He certainly wouldn't have to for the money; he was rolling in dough from the movies. Number five had just come out this summer, and had made him beaucoup millions, hadn't it?

Someone had snuck a camera into the play and then put the photos up on the internet. Abby didn't know whether to hide her eyes or lean closer. It was very strange, feeling fascinated and repulsed at the same moment; and she stayed stuck, looking sideways with her mouth open. Fortunately, in the scene with him portraying an unsuccessful attempt to have sex with a barn girl, they'd covered his...ahem...private parts with a cartoon witch's hat. Apparently, he then went and hurt the horses somehow...it seemed very twisted to Abby, and she couldn't see why Dan had publicized something so awful.

Penny pulled up the poster of the horse with him naked from the back, not a stitch on. Abby wasn't at all sure what to think about looking at Dan Radcliffe's naked butt. Certainly he seemed to have a nice body; but Penny and the girls were leering at it and making comments about going to see the play just to see him naked, as Jonathan Ross had encouraged people to do. The girls suggested Dan could try again with them after failing with the barn girl. This last was too much for Abby. She muttered, "Bathroom," and slid out the door.

She stood in the hallway for a minute, thoughts jammed, not ready to go downstairs and put on a polite face for company. She sought refuge in her room, as she did so often at home. Without a nook to retreat into, she laid down on the low pullout bed. She squirmed to get her bra straightened around; it had not shifted with her when she laid down. Her pinky finger chose that inconvenient moment to ache again; Abby sucked on it, feeling stupid. Her *HP #7* book stared at her from the foot of the bed, where she'd set it before dinner, and it amplified all of her whirling thoughts and emotions. She pulled the pillow up over her head and tried to sort it out.

No doubt Dan thought that as an actor he should do these things. She had read interviews in *Reader's Digest* with different actors who talked about stretching themselves as artists; but how many of them stripped for the world to see? Even Madonna, famous for her suggestive acts and lyrics, had worn a bikini thing in the old show Abby had once briefly seen, on a neighbor's TV, while going door-to-door for her school fundraiser.

What did J.K. Rowling think of him doing this? And wasn't he only seventeen when he actually did the play? Didn't you have to be eighteen to do naked stuff like that?

Voices interrupted her contemplation. She tried to ignore them but they got louder. Someone yelled. Were they yelling at her? Abby took the pillow off her head.

"You can't look at stuff like that. I'm telling Mom!"

"I can look at anything I want; it's my computer in my room!"

"Doesn't matter, you're not allowed! How would you like it if I was looking at naked *girls* on a computer?"

The voices belonged to Ricky and Penny.

"You wouldn't dare!" Penny lit into her brother.

"Yeah, I would too dare. My friends even find porno sites, too; so if you can, I can!"

"That's disgusting. I'll tell Mom!"

"And I'll tell her about your dear Danny boy!"

They were sword-fighting with no swords. Stab, recoil, slash, block …then a mutual silent retreat. After a moment, Penny's voice, although low, still reached under Abby's door.

"If you don't tell, I won't tell."

"Deal. Pinky swear."

Abby could just imagine them hooking pinkies and shaking on it. She shuddered to imagine the worst: one of them losing a pinky finger if they broke this solemn vow. But she didn't think they were the type to really carry through.

This only added to her confusion. They both thought it disgusting for the other to look at nude pictures of the opposite gender, but wanted the right to do so themselves. That's a double standard, maybe even being a hypocrite, Abby thought. It was messed up, almost as messed up as Reverend Gottle's fling with Mrs. Talinda. Did Reverend Gottle start his downward slide with things like looking at pornography?

Abby just couldn't try to be polite to people downstairs now. She looked into her backpack to see what she might find to do until bedtime. Half-started horse drawings peeked out at her. She dug around for her little pouch of colored pencils and allowed her drawing to take her off to much more pleasant places.

"Hey, why are you in here alone?" Jenn asked, opening the door.

"Um…" Abby said.

They understood each other so well. Abby knew that Jenn understood something had happened that was too big to easily put into words. And they both knew that the best way to solve this was for Jenn to wait patiently while Abby tried.

"Well, you know Dan Radcliffe?"

"Yeah," Jenn said in a quiet, neutral voice. Abby was grateful she didn't add a "doesn't everyone?" or give her own opinion about him.

They'd never talked about him, only said that they both liked the movies but thought, as usual, that the books were better.

"Penny had a bunch of interviews and pictures of him on her computer, and some of them were of him naked," Abby said.

Jenn raised an eyebrow but waited, looking away after a second to allow Abby to feel less scrutinized while she got her feelings put into words.

"Well I did think he was sexy, especially some of the pictures of him from last spring." Abby allowed herself to remember one shot of him being interviewed in the bleachers at a polo game. Seated, he was glancing over his left shoulder, flashing a fun-loving, high-energy smile full of attractive teeth. His hair was especially sexy in that shot, and his eyes were electric. But in later shots, he'd grown a strange wispy beard and moustache; he just looked too serious and too thin...the magic was gone.

"He handled adults and autograph sessions and crowds of photographers and screaming fans – no way could I do that – and he was really great, I really envy him that way. I wish I were that confident.

"And it was fun to imagine him with less clothes on. But when he actually was naked, it was kind of disgusting."

Abby fully expected her sister to contradict her or even make fun of her now that she'd said it. To Jenn's eternal credit, she did neither. She sat quietly and battled with what to say.

"I know what you mean," she finally said.

Abby realized that, as close as they were, they'd never had a discussion about these kinds of things. Mother had forbidden dating until after they turned sixteen. Jenn was old enough, but hadn't found anyone she was interested in.

There was a long silence as they both struggled with this new turn in their relationship.

"Maybe we shouldn't—"

"If you think that—"

They both spoke at the same instant, instantly re-establishing their close, easy bond. Both smiled.

Jenn became the valued big sister then, and Abby felt very grateful. She hadn't realized it until now, but she needed some help handling her feelings. Jenn was her only possible confidante.

"Children don't have sexual feelings," Jenn said kindly. "At some point, right about your age, their hormones start waking up and they start turning into adults, getting interested in sexual kinds of things."

Awake? Abby did feel like some things were waking up these days. She felt aware like she never had before.

"So maybe it's new to you to have sexy feelings at all." Jenn looked at Abby to see if this was correct. Abby allowed that maybe it was.

"And then there's the fact that very few of us walk around naked," Jenn added gently, "so nakedness is another thing totally."

That seemed about right, and Abby felt relieved. Which must have shown on her face, because Jenn smiled a bit and said, "My baby sister is growing up, then. Let me know if you need help on anything."

"Of *course* I'll need help; I can't exactly go to Mother!" Abby protested. "She buys me awful bras and forces me to shave."

"Yeah, it's hard enough without Mother."

"This horrible bra – I hate it. I can't get it comfortable. Why is it called a training bra, anyway? Do boobs need to be trained?"

"I don't know why they call it that, Abby. Breasts can be squeezed or lifted, but they are the shape God gives you," Jenn replied, smiling. Abby figured she knew what she was talking about, judging by Jenn's shapely curves.

Jenn offered to take a look, and after Abby said yes, gently lifted her shirt and showed her the adjustments on the straps. She also suggested making the hooks looser.

"The seams do kind of dig in," she shared. "Like on your socks. A sports bra, you could turn inside out; but these, I dunno." Jenn looked at the seams, evaluating wearing the bra inside out, then shook her head. She helped Abby to let out the shoulder straps and settle the rib band lower. It did feel better.

"What's a sports bra? And how am I supposed to reach behind me to hook it?"

Jenn drew a long breath. Abby didn't know anything at all, did she? Mother hadn't said or shown her anything, and Abby didn't even know what she didn't know.

"A sports bra is very stretchy with no hooks. You slide it over your head. You might really like them for riding. We could go find a kind you like. I'll get the money from Mother. This kind of bra with hooks, you can hook in front of you, inside out, then slide the hooks around to your back and turn it right side out. After it's in place, you stick your arms through the shoulder straps." She took a spare bra from her own suitcase and demonstrated on the outside of her shirt.

That way would definitely work better, Abby thought. And a bra-shopping trip sounded like a little bit of fun, actually. A kind of secret girl thing to do together. Plus, Jenn was braver than Abby, so surely she could get the money.

"When will I get my period? Is it going to hurt?" Abby asked. She hadn't intended to ask, didn't even realize it was on her mind.

"Not usually. Sometimes women get a sort of twinge when the egg releases, but the blood flows a couple weeks later; and unless you get cramps, it isn't so much painful as…a *pain*."

Jenn smiled at her joke. So did Abby. It was such a relief to have someone who did not boss or bully her, but just offered help and was patient.

"Maybe I'd better show you the, er, equipment before you need it. I remember a girl in sixth grade who stood up to hand in her test and was soaked in blood. I was just really glad I wasn't her."

Abby was horrified. How embarrassing!

"Yeah," Jenn agreed, "but that wouldn't be as bad as the nine-year-old who got pregnant and had the baby when she was ten!"[10]

Abby was even more horrified. "When will mine start?"

"I don't think there's any way to predict exactly. Hopefully, it starts out light and you'll see it on toilet paper or on your underwear. Could be anytime, anywhere, so let me show you pads and tampons. I'll give you a couple, and you can start carrying them in your purse."

Jenn went to her suitcase and got the supplies, laid them out on the bed, told Abby how to use them, and answered all her questions.

Afterwards, Abby got into the trundle with quite a mix of thoughts and emotions…the strongest one being relief that she had such a great sister. Her other one was that, in league with Mother and Jesus, her own body would soon betray her…all of them crouched, hiding, waiting to pounce on her and make her already-hard life even more difficult.

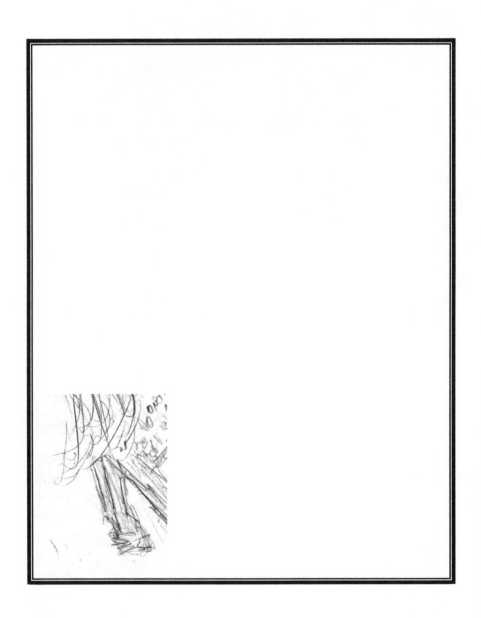

Chapter 8: Vacation

Sleeping erased yesterday's confusion and aches, and Abby woke with a gentle sense of being ready for whatever the day would bring. But what *would* it bring? She got dressed, including the more-comfortably adjusted bra and the weird-feeling deodorant, and went downstairs to see.

Jon was in the kitchen getting breakfast. He glanced up at her, then returned to making coffee.

"Good morning," he said.

"Morning," she replied. He was so much older than she was. She had never really connected with him, so was cautious. He seemed perfectly relaxed, though.

"What would you like for breakfast?" he asked without looking up from stirring artificial creamer into his coffee cup.

"I usually have cereal," she murmured shyly.

"Over there in the cabinet," he said, waving his dripping spoon and then hastily catching the drops.

Abby went to the upper cabinet he had indicated and saw a shelf full of boxes: Happy O's, Wiggy Niggys, and some high-fiber choices. She chose the Wiggy Niggys, then fetched milk. Jon brought her a bowl and spoon and joined her at the table.

"Sleep well?" he asked comfortably.

"Yes," she answered, thinking that perhaps she hadn't realized how much fatigue had affected her last night. "When did everyone else go to bed?"

"Oh, not that late. Around nine-thirty, I guess."

"And that was your girlfriend?"

"Um, yes; possibly a bit more serious than girlfriend," he said with a definite Look In His Eyes.

Abby didn't know what to say to this so she offered a small "oh" between bites of brightly colored circles.

"We've known each other for more than a year. She just gets more and more interesting," he said.

He seemed willing to share, and Abby took a chance.

"Um, like what?"

"Her heritage," he responded quickly. "Her mother is Native American, European, and Hawaiian; and her father is African American and Asian. She says wherever she goes, people think she's native-born." He smiled, apparently recalling some interesting stories about her travels.

Abby attempted to imagine anyone embodying more than two continents, but couldn't. "Interesting" would be an understatement for a heritage like that!

"She's also a member of the Bahá'í Faith," he added, then seemed to get lost in his own thoughts. He said it *beh-HAW-ee*. Abby tried to repeat it in a voiceless whisper; but it wasn't easy to say. In her own head, her attempt sounded more like *bah-HIGH*. A strange word, in any case. Probably a strange cult. But Abby felt welcomed to reply.

"What is that?" she asked.

He looked at her, unsure. "Uh, well, it's a really interesting religion she's been teaching me about. I don't feel like I know much about it yet myself, but, ah…" He trailed off, wrestling with how to voice what was unclear to him.

"At first, see, I thought it was some kind of a communal thing, like the Jewish communes in Israel; but it's not physical or geographical like that."

Abby must have looked blank, because he tried again.

"They don't live in communes or gather in one place like, say, the Israeli Jews or the Utah Latter-Day Saints," he clarified. Abby nodded her understanding.

"It's definitely a religion; there is a Prophet they follow who seems too good to be true. I mean, not to criticize, but I sure can't understand someone who did the things this Bahá'u'lláh did. He was either really from God or they're all lying about how forgiving He was…even to His brother who kept trying to kill Him for, like, twenty years. Also, how everyone seemed to just lose their minds…I mean, not go crazy but, like, go blank whenever they were in the same room as Him…"

Abby carefully repeated *beh-HAW-oh-LAW* to herself as she waited, Jenn-like, for Jon to sort out his thoughts. In her mind's ear, she could hear Mother's insistence that she repeat words, especially names, until she pronounced and remembered them correctly.

"And then there was His son, 'Abdu'l-Bahá…"

AB-dole-beh-HAW, Abby rehearsed silently while she finished her cereal, trying to smile encouragingly at Jon without dribbling her milk down her chin.

"You know those bracelets with WWJD? What Would Jesus Do?"

Abby nodded.

"Well it's not really fair, is it?"

"What do you mean?"

Jon was unabashedly spilling his thoughts now, and Abby was interested and honored.

"Well, according to the Bible and the Christians, Jesus was the son of God and even seems to be God Himself at times. So how could we possibly figure out what God Himself would do in a tough situation?

We're not God, for God's sake!"

Abby smiled, not knowing if he realized his own joke. Jon saw her, realized what he'd said, and also smiled.

"But 'Abdu'l-Bahá, he never claimed to even be a prophet. He was just…well not 'just,' but…well anyway, he was raised by Bahá'u'lláh, who *was* directly plugged in to God, you know; and so it's a lot more reasonable, we could say, to study 'Abdu'l-Bahá's life and try to be like him. And actually, he said we should."

"Should what?"

"Try to be like him. Do like he did."

"Are you?"

"I'm thinking about it. Well, I guess I already have, haven't I?" He laughed, his baffled look replaced by certainty. It was as if storm clouds cleared off his face.

"Hey, thanks!" he said.

"What for?" She was quite surprised.

"For listening, for asking honest questions. It really helped. Wow," his voice dropped to a whisper, "one of the Bahá'í months is named Questions. That must be pretty important if they named a month after it, huh? Sure helped me." He got up to put his spoon, saucer, and empty cup in the dishwasher. "She gave me a book. I think I'll go look at it now," he said. "See you later." And he was gone.

Abby was putting her own bowl and spoon in the dishwasher when Ricky came down to the kitchen, saw her, and grinned his goofy grin. His slightly curly, light-brown hair was combed. He wore a polo shirt and clean jeans.

"Hey!" he said. "Whatcha doin'?"

"Nothin'," she tossed back with the same smile he'd thrown at her.

He went to the refrigerator and got out a bag of English muffins, a jar of jelly, and a new stick of butter. Abby sat down again.

"I'm kinda in a hurry this morning," he said, ripping apart the muffin with his usual zeal and pushing the two halves into the toaster.

"Why's that?"

"Gonna go on a ride-along," he said.

"A what?"

"Ya know, ride along with the police. Or one policeman, anyway," he explained as he took a knife out of the drawer and peeled the paper off the end of the butter stick.

"Wow, really?" Abby was genuinely impressed.

"Yeah. I'm s'posed to meet a policeman at the station, and then we will go patrol for a few hours."

"I'd be scared of someone shooting at me," Abby revealed.

"Oh, I think that'd be cool. I'd get down low in my seat and watch. Waaayy better than watching it on TV!" Ricky enthused.

Abby watched him, dumbstruck for a moment. He grabbed the hot muffin halves out of the toaster, tossed them onto a paper napkin, sliced off thin squares of hard butter, and spread it on the hot halves.

"I might be a cop when I…you know, for my career."

"You would *want* to be a policeman?"

Ricky paused in his jelly-loading procedure and looked at her.

"Yeah, why not?"

Abby was not sure she should explain. Getting shot at, being in a rather low-status job according to Mother, having to handle everything from loose dogs to murders…it creeped her out. But he seemed very keen about it. She tried to gloss over any hard feelings with a small smile and a shrug. She hoped the shiver she felt didn't show.

Ricky fished a can of soda pop out of the fridge and brought it and the muffin to the table. He bit into his muffin, gulped soda, then burped the ABCs for Abby.

She couldn't help but laugh.

"Pop for breakfast?" she said, still giggling. Mother only allowed carbonated drinks for special occasions like birthdays.

"Absolutely," Ricky declared, puffing out his chest. "Starts the day off with a bang…or at least a lot of fizz!"

Abby admired his spirit if not his choice of foods, and they chatted about their upcoming school years while he ate. As he finished, Penny and Jenn came into the kitchen. Sofia soon joined them. Abby slid to the seat furthest in the corner. She found her willingness to speak was shrinking with each person who came into the room.

The kitchen bustled as everyone wished Ricky a fun ride-along and got food for themselves. Abby had not heard any prospective plans for the day, and it seemed no one had decided. Options included shopping, swimming at the public pool, a trip to the coast – which Abby silently favored – and having the neighbors over. Sofia turned to Abby.

"Penny says you might like to go riding."

"Oh! Um…"

"Vivi says you've been riding for several years now."

"Yes, I have," Abby said with a touch of pride.

"Well, there is a stable not too far from here that rents out horses. Perhaps you'd like to go on a trail ride or whatever it is they do," Sofia said, watching Abby for a response.

"Um, I didn't bring my boots," Abby said, once again bitterly regretting her cursed relationship with her mother, who thwarted her at every turn.

"I think they take people in tennis shoes," Sofia said.

"Well, if it works out, um, I really don't know..." Abby trailed off as she wandered off down mental pathways of horse smell, dusty trails, and scenes from movies with herself as the star. Her chin rested in her hands, elbows on the table, index fingers fiddling with the small gold hoops she'd so often worn since Mother had allowed her to get her ears pierced a few days after her twelfth birthday. She dismissed the nagging detail of no boots, and had trouble imagining her fantasy horse because she didn't know what it would look like. But she drew great courage from the idea of doing something so wonderful.

She came to earth to ask Sofia, "When would I go, please...if it all works out?"

"We'll have to check with everyone to make sure, but maybe even this afternoon," Sofia said with a smile. She seemed to understand that, although Abby didn't show it much on the outside, she was quite interested in riding. Abby liked Sofia, and she sometimes wished she'd been born into Sofia's family instead of Vivian's.

After breakfast, Abby followed Jenn into the family room.

"You okay?" Jenn asked Abby softly, giving her that coded look that meant: "Way down deep are you okay?"

"Yes, I am," Abby was able to answer truthfully. Boosted by the interesting breakfast conversations and the promise of riding soon, she was quite well indeed.

Chapter 9: Horseplay

Between grocery shopping and neighbors coming over that night, Abby's horsing around had to wait until the next day; and then it wasn't trail riding. Penny's friend Barb had arranged for them to see her sister "wiggle ropes and wave sticks" at her horse.

Penny drove Abby over to the stable, where they met Barb and her older sister Angie. Abby wasn't sure why Barb was there if she thought the whole thing was so kooky, but hoped the girl wouldn't criticize so much as to make a scene.

Abby felt strange in her tennis shoes and capris, but everything else was very familiar and comforting. The dingy barn, dirty and brimming with things Abby treasured. Horses and halters and hay that made her sneeze. Manure and leather and sweat. She even saw a chunk of hoof paring and picked it up, feeling the familiar hardness and noting that it must have been recently cut because it was not yet dried and curled.

Angie leased her horse. The owner required anyone who handled the horse to use this kind of training, so Angie had been learning it. She walked out of the barn carrying an orange stick and a long white lead rope clipped to a thin green rope halter, with a red string sticking out of her back pocket.

Why the different equipment? Abby didn't know how many questions Angie would tolerate and decided she'd better wait to see.

Angie led the group, trooping down the lane towards the paddocks. Abby expected Angie to go in and catch her horse, but she stopped at the gate. She whistled towards a medium-sized bay horse, who lifted its head and stared at Angie, then continued to nibble at sparse blades of brown grass.

"Ah," Angie said softly with a small smile. "The game is on."

Why did Angie seem to be happy about this disobedience? Weren't horses supposed to obey right away?

Angie slipped between the strands of twisted wire fencing, then ambled not towards the horse but in front of it, leisurely threading the red string into the leather loop at the tip of the stick. This was different. Abby was used to walking in a firm, hopefully boss-like, manner right up to the horse and catching it as soon as possible.

Angie bypassed the horse, but the bay gazed steadily at her, forgetting about eating. Angie changed direction, aiming beyond the horse's hindquarters. The horse took one step towards Angie, who stopped and began to back up. This was really bizarre. Abby was starting to agree with Barb, who whispered, "Told you she was nuts."

The horse dropped its head again, and Abby began to feel frustrated with its lack of cooperation. Abby felt like hollering that Angie should go right to the horse and catch it. She was glad she hesitated an extra moment, because the horse took another step towards Angie and she backed up another step. It almost seemed like the horse was in charge of being caught, and Angie was dancing with it in some kind of catching dance. Weird! Abby had certainly never seen anything like it.

The horse stepped again, and again, then walked steadily towards Angie, who laughed, her outstretched hand holding the halter and lead rope out like a treat. Then she ran backwards, the horse trotting towards her. For a second, it looked like a game of tag. Then the game was over, with a laughing Angie out of breath at the gate, and the horse – a mare, Abby saw – looking alive and happy. Abby was totally dumbfounded. What *was* this?

Angie began to stroke and hug the mare, explaining that Beauty and she had just been playing the Catching Game. It was part of the Parelli program of horse whispering, or natural horsemanship.[11] She slowly repeated the name: *pa-RELL-ee*. She rubbed Beauty all over with the halter and lead rope. It looked like she was searching the mare for any itchy spots. She did find one extra-itchy spot under Beauty's belly. She scratched it and laughed while Beauty stretched out her neck and upper lip and nodded her head like a dog. It looked like an oft-rehearsed and beloved ritual.

Angie stroked Beauty some more, but now it looked like an ordinary check of Beauty's legs and skin. Abby kept expecting the mare to leave, but she showed no sign of wanting to. One time, Beauty scooted backwards and then stopped.

"Oh, the old favorite, huh?" Angie said with a smile, scratching in the hollow in front of the shoulder. Beauty leaned into Angie's hands, asking her to scratch harder.

Abby fretted that the halter was still not on Beauty. Any moment now, the mare would push her way past Angie and escape back to her buddies at the other end of the paddock!

After what felt like eons, Angie knelt down on the ground, holding the halter open. When Beauty plunged her head into the halter, Angie quickly tied a knot. No buckle, no crownpiece slapping! Abby started wondering if this equipment was better and if she should use it. On her knees. But how would you get a horse like Moony to stick around? She would look for the right time to ask. Abby began to feel that if this was how catching the horse went, the rest of this Parelli stuff was going to be *really* different.

Angie stood up. She held a tidbit by Beauty's tail, stretching the tail forwards. Beauty bent nearly in half to reach the treat. It looked like horse gymnastics.

"Isn't she crazy?" Barb said, but now Abby detected a hint of pride in her voice. Finally Abby understood: Barb showed her admiration with teasing that sounded like criticism.

Angie bantered with Barb good-naturedly. "Yup, crazy as a dizzy duck!" "Crazy as a three-legged dog finding a corner in a round room!" "Crazy as a long-tailed cat at a rocking chair convention!"

Angie unlatched the gate while they joked, then pointed towards the opening. Beauty exited, turned and waited quietly while Angie shut the gate. Angie sent her down the lane, pointing with the hand that held the lead rope. When Beauty did not move, Angie wiggled the orange stick behind the mare, which made her walk on. Angie walked next to the mare's belly...on Beauty's right side. Wait, weren't you supposed to do everything from the horse's left side?

This was all so smooth and pleasant; so different from Abby's usual struggle with the horses she had to chase down, trick into a halter, and drag to the barn. There might be something useful here.

Beauty's nose arrived first at the cluster of sheds Angie had aimed at. Instead of tying her to one of the rails, Angie pointed Beauty around the rails...and even backed her between two of the tie rails by wiggling her finger like she was scolding the mare, but then hugged her and lavished love on her when she went smoothly. Abby began to feel that the surprises might never end.

Barb held the lead rope while Angie fetched a grooming bucket and bareback pad from one of the sheds. Abby had never seen anyone ride with a bareback pad. It seemed dangerous yet glamorous. Boarders at The Ride Place sometimes rode plain bareback, if they wanted a horse to carry them in from a pasture; they tied up the lead rope in a loop. But no one did anything very fancy riding bareback, nor for very long. Saddles seemed much safer. And where was the bridle?

Angie brushed Beauty, holding the middle of the long lead rope in the crook of her elbow. Beauty pinned her ears once, swinging her head around at Angie. Angie actually apologized, looked at the spot nearly underneath the mare, and found a swollen bug bite.

"Hmm, well, it's right under the cinch area. I guess no bareback pad today. I'll ride naked then!" She grinned mischievously at Barb, who reliably started in with jokes about how uncomfortable and risqué that would be.

Abby recalled Moony turning to bite at his sides. Only then, there'd been a saddle in the way. Abby's heart sank. Moony had probably had an itch under the saddle, and she'd *slapped* him for it. He'd pinned his ears at her because she'd been unfair. She hadn't meant to be; she just hadn't understood. Abby was beginning to realize there might be a *lot* she didn't understand about horses.

Angie stowed the grooming tub and bareback pad in the shed and then headed for a shortcut between pens, her entourage in tow. Horses in the pens approached, ready to make trouble with Beauty, but Angie whirled her string and stick over her head like a helicopter. That kept the rascals back! Beauty was not even bothered enough to lift her head, but walked calmly under the singing string, behind Angie and in front of Penny, Abby, and Barb.

They reached a round, pipe-panel pen. This time, Abby was not surprised to see Angie back Beauty through the gate, wiggling her finger.

Angie led Beauty to the middle of a round pen, scratched the mare's itchy spots some more, and cued Beauty's front legs and then hind end to glide away...first with a touch and next with just a look. It was so smooth, yet so fancy! Angie rubbed Beauty, cooed encouragement, and hugged her neck. It looked nothing like Abby's usual sessions – it looked like a lot more fun!

"How about Circle Game?" Angie asked Beauty, then waited as if the calm, attentive mare might voice a reply.

Beauty pressed her head into Angie's chest, and perhaps that was an affirmative reply. Misty-eyed, Angie caressed Beauty's ears, jaw, and cheeks, murmuring rapturously. Abby felt it was the most beautiful thing she'd ever seen. She couldn't imagine a horse ever giving its head to her, and envied their love. A matchstick of desire flicked against the grit of envy in her heart, caught, and began to burn. She so wanted that kind of relationship with horses.

Angie stroked the mare tenderly for as long as Beauty touched her. "Put my heart in my hand and rub her all over with my heart," Angie said softly.

When Beauty drew away, Angie stood tall, finger-scolded her back, and pointed to her right. Beauty circled the pen. Angie just stood there, passing the rope around her back or leaning on her stick. Abby had seen horse owners at The Ride Place lunging their horses. They faced their horses and kept their whips ready. Abby had assumed that was because the horses would stop if you didn't keep after them. Yet Beauty continued to walk with no prodding at all.

After two laps, Angie tipped her head to one side, smiled, and then reeled in the lead rope. Beauty came in to Angie for more praise, rubbing, and hugs. Abby's hand twitched, wishing to slap the mare heartily for its good performance; but Angie had not even patted Beauty, only stroked her.

She sent the mare out the opposite way for another two circles and brought her in again. Reaching Angie faster than the girl could reel it in, Beauty accidently stepped on her lead rope. Abby held her breath, waiting for the explosion. Horses panicked when they felt their heads being trapped like that. But when Beauty felt the tug on her halter, she calmly stepped off the rope. Abby had to wonder if Angie even noticed what Beauty had done; she'd been busy rubbing and praising the mare.

Next, Angie sent her to face the pipes. When Angie faced Beauty's side, stood tall, and pointed her stick at Beauty's shoulder, the mare glided sideways halfway around the pen.

It all looked like a conversation...not just love, but almost some kind of language between them. Once in a while, Angie would make some little comment to Beauty like "Good one!" or "No, move your hindquarters more!" She reminded Abby of a teacher leading a class. So, Abby reflected, there was love, language, and leadership all happening at once. Wow, this was something she'd *love* to learn. Angie was doing stuff Abby had never even dreamed of...and she dreamed about horses a lot!

After cueing Beauty sideways from each side, Angie softly mused, "Hmm, what for squeeze?" Looking around, she spied a cardboard box on the side of the lane. Barb fetched it, and Penny helped lift it over the fence. Angie dragged it a few feet away from the fence, stood next to it, and pointed to the gap.

Beauty seemed unsure about this request. Instead of smacking her or yelling at her, Angie stroked her and talked with her. Beauty's head bobbed up and down as if she were wearing bifocals and trying to read small print. Angie waited. Beauty poked her nose towards the box. Angie praised and stroked her one more time, then finger-scolded her backwards, away from the box.

Abby gave up trying to predict what Angie was going to do; Angie did the opposite of pretty much everything Abby had been taught to do with horses. But Abby loved it all!

When Angie again sent Beauty into the narrow space between the box and the panel, Beauty panicked halfway through and rushed forward. Angie was ready for it, though, and wiggled the rope hard; then she aimed her stick at Beauty's hindquarters, getting the mare to face her. The confident, relaxed brunette again praised Beauty and pulled another treat from her jeans pocket, this time asking her to bend way down between her front legs while Angie held the morsel just in front of her seeking mouth.

"That's to help her stretch, and maybe one day to bow," Angie said to the trio of watching girls.

Although stretching sounded boring, bowing sounded awesome!

But why was she rewarding Beauty for bolting through the opening? Angie sent Beauty back the other way. That at least was becoming predictable: Angie wanted Beauty to do everything from both sides, not just the left. This time, when Beauty went more willingly and did not rush through quite so fast, Angie gave her another treat. Hmm, maybe she was thanking the mare for trying. It seemed like Angie could see Beauty's thoughts and change them.

Angie asked the mare to go through the narrow space again, and Beauty went completely calmly. Abby was easily able to guess Angie would make a happy fuss over her accomplishment again, but she could never have foretold what Angie did next.

"Pick me up!" Angie told Beauty, climbing up the pipe panel to the highest rail. Nothing happened. Angie waved the stick at the mare's far-side hindquarters, bringing Beauty calmly close enough to slide a leg smoothly over her back. She was going to ride the mare using that same skimpy rope halter and that same lead rope, not even tied in a loop!

Angie looked ahead, lifted her rope-holding hand, and smiled; and Beauty obediently stepped forward towards her audience. Where was the kicking that Abby thought was required? The repeated clucking? Angie looked to her left, towards the middle of the pen; and as the pair passed in front of the girls, Abby thought she saw a slight movement of Angie's right leg. Beauty turned left into the middle of the pen. Angie seemed to slump, and Beauty stopped. There was apparently a better way to stop a horse than pulling back rather hard on both reins; but Abby did not know what that way was.

"What did you do to stop?" She finally asked her first question.

"Well, where Beauty and I are at in the levels, I let my energy down and then block her forward motion. But we're working on me thinking stop and she stops," Angie responded, twisting around on the mare's smooth brown back to answer.

Abby had been hoping for something a bit more useable, like "Pull the rein this way and give this cue."

"A truly Zen answer," Barb commented.

"What are 'levels'?" Abby ventured to Barb.

"In Parelli, there are levels of study. You can do the first three at home with the DVD kits. She has graduated Level 1 with Beauty and is doing her Level 2."

"Oh," Abby replied absently, watching Angie bend Beauty's head to both sides with some special rein cues. "Why are you doing that?" she couldn't help asking.

"This is my emergency stop; if she ever gets scared and runs off, I'll bend her with one rein like this. I should have done it when I first got on; but we were next to the fence, so I brought her into the middle. We did it at the halt now, and I also do it at the walk and trot. When we get up to cantering, I'll do it at the canter."

Abby realized this is how she could have handled Moony's out-of-control run during the Rescue Race. This was valuable information!

Angie asked Beauty to move her front and back feet with cues that Abby couldn't decipher but that the team seemed to know completely.

The duo began to walk around the pen's perimeter. Angie seemed to be turning Beauty with invisible cues from her body or legs, because the rope-rein never moved. They changed directions a few times. Then Angie asked Beauty, "Well, should I try trotting bareback?"

"*Try* is not a four-letter word!" Barb replied impishly.

Angie set Beauty ambling around the pen again. Angie seemed to be focused on something only she could see or feel. After a while, she lifted the rope, breathed in, sat up, and seemed to expect Beauty to go faster. At first, Beauty did not respond. After another moment, Angie made a kissing sound, then began to slap her own thigh. At this sound, the mare broke into a slow trot. Angie bounced and slid off-center.

Beauty slowed down to a walk again and seemed willing to stop, but Angie told her, "No, I've got it now," and sent her into a trot again while leaning back a little further. This made a big difference; Angie was well able to stay on. Even Angie's brown ponytail barely bounced. After one circuit of the round pen, Angie shrank down again. The mare stopped and received her rider's raving thanks and praise with a quiet grace that reflected her name.

Angie asked her into a trot going the other way, improving as she went, and ended by changing directions while the rope lay on Beauty's neck.

At their graceful stop, Angie laughed in appreciative delight. Barb clapped, and the other two observers joined in. Abby overflowed with admiration for everything she'd seen. She hadn't even known that such a willing, harmonious time was possible with horses. What she thought was right and normal was backwards compared to the cooperation and acceptance this happy pair was enjoying right in front of her eyes. She felt very, *very* privileged to have seen this.

Barb opened the round pen gate, and Angie rode Beauty out. Going forward for a change, Abby thought, catching the playful spirit. Angie chatted, happy and relaxed, as the complacent bay moseyed to her paddock. There was no tack to undo, it was so free and easy, the world just looked so different to Abby now…oh, what couldn't you do with boxes and fences and nearly invisible cues and a simple halter, lead, stick, and string? And a horse that seemed just as happy to do whatever you asked as to be back with its buddies?

Barb and Angie recounted how Beauty had used to be, before they started Parelli with her. Abby was again amazed, this time to hear of a completely different mare. One that could not be caught in less than an hour. That could not be ridden without a harsh bit, big spurs, a riding crop or two. That – even with a tack-roomful of restraints – was unpredictably spooky.

This challenged basic horse lore: "A horse's nature is set: it's unchangeable." "If a horse is a bolter, it will always be inclined to bolt." "If a horse is hard to catch, that's the way it is." People at The Ride Place always said things like that. Did this Parelli thing claim the ability to change how a horse *is*? Abby waited for a break in the conversation and asked that question.

"Oh yes, definitely," Angie asserted. "Of course, the human has to learn horse language first. But eventually, yes, we can help to change horses' minds about things."

"Isn't there anything that cannot be changed? Like, what about a horse that bites?" Abby had heard that once a horse has learned to bite people, it had best be sold, possibly to the killer-buyers, because that habit was impossible to break.

"I don't know if there are any horses that are hopeless, I'm not an expert," Angie said. "But Pat – Pat Parelli – says backing a horse away cures biting. Luckily, I can't speak from personal experience, because that's one thing Beauty didn't used to do. But beating horses into submission usually backfires, and they ignore us if we beg them to behave. We need to be firm, fair, and friendly as the situation requires."

She slid off Beauty's back at the bay's pasture gate, motioned her in, turned her around, gave her one last hug and kiss, and undid the halter knot. Beauty sashayed off sedately, first to get a drink and then to sniff her buddies.

Angie's explanations sounded so reasonable. So true! Abby just needed to learn how to do it. She decided she was going to. Somehow.

Chapter 10: Bookstore

Abby climbed into bed early, tired and happy, and fell asleep right away. She dreamt of horses…

∞ ∞ ∞ ∞ ∞ ∞ ∞ ∞

… spotted and painted horses swirl around her … they have no fear … she feels no fear … she stands smiling in their midst and they come to her … she hugs their necks and they hug her with their heads … smells them and they sniff her skin, hair … kisses them and they gently mouth her hands, cheeks … brushes them and they glow in beauty … laughs and they neigh in response … rides them sure-seated and they chase the wind … wondrous … glorious … magical …

∞ ∞ ∞ ∞ ∞ ∞ ∞ ∞

The magic stuck with her when she woke up. Dressing, she pondered getting hold of the Level 1 study kit and equipment. Angie had said it was worth it to use the Parelli halter and rope instead of nylon web and twisted cotton. She said it made it easier to communicate with a horse. The study pack plus equipment cost about four hundred dollars, an impossible amount of money to Abby. Maybe when she got back home, she could learn who owned the orange stick on the rack and see if they would share equipment or videos with her. Perhaps she could do chores in exchange.

Mulling it over, she entered the kitchen and nearly ran into Jon.

"Oh! Hi," she blurted out, jumping backwards.

"Good morning," he said lightly, apparently in no way affronted by her inattentiveness.

They fetched breakfast – she a glass of milk and a toaster pastry, he a cup of coffee – and sat down together.

"What are your plans today?" Jon asked.

"Don't have any," Abby replied, stowing a bite of Toasty Tart in her cheek before speaking. She spoke carefully so as to not spit food. Mother would be all over her like white on rice if she was impolite to her cousin.

"Do you want to come with us?" he invited. "Melissa and I are going to go to a couple of shops. One is a coffee shop we like, the other is a new bookstore. And maybe hit some last-of-summer sales."

"I probably could; I'll have to check with Mother," she said.

Jon mentioned needing to check the mouse traps in the pantry, as there'd been a funny smell. He mentioned a large disgusting roach one of the cats had caught in the kitchen, and they traded revolting house-vermin stories until Ricky walked in. Jon asked him how yesterday's ride-along had gone. Abby also nodded her interest.

"It was cool!" Ricky enthused, getting the last two Toasty Tarts and a can of soda pop. They had documented a fight between two special-ed kids at the high school. The teacher had said the kids taunted each other all summer session, but the budget didn't allow extra supervision. One kid had called the other an "ass pee," which Ricky assumed was some kind of retard-insult.

They had also investigated a report of a motorcyclist trespassing on someone's vacant land. The caller was in a Neighborhood Watch that had been trying to catch any of the bikers who'd been roaring around the field recently. Probably some bored kids looking for fun. Ricky had helped the officer record a description of the motorcycle and its rider.

"Well, I'm off to Brent's house," Ricky bubbled, tossing his empty can across the kitchen into the trash by the back door. "Three points!" He jerked the full trash bag out of the wastebasket and clanged out the back door.

Abby finished her milk and tart, cleaned up, and excused herself. As she left the kitchen, she changed mental gears. She might have to break a cardinal rule: Don't Wake Mother! The door to the family room was closed. Abby tested the knob, then opened it carefully.

Daddy sat on the edge of the bed in his underwear, taking earplugs out of his ears. Mother was lying down, her arm crooked over her eyes as she often did when "just resting." Daddy saw Abby and beckoned to her, putting his finger to his lips. Abby tiptoed to him, hesitated, then asked how he'd slept.

"It could always be better," he said, smiling sadly. His genial face looked haggard and he had bad breath. She felt sorry for him.

She whispered her request to go with Jon. Daddy whispered back that Abby could go where she liked today. He asked that Jon take his cell phone, then gave her a sleepy smile as she whispered her okay. She left the room quietly and went upstairs to get ready.

Jenn was just getting up. She said she would probably go shopping for school stuff with Penny and her friends, maybe check out some new CDs, hit the closest mall. She'd be back in time for dinner and would show Abby whatever she bought. Abby shared her newfound passion about Angie's "craziness" with her horse. Jenn gave her a quiet high-five and said it sounded really neat.

Grabbing the backpack that served as her purse, Abby found Jon waiting for her in the front hallway.

Jon worked at a burger place, Abby knew, in order to afford his car. Either the job didn't pay much or the car was too costly for him, even as shabby as it was. Three different colors decorated the passenger side, holes marked missing plaques, and dents and scratches competed with the rust. Jon wrenched the passenger door open for Abby and held the glove box shut long enough for her to sit. Duct tape and staples barely restrained the flopping fabric headliner, upholstery gave way to bulging foam, and bags of cans filled the hatchback.

"Morc welcomes you," Jon said.

"Pardon?" she asked. "N" was a hard sound to make with a plugged nose; she'd have to switch to "Excuse me."

"Morc – M-O-R-C, my Mobile Office and Recycling Center – welcomes you," Jon said louder. "Robin Williams would never be caught dead in here!"

It took a moment to figure it out, then Abby connected the famous comedian and his first famous role, the alien Mork. The last movie she had seen him in was *Night at the Museum*. He had played a serious part for a change, but he had jabbered away like Mork in one part of it. She had actually enjoyed that movie a lot, enough to watch it a second time with the director's comments turned on.

Jon coaxed the reluctant ignition into starting, and off they chugged emitting clouds of blue smoke. Rattles, squeaks, and loud engine noises made talking too hard, so Abby simply looked at Little Lily's tree-lined neighborhoods and stark strip malls. She hoped it wouldn't get too hot today, but it was promising to be a cooker, as usual.

Melissa was waiting for them on a bench outside her family's apartment building, working on something in her lap. Abby switched to the back seat, making sure that the springs showing through were covered by the cushion Jon gave her. Melissa expertly held the floppy glovebox door shut as she slid into the front bucket seat. When Abby asked her what she'd been working on, she pulled out a baggie and extracted two pieces of fabric and some colored thread.

"It's counted cross-stitch," she said. "Two different designs, see? One is 'World Peace' made from the peace symbol over the world. The other is 'No Hate' with the red line across the HATE." Melissa showed them to Abby. They were very attractive.[12]

"What will you do with them when they're done?"

"I think I'll make the World Peace one round and sew it onto the sleeve of my jean jacket, like a patch. And I might do one as a bookmark, or maybe a double-ended bookmark," Melissa explained in her soft Southern accent. Mother had trained Abby and Jenn to speak in an educated, slightly European way; and sometimes the various Southern accents took a minute to register. "I" sounded like "Ah."

"I've done some sewing, but never counted stitching," Abby said.

"It's not too hard," Melissa said. "I learned from the directions in the little kits I got at the mall. I bet you could, too…if you wanted to."

She showed Abby the chart and the thread symbols. True, it didn't look too hard, but Melissa's stitches were so very smooth. Abby knew it took skill to make it look that good.

Melissa tucked the project away as they parked at the coffee shop.

"We'll buy. Y'all didn't have any breakfast yet, did you?" Melissa asked.

"Oh, uh, yeah, I did," Abby responded.

"I left room for a muffin," Jon allowed, got out, and then held the door open for the girls, first at the car and then at the coffee shop.

Abby had never been in a coffee shop like this. It was more hippie, more back-to-nature than she expected. Mother would have instantly disapproved. Battered tile floors, mismatched wooden chairs, wooden windowsills supporting wild tangles of plants pressing against the front windows, neutral tan walls hung with artwork. Judging by the friendly greetings, there was quite a regular crowd, mostly young adults. Some of the patrons studied laptop computer screens. Others chatted or ate. Jon and Melissa bought apple and bran muffins and juice to share, then settled at a small table near the back of the store.

Abby looked at the artwork as they began to eat. A small white card explained each drawing, painting, or photograph. Children, still lifes, nature scenes; there didn't seem to be a particular theme.

By itself on the wall between the bathroom hallway and the back of the store, a large framed portrait of a smiling old man caught her eye. The black-and-white picture showed the most interesting expression she had ever seen on anyone's face. He looked into the camera; but it seemed he looked just at her, only at her, with an amused smile…as if he knew her secrets and thought it great fun to share them with her. Her first guess was that it was Albus Dumbledore from *Harry Potter*. His eyes twinkled as J.K. Rowling described, but lacked half-moon glasses. Definitely had the flowing white hair and beard, though, and robes.

But this wasn't a drawing of an imaginary person. It was a photograph. An actual photograph of an actual person!

The apple juice failed to reach Abby's mouth. Melissa and Jon both turned to see what had stunned her into immobility. Then they smiled.

"That's 'Abdu'l-Bahá," Melissa said.

"Who?"

"He's the one Jon was telling you about, the son of the founder of my Faith, the one who was a man we can emulate," she explained.

"Oh. Yeah, uh…" Abby struggled to remember what Jon had said. "He has a…a…an interesting look on his face."

"He had a lot of different pictures taken when he was in America, and in his other travels," Melissa said, watching Abby's reaction.

"He was in America?" He definitely wore robes and a hat in the style of the Middle East.

"Yes. He went coast to coast, and people wrote down what he said and did, took his picture, and even made some movies. The closest he came to here was Washington, D.C. They celebrate it every year."

"He looks happy, or maybe it's..." Abby could not find a word to name his expression.

"He has many looks in the different pictures. This is more a kindly, loving-father look, you might say," Melissa offered.

"Yeah, that fits it pretty well." It explained why he seemed to sympathize with her.

"The owners of this café are Bahá'í, that's why the picture is here," Melissa clarified. "Sometimes they have Bahá'í discussions and music here."

Abby looked around. Melissa intuited her intent and said that the owners would be in later.

"Are the workers all Bahá'ís?" Abby asked.

"I think right now only one or two are; the rest are not," Melissa replied.

Abby wondered if any of the employees she could see were Bahá'í. They all looked normal. Maybe Bahá'ís just looked regular. Certainly Melissa did.

They finished their food and got up to go, stopping several times to let people pass in the crowded aisles. Standing waiting for the path to clear a bit, Abby looked again at some of the art pieces, and guessed they were by Bahá'ís. One photo entitled "Children of the Half-Light" showed three children – black, white, and in-between – holding hands and passing under an archway towards the sun. An abstract painting, entitled "Order Out of Chaos," featured bright blocks of color. A pretty stained-glass star was called simply "Nine-Pointed Star." They seemed harmless enough.

She followed Melissa and Jon out and down the street, heading to the bookstore but waylaid by a fountain.

Melissa and Jon searched through their pockets for coins to toss in, combined them, and then divvied the kitty three ways.

Careful not to spill her coins, Melissa crossed all her fingers, two sets on each hand. While Jon and Abby laughed, she also crossed her legs and arms. Laughing with them, Melissa tossed all her coins high. They flashed, then splashed. Jon flipped his coins one at a time, trying to make them spin as many times as possible before hitting the water. Abby tossed hers in low and straight.

"Rats!" she said.

"Whatsamatta?" Melissa said, still happy.

"Forgot to make a wish!"

"You can share mine. My mom always had us wish for world peace with all our hearts; so when we were kids, we'd cross everything on our bodies. Sometimes we'd cross everything on ourselves and then cross the crosses with each other."

"Let's do it!" said Jon goofily.

"Yeah, let's try all three of us. Whatcha say, Abby?" Melissa turned her infectious smile to Abby.

"Yeah, so I can wish," Abby said.

Giggling, they piled their crossed pairs of fingers. They sat on the edge of the fountain to cross their legs over each others' and, finally, their arms. They resembled a human pretzel by the end of it; and Jon suddenly burst out laughing.

"Whazzo funny?" Melissa asked, half-guffawing herself.

"Where's our coin? And who can throw it?"

"Oh!" Melissa gasped for breath between laughs. "Okay, time for some creativity here. We'll just have to toss imaginary coins with our tongues; I think it's the only thing I can still move!"

Jon responded by crossing his eyes, making the girls laugh so hard they could barely keep *anything* crossed. Then they each pretended to throw in a coin with their tongue, the act made even harder because the fountain was behind them.

"Did anyone remember to wish?"

Groans and more shouts of laughter were the answer. But Abby had made her own wish after all: that she could have more fun times like this. She had precious few, and loved every second of this.

They fell apart, rubbing bits that were not used to being bent that way. Slowly they stood up and began to walk on to the bookstore, still smiling and giggling.

Jon's phone rang. He answered it, then listened silently. His face grew more and more serious. When he closed his phone, he was grim.

"It was Mom. There's a fire that started burning yesterday. Now it's spreading towards home."

The girls reacted instantly, blurting out concerns and questions.

"It's about twenty miles from our house, which is sort of at the edge of town, and they are concerned about all that dry brush catching fire. Right now it's headed towards us and, well, everyone is worried."

The group had stopped walking to ponder this information and its consequences. Jon said there was nothing they could do yet, but after the bookstore they should go home. If they had to evacuate, they'd have enough notice.

Abby had never been in a fire. She was quite worried about what affect it would have on Sofia's house and family, as well as on her own family's visit. Maybe the Wizes should leave North Carolina early… but Abby was counting on that horseback ride Sofia had offered.

Absorbed in worrying, she followed Jon and Melissa. To her surprise, the cement sidewalk had become new, green laminate flooring. Her friends were already out of sight, tracking down books.

Abby stood for a moment, unsure. Something sparkled next to the cash register: a tiny rack of beaded strings that caught the light beautifully. A little sign said they were bookmarks; but you could use them for jewelry, they were so pretty, with three or four beads on each end of a colored string. She fingered those for a moment, then drifted to a collection of miniature books at the end of the counter.

On the cover of *Zen Cowboy*, she saw a funny cartoon of an outlaw sitting in the full-lotus position in front of a cow and a cactus. A built-in bookmark ribbon ended in a tiny gold metal boot. Abby flipped through the pages and read jokes about Moo and Mu, Cowboys and Taoboys, Koans and Cow-ans. Someone had a great sense of humor, for sure! It was only $4.95, but Abby had only about two dollars. She put the cute book down reluctantly.

Another even-smaller book, *Native American Wisdom*, contained fabulous photos of Native Americans and even a few horses. As Abby scanned it, her eyes fell upon a quotation that seemed meant especially for her:

> I have noticed in my life that all men have a liking for some special animal, tree, plant or spot of earth. If men would pay more attention to these preferences and seek what is best to do in order to make themselves worthy of that toward which they are so attracted, they might have dreams which would purify their lives. Let a man decide upon his favorite animal and make a study of it, learning its innocent ways. Let him learn to understand its sounds and motions. The animals want to communicate with man, but Wakantanka does not intend they shall do so directly – man must do the greater part in securing an understanding.
>
> Brave Buffalo (late 19th century)
> Teton Sioux medicine man[13]

Abby read this twice. It was amazing. Of course, she instantly knew what her chosen animal would be…had been for as long as she could remember. And she had just seen that there could be actual communication between horses and humans, thanks to Angie the Angel. This

wise man was saying we *should* study what we are attracted to, and
learn from it, and let ourselves become like that animal or place. This
was confirmation: Abby should do what her heart was telling her to.

She wanted the book badly; yet after she'd emptied every last coin
in her wallet, and even dug into all the corners of her backpack, she still
had less than half of its $4.95 purchase price. Plus tax. Yet she knew
she would need the affirmation it provided her. She carefully folded the
front cover flap onto that page and carried it in front of her. She didn't
want anyone to think she was stealing it, but was unable to put it down.

Melissa and Jon browsed in their separate sections, Jon apparently
in the military section and Melissa in the history section. Abby looked
for the animal books, finding equines shelved among the pets. She carefully put her little book on the edge of the bookshelf and examined the
titles, delighted to find that she actually owned several. A few others
interested her only mildly. She picked up her small treasure and ambled
through the rows, looking for anything interesting.

The magazine racks held several horse titles. Some were familiar:
Horse & Rider, *Western Horseman*, *Horse Illustrated*, and *Young Rider*.
But there were many she didn't know: *Cowboys & Indians*, *Western
Cowboy*, and others. She squatted and looked at the ones on the bottom
rack, then leafed through the *Horse Illustrated*. She always enjoyed the
foldout, a tear-out poster of the month's featured breed. This month, it
was the Missouri Fox Trotter.[14] She'd heard of that one. It was like
the Tennessee Walker that was so popular in her home state. Hmmm.
Missouri, Tennessee, both gaited breeds…she wondered if the breeds
were closely related, maybe like cousins.

There wasn't anything else of great interest for her amongst the ads
for horses, saddles, and sprays, nor in the articles about building arenas,
barrel racing, small horse properties, or flying lead changes (whatever
they were; something about cantering, it seemed).

She put it back and picked up the unfamiliar *Cowboys & Indians*.
After a few pages, she understood why she'd never seen it before. It
featured some of the fanciest furniture, clothes, and jewelry she'd ever
seen, all Western-themed. She'd probably never in her whole life get to
even put on – much less own – the expensive strands of turquoise and
silver; or see – let alone live with – the antler-and-leather chairs. Every
page overwhelmed her more; so she began to turn several at once, past
the wine and restaurant reviews and articles about luxury resorts. Then
her eyes stopped dead at the gold word "Parelli."[15]

There were several small photos. Somebody – Mrs. Parelli? – was
sitting down in front of a horse she was apparently working with, smiling, holding an orange stick. Other photos showed a man – maybe Mr.

Parelli – working with horses in front of a crowd. Abby's nose nearly touched the page as she scrutinized the miniatures, mining them for information. The halters were the same as Angie's, and the horses did even neater things than she had: playing with a big green ball, standing on a platform, jumping barrels. The ad said they had actually been in Memphis, Tennessee last February. But they weren't going to be anywhere close to her for the rest of the year. Abby's heart plummeted as fast as it had soared. But maybe they'd be back next year, and maybe she could go if...

This was the key, she just knew it. Parelli was so cool. She *had* to learn how to do what she had seen Angie do. Somehow it had to work out, it just had to. She stood praying desperately to God, wherever God was, to please, please hear her...*Have to get hold of this stuff to learn this...money or no money...somehow...please...*please...*oh...*

She jumped when she felt a hand on her shoulder. Jon and Melissa looked quizzically at her.

"We're ready to check out. Are you buying anything?" Jon asked.

"Oh man, I, uh..." Abby blushed, embarrassed about not having the money to buy these two things she wanted so badly. This wasn't going at all well; now she was ashamed about being embarrassed! She looked down at her treasures, mumbling, "Don't have enough money."

"How much money would you need?" Jon asked after a questioning glance at Melissa and a quick answering nod from her.

"Um..." Abby totaled up the two items and said she would need around nine dollars more. Another signal passed between the pair.

"Bring 'em," Jon said. "We're buying."

Abby stood rooted to the floor, mouth open, stupefied. She'd never wanted anything so badly in her life, and had *never* had someone give her something like that just when she needed them to. Embarrassment, relief, and gratitude flooded through her in turns. She was also ready to be ridiculed for it, darn it! Mother's wonderful training...

But the pair waited patiently, encouragingly, until she stammered a heartfelt, nearly tearful "Thanks! Thanks *so* much!" Smiling with her, they approached the register.

As Abby laid her two prizes on the counter next to Jon's military career book and Melissa's Bahá'í book, a breeze from the open door blew the jeweled strings about. Without thinking, she touched them. The cashier asked her which one she would like. Abby, flustered and distracted, misunderstood the question and said she liked all of them.

"Well, you will need to pick *one*. Your purchase qualifies you. It's our grand opening this week."

Abby could not believe a word she was hearing. It was almost as if the heavens had opened up and admitted her to the select company of the blessed, today, now, right here. In a daze, she chose a light-green string with clear blue and bright green beads at both ends. The cashier quickly wrapped it in rustling tissue, taped it shut, put it and the books in a sack, and gave everything to Jon. To the assistant, it was a simple sale; to Abby, it was her personal blessing, a sanctified sendoff for the quest she had selected.

Chapter 11: News

The teens drove home singing. Melissa started the old "Titanic" camp song, which begged to be shouted at the top of their lungs.

Normally, singing about the doomed lifeboats would not have made Abby so happy; but today she was joyous about it. They all were. They dallied in the Holsworth driveway during the final chorus, Jon's deeper voice intoning the "sea" and the two girls taking the higher notes of the families lost.

They found a somber group of adults in the kitchen, getting a quick lunch together.

"What's the news?" Jon asked, immediately sobering.

Sofia, with Vivian and Paul, pieced together the fire's progress – burning steadily towards them but still a distance away. It was officially out of control now; but the fire department still battled it, especially near houses. Some residents had been evacuated.

They talked about how little news there was on the radio and TV. They wanted continual coverage, but neighbors provided more information than the media. They wondered how the fire started and why it got so big. It might have been some punk kid, a pyromaniac. Seemed like most years about this time, fires sprang up. Some fields could hide a kid and give a fire enough time to flare out of control. Sofia griped that no one needed extra stress from this threat. One neighbor had just learned she had cancer, another was caring for his elderly mother afflicted with Alzheimer's. The roll of woes flowed.

Ricky breezed in to grab a bite. As he heard them talk, he stopped dead in his tracks, his face white and his jaw open. Abby noticed him first. Gradually the room fell silent, everyone staring at him. He continued to stand, frozen.

"What's the matter, Ricky?" Sofia finally asked her motionless son.

It was a minute before he finally closed his mouth, swallowed hard, and murmured, "I heard about the guy who set the fire."

Everyone pelted Ricky with questions, and he described his new realization.

"On the ride-along. I heard the report about a motorcyclist roaring into a field. They've been having trouble with trespassers, with bikers being noisy. I bet anything that guy went in there and set it, way in the middle, and then got out of there. It was midday; it could have burned all afternoon without anyone seeing it unless they drove in there."

This added hours to the debate. Had the police gone back to look? Could someone have seen smoke? Why didn't the media broadcast the biker's description so that the public might help track down the rider or bike? Homes could burn down because of some arsonist on the loose!

Fear of what could happen to their own home – and if not theirs, to others – fueled radical talk about what should be done to arsonists. The adults were all in favor of jail at the very least...and more, if possible. It reminded Abby of Daddy's radio talk show. Ranting. She thought they were amping themselves up; but still, setting fires for "fun" was very, very bad.

When the adults started repeating themselves, Abby edged from the room, taking her books from the forgotten bag on the counter. The family room was empty, the stairs vacant, the upstairs rooms silent. Good. Penny had offered her computer to Abby; and now Abby definitely had something she wanted to look up. Her little Native American book slid open onto the desk as she laid down her valuables and sat.

> Conversation [she read] was never begun at once, nor in a hurried manner. No one was quick with a question, no matter how important, and no one was pressed for an answer. A pause giving time for thought was the truly courteous way of beginning and conducting a conversation. Silence was meaningful with the Lakota, and his granting a space of silence to the speech-maker and his own moment of silence before talking was done in the practice of true politeness and regard for the rule that "thought comes before speech."
>
> Luther Standing Bear, 1868?-1939
> Oglala Sioux Chief[16]

Abby imagined waiting around all the time for people to ask or answer. Wouldn't it make for awfully boring conversations?

Abby typed the Parelli web address into the ADDRESS field. Dazzling photos and bunches of subpages greeted her. Classes, instructors, an annual Colorado conference, equipment, rotating pictures of Pat and Linda Parelli. Where to start? Taking a deep breath, she yielded to her burning desire and clicked on Tour Stops. But the schedule ended at November of this year, so she couldn't tell if she could go to one next year. But she enjoyed clicking on photos and reading testimonials.

At first, whenever she wanted a new page, she shut down the whole site and re-entered it. But after a bit, she remembered Penny's navigation techniques and began using the BACK button, sliding switches, and several other tricks. Not being skilled at computers, especially the internet, she was proud of herself. Classes in school had covered only basic typing, clicking, and saving. They couldn't even print anything because paper and ink cost too much to give away to students. Navigating this site added to Abby's growing feeling of adventure and daring.

She clicked around the Parelli site, looking at the Level 1 kit in its beckoning red box and the happy people adoring their horses in clinics and courses. When she felt she couldn't look at them anymore without bursting with longing to join them, she clicked one last time on the little X-for-exit. Nudging her bra hooks aside, she leaned back against the wooden pressback chair, and mulled over what she'd seen.

The Parellis said they wanted to help horse owners' dreams come true. Wow. It was unreal but real, all of it. It was like a bubble – beautiful, special, and in danger of vanishing at any moment. Above all, she did not dare mention any of this around Mother. God only knew how Vivian would use this desire against Abby.

Which reminded her...Abby logged back on, entered "Baha'i" in the SEARCH field – she didn't know how to make the little marks over the two letters, but apparently didn't need them – and clicked on the first listing: Bahai.org. And there were more rotating pictures of happy people. No horses, but more skin colors than on the Parelli site, where everyone had been white. Hmm, wouldn't any people with darker skin want to do Parelli? Even in America? And what about the Native Americans; they were experts with horses!

Maybe it was a money thing, Abby thought. Horses are expensive, everyone knew that; and usually people with colored skin didn't make as much, everyone also knew that. Although, as Abby followed this train of thought, a little voice popped up in her head to ask: "But *why* do colored people make less money than whites?" Abby didn't know; she just knew it was so.

Wouldn't brown people love horses? Her heart said that girls with darker skin would love horses just as much as white girls do. How sad if their color prevented them from being with horses. Abby was quite sure she would not be the same person without horses in her life. They were her escape, her way to fly from everything that was sad and bad in her life. Oh! Fly from sad and bad, ride to glad! A babyish rhyme, but meaningful to her.

She looked again at the Bahá'í page and read the quotations from Bahá'u'lláh. About the earth being one country and mankind its citizens. About the world needing peace and security through the unity of all its people. And other quotes. It seemed to be serious business, Abby thought, and yet the people looked, umm, seriously *happy*.

Like Melissa. Jon's friend seemed to know where she was going in life, what she was doing – although Abby realized she'd never asked Melissa what her direction was – but she seemed to be having a good time getting there. That looked like an excellent way to be, and Abby vowed to be more like that. Headed where you wanted to go, having a good time getting there. Perfect.

Hours had passed. Mother called "Dinner's ready!" up the stairs. Abby quickly closed down the computer and, taking her books to her room, found a new sports bra waiting for her on her cot! Apparently, Jenn had bought it today and left it for her as a gift. She was almost as touched by the love it represented as by the usefulness of the item. She quickly peeled off her T-shirt, took off the old bra, and slid on the new one, trying it inside out as she was sure Jenn intended. It seemed like it would be great, including for riding. She would whisper her thanks to Jenn at dinner. What a great sister!

She went downstairs. And when she smelled the crockpot stew, she realized she hadn't had lunch and was ravenous. Everybody gathered in the kitchen to eat and complain about the fire. It was spreading, but there was no other official news about it. Phone rumors between friends flew rampant, fueling frenzied feelings. Neighbors raged about how the blaze was gaining headway.

As Abby joined the families at the extended kitchen table, Penny and Jenn were quizzing Ricky about the motorcyclist in the field. He racked his brain again, trying to remember every last little bit about it.

"Do you know the rider?" Penny asked. "Or think you've seen the motorcycle?"

No one had asked this question yet, so everyone waited for Ricky's answer.

"Hmm, well, I don't think...or maybe..."

His elders blasted him with questions, urging and insisting he think harder; but he frowned more and shook his head slightly.

"I guess not, no, probably not," he said, slightly irritated.

Abby thought he'd *almost* remembered something but lost it in the hubbub. Maybe if he'd been given "a space of silence"...

While the others roundly criticized the authorities' bungling of the fire, Sofia quietly told Abby that, if everything worked out, she could do that trail ride tomorrow morning. The adults could take her on their way to a street fair, assuming the fire didn't get worse. This was good news, and Abby began to daydream about it. She still missed her boots, and wondered whether she should try to do any Parelli on the horse she was assigned; but overall, she was sure it would be wonderful.

If only she'd picked up a Harry Potter crystal ball at the bookstore, she might have seen she was wrong. Almost dead wrong.

Chapter 12: Flying

True to her word, Sofia and Abby's parents took her to the Pleasant View stables for a nine o'clock trail ride. Several roads were closed due to smoke, making for slow going. That was fine with Abby; it gave her time to relive her dream from last night. She'd won a five-way coin toss for Baby Doll, the best lesson horse at The Ride Place...

∞   ∞   ∞   ∞   ∞   ∞   ∞   ∞

... in a big field, Baby Doll trots right up to Abby ... Abby ties a string around Baby Doll's neck ... plays ground games with her on the way to the dirt track ... Tag ... Follow My Leader ... Jump This ... many more ... Tony is waiting for them, grins handsomely, offers Abby an orange wand ... Abby accepts it ... leaps up onto Baby Doll's back ... cues the mare to turn ... walk ... stop ... trot ... jump over poles ... canter ... skid to a stop ... spin ... gallop a final lap ... oh! free, sticking like velcro to Baby Doll's back, Abby flies, unified with her horse, ecstatic ... fear doesn't exist ... every moment is a peak experience ... the lesson ends with jumping all the fences heading back to Baby Doll's pasture ... she hugs Baby Doll and the horse hugs back ... tucks Abby into her chest with her lower jaw ...

∞   ∞   ∞   ∞   ∞   ∞   ∞   ∞

Memory of the dream's horsey hug carried Abby through the rest of the slow drive.[17] But when they arrived at the trail ride, she felt like a tourist – improperly dressed in tennies and capris, unfamiliar with the horses and layout – rather than an experienced equestrienne. But at least her right pinky had healed and could manage the pressure of the reins.

Sofia and Dad waited in the car while Mother – with only minimal grumbling – paid for the ride, signed paperwork releasing the ranch from all liability, and double-checked the pick-up time; then the three adults left. The office girl stowed Abby's backpack in a cabinet. She'd brought Jenn's loaner supplies, her own wallet, an icy water bottle, and her *HP #7* in case the adults were delayed picking her up.

Abby met her mount, a gray horse with well-used tack. She bent to see if it was a boy or girl. Seeing the wedge of sheath near the back legs, she told him he was a good boy and patted him...oops, stroked his neck. Gunsmoke seemed mildly interested in Abby, neither rude nor super-curious. Abby liked him right away. He seemed to know the score.

The wranglers checked each rider's stirrup length by holding the stirrup in their armpits and placing their knuckles under the leather flap called the saddle jockey.[18] One wrangler shortened Abby's stirrups, although she could have done it herself. She did not want to talk about how much she knew. They might, if they were like Mother, quiz her or even give her a harder horse.

The wranglers helped each rider mount their horse from the left, get their feet in the stirrups, and hold the reins. "Kick your horse lightly to go," they instructed. "Pull back gently on both reins to stop. Stay well behind the horse in front of you. And don't let 'em eat on the trail."

Angie jumped unbidden to mind. Angie had never once kicked her horse to go nor pulled to stop; but Abby didn't know how to cue a horse in the new way. She decided she'd use the lightest cues she could.

Gunsmoke hadn't read the memo, though; he resisted any cues at all. The other riders headed out onto the trail, going towards the hill behind the stables, but Abby couldn't convince Gunsmoke to take even one step. Her stupid tennis shoes were too soft. And the fenders irritated her bare calves. She *knew* she should've brought her riding clothes!

The last wrangler twisted a green twig off a nearby tree and gave it to Abby to use on Gunsmoke's rump. This did the trick. Gunsmoke reluctantly headed after the herd. For a little while, anyway, until he was distracted by some tasty-looking weeds.

The wrangler smacked the horse with his long reins whenever the gray head bobbed down, which was at nearly every patch of weeds. Abby tried to pull Gunsmoke's head up, but just wasn't strong enough. She braced her feet against the stirrups to pull harder. Suddenly, her left foot slipped all the way through the stirrup, and her right nearly did.

Oh no! This was deadly! She remembered all too well some of the horror stories; if she fell off now, with her foot trapped in the stirrup, she would land on her head! Gunsmoke got in a bunch of extra eating as Abby wrestled her foot out, then kept the balls of her feet on the stirrups as she'd heard she should.

Once her alarm subsided, and she was ready to go again, Abby used her stick so long and so hard that she didn't think she could continue. Her arm was giving out. This wasn't the ride she had hoped for at *all*. Watching Beauty again would have been much better!

Gunsmoke shambled down the path, halfheartedly, only because of the wrangler's help. Once he smacked too hard and Gunsmoke jumped forward several steps, nearly unseating Abby, until an extra-appealing patch of grass stopped the horse. It was getting hot, her arms ached, and she was not enjoying her ride at all.

They continued to nag Gunsmoke until he was nearly caught up with the group. A cluster of trees grew into the path, and the riders had to slow down while ducking and leaning. This allowed Abby and the wrangler to catch up all the way as the trail started uphill.

"Just gotta show him who's boss," the wrangler asserted.

"Yeah, cowgirl up," Abby replied with confidence she did not feel.

Minutes later, the group stopped to enjoy the view from atop a hill. Gunsmoke immediately plunged his head into some weeds by the trail. Abby tried to tug his head up, but didn't dare brace against him for fear her tennies would again slide through the stirrups. He swung around to dig into another patch of weeds. That seemed to trigger a new thought in his one-track mind, for he began to walk past the wrangler and back down the path. This ride had gotten way too frustrating. Abby pulled hard with both reins. Forget gentle. Forget unity. Everything she did with this horse had to be with all her strength. It was a battle.

For some reason, hauling back on his bit didn't make Gunsmoke stop or even slow down. He broke into a rough trot. Abby bounced all over, painfully, slamming her most-private parts into the saddle, hunching, grabbing for the horn, nearly dropping the reins. She was terrified she'd fall. Bringing her worst fears to life, Gunsmoke began cantering; a choppy, hard-to-sit canter made harder for Abby by her rising panic that she could not stop him.

She screamed in fear and frustration, drowning in her inability to ride this monster. Voices shouted to stop him, but she was already trying to as hard as she could. Gunsmoke was hell-bent on running away with her, back to the stables.

Not even in her worst nightmares had she ever dreamed this scene. It was so wrong, she couldn't think how to deal with it properly. She could only continue to do what she'd been trained to do. Pull back on the reins. Harder. Frightened about her shoes, she clamped her knees, leaned back with all her might, and shouted, "WHOA!!"

It didn't help. Gunsmoke was fighting her every inch of the way. In sheer panic, she tried one last thing: what she had seen Angie do. She had no clue how to do it right, but...instead of pulling both reins up and back, she tried to pull the right rein down and back.

And it broke!

She wasn't sure how hard she could pull on the left rein before it also broke. Worse, the clump of trees loomed on the left. If she pulled on the left rein now, and he obeyed, he'd veer towards the trees.

She had no choice, though. It was do or die. She pulled with every last bit of her strength on the left rein, desperate to turn tightly before she hit the lowest branches. Gunsmoke did seem to be turning. Maybe it would be all right. But there was that funny unbalanced feeling, and a sickening sliding, and the horse went one way and she went another, and she was still heading towards the low branches, and oooohh this was going to hurt, this was going to...*Oh God, oh God, please, help, save me, get me out of here, nooo, God pleee...*

Chapter 13: Friend

Abby stood just past the clump of trees, blinking in the warm morning light. She was dazed. That was understandable, since she had just hit…er, not hit…um, how…where was the horse? She looked around. Where were the shouting riders? Why did the trees look so different, too? The stable had shrunk, or the changing light made it look smaller. It must be that she just didn't know the layout.

But where was the horse? Had he thrown her and run off? Had the others gone after him? But hadn't that one wrangler been right behind her? She looked around the other side of the trees for Gunsmoke and the wrangler. No sign. Surely she should at least hear some shouting. No, nothing.

This was way, *way* too strange. Did she black out and they were all back at the stables? The stables that looked like a house from this angle? Might as well head there; it beat just standing around here.

She walked past the trees and down the looking-different-now path; it had become a well-kept walkway rather than the rough, rocky horse path. Gunsmoke's clumps of grass were now plants and flowers at the verges. By the house, someone stooping in the yard glanced up. Looked again. Seemed surprised. Set their trowel down next to a bucket and straightened up. Lifted their hand to their ear. Someone wearing strange clothes. Not ranch clothes, more like earthen-colored, Chinese peasant clothes. Loose clothes, a loose stance, a free hand waving at her.

"I fell off!" Abby shouted.

The person – apparently a woman, or girl – didn't answer but lifted her watch, lips moving. Still, she smiled; that was something.

Abby walked further and cupped her hands to her mouth. "Where is everyone? Did the horse come back?"

The woman smiled again and called, "It ees ahkay. Come dawn!"

Hmm. She must be Chinese; she had a funny accent. But up closer, she looked a lot like Melissa. Maybe part Asian, but also a lot of other things. Abby descended the last slope to the barn…er, house…and approached the woman. Girl. Whichever.

"Where is everyone?" she repeated. "Who are you?"

"I eir, is, are Dali. Dali Puerta," the lady answered. "End you eir?"

What an odd last name: *p'WHERE-tah*. "I'm Abby. Abby Wize."

"Wise?" Dali Puerta looked at her for a long moment, as if *Abby* had a strange last name.

"Yes, Wize. Well anyway, Mrs. Puerta, Miss Dollie, uh, I must've gotten lost. I fell off a horse. I mean, I was going to fall off and then, um, well, I lost everyone. And the horse. Did you see them?"

Dali Puerta held up her watch again. And it seemed to whisper to her. Abby stared at the watch. She knew she was behind the times on iPods and Blackberrys and Bluetooths and all that, but she had never heard of a whispering watch.

"Help let you with all embracing vision," Dali said nonsensically. "Coming in for now?" Her watch whispered again; and she held out her hand to Abby, clearly inviting her inside the little house with a word Abby didn't catch. They stepped through a wooden doorway, past the thick earthen walls, into the cool living room.

The ceiling slanted up to a vent that drew air through the open windows and doors. A screen appeared across the doorway, the same kind of screen as on the open windows.

Doors led into a bedroom and bathroom. Low walls revealed the kitchen and a couple of other areas Abby couldn't identify. It seemed even more back-to-earth than the coffee shop she had gone to with Jon and Melissa. Plants, yes, and wood. Some decorations. But also colored glass for doorknobs, and metal shelves with hammer marks, and pottery and quilts and weavings for show or maybe for using.

"I like your house," she said a little guiltily when she realized she'd been peeking more than Mother would consider proper.

"I are glad that you liking it," Dali said, smiling and listening to her whispering watch. "Could you like...no, would you like some...thing to drink?"

"Oh, I have water back in..." Back in where? The small house sat where the stables had been. She had ridden up that hill and just now walked down it. "Where are we?" she blurted out.

"Would you pless sat down?" Dali asked politely. She held out a very pretty multicolored glass of what looked like cool water. Abby accepted the glass and, still standing, sipped from it appreciatively.

Her capris passed a quick inspection for dirt. She apparently hadn't been on Gunsmoke long enough to get very dirty. She blushed, ducked her head, gingerly sat down, and pretended to look at her chair.

"Are you all right?" her hostess asked, concerned.

"Ye...um, I'm, uh, not sure. I'm not hurt anyway, that's good; but I have to say I am very confused. You weren't here when I came before. Are your parents home?"

"Ah...is different..."

"Um, well then, where am I?"

Dali took a deep breath and seemed to be deciding what to say. Her almost-always-whispering watch stayed silent this time.

"You are...where you were...before."

"I'm in the same place I was?"

"Yes, I have belief so."

Abby could tell her hostess was worried that this would be unhappy news for Abby; and somehow Abby did not think this was a joke or a lie. Hesitant to make a fool of herself, she asked her hostess to explain. The watch began whispering again.

"I am not entirely sure what happened, but you have come a long way from where you were."

It seemed to Abby that Dali's English was getting much better by the minute. The whispering watch, no doubt. Some kind of translator she wore? While she was…weeding?

"I thought you just said I am where I was before. Which means I didn't come very far at all!"

"I'm so sorry. I mean, you came a long way in time. How would you call that?"

"I don't know, yeah, far, I guess. How far, do you think?"

Dali looked at Abby, again seeming to decide something. Silence from her watch. Dali was on her own for this one, whatever it was.

"What year is it when you came?"

"Year? 2007, why?"

"2007? In what calendar?"

"What do you mean, 'what calendar'?" Abby was beginning to get quite frustrated. Her confusion was growing, not lessening, with the discussion.

"I am so sorry. Do you need to… take a break?"

"Break? No, I need to know where I am, where everybody went, that's all." Abby began to change her opinion about Dali. She'd seemed a fast learner, but now she appeared rather slow.

Dali smiled and stood up smoothly. When she came to pick Abby up and met Dali, Mother would at least approve of her graciousness and gracefulness. Abby hoped that Mother would not then badger Abby to act like Dali.

First, though, Abby would need to figure out how to meet the car, regardless of where the wranglers and horses had gone. Mother would never let her forget it if she was off lost somewhere.

Dali opened a wooden box on a wooden table, touched something inside, and shut it gently. Several beautiful painted horses next to the wooden box reminded Abby of the TRAIL OF PAINTED PONIES statues she often admired in horse catalogs.[19] The sound of drumbeats began to fill the small house. They became hoofbeats, and loud nickering. Brassy bugles sounded, blending into neighs. Other instruments followed, and other horse voices…a little foal answered a happy clarinet…

Dali had glided off somewhere. Abby had nothing to do but sit in this soft, remarkably comfortable chair and listen to the horse music. She rested her heavy head on the back of the chair, which seemed to adjust instantly to hold her head just right…just right…

∞   ∞   ∞   ∞   ∞   ∞   ∞   ∞

… and horses … her favorite escape … sunshine on their shiny coats … their smell … oneness with them … beautiful, majestic horses obey her very thoughts … no reins, no saddles needed … cantering up and down hills … a bunch of trees in the path …

∞   ∞   ∞   ∞   ∞   ∞   ∞   ∞

Her eyes flew open to reveal Dali sitting opposite her again, regarding her while the watch whispered away. Abby relaxed again.

"Do you feel better now?" Dali asked, smiling slightly. "You were getting upset. I thought that would help you calm down."

"I do feel better, thanks. I was just confused."

Dali looked at her a long moment, then shrugged.

"Do you want to talk about your…situation…again? Or would it be too…confusing?"

"Um…" Honestly, even thinking about her situation was upsetting; who knew if talking about it would send Dali to her little sound-box again. She was supposed to have crashed into that tree and didn't; and now the stables were gone and she had traveled a long way…in time?

"How about if we talk about you for a while, Dali?"

"All right, Abby, I will tell you what I th…what I can," Dali said earnestly.[20] "I told you my name already: Dali Puerta. And my age is eighteen. This is my aunt's house that is now mine. I work…um, part-time. And my bliss is to grow the plants such as you saw on the hill."

"And where are we now? Are we in North Carolina?"

The watch whispered again on Dali's wrist. She had propped up her elbow on the arm of the couch, the better to keep the watch by her ear.

"We are in the, ah, area of North Carolina, yes."

Abby wasn't sure why her hostess said it like that; but at least she was where she was supposed to be. Just not when.

"For me, it's Friday, August 17, 2007. What…um, what year is it here?" Abby's statement set the watch to whispering again.

"I think you use the Gregorian calendar. So your date translates to Istiqlál, 17 Kamál, 164 BE. You're from the mid-2nd century."[21]

Abby felt stupid. She knew there were other calendars in the world: the Chinese New Year, and Moslem lunar months, and stuff. But to not even know what her own calendar was called, that was just plain pitiful. She hadn't even thought to say she was from 2007 *AD*.

Dali didn't seem to think Abby was stupid. On the contrary, she was smiling as if she'd solved a hard puzzle. Her watch whispered non-stop. Abby was very glad that the little mechanism was helping Dali to help her.

Then Dali looked at her seriously again, and said, "I can now tell you how far you've traveled, but you may not want to hear."

"Try me."

"Pardon?"

"Yes, I would like to hear."

"Today is Jalál, 17 Kamál, 864 BE. It's a...Saturday this year. You have traveled *exactly* seven hundred years into the future."[22]

Abby stared blankly at Dali's unusual face, trying to grapple with her extraordinary announcement. Glancing at the very unusual house and recalling the morning's unusual events, though, she realized it was probably true. She had no idea how; but the facts in front of her eyes indicated that she had left 2007 and was now in...2707? Wow! It sure explained the whispering watch, anyway. She wondered a little crazily where the spaceships and aluminum-foil suits were.

But...Jenn would never know what happened to her. She hoped it had not been too painful for her only true friend. She had never even thanked her sister for the bra; dinner had been too noisy. Jenn's face swam in front of her, gazing concernedly at her. Slowly it transformed into Dali's face, also showing deep concern. Same sisterly care, new face. Reminiscent of Melissa's face, too. A blend of many different cultures...and times.

Well, if this was the face of the future, it was a good one. The dire predictions from *her* time about *this* time were apparently wrong. Best put on a good front and be glad that she had a helper while she tried to figure things out.

Abby flashed what she hoped was a winning smile.

"You will have many, many questions. I am not sure I can answer them all," Dali said, looking relieved.

"Well, I bet you'll do the best you can, and that'll have to be good enough," Abby said, trying to adopt a mature tone but surprised at how much her words sounded like Mother. "I should just be glad that I'm not dead." She lumbered on, trying to sound more like herself. "Um, I'm not, am I?"

"Oh no, *that* I can answer. You are definitely not dead." Dali said, a very pretty smile emerging through her worry. It reminded Abby of something she had once read in a teen magazine back in Surely, while waiting for Jenn to get her hair cut: a smile was your best business card ...a cheap, instant beautifier.[23]

"What time is it? What are you going to do today?"

"It's coming onto noontime." Dali looked keenly at her for a few moments, saying nothing.[24] Just before Abby began to feel uncomfortable, though, Dali added, "I work some this afternoon. Tonight is scheduled a...gathering."

"How do you get to work? And where is the gathering? Aren't you afraid to live out here all by yourself?" The last question had popped into Abby's mind as she tried to imagine Dali's living arrangements. She hoped it wasn't too personal.

But Dali smiled wide again and answered, "I'm not afraid to live out here; it is quite safe. I love it very much. The gathering is close. My work is further away, in the nearby village. We could walk or use a... bicycle."

"Are there horses in your world? Would you ride one to work?"

"Oh yes," Dali replied instantly, with a thoughtful look. "We have horses and other animals; but it is rather different than in your time, I would imagine. You may like to see. I suppose a person could ride a horse to go places, but..." She looked doubtful. The watch whispered. "As in your world, it is not commonly done."

"If I can, yes, I would like to see," Abby wondered how the animals would be different. "Is it a horse show, or a rodeo?"

"Perhaps more like a show. What is rodeo?"

"Riding bucking horses, roping steers, you know, barrel racing, that kind of thing," Abby tried to explain.

Dali gazed at her for a moment, her brow slightly furrowed, then blinked long and slow. After a couple of seconds, she said, "There's no need to 'rope steers.' Once in a while someone might ride a bucking horse if they're feeling foolish and...ready to be injured. Racing, we sometimes have; but not in the show you'll see."

"Oh."

After another thoughtful pause, Dali said, "Do you like food?"[25]

"Um, do you mean do I like eating? Yeah, doesn't everyone? Or do you mean do I like to cook food? Well, Mother doesn't..." Mother. If she ever got back home, Mother would probably kill her even if Gunsmoke hadn't. Better she stay here in the future until she had a really good explanation.

"Are you hungry?" Dali asked.

"A little, I guess."

"Would you like to help make our noon meal with me?"

Abby looked at Dali's face to check on meaning. Could she say no? Or did Dali expect her to help, like Mother would? It seemed that Dali was waiting for her honest answer.

"Maybe I can help. I'm not very good at fixing complicated stuff."

"I'm sure you'll do well," Dali assured her.

She led the way to the sink, where both girls washed their hands. Counters and cabinets stretched between the sink and a refrigerator-looking panel. Three chairs, two stools, and an eating table set against the low wall into the living room completed the small, tidy nook. At least Abby could identify that much, seven hundred years in the future.

Dali pulled open a small panel in the lower row of cabinets. Abby was enveloped in the smell of fresh-baked bread, a smell she'd never been able to resist when they passed Cinnabon in the mall...and could not resist now. Dali straightened up with a pan of hot bread.

"It will settle while we get our salad," she said, setting the pan on a colorful trivet.

She went to the biggest panel, swung it open, and took out lettuce, some colorful vegetables, and several dressings.

"Would you like...cucumbers on your salad? Carrots? Radishes? Well, here, come look and put in what you wish."

Abby was not terribly fond of salads, but this would at least fill her stomach. Dali got Abby started, then shook the bread out of the pan, put the loaf into a cutting rack, cut off two slices, and put them onto two pretty pottery plates. The bread Abby loved was usually white, not dark brown with chunks.

"Give us this day our daily bread," Abby muttered.[26] Plain bread and salad didn't seem like a complete meal, but Abby didn't want to be rude to her gracious hostess.

"...and grant Thine increase in the necessities of life, that we may be dependent on none other but Thee," Dali responded.[27]

"What?"

"Oh. Sorry; never mind," Dali said quickly.

Dali made her salad and offered the salad dressings, describing one new bottle and asking if Abby would be interested in trying it with her. When Abby agreed, Dali unscrewed the lid and poured. Abby noted that there was no safety seal inside the lid, and asked about it.

Dali poured the dressing silently, watch murmuring. Had she not heard? Was it a rude question in this world? Abby was gathering her apology when Dali gently asked her why bottles needed safety seals.

"Well, because, um...to show you if someone has messed with your bottle," Abby said. Bottles just had them, had always had them.

Again, Dali seemed to blink really slowly. "Safety seals began in your 1980s, after seven people died from poisoned pills," Dali noted quietly. "Anonymous murderers randomly poisoning totally innocent strangers.[28] It marked a milestone in America's decline."

"And now you're not worried about anyone poisoning you?"

"No, we're not," Dali confirmed. "One of many wonderful things about our time."

They sat down together. Abby watched her hostess, ready to follow her lead. Dali simply squeezed her hand, looked directly into her eyes, said, "I'm glad you're here," and tucked into her bread.

Abby bit into hers. The bread was moist, very flavorful and, due to the various grains and chunks, different with every bite. The salad and dressing were also easy to get used to. Its lettuce was very dark-green, and not quite sweet but...interesting. In both color and flavor, the head lettuce back home paled in comparison.

Abby was glad she had some clue about proper table manners. This unexpected meal with a complete stranger made her feel self-conscious, even though Dali was only warm and accepting.

A beautiful chime sounded. After three repetitions, Abby began to count, ending at twelve. The last few sounded more like a wailing siren. Abby wondered if it was faulty, but Dali seemed not to notice.

"Noontime, thank God," Dali said.

"Why? Is noon special here?"

"Every time is special here," Dali replied, "but starting at noon, we can say the noontime prayer."[29]

"Oh," Abby said. She had not thought about the spiritual practices here. "Why is every time special here?"

"I will try to show you the answer to that while you are here," Dali said. "I'm just afraid of...overwhelming you."

It was Abby's turn to look at Dali searchingly. She was not used to someone being so concerned about her mental state. Emotional state. Even physical state, for that matter. Come to think of it, she should add spiritual state to the list as well. She had traveled to the future, where she was being totally cared for by a total stranger. How much stranger would it get? She could not guess.

Chapter 14: Town

"I usually ride my bike to work. But I only have one bike, so we'll walk; is that all right?" Dali asked as they cleaned up from lunch.

"I guess so. Is it far?"

"About five times as far as you walked this morning, I think."

Abby looked sharply at Dali. How did she know how far Abby had walked? Dali wouldn't have been able to see her that far away. She did not want to argue with her hostess, however, and let it slide.

"We may be able to borrow a bike for the return trip. You'll be tired by then, probably. Unless you already feel tired and would rather rest here at home."

"No, I'll go," Abby replied quickly. She couldn't imagine staying here alone, and was a little surprised that Dali would consider leaving a stranger alone with her whole house and all its possessions.

"Good. Let me just get my bag. Do you think you'll need anything before we go?"

"Not that I know of." In truth, Abby had no idea how to prepare for their afternoon, because she had no idea what it would be like. So she added, "But if you can think of anything…"

Dali studied her. "You might want to visit the restroom first." She held her watch up to her ear and it whispered again. "Yes," she added decisively, "let's show you the bathroom."

Past a painted wooden door stood a boxy toilet and a bath/shower installation. Towels on a rack and tall, decorative, wood-and-painted-tile cabinets filled the far wall. Above the toilet, a color photograph of a pair of pretty, bright, brown eyes against light-brown skin supervised the sink opposite. Dali's face? Abby looked away from it lest she fall into Dali's eyes as she had into her own.

"In your time, toilets have water and pipes from and to outside the house, yes?" Dali asked.

"Right."

"Most houses do not bring in water like that. There is no water to toilets. When you…go, swing the little door out of the way, like this," she said, pressing a lever. "Everything will drop down the hole."

"Like a porta-potty then," Abby said. "With no water."[30]

"Maybe so," Dali said. Abby noted that the watch was silent about porta-potties. "After, press this button to start the waste breakdown."

Abby hoped she'd get everything right. Dali saw the concern on her face and said, "The instructions are printed…oh."

"What's the matter?"

"The words are in UL. I'm afraid you won't understand it."

"What's, um, *yule?*"

"U-L, the universal language. It's the worldwide secondary language that we all learn in school." Her watch coached her quietly. "It includes a lot of English, but it's not close enough to your American for you to read. Even my American is very different from yours, just as the English of your 1300s is very hard for you to read in the 2000s."

Abby had seen some of the English from the Middle Ages. It was indeed nearly unreadable. She'd just have to try her best...she remembered Barb's joke about *try* not being a four-letter word. Dali went out, softly shutting the door.

Abby thought she figured it all out pretty well. Then she washed her hands and, glancing in the mirror above the sink, decided to wash her face to erase the last traces of the recent/long-ago trail ride. The soap pump was a work of art in itself. As she admired it, her mother's voice called it *cloisonné* in Abby's head. Dali tapped on the door just as Abby was drying her hands on a soft, rust-colored towel.

"I'd like to offer you some clothes before we go," Dali said, handing her the folded garments. "You'll be more comfortable in these. I kept some favorites from when I was your height, and it would be so pleasant to have someone enjoy them again."

"All right," Abby replied, accepting a tan slip-on shirt and golden stretch-waist slacks with some embroidery and stamped designs. They were loose, cool, comfortable, and surprisingly soft. Abby had thought the woven fabric would be stiff like her mother's linen suits.

Bringing her dirty clothes, she found Dali in the clean, simple bedroom. It smelled nice, too. Like Dali herself. Not at all, um, fake-y like deodorant, but more how the outdoors smelled. Earthy...no, natural.

"Uh, I don't have any deodorant, or spare underwear," Abby said.

Dali pondered this, with her watch whispering away. "You should be able to get along without deodorant, here," she finally said.[31] "We can wash your underwear whenever you wish.

"Oh, and I used to wear some gold butterflies in my hair with this outfit, would you like them? I think they will look even better in your brown hair than my black."

Abby put two butterfly barrettes in her hair, one on each side.

"They look good on you," Dali said approvingly. She even turned Abby around to admire the back. Wow, this was as good as the all-too-rare sleepover – new clothes and an admiring friend!

Dali didn't have any shoes in Abby's size, and so her once-white canvas sneakers had to serve. If she got them dirty enough, they might even look more natural and blend in better.

"You'll also need a bag. I have just the right one," Dali murmured, pulling open a drawer in the simple wooden bureau. It was a knotted, macramé-like, light-brown purse, with handles long enough that she could wear over her shoulder. It went perfectly with the outfit. It was, however, empty. Abby just hoped that she wouldn't need the supplies Jenn had given her, which were "back home" in her backpack.

"Thanks, this is so nice! And thanks for...finding me."

"It is my privilege to help you." Dali's manner was so gentle, her smile so warm and sincere, Abby felt like she had gained another big sister, even though they looked nothing alike. She was pretty sure she could muster her courage and ask Dali for anything she really needed.

The watch whispered, and Dali's face sobered.

"We're late; we'll have to take the bike," she said. "Can you...did you ever...are you okay with riding double on a one-seat bicycle?"

"Yes," Abby said, wondering how to avoid ruining the beautiful slacks in the bike chain, even if she avoided falling off. One of the girls would stand on the pedals, even when not pedaling; the other would sit on the seat, legs hanging in midair, holding the pedaler's waist.

"It might work," Dali said.

The girls left the house, Dali murmuring a few words. Click! The door swung shut – a really beautiful front door made of carved wood with three tall, clear, lead-glass panels inserted. While Abby looked at the door's attractive clear glass doorknob and reflected on the voice-activated closing, Dali retrieved a bicycle. It looked surprisingly like a regular woman's bicycle, with baskets in front and back. Instead of a greasy, pants-leg-eating chain, she saw a clean, clear tube. Unfamiliar gadgets adorned the handlebars.

"I think if you pedal and steer, you can sit on my lap to rest. You're lighter."

Abby thought that Dali should steer, since Abby had no earthly – or other-earthly – idea where they were going. Before she could say anything, though, Dali added, "I'll give you directions; it's not hard."

After a few false starts, they arranged themselves and lurched down the road. Soon they were both laughing.

"I knew I should've gotten the seat to fit across the back baskets," Dali said after they'd wobbled to a stop for the tenth time. She strained to touch her tippy-toes to the ground, balancing the bike for Abby, who prepared to simultaneously jump onto the pedals, pedal off, and steer straight. "We should always listen to those divine promptings."

"Can you still get a seat? If we have to come home like this..."

"I've already arranged to borrow another bike," Dali said. "Wait!" Reaching down, she unfolded the top bars of the pedals, making them twice as long. "Now we can both pedal. I forgot I had those."

Abby was glad for the pedaling help. She realized, though, that she hadn't heard Dali phone anyone, nor had she seen anything that looked like a phone.

Once they were truly coordinated, Dali sang a song Abby did not understand – a good biking song, she supposed. Dali directed her down the road that could have led to the stables hundreds of years ago. It sure looked different; the plants were more orderly, the road better tended. It had been brown dirt in Abby's time; now it was paved. Not with black asphalt, but with a surface that stayed cool and let the bicycle tires roll easily. Like special rubber and brown North Carolina dirt together. And the fire had been raging just over *there*, she thought, looking left towards where Little Lily should have lain. She didn't see any smoke. She seemed to catch the smell, though, and was momentarily alarmed.

Some twenty minutes later, topping a hill, she saw more houses. The only other traffic was a couple of bicycles and a small, canopied tricycle. Dali waved at all of them, calling out a greeting in her own language – New American, Abby supposed. A woman sat in a porch chair, working with something in a large pot. A man hung up laundry outside. Dali waved at them, too.

Everyone waved back warmly, gazed wonderingly at Abby, then went on with their business. After the fifth time, Abby asked why they were staring. She'd put on the clothes of the time; what was wrong?

"They're just curious. They don't know you, and I didn't tell anyone I was expecting a visitor. Also, most everyone has darker skin than you. So they're trying to figure out where you came from and who you are. Everyone knows everyone around here. It's a small town."

"What's this town called, anyway?"

"Lodlan." She pronounced it *LOAD-lun*. "L-O-D-L-A-N."

"And most people are darker than me?"

"Yes. As people intermarried farther and farther from their original cultures, all the skin colors started to genetically mix. But there are always some people with darker and others with lighter skin. Very rarely, someone has skin as light as yours or as dark as, say, my Uncle Arno's. Both of your colors are considered quite exotic, special, and attractive."

Surprised, Abby pondered the thought that she – as well as a really dark-skinned person – would be so rare and thus especially good-looking.

The houses they passed were similar to Dali's, with some variation and less land around them. Several were U-shaped, a few were many-sided, some were two-storied, a couple had a double yard. Like Dali's, all of them looked made of earth and wood. And the attention to plants was obvious; they had a pleasing variety of flowers, gardens, trees, tidy fences, benches, attractive statues, and lights on posts or strung from the eaves. Cats and dogs watched the pair cycle by; Abby was glad to know that pets had accompanied people far into the future.

In the yard of a wide, three-storied house with a wraparound porch, Abby saw about ten adults, two of them holding babies, and a pair of teenagers. They were pointing at and seemed to be calmly discussing something about their roof. Another half dozen smiling kids of various ages sat nearby in a grassy circle and played a quiet game with a ball. It looked to Abby like maybe four generations of one family. She wondered if many extended families here lived all together in one house – something Daddy had told her often happened in bygone days – whether they were happier together or just could not afford separate homes, and how anyone managed to get any privacy.

All the houses and streets were very clean. One small house, however, was not as attractive as the others. It was definitely older and in worse repair than others, and the yard was mostly dirt, devoid of fences and flowers but dotted with kids and dogs.

Several small, slow, nearly silent, enclosed four-wheeled vehicles shared the road with some more trikes, both canopied and not, and a few small trucks. A buffer of empty land bordered the edges.

"What are those shiny lines?" Abby gestured towards the gleaming strands peeking through the road surface.

"Those are the, ah, let's say, 'guidance channels' for when someone drives a wreckless," Dali replied, pointing to one of the small vehicles.

"What do you mean, 'guidance channels'? And are they reckless a lot?"

Dali listened to her watch for a moment.

"Are you familiar with trolleys that run on tracks in the road?"

"Yes. I've seen pictures, anyway."

"These wires guide our wrecklesses – oh, I remember, you called them autos or cars, right? – like trolleys on tracks. It might be a better comparison to consider train tracks. Or air traffic controllers, who monitor each airplane and prevent any two from colliding. Those wires… monitor all the cars in the area and help prevent things like collisions, running off the road, or going too fast for conditions. Drivers see a display panel of all the necessary information. They can also let the road itself drive their car."

That was *some* kind of cruise control, Abby thought.

"Our cars are gyroscopically stable, expandable, have air-pressure bumpers all around, and can be powered from several sources, including recycled, ahh…plastics. Not the same plastics as from your time, though."

"They're expandable? How?"

"We make them bigger or smaller by sliding out panels and beams. Most of them hold two to six people, or the same amount of…what do you call it…stuff."

Abby smiled to hear such slang coming from her.

Tall trees blocked a large, unusual building from Abby's view until they pedaled almost right up to it. It presided over the large gardens that surrounded it, much the way small-town courthouses reigned over their town squares. And it also looked to be in the center of town, like a town square. But this building did not look like any courthouse she'd seen; it had more sides and an arched roof.

"Turn counterclockwise at the House of Worship, then right again onto School Street," Dali instructed, pointing past the building.

Abby looked around while she pedaled down School Street, with its sign that she couldn't decipher. The traffic was light, and the cars very small compared to her world. She saw several buildings that looked like businesses, but didn't see what they were selling.

"The Dependencies," Dali said, pointing to them.

"The what?" Abby said.

"Oh. Sorry. Hospital, medical clinic, university, traveler's hospice, orphans' facility, home for the elderly, and such."[32]

"All in one building?"

Dali smiled. "Well, in small towns like ours, some are combined and some are shared between towns. And see that separate building," Dali pointed left, "with the big windows pointing northeast? That holds the meeting chambers of both the local House of Justice and Lodlan's town council." At Abby's questioning murmur, she added, "The local House of Justice guides and administers Lodlan's Bahá'í community; and they and the town council often consult and work together."

"Where do you work; where are we going?"

"I work at a school – in the library and sometimes the office. See up ahead? With the student artwork?" Dali pointed down the street to the right, at a building festooned with colorful murals. Abby was impressed with the quality of the art – nature scenes, imaginary scenes, and what were probably favorite teachers and important events – and said so.

"I'm glad you like it. The youth repaint sections once in a while. It is always something interesting, uplifting."

"Don't you worry about graffiti?"

Dali consulted her watch again. This time, it didn't help her.

"Would you please explain who graffiti are?"

"Not who; what…like, someone paints their name real big all over the artwork, or a big moustache on the face of one of the people. You know, graffiti. To be mean or flashy or they just don't care."

"People do this in your time?"

"Uh, yeah." Abby had a hard time not sounding like a Valley Girl, and nearly added "duh!" to it. Do they do graffiti in 2007? Is rain wet?

"No one would think to do such a thing now. It is an outrageous idea and would cause a great deal of hurt."

"Yeah, it does."

A local artist in Surely had painted a fabulous landscape on a store wall, Abby remembered. Within a month, it was defaced by graffiti. As soon as they saw the artist start painting, everyone knew what would happen. Its predictability didn't make it any more welcome.

Dali directed Abby to the bike rack, which held two other bikes. They coasted smoothly to the rack, and Dali dismounted, then Abby.

"School starts this week. I choose to work five half-days a week. I use Thursdays for long personal projects, or for something fun. Friday, yesterday, was our primary day of rest. We learned, partly from your time, what too much work and no play can do."

"But don't you need the money?" Abby's father had once said that people worked to pay for houses, furniture, cars, clothes, food, utilities, health care, college, vacations, and on and on.

Dali consulted her watch as she parked the bike, got their bags from the rear baskets, and headed towards the door. She didn't lock the bike, Abby noticed, nor were the others locked. That would be cool, not to worry about everything getting stolen all the time!

"And what *is* that watch?"

"Watch? For what?"

"No, your watch."

"I need to watch?"

They both stopped, realizing they were speaking from two very different worlds. Abby knew from her experience with Jenn that the best solution was to wait. Dali pulled open one of the doors, turned into the room to the right, pressed her finger to an electronic pad, and greeted the other office workers. They walked back out into the hallway and headed down the second corridor to the right.

The watch whispered.

"Oh, you think this is a wristwatch?" Dali finally said, relief flooding her face.

"Isn't it?"

"Well, it does tell me the time, but it is soooo much more than a mere timepiece," she said with conviction. The girls walked as Dali listened to the watch.

"We call them Yuters."

"*What?* Uterus?" It felt obscene to even say it.

"Just a Yuter." She carefully repeated it. "*YOU-ter*. Originally, it was the Old American word *computer*. Now, it delivers almost all our knowledge in this world; so I think it is fitting that it also sounds – as you said – like the old word *uterus*." Smiling, Dali checked to see if Abby was still with her, mentally and physically.

She was, but just barely. "Go on," she said.

"Your computers had internet, email, games, pictures, documents, dictionaries, calculators, and so on, right?"

"Yeah," Abby replied, momentarily – and unhappily – reminded of some computer pictures she didn't want to see.

"Imagine one computer that can do much, *much* more...and fits on your wrist. Of course, there are also various larger Yuters that serve homes, schools, medical facilities, businesses, governments, and so on. But this model – the Wristlet Anagojal Esthezic Recoursive Yuter, or WaerY – this wrist-Yuter serves individuals."

"Oh." Abby thought about this while repeating the strange words to herself: *an-ah-GO-jell ess-THEEZ-ic ree-CORE-sive*. "So when your *WARE-ee* whispers, it's..."

"Answering my questions, mainly from a global database."

"How do you ask it?"

"Out loud. Or mentally. I can ask it something in my mind and it can understand, and it looks it up and answers back in my mind. But I prefer to speak with it. Especially now, when I need to clearly hear how to pronounce some of your words."

"Wow, cool!"

"Is it too chilly for you in here?"

"No, cool means it's really neat...um..." all the words Abby could think of to define 'cool' were just as unhelpful as the original. Groovy, neat, boss, hot, tight, sweet, phat, rad...what a strange thing, not to be able to define something you approved of. "It means I like it a lot."

The watch whispered again and Dali said, "In UL – that's the universal language, remember – we say bonega."

"Um, *boe-NAY-gah*? Your watch told you that?"

"It told me what you were trying to say."

"Man, that would be handy! Does everyone have one?"

"Almost everyone. But they are not free, and some people who are very poor cannot afford one."

"You have poor people?"

"Always. They are a trust to be guarded, of course."[33]

"Of course," Abby echoed, clueless.

"My work," Dali announced, turning and pushing through swinging wooden doors into what appeared to be the library.

Chapter 15: Library

"Anyway, we are careful to live so as not to need lots of money," Dali said, putting her bag into a cabinet and indicating that Abby should do the same. "We also learned this from your time. Wasn't there a saying then: 'Don't let your possessions own you'?"

"Yeah, something like that," Abby replied, looking around.

The book section looked familiar. The cubicles housing expensive-looking screens, not so much. The library was fancy; all the artwork on the walls helped it appear inviting. Even in the hallways. Weren't kids still kids here? Didn't some juvie ever wreck stuff, pull the fire alarm, steal the paintings?

"What age of kids go here?" Abby asked.

"This is a regular second school, so about eleven through fifteen in normal studies," Dali said. "Higher-level studies are at another school. I'll be readying presentation and discussion materials for the teachers. Would you like to look at the library displays, or would you prefer to spend some time on a Yuter?"

"Um…which is the best one to see what this world is like?"

"The Yuter," Dali said firmly. "You could start with Local Events and Features."

Dali consulted her WaerY for a moment, then led Abby to a small desk and chair. She invited Abby to sit down. Once Abby was seated, the chair slowly molded itself to her body. Then she reached under the desk and swung a board up, making a back on the desk, and pressed a large, transparent, wire-framed rectangle against the backboard. The WaerY whispered constantly as Dali touched the edge of the rectangle, bringing it to life, then touched several more places on what Abby now realized was a Yuter screen.

"There, that's as good as I can get it. We don't have many people asking for translation into the Old American of the mid-2nd century." She smiled gently.

"Remember I told you about larger Yuters. This screen is part of the school's ALLY," she continued. "Just like I have a household ALLY. The name originally came from the term "all-purpose Yuter", but it's such a blessing to have this kind of helper that people started calling it *AL-eye* instead of *ALL-ee*.

"Anyway, I've made this as close as I can to the computers of your time." She showed Abby where and how to touch the screen to command it, then left her to explore the news of 2707.

The first screen showed videos, text, links, two articles, and a TV schedule. So it was still called TV? Oh, maybe not; this was translated, antiquated. Abby tried to picture Dali's living room…didn't remember a TV or screen. She guessed they wouldn't be watching any shows.

There were lots of programs, some curiously named. Many of them described special interests. Gee, was there a Horse Channel? She didn't see one specifically for horses, but there was an animal one. Also ones for food, gardening, news, drama, and live cameras, but no sports, talk shows, or reality TV. Instead, listings included Consultation, Games, Homebuilding, Gathering Ideas, Feast Results (what could the result of a feast be? indigestion?), Holy Day Suggestions, Travel Offers, Looking For, BrainBank, and more that Abby could not fathom.

Abby chose Games, and touched its icon. She had not necessarily been expecting Solitaire, but she was surprised to see a video of many laughing children and clapping adults playing a game that looked like a cross between Musical Chairs and Country Line Dancing. When the music started, the kids stood up and danced almost gracefully between their chairs, retrieved something small from the laughing adults dancing around them, then dodged and spun back to the chairs. When the music stopped, everyone froze, an announcer seemed to give the results, and everyone unfroze and laughed and clapped.

It looked like a lot of fun, whatever it was; and no one seemed to lose and leave, either. Abby had always disliked games that eliminated people, mainly because she was not the pushy type, which usually eliminated her early.

Anyway, the people of the future obviously loved to laugh and have fun, Abby thought. Did away with the Spock-like portrayals, for sure. Nary a pointy ear in sight! A whole garden variety of colors, though: eyes, hair, skin. But probably nobody with green blood, Abby chuckled to herself.

She meant to select Homebuilding, wondering whether it would detail building a house like Dali's or contain clues to a peaceful home life. Instead, she accidentally opened Consultation. A wheel of words rotated and swelled on the screen:

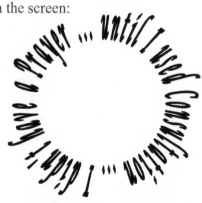

The words circled around and around, then shrank and faded to the growing title:

Consultation Today

Next, a gray-haired man appeared, wearing tighter-fitting, more formal-looking clothes than Dali's. He was darker-skinned than Dali, too, and had almond-shaped blue eyes and an authoritative announcer kind of voice. When he spoke, the translated words didn't match his mouth movements. Abby suspected she was somehow hearing his real voice, though.

"Welcome to Consultation Today. I'm your host, Ling Modderay."

The camera zoomed out to show several people in soft chairs, looking very relaxed to Abby and smiling at Mr. Modderay. Hey, his name sounded just like *moderator*, only minus the final syllable. Interesting coincidence.

"Today we have a very interesting topic for our consulters to dig into," he said eagerly. "The topic posed is 'My son says he's unhappy in school, but won't say why. What should I do?'

"So, group, let us get started, then. A child is unhappy in school. Please begin."

All five people in the group settled into their chairs, bowed their heads, and closed their eyes. For long seconds, there was no sound or movement. That surprised Abby; in 2007 no one in talk-TV would ever allow such a lull. She was also surprised that the consulters hadn't first been introduced. Were they that famous? Or did they just not care about personal fame?

After a short while, the second consulter from the left, a woman, sang a short song. When it was done, again no one moved. Translation was perfect; but Abby hadn't understood several words and, while trying to sort them out, lost others. The bits she did get were "God...above all things, and nothing in the heavens or in the earth but God...Himself the Knower..."[34]

The camera did not zoom in, replay, inset smaller shots, use a split-screen, or do anything dramatic at all. It continued to show five consultants, sitting quietly. One of them began humming something, and the others seemed to join in. Then that stopped. One by one, they opened their eyes, but remained quiet until the last one opened his eyes. They all smiled at each other, more relaxed than ever.

"I'm remembering," said the woman on the far right, "that 'Abdu'l-

Bahá wrote—"

Abby gasped. She knew who 'Abdu'l-Bahá was! Dear Melissa! And Dumbledore's picture in the coffee shop! Oh, but she had lost part of what the woman was saying. Abby dragged her focus back to the screen.

"...must give him learning, and at the same time rear him to have a spiritual nature. Let the teacher be a doctor to the character of the child, thus will he heal the spiritual ailments of the children of men."[35] The woman was reading, Abby saw, from what could be a ALLY screen... like she herself was watching right then. They all seemed to have one. Abby bet the ALLYs had all kinds of things they could pull up for their consultation.

"It is wonderful that the parent is so concerned about sia child. We all agree that the parent is to be commended for caring for sia little one so well?"

Abby thought the Yuter was translating well; but she was pretty sure she'd heard "see ya" twice from the man second from the right. Must have meant *his*...with some unusual accent.

Everyone murmured agreement. A smaller inset shot appeared, with a man – serving as secretary, apparently – sitting at a kitchen table and showing several attractive certificates to the camera.

Wait, that didn't look like a TV studio. It looked like somebody's real home. Abby quickly reviewed her meager understanding of TV production. Didn't they need room for the big cameras, lights, wires, and people? Apparently, they'd figured out how to make it all fit into regular spaces. No wonder they appeared so relaxed.

A woman's voiceover broke in quietly. "If you're viewing this program live, you're welcome to yuter words of support for the back of the certificate the consultants will send. Key to episode 864-22. You may use Key 864-22-PF to yuter us post-program feedback."

Next, the man on the far left spoke.

"One other Writing that may help in this instance is 'How wonderful will it be if the teachers are faithful, attracted and assured, educated and refined Bahá'ís well grounded in the science of pedagogy and familiar with child psychology; thus may they train the children with the fragrance of God. In the scheme of human life the teacher and his system of teaching plays the most important role, carrying with it the heaviest responsibilities and most subtle influences.'

"That was 'Abdu'l-Bahá, quoted in Star of the West, Volume 17, on page 55," he concluded.

The panel sank into silence. Abby almost selected something else, thinking the clip was finished; but then the woman second from the left spoke up.

"Has the parent already consulted with the teachers about sia unhappy child?"

Several others nodded their heads, and one said, "I was thinking the same thing. More fact-finding."

One of the women said, "It may be something simple, if everyone will come together for the good of the child."

"Yes, has the parent consulted with everyone who interacts with the child?" another asked.

"How about checking on how well the child is sleeping? It could be something physical."

"Has the child voiced the reason to a playmate who could be encouraged to share?"

The camera had started doing close-ups. Voices flowed so quickly Abby couldn't tell who was talking. She'd thought no one was coming up with any answers. Now, they were happily offering solutions left and right. It again reminded her of the Native American quote about allowing time. Pauses might mean that great realizations were hatching.

The secretary touched spots on an ALLY screen that Abby couldn't quite see. Abby's screen now dwelt half on the secretary's collection of the suggestions and half on the consultants themselves, shifting from one bright, excited face to another.

Silence fell again. Ideas seemed to have run out. Each consultant looked like they were listening to a voice from within; but when there was nothing new, they looked at each other with satisfied expressions.

"The final thought I have," second-from-right man said at last, "is that perhaps the school the boy attends is not a good match for him, and that he may find happiness in a different school. After all, unhappiness in a school is grounds for transfer."

Abby was amazed. If a kid was unhappy in school, they called a meeting, put it on TV, and talked about automatic transfer?

Every kid she *knew* didn't like school. A lot of them only went because they had to. Some talked about dropping out just as soon as they could. The hard-core cases dabbled in failure by repeatedly skipping school. So what did they do in the Lodlan schools to make things so different?

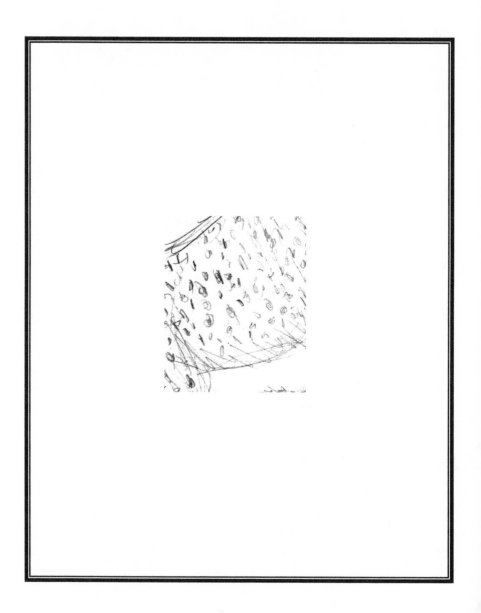

Chapter 16: Pollution

Abby spent the next several hours learning that the world of 2707 seemed to be mostly Bahá'í and that learning and helping were highly valued, as were good clean fun and an open mind. She was just feeling overloaded, when Dali said it was almost time to go.

"Good," Abby said, standing and stretching. "Where do we go from here?"

"Well, I was going to a gathering at a neighbor's; but I am thinking I should get you to bed. You must be exhausted."

Abby's only response was her biggest yawn ever.

"I thought so." Dali flashed her pretty smile again. Abby could get used to making her smile; it was such a rewarding experience. "Let's get dinner when we pick up your borrowed bike."

It was after four o'clock, and the school was closing. Dali chatted with several departing teachers. She tried to include her guest; but since Abby didn't speak their version of American, she was unable to participate. When they reached the bike rack, though, they doubled up easily and started pedaling back down School Street towards the business district.

Abby caught a better look at the House of Worship as they biked towards it. Each of its many sides featured a large, clear glass door surrounded by glossy, attractive, carved wood. The edifice was built of the same earth as most of the local structures, but with additional wooden accents. As they biked nearer, beams of lustrous hewn wood appeared like ribs between sections, reaching to the peak of the building. They looked to Abby somewhat like those European houses with the beams showing on the outside. Like the houses she had seen in the movie *Ella Enchanted*. What had Mother called them? Timber something? Half-timbered, Abby thought; she could almost hear Mother's voice.

Up closer, some of the burnished wood looked like actual branches coated with something protective. Surrounding gardens offered glimpses of decorative bushes, grasses, and flowers. Even though it was so dry, the garden had been cleverly planned to show dried grasses and ripening fruits to full advantage. Abby saw part of a simple stone fountain through the nodding branches of huge evergreen trees.

The heat brought out the wonderful smell of the pine trees the girls passed. Birds flew and chirped busily. Several people walked on the garden pathways. Two people sat on a bench under a tree, talking and enjoying the coming of evening.

"What goes on in the House of Worship?" Abby asked.

"Every morning, the elected go and pray. Anyone can join them, of course. We commemorate all the Holy Days with prayers and hymns. Voices only, no instruments or recordings. The acoustics are wonderful. It is quite an experience."

Abby doubted listening to prayers and hymns here would be much different from her boring church in Surely, wonderful acoustics or not. But to be polite, she didn't say so.

"Do you see that it has nine sides?" Dali asked.

"I wondered how many."

"Nine is a special number in the Bahá'í Faith.[36] It is the highest single number, before you start using them over again."

"How did the world come to be Bahá'í? I'd never heard of it before this week."

Dali directed her to again go counterclockwise partway around the House of Worship and then to turn right onto another street. Then she asked Abby, "What religion are you?"

"Episcopalian."

"Is that Muslim, Buddhist, Hindu…?"

"Christian."

"Oh, how wonderful that you're familiar with the Holy Bible. Did the Old Testament promise that when the children of God were in need, One would return to free them as His Holiness Moses had?"

"Um, I think so."

"So could you say that Jesus, the Blessed Christ, was the return of Moses…*spiritually*, not physically? To free *souls*, not just bodies?"

"It sounds right." It seemed to mesh with what Reverend Davison had said over the years in church, and it made sense.

"And did Jesus promise His disciples that *He* would return?"

"Yes." Reverend Davison had definitely said that.

"God has *always* sent Messengers to humanity to guide us.[37] Sia changes the *social* teachings each time, things like dietary or marriage laws. But the *spiritual* teachings are always the same, like the Golden Rule, our souls living on after our bodies die, praying and meditating, and so on. Some of them may not always be emphasized, but they're always there."

"What does 'sia' mean?"

"He or she. Her or him. Hers or his. One or one's. God has no gender, being all spirit and no body. You say *He*, though, don't you?"

"Yes…" Always so much to think about here. "Go on."

"All religions, all Holy Books, also carried God's promise of peace on earth. That promise is in your Lord's Prayer, correct?"

Abby could not recall there being such a promise, so she recited the Lord's Prayer rapidly in a low monotone…

Our Father, who art in heaven,
hallowed be thy name.
Thy kingdom come,
thy will be done,
on earth as it is in heaven.
Give us this day our daily bread.
And forgive us our trespasses,
as we forgive those who trespass against us.
And lead us not into temptation,
but deliver us from evil.
For thine is the kingdom, and the power, and the glory,
for ever and ever. Amen.[38]

Had she missed it? She began to say it over again, trying to slow down the rush of words she'd said almost without understanding them, a rote drilled into her since babyhood.

Before she'd repeated more than a few words, Dali said, "It's in the part about 'Thy kingdom come' and 'on earth as it is in heaven.' God's Kingdom is on earth when we do Sia Will all over the earth."

Abby felt stupid that Dali knew the prayer better than she did; but Dali said soothingly, "All religions prophesied a time when there would be blessed, heavenly peace over the whole earth. That wasn't possible until about your time, when communication and travel finally brought all the separate parts of the earth together enough for that idea to mean something. And then, you *had* to learn how to get along, yes?"

Abby flashed on Nine-Eleven, war, starvation, pollution...so many global problems with no perceivable way to solve them.

"Well, yes, but it's not all bad..." and she trailed off, remembering several personal crises. Money disappearing at the ranch. The fire bearing down on her family. Set by a punk arsonist, probably. She could almost smell the smoke, and frowned. Oh, and Mother! She felt overwhelmed, vulnerable, scared.

But here in Lodlan, she was safe. Wasn't she?

"Good, here's the spare bike," Dali said, glancing at a silver bike parked in the rack in front of the café she had indicated.

As they dismounted, Abby turned troubled eyes to Dali.

"So, does it end? I mean, I guess we didn't blow up the world, because here you are, in the future; but..."

"Don't misunderstand; it was a close thing," Dali said. "And we are still cleaning up some of the toxic waste from your time. There are still unacceptable levels of pollution in some waters and lands. There are still forms of physical and mental illness lingering in the...gene pool...

created in your time."

"*Mental* illness created by toxics? Toxic stuff?"

Dali's WaerY whispered.**[39]**

"Is there something in your time," Dali asked, "about...let's pick, say, autism increasing greatly?"

"Yeah, there is. Every year we've gotten a couple more autistic kids in school. Daddy even heard a radio program about it growing."

"Yes, there were warnings even then, saying toxins caused autism and other problems in the brain. Now we know that excessive and impure vaccines, drugs, surgeries, irradiations, chemicals, and many other pollutants cause such illnesses. They can even change peoples' genes, which may then get passed on to their children.**[40]** The Industrial Revolution triggered a massive increase in both the amount and the types of pollutants. Perhaps the most extreme example was England, especially London; but America was also badly affected. Soon thereafter, people were handling mercury and asbestos and other bad chemicals in ignorance. Ingesting various chemicals followed, including a real blow to human immunity: feeding babies formula."**[41]**

Engrossed in conversation, they continued to stand next to the bike rack of the little café.

"One of the worst effects of all this internal pollution was that many people started...disconnecting...from each other emotionally. For instance, many people seemed unable to give or receive love." Dali looked at Abby piercingly. Abby thought Dali was giving her a message of some kind, but didn't know what it was. She looked back blankly.

"For example," Dali added, "parents might be perceived as hating their children."

Comprehension dawned. Her own mother! Abby had long thought that Mother hated Jenn and herself. Dali was saying pollution cut off Vivian's ability to show love. Maybe Daddy's, too. That explained the problem! The girls were nurtured physically, sure...there was enough food, and better than a lot of families had; they were always dressed, rather well-dressed compared to some. But from there on, it was criticism and coldness.

Abby didn't know what kinds of pollution her mother might have absorbed, or her parents before her. She did know that Granny was always catty, pitting family members against one another. It still made for some tense moments when the families got together. Mother's dad had died of liver failure...from drinking! Could that pollute the genes that Mother had gotten from him? There was a lot to think about. Too much to figure it all out here on the sidewalk.

Abby looked back up at Dali, her brow creased. Dali correctly interpreted this as a sign of overload. They stepped into the café in silence.

The room looked very much like the coffee shop back in Little Lily. Wood floors, plants, some tables, friendly people. Even large artwork pieces on the walls. The menu was in UL, so Dali translated.

"Steamed veggies on brown rice with your choice of sauce; spinach pizza; falafels; soy loaf and gravy; baked potatoes with different top-pings; stir-fry; curried green peas with bread; salad—"

"Are you guys vegetarians?" Abby asked.

Dali smiled at her comprehension. "Eight hundred years ago, in your year 1907, somebody asked 'Abdu'l-Bahá what the food of the future would be. His answer included this statement: 'Medical science is only in its infancy, yet it has shown that our natural diet is that which grows out of the ground.'[42] He also wrote that meat wasn't forbidden and was even needed in certain cases, but that it was better to be con-tent with earth-grown foods.[43] You know, vegetables, fruits, grains, nuts, herbs, and so on. What you called *vegan*.

"Yes, that's another lesson from your time, and described in some detail in the Bahá'í Writings: that – except, of course, for mother's milk – our bodies are not actually all that well-suited for regularly digesting animal proteins. There was much illness in your time that we now know was due to consuming animal products. And especially over-consuming them. So," Dali finished with a wink, "what veganish dish would you like to try?"

"I might like the soy loaf, but I don't have any money."

"I know, and I'll buy," Dali said. "My treat. I'm enjoying this a lot, and the food is affordable. You'd also like mashed potatoes, yes?"

How did Dali always know just what Abby was feeling and think-ing? She'd just been feeling like a burden to Dali, and then Dali tossed in that she was enjoying their time together. She was amazing. And yes, Abby did want mashed potatoes!

After getting their food and finding a table, Dali gently continued, "We can learn to read others' thoughts when we try to become like the Master."

She was doing it again! "How? Who's the Master?"

"'Abdu'l-Bahá. The Master. He said to try to be like him."

"That's one of the only things I do know about Him."

"Good for you!" Dali was genuinely pleased. "He could read minds, or perhaps you'd say he could read hearts.[44] I guess it seems to you like I can see your thoughts."

"Yup. About five times so far today."

Dali laughed a long, delighted laugh.

"I'd say my WaerY reads my mind, too, but I don't think it really does. Still, it can pick up the slightest breath, brain waves, eye flicks, muscle micro-movements, and such; match them with my past words and actions; and put them all together into an interpretation of meaning. What I'm really doing with you is using what I know about reading expressions, interpreting words, and understanding body language. And a large dose of spiritual guidance."

"Yeah, I should be able to do that in about seven hundred years," Abby retorted with a grin as the server brought their food. "Um, why do you call him 'the Master'? It sounds kind of like, uh, I'm not sure, like a dictator...or a slave-owner."

Dali seemed taken aback, then smiled gently as she listened to her WaerY whisper.

"Oh no, not like that," Dali answered. "I agree with you, that would be terrible. No, it's more like when you say a person masters a skill or masters their emotions, or gets a Master's degree, or the way a master key opens all doors. From a very young age, even, 'Abdu'l-Bahá had a masterly understanding of his Father's teachings. He fully mastered the skill – the *art* – of living the Bahá'í life. That's why we should try to be like him. Actually, Bahá'u'lláh Himself called His teen-aged son 'the Master.'"[45]

"Hmmm," Abby murmured around a mouthful of food. The soy loaf tasted almost like other meat loafs she'd eaten...but less, um, greasy. The vegetable gravy was great. A small rack of seasonings offered some interesting possibilities, but Abby wished for some butter to put on the potatoes.

"We have butter-like vegetable spreads," Dali said.

"Stop it!" Abby cried, laughing.

"They're good. I'll get you some." Smiling, Dali went over to the counter, and came back with a small bowl. "Here's a little, shall we say, *vutter* to go with your deep-dish questions."

Abby was only just catching on to Dali's quick, dry sense of humor, but thought she could enjoy it.

"Which question were we on?"

"Originally? The one about how the world got to be Bahá'í."

"Still?"

"We'd just gotten started on it."

"If you say so." Abby listened as she ate hungrily.

"Each of the special Prophets promised that They would return and bring peace to earth. But since They had passed away centuries previously, how could Their decayed bodies return? They couldn't. It was a spiritual return, not a physical one."

Abby paused mid-bite. She realized she had always imagined that

Jesus physically floated up from the earth into the clouds. And was still there, watching, biding His time until He returned. But that wasn't very logical, even accounting for miracles and God breaking the usual rules. People in Jesus' time thought that heaven was an actual place above the clouds and that He'd gone there. But science showed us that heaven is not in outer space. If Jesus' ascension was spiritual and not physical, though, that explained it. His soul went with everyone else's soul, to someplace we couldn't see with our physical eyes.

Dali had been watching Abby's mental cogs turn.

"This might be the first time you have considered that science and religion can be – are – in harmony," Dali ventured, and Abby nodded. "Let me know if it gets too overwhelming," Dali added gently. Mouth full, Abby gestured Dali on with her spoon.

After a bite of her own stir fry, Dali continued, "God has promised humanity that Sia will keep sending us these special Messengers, like teachers for the next level in school."

Being in school, passing from grade to grade and teacher to teacher …that image made sense to Abby. She could really see that.

"Finally," Dali went on, "in the Year One – 1844 by your Christian calendar – everything needed for world peace was set into motion. But unfortunately, many people in your late 1800s were so ignorant of or threatened by Bahá'u'lláh's exalted station that they tried their best to kill Him…the same treatment almost all the Blessed Founders of the world religions have endured. But He and His son, 'Abdu'l-Bahá, both lived into old age and left many Writings to guide us.

"Of course, everybody investigates the various Faiths and makes their own choice. And our Houses of Justice govern only the Bahá'í community; civil law governs the people of all Faiths. Still, no matter what Faith people belong to, everyone eventually could see both the need for world unity *and* the unifying value of the Bahá'í principles.

"The value of sending all children to school, for example. Whether they want to go or not." Dali grinned. "Though, of course, 'most all of them do. The value of having a secondary language that everyone in the world can speak. Of treating men and women equally. Of eliminating prejudices and the extremes of wealth and poverty. Of having a world government to help the nations solve differences and work together on world issues – like the United States government involving all the states on national issues.[46] But spiritual values prevail. Protecting the rights of individuals. Keeping the world government, the educational system, the financial markets, and so on balanced and free of bickering, favoritism, corruption, greed, laziness, and so on."

"Wow! And who started this?" The name was so different, Abby hadn't memorized it yet.

"Bahá'u'lláh, an Arabic title that means *Glory of God.* He brought God's teachings for the Golden Age of World Peace, which you're now …visiting."

"No way!"

Dali listened to her WaerY, then beamed. "Way!"

Abby was too amazed to smile back. She could not even begin to think of all the questions she should ask.

"Don't worry, I'm sure you'll think of things. Seven hundred years is a lot to catch up on in one meal."

They finished their dinner, mounted their bikes, and pedaled home in near-silence and near-dark. Abby was overloaded with new ideas; her brain felt jammed. So she simply enjoyed the cool, and noticed small things like the bike's clear tube now glowing. Fireflies also began to glimmer, and crickets to chirrup. It was a very soothing ride for a be-fuddled soul.

Chapter 17: Dream

Dali made up a bed on the sofa and gave Abby some too-big PJs. Also an interesting teardrop-shaped device that – when she pointed it into her teeth and pressed a colored spot – completely cleaned and refreshed her mouth. Then to bed. And Abby was indeed exhausted. All those centuries packed into one day! As she drifted off, she heard a low murmur from Dali's room. Was her hostess on the phone to someone? Soon deeply asleep, occasionally shifting on the couch, she dreamed Dali was calling her mother to tell her where Abby was...

∞ ∞ ∞ ∞ ∞ ∞ ∞ ∞

... and how to get to the earthen house ... 'Prank call!' Vivian sneers, hangs up ... **ZZP** *... in a courtyard, boys climb down from a tree-house ... younger kids wait below ...* **ZZP** *... a ragged line of agitated kids files noisily into a classroom-amphitheater with chairs parked on cement tiers rising up from a stage ... organized chaos ... kids scamper out of their chairs ... not-teaching teachers swap places ... everyone earnestly discusses where to sit ... some kids say they just can't concentrate in their seats ... Abby climbs up the tiers to stand near the complaining kids and, surprised, hears distracting noises coming at her from two directions ... realizes the noises are inaudible in other parts of the room ... explains her discovery to the teachers, who encourage the kids to move to better places ... watches the kids yammer about, shoving chairs ... wonders at the high noise level and the lack of learning that none of the teachers seem the least upset about ... and lo, the kids make order out of chaos ... amiably find new seats ... shift their belongings ... all quiet down and focus on the teacher, who resumes the lesson ... so the class had been stopped to do some real-life consulting, honoring others' needs ... must be a dream ... this would never happen in real life ... Abby walks out of the room ...* **ZZP** *... under the tree again ... the boys, grown into men, come down from the tree-house with a problem ... head off in different directions ... several of them head into a meeting room ... call Abby to come with them ... say they need to* clarify *(whatever that means) ... a loose-ranging discussion on something Abby has missed the main points of ... a newborn baby? a fellow student? an elder? ... she cannot hear a word, and yet ... and yet ... they all show amazing abilities to discover the truth and the inner realities of things just by focusing ... they are confident ... determined ... beautiful ... spiritual lightning rods channeling divine energies into divinely-inspired suggestions ... the group finds an agreeable solution ... pledges to implement it ... streams out the door to undertake their mission ... though their words never reached her ears,*

an amazing feeling fills her ... the feeling of working together ... honoring each other... seeking the best, the brightest way ...

∞   ∞   ∞   ∞   ∞   ∞   ∞   ∞

Abby woke with a strong feeling of community and of living in the God-promised paradise on earth. She lay still a little longer, relaxed, relishing the feeling. She was used to fighting uphill battles for whatever she wanted. Being helped by people who delighted in devising solutions to problems – hers or anyone's, without blame, with *joy* – was a new and powerful experience.

If only the power, the inner knowing that she'd lived in her dream, could become reality. What a different life Abby would have if only she could keep that dream-world perfection with her during the day.

Abby's eyes flew open. Dreams *can* come true! Parelli promised it. 'Abdu'l-Bahá *wanted* us to be like him: a perfect person. And Dali did amazing things. How could Abby get some of that happiness, that confidence, that spiritual sight?

Dali had said she used a lot of spiritual guidance to read Abby's thoughts. With the last bits of the dream-feeling draining away, Abby wondered how to keep in that mode. The dream mode. Dali's mode. The one 'Abdu'l-Bahá lived in. Which, actually, would give you superpowers. Not physical ones. Better. They'd be spiritual. You'd know things before they happened, maybe. Probably solve difficult problems easily, happily, like on *Consultation Today*. Find hidden truths quickly. Read peoples' minds, hearts, souls. For good purposes only, of course.

Awake and aware, Abby pondered how to learn that spiritual mode. Nothing in her world said it was possible, but she was away from that time. Everything in this world encouraged it. Her own powerful wish, her will, could help it come true. She'd just need to keep an eye out for whatever could bring it to her, to grab and hold onto it when it came her way. Ideas like Dali shared. Or actual tokens like the books from the bookstore.

Abby felt as if she'd cast a fishing net of questions into an ocean of possibilities. What she would catch, she did not know. But she'd hold onto the net with the hand of faith; and as long as the winds of doubt and difficulties did not blow too strong, she was quite sure she'd haul up some interesting and helpful things.

Pleased with her strong mental picture, she sat up. Today was Sunday. Dali had to work again. Abby's agenda was simply to enjoy the age awaited by everyone for thousands of years: Peace On Earth. She wondered if lions actually did lie down with the lambs, as she'd heard they would when heaven came to earth. If they did, maybe she would see it when she saw the animal show.[47]

Chapter 18: Service

The girls got up, dressed, and ate. There were no Fruity Rings or Puff'ems, only whole-grain cereal with rice milk. Different, yes, but acceptable-tasting.

"Why the health food?" Abby asked. "All the food I've seen is what we'd call health-nut food."

Dali spoke after listening to her WaerY. "I mentioned last night that our bodies are not that well-adapted to eating animal protein. We also learned that the more processed food is, the more unnatural, the more chemicals and colorings in it, the worse it is for us."

"I eat those and there's no problems."

"May I assume you've had cow's milk?"

Abby nodded, trying to remember what Dali had said yesterday. She had been so tired; plus, what Dali had said about animal products had seemed a tad extreme.

"Cow's milk is, of course, an animal product." Dali appeared to be deciding whether to go into more detail about milk. "Did you ever notice a thickness in your throat or nose afterwards? Or have repeated ear infections? Get rashes for no reason?"

Abby searched her memory. Those things did ring a distant bell. She hadn't had them for a long time, but she had been "born sensitive." Sensitive in every way, her mother complained on a regular basis, adding that she had not wanted to live with The Princess And The Pea in real life. Abby's newborn rash evolved into toddler eczema, then into full-blown childhood allergies magnified by periodic colds and flu. The doctor said these problems often accompanied fair skin and reddish hair like hers. But she did drink milk every morning…and every morning her nose was stuffy. But things like that just *were*; they didn't have a *cause*, did they? What a bizarre idea.

"Yeah, maybe," Abby finally answered.

"It was known in your time that many humans could not tolerate cow's milk," Dali said.[48] "There were even reports of children who had gray teeth from repeatedly taking antibiotics to treat the ear infections they got from drinking milk, which they didn't know they were allergic to.[49] That must be very sad."

Abby had seen kids with gray teeth. Was that why?

"Chemicals and colorings in your foods contributed to cancer and other illnesses," Dali said.[50]

When Abby looked doubtful, Dali added, "Did anyone around you ever wonder where allergies came from? Parkinson's? Alzheimer's? Multiple sclerosis?" The WaerY whispered a long list. "Diabetes? Hay fever? PMS? Flu? Common colds, even?"

"Well, there's germs. And heredity. And..." Abby stopped. She had never heard of a cause for many of those conditions. The usual claim was that the cause was unknown, but that diet changes might help.[51]

"The Master told us that when we eat complex foods that are not healthful, the result is 'diseases both violent and diverse.'[52] He said that from the day of birth, children must be provided with whatever is conducive to health...starting with breastfeeding, if possible.[53] But the level of pollution got so high in your time that illnesses were more prevalent than health. Isn't that your experience?"

"No, I don't think so."

"So everyone wakes up happy, refreshed, clear-minded, and stays energetic through a long day plus one emergency?" Dali asked, adding at Abby's quizzical murmur, "Our common definition of health."

Abby felt the kids were pretty healthy – except for the ones who were sick – but she'd noticed the adults were often under the weather. Mother was off wheat and never happy. Daddy had trouble sleeping. She herself never woke up energetic...and often felt mentally foggy and physically sluggish, especially if she'd slept a long time. Sofia's neighbors could occupy an entire hospital wing.

"I guess not, then," Abby admitted.

"Here is another quote from Abdu'l-Bahá. It is very inspiring."

Dali laid her left arm on the kitchen table. From the WaerY, Abby heard a clear, soothing, man's voice reciting a passage.

"Quoting: 'Make ye then a mighty effort, that the purity and sanctity which, above all else, are cherished by Abdu'l-Bahá, shall distinguish the people of Bahá; that in every kind of excellence the people of God shall surpass all other human beings; that both outwardly and inwardly they shall prove superior to the rest; that for purity, immaculacy, refinement, and the preservation of health, they shall be leaders in the vanguard of those who know. And that by their freedom from enslavement, their knowledge, their self-control, they shall be first among the pure, the free and the wise.' End quote. From *Selections from the Writings of Abdu'l-Bahá*, selection 129, page 150."

"When we know better, we do better. Sometimes big changes, sometimes little by little." Dali smiled, then busied herself with her cereal. Abby also chewed, granola with her mouth, the new ideas with her mind. The people of Bahá...*beh-HAW*. Pure. Refined. Healthy. Free.

As they cleared the table, Dali said that they had a few hours before work. She asked Abby if she wanted to go to work again or stay home. Abby didn't want to hang out alone in the unfamiliar house today any more than yesterday. She'd really enjoyed everything she'd done with

Dali the day before, and told Dali so. Dali looked pleased and, hand-washing the bowls and spoons, said Abby would be welcome at work again and could spend more time on the school ALLY.

"You have to wash your dishes by hand? Don't machines do everything for you?" Abby asked. Not having to do any work was what most people thought of when they imagined the ideal future.

"Simpler is usually better. Machines burn energy, require maintenance, and cost money unnecessarily," Dali replied. Abby thought that Dali's mouth might be twitching. Was she trying not to laugh? "I am sorry, but your fantasy is a little unrealistic." Dali chuckled.

A little miffed, Abby began to defend the "fantasy."

"Just the laziness in human nature, I suppose," Dali said, amused, still washing dishes. "But if you carry out the fantasy, you'll soon have to picture a world full of overweight, out-of-shape – what do you call them? uh, potatoes people, yes? – with no perseverance and few skills. Moderate work is very good for people. Too much or unhealthy or demeaning work, no. Key devices that advance mankind, like Yuters, yes."

"I suppose," Abby grumbled. It was just hard to have all your basic assumptions wiped out overnight. "And it's 'couch potatoes.'"

"Oh. Thank you!" Dali finished tidying up the kitchen, then added, "Well then, what would you like to do before we go to work?"

"Um…what are my choices?" Abby asked.

"We could garden, take a walk, clean the house…oh! Today is also a Public Service Day!" Dali exclaimed.

"Can I do that, too?"

"Yes, of course. Let me just check the something." Dali approached a small table in the corner of the living room, above which hung a large framed photograph of a sunset. As Abby watched…

"It changed!" she exclaimed. Now it showed Dali smelling a cluster of colorful flowers, perhaps ones that she'd produced on her property.

"What? Oh, it's…" Dali listened to her WaerY whisper, "…like a slide show." Dali touched a spot on the frame, studied what became a Yuter display, and touched the screen to select a link.

"Today's Service is at Mr. Sawqui's house." Another strange name …*SAW-kwee*. "That's good, it won't be too far to the school afterwards. Let's take our lunch and water, and ride the bikes," Dali planned aloud. "Oh, and tonight after work, some of my friends are getting together at The Draggin' Dragon. If only you could understand them…oh! Yes! That could work!"

Abby gave her a quizzical look but figured she would say what was on her mind if she wanted to. Dali scurried off. Abby heard her rummaging in the bedroom.

Wanting to be helpful, Abby searched the kitchen for portable food; there were pictures on most packages and cans. She saw soup. Were there crackers? And throwaway utensils? Though they probably would not be real plastic. Or would they need to pack the metal spoons and then bring them home? She contemplated the innards of the silverware drawer. Dali entered, looked at the soup, fetched crackers from a wall cabinet, and joined Abby in peering into the drawer.

"Yes, we have recyclable utensils. They're in the back," Dali explained, groping behind the metal utensils.

Abby put two spoons and several napkins into a plastic bag. Well, actually, it felt like a mix of plastic and fabric.[54]

"It's sure to be hot today." Dali added two bottles of juice and three of water to Abby's bag, plus spare clothes for both of them. They went out, locked the house, and rode their bikes down the road.

Dali sang again. It sounded like yesterday's song; and when she was done, Abby asked her about it.

"It's the Traveling Prayer," Dali said, smiling and obviously glad Abby had asked. "There are many, many prayers, a lot of them straight from Bahá'u'lláh. We learn most of them when we're young, usually by singing them. Then we spend the rest of our lives figuring out how to live them. I'm quite sure many of these same prayers were put to music in your time. Maybe we're still using some of them now!

"Would you like me to sing it again? I could try to translate it to your American. In fact, it was *originally* translated into Old American."

"Sure," said Abby.

Head held high, with a bike-generated breeze blowing her straight, shoulder-length, black hair, Dali began to sing with the WaerY…

> ♫I have risen this morning
> by Thy grace, O my God,
> and left my home trusting wholly in Thee,
> and committing myself to Thy care.
> Send down, then, upon me,
> out of the heaven of Thy mercy,
> a blessing from Thy side,
> and enable me to return home in safety
> even as Thou didst enable me to set out
> under Thy protection with my thoughts
> fixed steadfastly upon Thee.
> There is none other God but Thee,
> the One, the Incomparable,
> the All-Knowing, the All-Wise.♫ [55]

It was a quick tune, and the girls both pedaled in time to the beat, Abby's energy picking up as Dali sang. Abby thought how different it was to have prayers for little things, not just for the big formal times inside churches.

"What are some of the other things you have prayers for?" Abby asked as they approached the edge of town.

"Oh, there are many kinds!" Dali rattled off, "For help, healing, families, children and youth, safety, spiritual insight, unity, meetings, work and looking for work, detachment from everything *except* God, praise *to* God, Holy Days, the obligatory prayers—"

"The what?"

"In every religion, God has commanded Sia believers to fast, pray or meditate, learn Scripture, and follow other spiritual practices. In the Bahá'í Faith, God tells us to offer up – in addition to whatever personal prayers we say – one of three special prayers every day."

"Really? For no particular reason? That all seems like a lot. Outside church, we usually only say a prayer before eating…you know, to bless the food."

Dali was quiet for a while, perhaps thinking how best to respond. Abby remembered the quote from her *Native American Wisdom* book about not pressing for a response. Suddenly, it didn't seem boring at all, but helpful to everyone. Less frantic. And she remembered how Ricky's train of thought had gotten sidetracked when he was pressed for a response. It made a lot of sense to stay relaxed. To not rush. Getting all uptight just cut off the Divine. Oooohh, this was a clue on how to stay in the spiritual, the powerful mode!

Dali introduced her next clue.

"Did you ever have a time when you wished you were more clear about something? Or needed to stand firm? Ever had to handle something really difficult?"

"Well…yes." Abby was a little embarrassed to admit it.

"We all have," Dali hastened to say, sending an encouraging smile Abby's way as they rolled towards Service Day. "The Bahá'í teachings give us much guidance on how to live, and how to stand firm and stay true to our beliefs. So we read from the Bahá'í Writings every morning and evening to receive these teachings. We also pray and meditate. All of these help us become…centered. Strong inside."

"Centered," Abby repeated. Yup, it felt like another clue. Sounded good, too. She thought she could figure out how to pray outside church, though doing meditation seemed completely foreign. "What should we pray and meditate *about?*"

"That's a great question," Dali replied warmly. "It has no single correct answer. You could choose a difficulty you are having in your life. Or focus on, maybe even research, something you wish you were better at, some virtue you feel you could improve. I often ponder clues or signs I think God is giving me, to see if I can progress in my current test, or if another one is coming. These days, I am meditating on the quote: 'God hath never burdened any soul beyond its power.'"[56]

The words made sense; but Abby was so unused to such thoughts, she felt the concepts slipping out of her mind as quickly as she heard them. She thought of all the TV shows that said "Don't try this at home" and wryly added that Reverend Davison should have said "*Do* try this at home." And she didn't think saying grace at meals really counted; it seemed like just rattling off words with no feeling.

"What do you mean, 'tests'? Not tests on paper, like in school…"

"God provides us with tests, challenges, hurdles, whatever word you like. They help us to grow. Oh, here we are!"

They came upon the run-down house Abby had seen the previous morning. People were arriving on foot, by bike, and in the little cars and heading to a folding table in the right-side yard.

As they parked their bikes at the curb, Dali held out her hand and whispered to Abby to put it in her ear. Abby's Old-World mind heard Dali telling her to "stick it in your ear." She was taken aback by Dali's unexpected rudeness, but saw only the usual sisterly expression.

Dali repeated herself, showed Abby the tiny, nearly transparent bud she was holding, and helped Abby insert it in her ear. It hovered, unfelt, in but not touching her ear canal. Dali tested the ear-Yuter, speaking New American, then UL. The bud translated Dali's voice perfectly. It was odd seeing and hearing other languages come out of Dali's mouth while listening to her voice in Old American in one ear.

Dali ended the test with Old American, saying, "'Let us encourage each other, and set all in motion.'"[57] Abby threw her a thumbs-up, and Dali returned the soul-happy smile Abby had grown so fond of.

"This AerY," Dali pronounced it *AIR-ee*, "or Audile Essential Reference Yuter, doesn't have all the functions of a WaerY. It translates well, though, so you should be able to understand everyone. I forgot I still had it. Communication and knowledge are so vital to world unity that every child gets a free AerY when starting school. But when I got a WaerY, I just stashed my AerY away and forgot about it."

"Oh. How come you ever learned to speak Old American?"

"We Erdeans treasure our cultural heritages, so I studied the old language in school because most of my ancestors were American. But now I think God wanted me study to it so I could speak with you when you came! When you first came down the hill, I needed the Yuter to understand, as I was out of practice. It's wonderful when doing God's will is so pleasant."

It blew Abby's mind to think that God had prepared Dali for her. It also scared her to think that God managed things that closely. She was used to a remote God, uninterested in peoples' petty concerns. But this God was all around you, at your fingertips, even inside you. It would certainly make a person more conscious of what they did if they lived with that awareness, Abby mused, following Dali up the brick walkway to the sign-up table. Was this what Reverend Davison meant when he spoke about living as if Jesus might come back and see what you were doing? Only, that felt different from this.

But, she mentally challenged herself, *how* was it different?

Well, Reverend Davison's vision felt like the guilt trips that Mother laid on her. This version wasn't so judgmental. It was loving. Here, she *wanted* to try. Back home with Mother, she couldn't win no matter how hard she tried. Here, there was actually a chance she would be accepted and welcomed for her efforts.

But, Abby argued back inside her head, people are human. They're going to mess up. What happens then? In her world, in the Old World, people seemed to exclude God from their everyday lives. Here, people seemed to be constantly checking in with Him...Sia...before, during, and after everything they did. And they seemed to feel...secure. Happy. Centered. Sure of guidance and, Abby supposed, sure of acceptance. She realized it would change *everything* if you lived that way. That was a new thought, one she'd have to keep figuring out. Would it be something to meditate on? Was she meditating now? Or did you have to sit cross-legged with candles in a quiet, dark room for it to count?

If Mother had been there, she would have criticized Abby for woolgathering. Abby looked around the plain yard, concerned she'd missed something, but there was no need to worry. Since Abby didn't care what job they did, Dali had signed them both up for digging, and was now reading messages on an ALLY screen on the table. The front door of the weathered house opened, and an ancient man emerged.

Abby had never seen anyone as old-looking as this man. Compared to most of the community, he had noticeably darker skin, which stood out starkly against his snow-white, wooly hair. Two well-used canes helped him navigate the three steps into the front yard.

"Mr. Sawqui takes cares of himself and of the house, pet-sits, and regularly looks after several generations of children," Dali explained quietly. A younger man assisted Mr. Sawqui down the steps. A woman in the yard brought a chair to the shade at the bottom of the steps. And another clapped her hands and called everyone over by Mr. Sawqui.

"Thank you so much for coming today for Service," she said. The AerY translated almost as fast as the woman talked. Abby recognized some familiar-sounding words, but was glad for the translation.

"We helped Grandfather repair his house last year, and he says the repairs are lasting quite well." Cheering and clapping greeted this announcement. Abby guessed that some of these workers had helped last year. "This year, we'll help him with his yard. He said he would love to have some roses to enjoy, if only the kids didn't tear everything up; so we'll start with a strong, decorative fence for flowers…and a bench. We're also going to fence in his back yard."

The crowd expressed sympathy and agreement.

"The roses will go here, and the bench will sit here," she said, as a sketch of the front yard unfolded on the ALLY screen. "We'll plant the roses in the fall, when the weather cools and rains return.

"Fence posts go there," she continued, pointing to stakes marking a rectangle in front of the large living-room window and another around the back yard. "We need to do all the fences first. The cement, wheelbarrows, shovels, and everything else is ready over there." She pointed again, to the supplies in the side yard. "Any questions?"

There didn't seem to be any questions at the moment, so the woman said, "You've each signed up for a task. If you'll gather your supplies, we can get started."

"Hooray for digging!" Dali cheered, as she and Abby picked up shovels and joined the front yard workers. Diggers, holders, cement mixers and cement pourers were all sorted. Most interestingly to Abby, someone had volunteered to play music. This seemed like a strange job; but Abby reasoned that if they were doing this project back in her time, there'd almost certainly be a radio. Live music had the advantage of no commercials, and it would be, well, live! Sure enough, several people suggested appropriate dirt-digging songs with good-natured teasing.

Dali and Abby took turns shoveling while two other teams dug close by. Abby didn't know any of the songs, but everybody else was humming along to the mandolin-sounding instrument and pleasant singing. It was almost fun, at least until the shade vanished.

"Anyone for a spray?" A middle-aged, bronzy-faced man with a big smile pointed a sprinkler-headed hose at them, ready to wet down anyone who said the word.

Half the group, including the musician, moved out of the way; and the other half stood like scarecrows. Abby stepped up to get sprayed, and her squeals joined others as a light, cold spray hit their hot bodies.

"Stop, stop, we're making mud!!" one of the ladies shrieked, shoes squishing as she stepped out of the damp dirt. There were some good-

natured threats about a mud fight, and smiling promises of a good one
next time…unless the kids stopped ruining the grass by then.

Two more people had come by on their morning walks and offered
to help for a while. Dali and Abby gladly handed over their spot to the
reinforcements, then sat in the shade of the house sipping cool water
from their lunchbag.

"How old is Mr. Sawqui, anyway?" Abby asked.

"Mmmm, you know, I'm not sure. I think I heard he celebrated his
one-hundred-twenty-fifth birthday about ten years ago by going on pilgrimage," Dali answered her, watching the frail man smiling, talking,
and thoroughly enjoying his morning.

"So now he's a hundred and thirty-five! You're joking, right? And
where's pilgrimage to?"

"Israel; and I'm not joking. Since we learned so much from your
bad example," here she nudged Abby to emphasize her polite teasing,
"oldens often live to one-hundred-fifty.[58] But most choose to live in
an olden-aid home after they reach one-hundred-thirty.

"Mr. Sawqui's wife passed away a few years ago, but he has a lot
of family around here. They gather here for dinners and celebrations.
The lady who organized us is Sue Lee Sawqui, his granddaughter."

Abby looked at the patriarch in amazement. He looked perfectly
happy, speaking with various volunteers who came and chatted with
him for a few minutes. Wow, she'd be doing well to even draw breath
at that age, let alone live in her own house and host a big project! Perhaps because she hadn't grown up close to her grandparents, she felt a
great fondness for him. No wonder people were delighted to come and
help him. He was a treasure just by living here, she thought, as she went
to help mix cement in a large tub.

About noon, most of the fence posts were in. People taking a lunch
break rinsed themselves off using the hose at the front of the house,
some turning northeast and murmuring as they did. Abby tried not to
stare; still, it was so odd that she couldn't help but sneak looks at them.

"The Medium Obligatory Prayer," Dali whispered. "It's one of the
three I mentioned. As we start it, we rinse our hands and then our face
with clean water…three times in a day: morning, noon, and evening."

"Which one do you say?" Abby whispered back as they got their
lunch sack and spread a thin, shiny, colorful cloth on the dirt under a
tree on the west side of the house.

"I usually say the long one before I go to bed. We say that one once
a day. You may have heard me saying it last night."

"Why don't you say it silently?"

"Because saying it out loud gives it more power and lets it carry further."[59]

While Abby was thinking about Dali's words, she noticed how soft, cloth-like, even plushy, Dali's picnic blanket felt...not at all the thin, plasticky feel one would expect from looking at it. She also realized, as she fingered and turned an edge, that dirt and grass didn't stick to it.

Dali showed her how to pop open the top of her chilled soup and eat it straight out of the can. When Abby tried to express how wonderfully refreshing the cool liquid was, Dali showed her the spots on the lid for heating or cooling the contents. Dali had pressed the cooling spot in the kitchen. Abby dipped her whole-grain crackers into the broth and scooped up rich tasty vegetables with the spoon, enjoying the simple, pleasant picnic.

After a bit, a young man came over and asked to join them. Abby gulped; what should she do? At least she could understand him, thanks to the invisible AerY, but it wouldn't help her know how to speak, or what to do with someone who didn't know...who she was.

"Please, join us," Dali said, arranging the little group into a triangle on the blanket. "Abby, this is Tonba Sayre. Tonba, this is Abby."

"Alláh-u-Abhá, Sister Abby," Tonba said, giving a slight bow before he knelt down, feet under his bottom.

Abby didn't know what *al-LAW-hoe-ab-HAW* meant, and the AerY was silent. She nodded, simply repeated his name – *TONE-bah SAY-er* – and smiled at him.

"How are you? It's very good to see you," Dali said respectfully.

"I'm doing very well, thank you. My walk has been full of beauty lately," Tonba replied. Abby recalled, from her little wisdom book, an Indian describing walking in beauty. An *American* Indian, she mentally corrected herself. Here, everyone had ancestors from all over the world and might have come from anywhere in the world.

"I would be pleased to hear whatever you wish to share," Dali said.

"This past Honor, I traveled to the Land of Tá to help celebrate my gee-four grandparents' hundredth anniversary. It was very fitting they were married in Honor, as that virtue was much in evidence during my entire time there. We also made our pilgrimage to the Holy Houses; and I made many supplications for the health and welfare of my friends, including yourself."

Abby was sure the AerY was working just fine, but she still didn't understand half of what Tonba was saying. She looked to Dali and was alarmed to see tears in her eyes.

Dali took Tonba's hand in both her own and was, for a moment, overcome with emotion, teardrops tracing a path down her face.

Tonba also was struggling to contain his emotions, and Abby felt completely left out of whatever important event was transpiring. When the tricky moment had passed, Dali patted his hand, let it go, and whispered with some emotion, "I'm sure you felt aweful."

It might have been a lot of things, but *awful* was not what Abby would have guessed about Tonba's pilgrimage...and wasn't that supposed to be in Israel, not Tá?

She was completely confused, and gave up trying to understand. She fiddled absently with the nearly-empty soup can, pulling at a loose corner of the label to see how it was fastened on.

Suddenly, the can was a limp, wet film in her hand. The last bits of broth and vegetable spilled onto her slacks and the blanket. She yelped and scooted back. Dali and Tonba jumped as well, not knowing what was wrong. Dali saw the dripping label in Abby's hand and laughed.

"Never mind, Abby; no real damage done. We'll just shake out the cloth. It's time to go anyway."

They all got up, Abby wiping her slacks clean, surprisingly, with a napkin. Turning to Tonba, Dali bowed to him as he had to her, and said, "I will carry with gladness the blessing you have brought me."

He bowed back and replied, "The gladness is mine. I will look forward to telling you more if the time becomes convenient."

They wished each other goodbye, which the AerY pronounced as *god-BEE*.[60] Then Dali turned to Abby.

"I'm so sorry you were left out. I'll explain now.

"The Bahá'í calendar has nineteen months, with Arabic names. Last winter, in the month of Sharaf, or *honor*, Tonba went to the Land of Tá – to Tihrán, the capital of what you call Iran – for his great-great-great-great-grandparents' hundredth wedding anniversary.[61] And it was all very honorable...full of honor for them and everyone."

Abby nodded her understanding, and for Dali to continue.

"Bahá'u'lláh was born and reared in Tihrán. In His thirties, He was exiled to Baghdád, the capital of what you call Iraq, and His home there is also designated as a place of pilgrimage.[62] In your time, Iraq was a country of great turmoil, yes?"

"Oh yes, it's a real garbage pit right now...oh, I mean..." Abby had not meant to be so rude, but it was true. Men in Surely sometimes spit on the ground when Iraq was mentioned. The war against Iraq and in Afghanistan was going strong back home. It was the number-one topic on all the talk-show airwaves.

"Tonba's family is mainly Middle Eastern, way back, as well as subcontinental Indian *and* American Indian. Some of my family were neighbors with his family years ago. Now I'm here. And his sisters also live here, so I see him once in a while. He's such a noble spirit, almost like the brother I wish I'd had. But we're all fortieth cousins anyway," she ended lightly.

"And the can?"

"Yes, the can. Once the lid is off, if you press this other spot here," she demonstrated with her own can, "and pull the ripcord on the label, it pre-decomposes. I forgot to tell you to watch out for that."

"And what did he say when he greeted me?"

"Hm…Yuter, please repeat Tonba's greeting."

"Alláh-u-Abhá, Sister Abby."

"Right. Thank you. That means *God is the All-Glorious*. Most early Bahá'ís grew up in Islam, so later they gradually replaced the Muslim greeting Alláh-u-Akbar – or *God is Greatest* – with Alláh-u-Abhá."

"And he said his time was awful?"

"Yes, he did."

"But he'd been saying it was so honorable, and then it was awful?"

Dali stared at her, then asked her WaerY a question. A voice spoke softly in Abby's ear and from Dali's wrist, "One: A-W-E-F-U-L, AWE-ful: full of awe; a reaction to something awesome. Two: A-W-F-U-L, AW-ful: full of distress; a reaction to something very unpleasant."

"Homophones!" Dali exclaimed cheerfully. "Words that are spelled differently and mean something different, but sound the same. Well, that clears *that* up."

As lunch break ended, other helpers began working on the fence again, or taking their leave. Dali and Abby got on their bicycles after calling "Godbee" to everyone, and headed towards school.

"I liked it, thanks for taking me!" Abby exclaimed. "And thanks for the AerY!"

"You're welcome. I just love when I can receive divine inspiration *when* I need it instead of *after* I need it."

They soon arrived at school, parked the two bikes in the rack, and went to the staff bathroom to clean up and change.

"Oh, before I forget," Dali said from her stall, "Tomorrow afternoon is a performance of the animals. I reserved two seats for us."

"Sounds great! Wow, I could really get used to life here!"

"And I could get used to having a little sister to boss around," Dali responded with tender affection in her voice. Abby was too grateful for the overwhelming care Dali had shown her to say anything; but she assumed Dali was, as usual, able to…um, *divine* her thoughts.

Chapter 19: Creation

"Here, blow this on yourself," Dali said, holding a cordless hair dryer over the stall wall. "Before you put your clothes on."

Abby pointed the dryer at herself. Nothing happened. "How do I turn it on? Or does it turn on?"

"Ah, yes, press the green dot on the handle. You'll know it's on if you feel it."

Abby pushed the dot, turned the dryer on herself, and felt as if a silent wind or invisible shower were passing over her. It was a fantastic experience; wherever she pointed the open end, all the dirt and sweat seemed to fall away.

While Abby was cleansing herself, Dali called out, "You know, I just had a sort of funny thought."

"What about?" Abby asked.

"Well, you know how we got all confused over 'full of awe' and 'terrible' when Tonba was talking? Telling homophones apart? I was just remembering another conversation we had where I think the same thing happened. When I was explaining about cars. You asked me why a car was wreckless here and I told you about the safety features. Now, I said wreckless with a 'w'; did you, though, hear reckless without a 'w'? So that when I used their common name these days, meaning it's almost impossible to wreck them, you thought I meant people drove them dangerously?"

"Hey yeah, I forgot about it then, but you're absolutely right. That *was* what I thought." She laughed and shyly ventured to joke, "Guess we'd better talk and listen less rrrecklessly if we want to communicate more wwwrecklessly, huh?"

"Oh, good one, Abby," Dali said, laughing with her.

Finished with her cleansing, Abby pressed the red OFF dot and laid the blower on the back of the toilet, then got dressed. She rolled up her dirty clothes and brought the blower out to the waiting Dali, who hung it in its cradle on the wall.

"It's pleasant using the staff bathroom, isn't it?" she noted. Abby agreed. Astonishingly clean, fragrant soap in decorative containers, low carpeting and comfortable chairs in a lounge area, fresh flowers on a small table in the corner…a stark contrast to the smelly, grungy, graffitied bathrooms she was used to at school.

"Schools have top priority for money, of course," Dali said gently. "Children are the most important."

This was so opposite the invisible, third-class-citizen status she was used to that she felt something both break and bloom inside her. That was how it *should* be, she knew. But would it be seven hundred years before children would have their rightful recognition?

Dali saw the emotions tangling in her, and waited patiently.

Abby worked through it, and signaled her readiness to move on by looking at Dali's pretty brown eyes. Abby noticed for the first time that Dali wore little if any makeup. She realized with surprise that, although Dali did not primp like the Old-World supermodels did, she seemed beautiful. The beauty came from inside. Abby thought that *that* was a kind of beauty worth copying.

"Are you ready? Good then. I thought you could either...how do you say?...cruise the Yuter again, or I could find some crafts for you to try."

"Browse or build, hmmm? Surf or shape?" Abby surprised herself. Not only did she seem to be thinking better, using words in interesting ways, she was even offering Dali a correction without actually correcting her. It felt *good.* "Maybe some of both?" she ventured.

"An excellent answer!" Dali clapped as she said it. "Let me get you started on the Yuter, and then I'll get some crafts supplies."

Dali led her to the same table as before and started the ALLY.

"What should I look up today?" Abby asked.

"I think you might enjoy Auntie Zoray," Dali opined.

"Who's Auntie *ZOR-ray*? Never mind. Whatever you think," Abby said. She trusted Dali with her life, so letting her pick the computer programs was a no-brainer.

Dali pulled up a page that, sure enough, touted "Auntie Zoray" in big. zany letters across the top. A cartoon of a Middle-Eastern-looking woman peeked out of the 'o' in Zoray, showing a colorful shirt, shiny black hair, bright head-kerchief, big round earrings, and a welcoming white smile. She waved from under the 'r' next to her head, her fingers and wrist clanking with rings and bracelets. It was hard not to smile just looking at her, so Abby gave in and smiled back. And somehow, smiling elevated Abby's own emotions, as if the smile on her lips was also making her brain smile. Which made her smile even more. Interesting, how a happy smile could be so infectious.

Abby touched the ALLY screen, which felt like plexiglass, to select the first topic, "Sharing Dorm Room." And as Abby watched, the text switched from New American to Old American.

Dear Auntie Zoray,

I'm in university. I'm a neatnik and my roommate is a slob. I tried consulting with him. He said he'd try; but it's no better. I finally put a line of tape down the middle of the room. I'm just about to put up screens so that I don't have to look at his books, sports gear, clean and dirty clothes, just *stuff* spreading all over his half of the room and creeping into mine. But I'm not sure if this will do any good. It bothers me to see mess. 'Abdu'l-Bahá said: "The home should be orderly and well-organized."[63] And Bahá'u'lláh said: "Wash ye every soiled thing" and "Be ye the very essence of cleanliness amongst mankind."[64] I'm at a complete loss! What can I do?

~ ~ Bothered Brother

Oh brother, Brother,

You do have a problem, and you are right about what the Master and the Blessed Beauty said. Some people really don't care how messy their place is, and reminding them is like wind blowing outside their dirty windows. So let's roll up our mental sleeves and think hard. Can you get another roommate? Move out yourself? Declare a day that cleanup will happen, even if it is only once a month? Clean it yourself, if he'll let you? Trash out your side of the room and see how he likes it? (Just kidding; what if he *likes* it??!!) Consult with your Resident Assistant? Keep your back turned, and buy yourself some eyeglasses that will block your peripheral vision? Say a bunch of prayers to not be bothered anymore? (Those would be in the prayer book under "Detachment.") Good luck, and let me know what happens!

~ ~ A't Z

Abby thought Auntie Zoray was a hoot and a holler, as they would say back in Tennessee. She felt a stab of homesickness in her heart… how would she get back home? What if she never got back? She could almost see Jenn's dear concerned face in front of her. She closed her eyes and it got clearer…hung there before fading. Maybe it was the hormones kicking in, but she seemed more emotional these days. She wiped a tear, took some deep breaths, and clicked on the next item: last week's letter.

Dear Auntie Zoray,

About ten years ago, we planted a fruit tree in our yard. We knew it would grow large enough to hang over our neighbor's yard and maybe drop leaves and fruit there, so we got permission from them to plant it. They said they'd be happy to have us plant it, because it was a ManyFruit tree, with grafts of different fruits all growing on the same trunk.[65]

But those neighbors moved, and our new neighbors are not happy with what they call "trash" dropping into their yard. We like our tree, and so do all the other neighbors who get to come over and pick the peaches, plums, and apricots when they are ripe. We make wonderful jelly.

We've tried to consult with our new neighbors, but they just don't want to talk. Do you have any suggestions?

~ ~ Fruitless Strife

Dear Fruitless,

Too bad you're not growing cucumbers; then you could be in a pickle instead of a jam. So you have some sour neighbors? Maybe they wish you'd planted a lemon-lime tree so they could suck on lemons. Or maybe they already do! How about growing a sugar tree to sweeten them up?

Okay, more seriously, might they give you permission to come on their side and get the fruit they don't want, and rake those leaves? And you offer them some jelly in exchange? Or how about if you install a net, so the fruit either collects without dropping or rolls back onto your land? It usually works better if you can approach people with a proposal ready to go, instead of asking them to solve your problem – or anyway, one they think is yours. However it turns out, do enjoy the fruits of your labor!

~ ~ A't Z

Abby read a couple more and enjoyed Auntie Zoray's wacky sense of humor. It could not be said that the people of the future had no fun!

She checked the daily online paper and saw a small notice about the get-together tonight at The Draggin' Dragon near the Temple. It was to "Celebrate The Declaration Of Elle Tulia," whatever that was.

She looked around. She didn't see Dali, but saw several new bags on a table behind her. One looked like a baggie of clay; another was a sack of fabrics. The third looked like wood, possibly to carve; and the last held colored stones and a large tile.

Dali was still nowhere to be seen, so Abby got out the wood. There was nothing else in the bag, certainly not a burning or etching tool. She pressed it with a fingernail, and it seemed to be soft wood but nothing more. No instructions came with it, and she would not be able to read them even if there were.

She put the wood down and spread out the stones. With no plan in particular, she placed the stones on the tile, then accidentally knocked the wood onto it…and why not? She arranged the stones around the wood. There seemed to be room left over, so she rolled the clay out into snakes and balls, adding them to the tile. What would the fabric do? Loose threads around the edges of the fabric invited pulling. They came off in her hands and, without thinking, she dropped them on top of the design. She liked it and pulled off more threads, dropping and poking them here and there. Some nestled down on the tile, some lay over the chunk of wood, some bent in half, poking up between the stones. She was thoroughly absorbed in her design when she heard a soft sound next to her.

"This is amazing!" Dali said...awefully.

"Is it?" Abby replied, coming out of a dreamlike place of creating. "I'm just messing around."

"I'd never have thought of combining everything."

"Am I not supposed to?"

"In creating, there are many right answers, and rarely a 'supposed to,'" Dali supplied. "The important thing is, have you enjoyed it?"

"No, not at all," Abby said with a straight face.

"I can tell," Dali matched her without missing a beat. "We elevate ourselves when we create. One of the main names of God is Creator; and whenever we...participate?...in one of God's attributes, we feel closer to Sia."

"What do you mean?" Abby inquired, putting the final shreds of thread on her creation.

"Let's take another of God's attributes or qualities. Give it a try; name one."

"Knows everything?" Abby ventured.

"All-Knowing, Omniscient; yes, wonderful. We can't know everything, of course; but don't you like it when you learn something? Don't you feel *more,* somehow? It's not merely increasing your knowledge; it also somehow increases your spirit."

Abby turned towards Dali, considering what she had said. It was a completely new idea: that doing these things was taking part in God's attributes.

"I'll have to...um...meditate on it," Abby finished lamely.

Dali smiled brilliantly, patted her arm, and said that if they sprayed the tile with the right liquid, everything would stick to the tile. They went to a workroom, where they sprayed and parked the tile.

Then Dali said they were ready to go to the party at the restaurant, so they biked around the left side of the House of Worship and down a new street. After a couple of blocks, Dali motioned her to a crowded bike rack on the right.

"You'll have the AerY," Dali said, "but let me also teach you a few words in UL. There may be people from other countries here, so that'll be a safer bet than teaching you our current American."

At Dali's prompting, Abby carefully repeated words like: "Jes" (it sounded exactly like what it meant: *yes*), "Saluton" (*sah-LUTE-own*, meaning *hello*), and "Kiel vi fartas" (*KEE-ell vee FARR-tahs*, meaning *how are you*).[66] But Abby couldn't stop laughing after that last one. She was just glad Dali didn't press her as to why.

"Oh, and if people ask your name," Dali advised, "don't say your second name, your family name."

"Why not?" Abby asked, still giggling.

"Usually, in this Age, when people discover their calling in life, they change their childhood last name to reflect that."

"What do you mean, 'calling'?"

"The Blessed Beauty, Bahá'u'lláh, said: 'True reliance is for the servant to pursue his profession and calling in this world.'[67] Also: 'The best of men are they that earn a livelihood by their calling.'[68] It's like a job; but *calling* has the extra meaning of being the fulfilling work God has nurtured you for."

Dali checked Abby's face for signs of understanding or being lost. Abby smiled; and Dali continued, "My last name is Puerta. Soon after I turned fifteen, I realized my calling is opening doors for people who want to learn something. That's why I chose to work in a school."

"Like you've been helping me. Puerta means *door*?"

"Yes, in Old Spanish. I liked the sound of it."

"So do I." Abby realized Mr. Modderay's name hadn't been just a coincidence after all. "But what's so important about turning fifteen?"

"In the Bahá'í Faith, the beginning of maturity is age fifteen. To-night's party is because one of my friends turned fifteen just a few days ago. Spiritually, she's an adult now, and wants to reaffirm her faith."

"Why would you reaffirm your faith?"

"It's a wonderful concept. In the past, children inherited their parents' faith. In the Bahá'í Faith, one of the principles is that we should investigate such things for ourselves, instead of just accepting whatever someone hands us...even if it's from our parents. Most of us are raised Bahá'í, and that is wonderful indeed; but we're also able to say for ourselves whether we accept it or not. Then too, there are laws to follow; and some youth aren't sure yet at fifteen that they can follow them."

"Like what?"

"We are to observe the Fast, say the Obligatory Prayers and read the Writings daily, avoid alcohol and other drugs except for medical need, have sexual relations only in marriage, shun gossip—"[69]

"No gossiping? That's different."

"I understand that, in your time, gossip was not only practiced but enjoyed widely by people everywhere."

"Yeah, that's an understatement," Abby muttered, remembering the rumors at the ranch.

"It has very destructive results, as you've apparently experienced," Dali said kindly. "Anyway, we also have many teachings that are not actual laws, but guidance. There's plenty to go on with."

"Um, but back to the names thing. That man at Service today, what was his last name?"

"Sayre."

"Is that his calling name?"

"Yes. He is an eloquent speaker. He *says* many marvelous things, you see."

"And your friend tonight?"

"She hasn't chosen another name yet. And she doesn't have to. Her name now, Elle Tulia, is beautiful. But your last name, Wize? Well, can you see how that's quite a claim? And people may not know if you're fifteen and chose your name, or…well, it's going to be easier if you just don't mention it."

"You're saying people in the Golden Age lie? And won't they find out my name anyway?"

"I'm not asking you to lie. We can simply – gently, graciously, and truthfully – steer the conversation away from awkward topics," Dali said, turning to open the restaurant door. "And the Yuter doesn't reveal personal details that you don't wish it to."

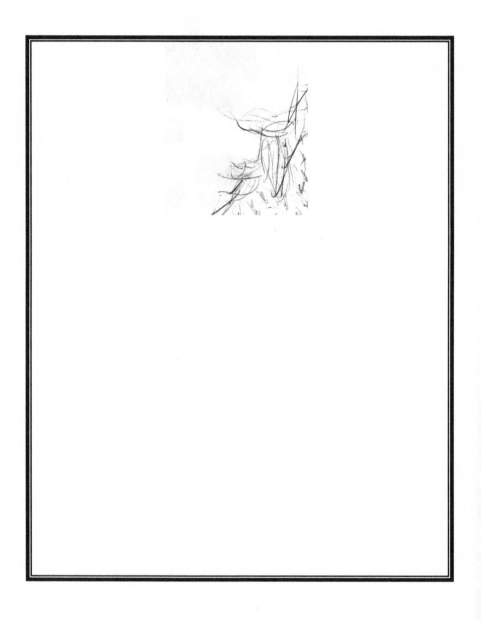

Chapter 20: Party

They stepped into the most interesting restaurant Abby had ever seen. To the left stretched a long counter. To the right stood glass-topped pedestal tables with chairs, several machines with controllers and colored screens, and some tall, blank wall panels surveying vacant floor space. Beyond these, Abby could also see part of another large, bare room.

The most eye-catching thing, though, was the very lifelike, scenic wallpaper running around the top third of the whole place. And amazingly, it was animated. It depicted a large grassy sward bordered by tall, dusky trees. The sun-bright clearing was dotted with couples and groups of people and animals...meandering, meeting, greeting, dancing, riding, wrestling, playing tug-of-war.

To Abby's delight, horses abounded. Here, amidst the trees, several sinuous Asian dragons – wingless, yet able to fly – played a gliding game of hide-and-seek with valkyries astride soaring cloud-horses and medieval knights on mailed chargers. There, on a low knoll, maidens – some in kente-cloth kaftans, in embroidered kimono, in flowing gowns, in long-fringed buckskin – read to grazing zebras and a pair of lazing, winged, European dragons that seemed as friendly as their Asian cousins. Elsewhere, by a stream, samurai collected viney flowers, which young ladies twisted into stiff leis and tossed in a nimble game with ebon warriors and several spirited unicorns of both the caprine and the equine kind.[70]

Abby was amazed. It was mega-cool. And it blended races and cultures in ways she'd never even thought of.

Dali's name rang out from several directions. Abby shyly peered around at young singles of both genders, all with middling-dark shades of skin, sporting various colors and styles of hair, dress, and jewelry. Abby was pleased that she was not the youngest; several little kids had broken away from older siblings or young parents and were playing tag in the big room.

"Dali!" squealed a girl from a group at the middle of the counter. Dali immediately hello'd back – or rather, saluton'd and kiel vi fartas'd – while Abby tried hard not to laugh again.

"Good practice to keep a straight face, Abby," Dali whispered out of a corner of her mouth. "People can also have unusual names."

"Like what?" Abby murmured, weaving her way behind Dali.

"I knew a young man in professions training whose first name was Metric. That seemed odd, but who was I to say? It was an old family name, he was proud of it, and I realized how discourteous it would be to laugh."[71]

"Oh. Okay, duly added to my list of things to meditate on: how to keep a straight face when people have odd names or when languages sound silly," Abby said.

"That's the spirit," Dali said. Then she and the delighted girl by the counter gave each other a long and heartfelt hug.

"Abby, this is Elle Tulia, my close friend since babyhood," Dali said. "Elle, this is Abby."

In response to Elle's greeting, Abby nodded, smiled, and offered *ELL too-LEE-ah* a "Saluton" and a "Kiel vi fartas?"

"I'm very well, thank you. And you? And where are you from?" Elle's question was translated through the AerY.

Dali came to her rescue. "She's my distant cousin; her family hails from north Europe. She has an AerY to translate our words, but can't speak UL very well."

Abby thought that was an excellent white lie. In fact, she reconsidered, it wasn't a lie at all. Dali said the whole human race were cousins, however many times removed. And, as Mother frequently said, Abby's family tree did originate in Europe. Abby was impressed with Dali once again.

"Ah, okay," said Elle. "Well, are you hungry yet? Just come from work?"

"Uh huh," Dali said, taking Elle's proffered arm and leading the way to order dinner. Abby hoped there were pictures of the food.

"Do you know what you want yet?" asked a voice behind her. It belonged to a shortish young man standing next in line, wearing loose purple pants and a comfortable-looking, embroidered, yellow zip-up shirt. He was good-looking and well-mannered; and as he turned towards her, she saw tattoos around his ears and eyes. He in turn seemed to be studying her skin, definitely lighter than anyone else around. She pulled her eyes away from his intricate tattoos and saw thick, slightly wavy, dark-brown hair secured in a short ponytail. Beads shone on his head. She'd never seen anyone like him, but found him and his adornments attractive. He handed her a menu from a stack on the counter.

"I'm sorry, but I don't read UL," she said, then panicked. He would not understand her. She looked at Dali, who was engrossed in conversation with Elle, her back turned to Abby.

The young man, though, saw that Abby did not even look at the menu, read her face, and asked, "Do I understand that your AerY is translating?"

"Jes," said Abby, heart racing, palms sweating, feeling caught.

"Would you allow me to read the menu to you, and you can tell me what you'd like?"

"Jes, um, please," said Abby, heartily wishing she hadn't fallen apart so soon into her UL lesson.

This fellow seemed to be as good at reading minds as Dali, though, as he said, "You're doing great. The UL word is plaĉi. *PLAH-chee.* But I understood you just fine anyway."

She was very grateful.

"My name is Kreshi, I'm pleased to meet you, Abby," Kreshi said.

Kreshi? Like "FRESH he"? Kinda cute, that. "Me, too. What's your last name?" Abby responded, her interest overshadowing any concerns. He looked at her thoughtfully and then snapped his fingers and looked at his WaerY. In a flash he had it off his wrist and – after pushing two places on its case – wrapped around his ear.

"There! See, I find it takes a lot of concentration to communicate mentally with the Yuter; this will whisper where I can hear it," he said, smiling for the first time. Oh my, even his teeth were tattooed; that was *quite* fascinating. Abby had read about unusual ways to beautify oneself, but to meet such a person face-to-face…what an experience!

"What did you ask?" Kreshi inquired gently. He had been looking at her pierced ears with small gold hoops in just the same way she'd been looking at his facial tattoos. Didn't people here pierce their ears? She hadn't noticed.

"I was wondering what your last name is," Abby replied, trying to be her most polite.

"Ah. It is Tender," he said. "And yours?"

Abby's face fell. She'd trapped herself! Now what?

"Abby, what do you want to order?" Dali interrupted. Bless that girl, she rescued Abby thrice a day every day. Dali was going to have to change her name to whatever the UL was for Rescuer. "Do you want something substantial or light? They have tacos, would you like that? That's medium-heavy," Dali prattled on, steering the conversation onto food.

"Sounds great. Do they have fried rice, too?" she asked on a whim.

Dali smiled. "That's fun, mix and match."

They all ordered their food. You could pay through your WaerY or with cash. The money some people placed on the counter had really interesting designs and colors. The bills were smaller and more colorful than dollars, and the coins were really different. She picked up one and was amazed to see a tiny feather encased in the coin's clear center. She turned the coin over; yes, it was a real, miniature feather. She saw a bit of red dirt in another coin's center, and a tiny bit of green in another.

"Those are the current Kingdom coins," Kreshi explained.

"I'm sorry, I haven't seen them before. Could you please explain?" asked Abby, hoping her excuse would work, as she put the feathered coin back on the counter.

"Well, you know, the Kingdoms of Creation. Coins with bits from each Kingdom." He pulled a small handful of coins from his pocket and sorted through them.[72] "See, here's a mineral kingdom coin, this red volcanic soil from Hawaii; they even dye shirts and hats with it. And here's a vegetable kingdom; I think this one's a bit of needle from the world's oldest living thing, the bristlecone pine in California. Then for the animals, this one's a molted feather from the world's smallest bird; let me see if I can read...yup, the bee hummingbird of Cuba. For the human kingdom, here's one with a bit of hair from Marta Kair; she's a Teacher of the Year. And finally, the kingdom of the spirit is always represented by light. This one has a micro light bulb powered by the warmth of your hand, see? And this one has a tiny prism that forms a rainbow in bright light."[73]

Abby enjoyed his easy rambling as much as the beautiful coins. She thought them the coolest thing in numismatics since the time she read in *Muse* about some islanders using huge stones as money.[74]

"Hey, there's Kwan!" Elle called as she waited for her food. "Kwan! Penda! Over here!"

More people joined the group and stood in line to order while they greeted each other and chatted. Abby looked at all the interesting variations in appearance, hoping no one else would speak to her.

Kreshi, Elle, Dali, and Abby got their food and moved to a table close to the game machines. The other three chatted as Abby crunched through her warm, crispy, scrumptious tacos. For some reason, the taco innards didn't spill all over. She looked more closely, saw an almost invisible and obviously edible wrapper around them holding everything together and maybe keeping them warm, and marveled at the practicality, especially as the flavor was apparently unaffected.

Seeing Abby's examination of the tacos, Dali whispered to her, "I assumed you didn't want to be all messy here. You see, tacos and other messy finger foods normally come twrapped. But you can order them twrapless if you want to; some people do sometimes because they say a taco that doesn't fall all apart just isn't as much fun." She chuckled and turned back to her three-way conversation.

Abby mentally replayed what Dali had said. Dali hadn't really said "trapped"; she had pronounced it funny, like *twoo-RAPT*. Abby stopped chewing as she thought hard for several moments, then smiled as she figured out what the word might really be. She would just bet it was a New American word made up of the letter "t" to indicate taste-free or tasty or tofu or something and the word "wrapped" but with the "w" pronounced more like a double "u." Hey, figuring out new words was fun...more fun even than the fall-apartness of an untwrapped taco.

As Abby continued eating, she again gazed up at the animated wall-paper circling the room. The scene had changed. Now all the previous people and animals were at a seashore, some of them picnicking on the sand and others resting on rocks or playing tag and a gentle version of monarch-of-the-mountain among grassy dunes.

In the ocean waves, Abby could also see several people in unusual but modest swimsuits splashing about, swimming, surfing, and riding playful dolphins and sea serpents. Oh yes, of course; sea serpents could be a kind of dragon, couldn't they? And one rider was astride a black horse prancing across the tops of waves; Abby decided it must be a friendly kelpie. Kelpies – Celtic water horses – were not usually considered kindly creatures, of course; but apparently they were depicted as such here at the restaurant.[75] Just like the European dragons.

Abby was entranced with the way the wallpaper mirrored the cheerful mood of the restaurant. Maybe it even helped set the positive tone. Using her fingertip to finish the few taco crumbs that had escaped the twrap, she noticed that whenever the animated swimmers exited the water, their hair was immediately dry and neat. She wistfully wished hers could do that, but doubted it was really possible, even in Erden.

Suddenly, Kreshi invited her to play one of the games.

"I don't have any money," she replied, startled.

"And no credit, either, I'm guessing? That's okay; I'll pay," he said graciously, listening to his WaerY translate her words. Abby could hear her own voice whisper in a language she'd never spoken. Weird! They finished eating, made sure the table was clean, carried their trays to the end of the counter, and sorted all the organic scraps, recyclables, and washables into their designated bins.

Going to the bathroom to, um, wash her hands after the tasty meal, Abby passed by the large room at the back of the restaurant, and paused for a minute to watch a boisterous group game. It looked sort of like martial arts group-fighting, except all the moves were stylized and set to music. A circle of five people "fought" back-to-back; other dance-fighters approached them regularly, sparred symbolically, then backed off. Someone might be calling out the moves; Abby couldn't hear well enough over the laughing and chatting of the people.

Without getting underfoot, the littlest kids watched, played with their friends, and toddled comfortably around the room. The scene had such a great feeling to it, yet something was missing. She stood watching, trying to figure out what it was. Finally, she realized that in her time, the room would've contained a cloud of toxic cigarette smoke looming over a raucous crowd of adults drinking and arguing while their hyper kids raced around the room. This was so different, made possible by everyone's different behavior. The dance, the people, the room itself had a different feel to Abby.

When she returned from washing up, Abby found Kreshi at one of the blank wall panels.

"Do you like to dance?" he asked.

"Um…" Abby wondered how *that* translated. Her face must have carried the message, though, because Kreshi said, "This is easy to learn. Here, watch me."

He took his WaerY off his ear long enough to hold it up to a small scanner by the floor-length screen. The screen lit up with a human silhouette, black with a green outline, which pointed to the patch of floor in front of the screen. Kreshi stood on the indicated spot and flexed his knees. "Easy, please," he said to the figure. It nodded and started to move to fairly slow music.

To Abby, it looked like a futuristic DDR – Dance Dance Revolution game – but without a footpad, with arm movements, and following the figure instead of arrows. Whenever Kreshi matched its movements exactly, it gave a thumbs-up as it danced. The first song ended, and another slightly faster one started. Kreshi was keeping up pretty well, and the figure glowed brighter and acquired more detail.

Laughing at his own efforts, Kreshi finished that song. He offered Abby a turn, asking the game for another easy song.

Abby had had very little dance experience, one of the memorable times being square-dancing in gym class. She had not felt very successful at it. But this song was slow. Kreshi called encouragement, and at least the figure did not grow dimmer or give her a thumbs-down. When she finished, Kreshi clapped for her. The figure also spoke. "Very good, Abby!"

"How did it know my name?" Abby asked, laughing with Kreshi.

"It must have heard me saying it," Kreshi said. "I've never heard it do that before, though."

"That was fun! Thank you very much." Abby gave a little curtsey.

"You're so pretty when you smile, it's just fun to get you to smile more," Kreshi said. Abby blushed and found she could not look at him. She also felt her tacos and rice give a funny lurch. She knew then that she liked him, but immediately thought that there was no way it could work.

Attraction mixed with regret. Which must have caused a strange expression on her face, because Kreshi asked, "Would you like to dance again, or do you need to sit down?"

"It might be good to sit for a minute before I try something else," Abby said, thinking perhaps she could balance her thoughts again.

"Okay, here's an empty table. And would you like a drink?"

"No, I'm not old enou...oh! I mean, sure. I'll have whatever you choose," she said, sitting down. She really needed to get her worlds separated better, she thought. Drinking never meant alcohol here. If she continued putting herself in spots like this, she would be writing Auntie Zoray with the strangest story that jovial woman had ever read.

Kreshi brought back two beverages: an orange-colored iced drink with a straw spitting colorful sparks, and a scarlet one sporting a wedge of bright-red tomato sprinkled with dark seasoning. He held out two spoons.

"Here, taste each one and then choose whichever you like."

Now, along with her stomach flipping, her heart was melting. If everyone was so eternally polite in this world, how could you tell the difference between regular manners and flirting? She wasn't sure the AerY could help her with that, and Dali was sitting several tables away chatting vigorously with her friends, who kept on arriving in a steady stream. The restaurant was now quite full, although it didn't seem to be excessively noisy. It was very nice to be part of the celebration. She usually felt shy in groups, but everyone was always so welcoming and helpful in this age that she felt her courage growing.

Kreshi encouraged her as she spooned up one concoction and then the other...sipping water and waiting a bit between them to – as Mother said when tasting wine – clear her palate. There seemed to be no rush to decide; the emphasis was on enjoying the process. She deeply enjoyed the drinks...and the company!

The red one was more vegetablish, the orange one fruitier. She felt like having something sweet, so she chose the orange one, watching the straw-sparkler until it fizzled out. Kreshi took the red one, biting the spiced tomato and sipping his juice as she savored hers.

"Are you employed?" Abby had had to work out the most polite way to ask him what he did with his time.

"My calling is to tend things, including plants, animals, children, families, ideas, conversations, and projects," he said. "Right now, I lead low-impact outdoor expeditions for families and groups seeking a unifying experience, usually in mountain areas. I've been leading tours in the Appalachian Mountains. I'm a friend of Elle's – of Dali, too – and was close enough to take a train for Elle's party."

"Is it too rude of me to ask how old you are?"

"Not to me. I'm sixteen."

"And you're out on your own?" she blurted out.

"Why not? I reached the age of decision last year," he said.

She would have to stop sticking her foot in her mouth. Dali had told her that age fifteen was the beginning of maturity here.

"And is turnabout fair play? May I ask how old you are, what you do, and what your last name is, Abby? Or will Dali leap to your rescue again?"

She was really stuck now. She took a deep breath and plunged in.

"I'm thirteen, almost fourteen, I'm still in school; my passion is horses, and my last name is Wize, W-I-Z-E, but I didn't choose it, it's a family name," she responded in one breathless rush.

"A very 'Wize' answer, however, Abby." Kreshi smiled and raised two fingers to his temple. "And I salute your courage in telling me when you weren't sure if I'd like it."

Oh my. Would having your mind read in this world ever get any easier?

Chapter 21: Dragons

Just then, another young man, thin, wearing a net vest with pockets holding little cases, joined them. Kreshi said, "Saluton, Rykeir!"

"Hi!" The young man turned to Abby. "I'm Rykeir Gamero. And you are?" he inquired politely, touching his hand to his head and then presenting her with his palm. As he did so, Abby noticed that his black hair, braided close to his head, was entwined with tiny blinking lights.

"Abby," she said. "Saluton, *RYE-keer gay-MARE-oh.*"

"Abby is Dali's cousin from...your family's from Northern Europe, did she say?" Kreshi asked, frowning slightly.

"Yep," Abby said.

"Kio?" asked Rykeir. Abby heard him say *KEE-oh*, which came through her AerY as "What?"

"Oh, she isn't well-practiced in UL," Kreshi intervened. "She has an AerY and, as you can see, I'm using my WaerY in this attractive fashion." He turned his head so Rykeir could see the thin strap wrapped around his tattooed right ear. "Got yours?"

"Sure, love it!" said Rykeir with an adventurous grin. He touched a couple of places on his WaerY case and, with Kreshi's help, strapped it on his ear. "Soooo stylish, don't you think?" he grinned, modeling with exaggerated head and hand poses.

Abby noted what a difference a smile made for Rykeir. Though he hadn't seemed at all attractive, his clean white teeth and lighthearted spirit changed him entirely. Tooth care must be a global sport here, she thought. And no one seemed to worry excessively about whether their outsides were attractive, but there was a lot of attention paid to inner beauty. That was handy. There was only so much one could do about the face one had been given at birth, but everyone could work on their personality...their spirit. Rykeir and Dali had shown her that the warmth from inside could also transform whatever face a person had.

"What are y'all up to?" Rykeir asked.

"I was about to invite Abby to accompany me on her first dragon-guided tour of Dál Riata," Kreshi replied immediately.

Abby heard Kreshi simply say *DOLL ree-AH-tah*, but the AerY explained that the name came from a Gaelic overkingdom covering a goodly portion of Scotland and a bit of Ireland two millennia earlier.

"Excellent! May I come along?" Rykeir said, lifting his eyebrows and bugging his eyes at his two companions.

"Only if you tell me how you got those fabulous lights in your hair," Abby said, feeling as impish as the two young men were acting.

Both guys burst out laughing at her chutzpah, and Rykeir said, "I'll tell you if you don't fall off your dragon. Deal?"

"Deal," Abby said, trusting they wouldn't purposely set up a game that would humiliate her.

"Three-player format it is," Rykeir said. "Give me just a second to retrieve the table diagnostic I came to get, and I'll start the game. I also have a new game to install, but I'll do that after we finish, okay?"

"Okay," Kreshi and Abby chorused; and almost before they were done, a 3D grass field popped up on the table surface.

It was way better than anything Abby could ever have dreamed of. It looked real – really real. Even more real than the wallpaper border. She reached her hand into the image to see if she could feel the grass, but it was without form.

"The beginners all do that, don't they? Tsk tsk tsk," Kreshi declared fake-sadly, shaking his head and touching various spots on the table.

"Every last one," Rykeir solemnly intoned, rummaging in several pockets.

"I wonder if either of you would like an ear-piercing. It's all the rage where I'm from. But I'm not very good with my aim and I might get your nose or eyebrow instead. I do need the practice, though, and I think I have a stapler right here." Abby had a very hard time keeping a straight face as she reached for her bag, amazed at her own gall, as Mother might've put it, but thrilled that she was keeping up with them."

"I have been thinking I'd get something pierced, but not just now, thanks," Kreshi parried lightly, then looked at Rykeir.

"Game on. Dál Riata Dragon Tour," Rykeir commanded. "Three dragons. Beginner level, please."

Three winged dragons appeared on the grass field...a long-necked pearlized gray one directly under Abby's hands. For just an instant, she thought it was a horse; but as it turned to look at her, she saw that, no, it was a square-headed dragon. She looked to her left at a stout, mottled-tan creature; her own dragon's head also swung around. Experimenting, she looked right, at a black dragon emitting smoke from large nostrils. Again her dragon's head moved to match hers.

She glanced left again just in time to see Kreshi appear on the compact tan dragon. She continued to look at him and, in a moment, felt her dragon's whole body turn towards him. On a hunch, she leaned back in her chair – which now felt exactly like a saddle – and sure enough, her dragon backed up. While she tested out several more maneuvers, the scene grew until the restaurant disappeared behind the guys and became the hills of Dál Riata. Her only wish was...

"A horse instead of a dragon?" Kreshi asked, smirking.

Abby ducked her head in sudden embarrassment, which made her mount sink into the grass. "Whoops!" She got it to stand again by sitting up straight. "Sorry, yes, I did wish that...no offense to Sir – or is it Lady? – Pearl, here." She reached down to pat its neck and felt a mane! Not daring to incline her head, she cast her eyes downwards and, to her utter delight, saw she was now astride a pegasus! Its lustrous coat, hair instead of scales, was still pearly. Her comfortable saddle sat behind powerful, pearly-feathered wings coming out of its shoulders. It turned to eye her; and she saw a capable, proud face that humbled her with its willingness to partner her, even for a game.[76]

"Might as well all ride variations of your favorite theme." Kreshi's grin threatened to take over his face. He laid a gentle hand on the dazzling golden unicorn he now rode. Its pointed brown horn was smooth, not spiraled as she'd seen in many drawings. Its darker legs, muzzle, mane, and tail reminded her of a buckskin's coloring.

Rykeir now rode a dragon-horse, its sturdy black body covered with saucer-sized, diamond-shaped scales. Pores on its neck and thin snake-tail spouted smoke instead of hair. It tossed its head, flapped long black batwings, and pawed the air with flashing hooves.[77]

"Everyone ready? Everyone's earrings firmly in?" Kreshi asked, smirking and winking at Abby. Her tacos flipped. He was irresistible. Did he know how she was becoming enamored of him?

"Ready," Abby replied, sure she would enjoy it.

"Okay, Lung-Ma, lift off," Rykeir told his hybrid creature, whose glistening black wings took over from its galloping hooves, trailing a magnificent stream of smoke. Kreshi's unicorn did not have wings, but simply rose into the air behind Rykeir. It wasn't a dream; but, like her own dreams, it seemed entirely real. Thrilled, Abby looked skyward. Her pegasus also looked upwards, but did not rise to join the other two.

"How do I do it?" She saw no joystick, reins, or means of control.

"Just think it," they both said.

Now she understood. Angie's Parelli session all over again...her riding dreams in new form. She envisioned her goal, willed herself to lift off, soared high, and hovered exactly where she'd planned to. She could see far ahead now. She looked right without willing to go right, holding her body still so that her pegasus didn't turn, and was able to view low hills and irregular outlines of farmers' fields. Careful of her thoughts, she turned her head to the left and saw cliffs and ocean.

"Oooo, the little mutilator learns fast," Rykeir said.

"This is fantastic!" Abby's cheeks hurt from smiling so big.

"All the first-timers say that," Kreshi said.

"And all the tenth-timers, if I've done my job right," Rykeir said.

Abby turned her head towards Rykeir, stopping midway to ensure the move wouldn't make her pegasus spin. "Why, what's your job?"

"Three guesses, and the first two don't count."

"You make games? You made this one?!"

"Helped make it," Rykeir corrected, wisps of smoke wafting around him.

"What's your last name again?" Abby asked, having forgotten what he'd said earlier.

"Gamero," Rykeir said, all the lights in his hair blinking at once.

"Ahhhhh," Abby breathed, understanding…and glad for that. She smiled and turned her head back to her mount as Rykeir said, "Shall we tour the coastline or the mountains? Ladies first."

Abby totally reveled in the adventure. She willed her steed forward along the coastline, accompanied by super-real sound effects: wind, birds, ocean. Willing it correctly, she turned her head to check on her companions; her steed's head turned, too, but not its body. If she wanted the pegasus to turn, to change direction, she twisted slightly in her saddle with the intention of turning. If she wanted to go faster, she sat up a little taller and thought of more speed. If she looked, thought, and leaned down, it sent the pegasus lower. If up, the pegasus climbed. After quite a few minutes of experimenting, she found that her lower back was stiff. Trying to relieve the ache, she scooched backward in her saddle…and the pegasus skidded to a halt in midair!

"Hah, first near-wreck was at time code 06:23," Rykeir said. "You didn't fall off, though, so that's saying something. You *sure* you never played this before?"

"Never," Abby answered. "Honest." She saw Rykeir's raised eyebrow. "I swear!"

"Oh, so if you tell me three times, then it's true?" Rykeir fired back with a chuckle.[78]

"Yep; absolutely; fer shur," Abby retorted, grinning.

"Okay, okay, okay!" Rykeir waggled his hands at her. "But since you're apparently fibulous about your experience, we'll need to test you further," he continued to tease her. "Game, course 4C, please."

Several obstacles appeared. Lights blinked in a line, showing Abby where to go.

"Whenever you're ready, go ahead. I'll be right behind you," he added grandly, "to pick up the pieces."

Abby set off at a moderate pace, carefully watching the route as her magnificent steed approached the first obstacle: five horizontal poles about sixteen feet apart, hovering some four feet off the ground. The guide lights showed she was supposed to touch down between the first and second poles, jump over the second and third and fourth poles, and soar away over the fifth.[79]

Wow, could she do all that without touching any of the poles? She had never jumped with a horse, and certainly never flown on a winged creature. Summoning her courage, she decided slow and easy would probably be the best approach. She wasn't sure what would happen if she fell off, and she didn't want to find out. As she descended towards the first pole, following the arcing lights, she saw the initial touchdown spot marked with a large numeral 1 in a circle. She realized her pegasus would have to jump again – wings folded – immediately after landing. This was going to be tricky. But if she could match her body's signals to the suggestions of the lights, she might just make it.

Easy now…the first landing was a little bumpy, but she stayed on. She leaned forward slightly, willing her steed to jump each pole, and firmly hunkered down to land. Her steed's massive muscles bunched and rippled under her as it alternately coiled and released its mighty frame to do her bidding. Never once did she fear for her safety; they were united in thought and motion. After nailing the third jump, they soared off again, a whoop of ecstatic delight gushing up from her soul and out through her mouth.

The game's sounds told her that Rykeir and Kreshi were just behind her. She heard them reach her height, so she twisted to her left, leaned back, and threw out her arms as she came to a tidy halt.

"Yup, you're a certified fabulous fibber," Kreshi said. "I'd put her at the intermediate-plus level; what say you, Rykeir?"

"I say if you ever need a job testing games, Abby, let me know," Rykeir said admiringly. "*Nicely* done, fibulosity notwithstanding."

It was amazing how much good that little bit of praise did for Abby. She felt on top of the worlds, both of them. It was all her best dreams come true.

The rest of the game was just as phenomenal. They tackled stationary, then moving, then flaming hoops. Squeezed through empty, then caving-in, then exploding tunnels. Outran arrows, then cannon balls, then flying saucers; Abby, using a technique she had seen in an old movie, led the saucers into each other.[80] Finally, they just enjoyed flying over the mountains, her two friends pointing out pretty lakes and historic castles. Her steed never tired, never balked, always obeyed her slightest cue. Abby felt she would burst with euphoria.

"Touch down near that little town," Rykeir suggested. As they did, the game ended; the restaurant and their table and chairs reappeared. The three players grinned like idiots, bonded as close friends. They sat smiling at each other, reliving the experience delightedly, silently.

Finally, Abby turned to Rykeir. "So what brought a world-class game maker to…Lowland? What's the name of this town?"

"Lodlan," Rykeir answered lazily. "I travel all over checking on new installations of games. It's great; I have BFFs everywhere."

"And now you have to tell me," Abby commanded Rykeir.

"Tell you what?"

"How you did those lights in your hair. I might want some."

"Ha! You'll have to tell me if you're ever in the same city, because two makes a trend, which we wouldn't want to start," Rykeir said. "But okay, it's just white micro-lights in thin strands of solar wire."

"Can I get the lights from you?" Abby asked. "I would want peach-colored, though."

"Um, I'll have to work on that," Rykeir said. "Next year's Ayyám-i-Há present, probably."

"A Yamaha? What's motorcycles got to do with it?"

Both guys blinked, long and slow, and then laughed so long and loud that everyone nearby looked over. Dali, holding a charming little girl on her lap, was one of them. She threw Abby a big grin and clapped briefly. She understood that Abby was having a fabulous time.

"The Days of Há, the days in between the calendar, *eye-YAWM-ih-HAW*," Kreshi said. "A bit like your Christmas season, I'd think, but actually completely different."

"Now that's clear as mud, Kreshi. Good job explaining," Rykeir growled. "Yuter, please explain Ayyám-i-Há."

Into Abby's ear came a soothing female voice.

"Ayyám-i-Há, also called Intercalary Days. The four days or five before the last month of the Bahá'í year, the month of fasting. In your culture, using the Gregorian calendar, this festival runs from sundown February 25 to sundown March 1, thus aligning the Bahá'í year with the solar year. The believers feast, show hospitality, hold charitable events, give small gifts, and prepare for the Fast.[81] Say 'repeat' to repeat."

"Repeat," Abby requested, as the guys sat watching her with small, silly smiles fixed on their unself-conscious faces.

The definition repeated. Abby could see how it was like Christmas but totally different. The feasting and gift-giving were the same on the surface. Only, it said *small*. She would bet they didn't overindulge now as they did in 2007. People in her time groused about getting into the Christmas spirit…of excess. Advertising fueled an image of the completely redecorated holiday house with mounds of absurdly expensive presents under the picture-perfect tree. Parents fought each other for Tickle-Me-Elmos. Guilt tricked people into overspending. And not just money – Abby struggled to comprehend – but time, energy, emotions. Too much eating, too much drinking, too much of everything, really. It all seemed ridiculous from this vantage point.

"How do I get the Yuter to tell me other things?"

They told her to command it, aloud or silently, using the initial key words "Yuter" and "please" and the closing key "Thank you." They added that silent yutering wasn't *exactly* mind-reading, and also that the Yuter might even respond to her *intent* to use the key words.

"When people really concentrate on thinking about something," Kreshi explained, "they usually tend to subvocalize it...say the words soundlessly with some of their throat and tongue muscles without ever opening their mouth. Their inner ears seem to hear their 'thinking' in their own voice. The Yuter can also hear that subvocalization, and can silently answer via bone conduction or micro-targeted air pressure."

"Wow. So if the Yuter tells me something silently, it'll seem like my own voice?"

"Yes, if it determines by your reactions that you will respond to that best. Unless it's quoting someone, of course. It will converse with you and provide all kinds of information. You can even get it to compare two cultures and translate any language...including Old American." Rykeir, ever the techie, then told her the commands.

"Thanks. But...how did you know..." Abby trailed off, concerned that her cover was blown.

"Don't you know?" and "We can read minds!" they said over each other.

"Not!" Abby retorted. She was sure they were pulling her leg.

"Of course we can, with the help of our Yuters!"

"You were spying on me through your Yuters?!"

They looked mock-offended. "Helping! We were *helping*!"

"Seriously, can you read minds? Dali said she can."

They looked serious for a change. "Of course, never as perfectly as the Master, though we try," Rykeir said. "Just now, we simply had our Yuters pick up what yours was telling you. They can do great stuff, like take pictures, pull up information on any subject, find people or animals, note—"

"Aaaahhh." Abby suddenly understood how Dali knew that she'd appeared by the tree. That was one smart girl. She'd been weeding her garden when Abby had dropped in from nowhere, looking and talking totally foreign...jabbering about horses, no less. The WaerY had helped her figure it all out. She'd said she preferred to converse out loud with it; that's why it whispered.

Abby slumped in her chair, dumbfounded with how hard and fast Dali had scrambled to speak with her, to decide what questions to ask both her and the WaerY, to not scare her since she'd had no idea what had happened...all while remaining smiling and gentle. Abby remembered how frustrated she'd been, and how Dali had defused it: picking up on Abby's mention of horses, playing calming horse music, then removing herself so as to not be around to argue with. Abby blushed when she remembered how she'd denied she was upset. She'd been plenty upset, especially compared with the fine-tuned awareness and consummate control she now knew the people in this world had.

Abby glanced up at Rykeir and Kreshi, and they smiled warmly. They apparently enjoyed supporting her through her recollections, her realizations. It was so wonderful to feel supported. To know that everyone cared about her progress. Towards learning, towards being a better person, towards having fun whenever possible without breaking any laws or harming anyone or anything. This was, indeed, heaven on earth.

"You know, 'Abdu'l-Bahá placed great importance on being happy," Kreshi said gently as Abby reached a stopping point in her thoughts. "He often asked people if they were happy. Try asking your Yuter to pull up the 'for what age are you waiting' quote."

She closed her eyes to concentrate better.

—Yuter, please pull up the 'Abdu'l-Bahá quote on 'what age are you waiting for.'—

There was a brief silence. Then the AerY responded.

—Sorry for the slight delay to find the intended passage. Quoting: 'Do ye know in what cycle ye are created and in what age ye exist? This is the age of the Blessed Perfection and this is the time of the Greatest Name! This is the century of the Manifestation, the age of the Sun of the Horizons and the beautiful springtime of His Holiness the Eternal One!

—'The earth is in motion and growth; the mountains, hills and prairies are green and pleasant; the bounty is overflowing; the mercy universal; the rain is descending from the cloud of mercy; the brilliant Sun is shining; the full moon is ornamenting the horizon of ether; the great ocean-tide is flooding every little stream; the gifts are successive; the favors consecutive; and the refreshing breeze is blowing, wafting the fragrant perfume of the blossoms. Boundless treasure is in the hand of the King of Kings! Lift the hem of thy garment in order to receive it.

—'If we are not happy and joyous at this season, for what other season shall we wait and for what other time shall we look?' End quote. From a letter by 'Abdu'l-Bahá to the Spiritual Assembly of Samarkand, Russia; found in *Tablets of 'Abdu'l-Bahá*, volume 3, page 730.

—Say 'more' to hear more at this time. Say 'hourly' to hear a quote on happiness every hour. Say 'daily' to hear a quote on happiness once a day. Say 'other' to hear quotes on other topics.—

"Hourly," Abby said aloud; then —Hourly,— she practiced silently.

The AerY's response was also silent – or subvocal, anyway – although it still seemed warm and friendly.

—Making the usual exceptions for sleep and other necessities and obligations?—

—Uh, yeah, sure. Thank you.—

—You are welcome.—

"Wow, I need a Yuter of my own!" Abby exclaimed.

"Spoken like a true air dean," said Kreshi.

"A what? Oh. Wait!" Again, Abby briefly closed her eyes to begin concentrating. She didn't have to keep them closed this time, though.

—Yuter, please translate…that…into Old American.—

"*AIR-dee-yen*, E-R-D-E-A-N," the AerY pronounced aloud, then continued silently.

—It is already translated from New American. It is a citizen of *AIR-den*, E-R-D-E-N, your planet Earth after the Most Great Peace.—

—Explain Most Great Peace, please.—

—Caution: response to this request will be long. Say 'later' if you prefer to hear it later.—

—Later, thank you.—

The guys clapped and whistled softly. "Well done!" "Brava!"

"It's going to take a long time to get the hang of everything," Abby admitted ruefully, "especially having my mind read." She thought about Mother's invasive probings. That was so different, though! Mother took potshots at Abby, hurling accusations, sometimes hitting the mark. The Erdeans blended with Abby, seeking to assist, understanding where she had come from and where she was trying to go.

"About that," Kreshi shifted uncomfortably in his seat. "I suspect our world's idea of reading minds is very different from how your culture thinks of it. We are taught to read vocal tones, expressions, body language in animals and people. And, in our time, people's minds are more predictable."

"Sorry? I don't understand."

"In your time, you had people who were mentally ill, criminals, addicted to drugs, doing bad things, right?"

"Oh yeah, big-time, roger on that one," Abby said soberly.

"Here that does not happen. Virtually no one is negatively addicted to anything."

Abby wondered if you could be addicted to something in a positive way, but decided to hold that thought…hey, could her AerY hold it for her?

—Yuter, please hold the thought: 'Can someone be addicted to anything in a positive way?' for later. Thank you.—

—Noted.—

Way, way too cool. Abby wondered what this gadget would cost back home. Millions, no doubt, if it were even possible. But it wasn't; the technology didn't exist yet. She sighed and turned back to Kreshi.

"Similarly, no one has bad intent. No one is going to try to steal things, or cheat someone else, or flout laws."

"No one at all *ever*?"

"Well, once in a great while someone does, but it's rare. Of course, children might, but their Yuter will tell them and their parents. Kids' Yuters are great babysitters."

"Don't the kids just remove them if they really want to steal candy or soda pop or something?"

Both guys looked at her strangely.

"Is this how you people think back in your time?"

"Yup, a lot of them, anyway. Um, aren't you surprised that I'm a time traveler...or whatever you'd call it?"

"Only a little. It's actually really...cool, though," said Kreshi. "My WaerY told me you were speaking Old American to Dali, so I got in line behind you and found a chance to speak with you. I thought it'd be interesting. As foretold, we've seen life on other planets for centuries now.[82] And lots of stories and scientific ruminations have been written about time travel. So why couldn't it be possible? At least you're human, not an alien species, so you are quite easy to talk with!"

"Of *course* I'm not an alien!" Abby pretended to take offense.

Kreshi chuckled, then looked blank. At once, his WaerY whispered to him. By wishing she could hear it, she heard it reminding him: "Kids taking off Yuters."

"Is everyone this easy to eavesdrop on?" Abby interrupted.

"You can silence your Yuter," Rykeir said. "But I ask that you not. It's easier to help, and learn from, you if you let us hear your thoughts. Don't worry; there are certain personal ones that won't be transmitted," he said, again winking outrageously.

"Yep. Back to the kids, though?" Kreshi fended off yet another sidetrack.

Abby noted how easily he monitored the conversation, and saw that, indeed, he was good at Tending.

"In my time, when a kid wants to do something and not get caught, they'll often figure out what will get them caught and work around it," she explained. "If the Yuter monitored them, they might remove it."

"Sneaky little fiends, huh?" Rykeir said. "In our time, there are a few more safeguards. One is that everyone helps everyone, especially with kids. If a kid is tempted to, say, steal sweet-fruit – we really don't have much candy and soda pop; don't you know it's bad for you? – and their parents don't see it, another person might, and will tell the parent, who can then educate the child about it. If for some reason a child is alone and doing something they shouldn't, there are special kid-Yuters that only approved people, like the parents, can remove. That pretty much catches the rest of them.

"But basically, kids now have what they need. And they are very much loved, well cared for, and well taught. So it'd only be a childish impulse that would make them steal. It's pretty unlikely they'd plan for the crime in advance."

There was a pause as everyone reflected on the difference in the two worlds. Abby slowly rubbed the edge of her simple wooden chair. Kreshi blinked, absorbed in thought. And Rykeir fiddled with wires and bits in his pockets.

After another slow blink, Kreshi said, "All that was background for how to read minds. See, nowadays there's a much smaller – or perhaps I should say *saner* – range of stuff people think about now. Everyone's mind is more predictable, now that they all have thorough training and pure nutrition from the start. With all the clues that peoples' faces and bodies give, what they say and how they say it, and sometimes with help from the Yuter, it's not too hard to guess what's on most peoples' minds. The longer you experience patterns of life and types of people, the easier it gets to make accurate guesses about what their history is and therefore what is going on for them in the current moment. And then there are divine promptings."

"Please explain," Abby invited. Dali had said much the same things, but Abby wanted to hear it from these friends also.

At a nod from Kreshi, Rykeir explained as he twisted wires into a tidy circle. "There's a piece of the Divine inside us all. Our eternal soul, our inner knowing, those are other names for it. It's what Bahá'u'lláh was talking about when he declared: 'O Son of Being! Thy heart is My home; sanctify it for My descent. Thy spirit is My place of revelation; cleanse it for My manifestation.'[83] Will you accept that proposition?"

"Yeah, I guess so," Abby replied.

"The Master said we can develop the qualities he had; and his soul was so connected to the Divine that he had truly amazing knowledge and abilities. Many of the Bahá'í Writings talk about having spiritual insight, heeding the suasion of the spirit, things like that," Rykeir continued, spreading out some tiny electronic parts on the table.[84]

"Looking at the Master's life and words, we can see that a lot of what he did and said was based on his ability to listen to God by keeping his connection with God clear. It was almost like he had a mystical crystal ball inside himself. Whatever information he reached for was always there. He hinted that we all should strive to have that kind of connection."

"Did he – do your scriptures – say how we should do that?" Abby asked Rykeir, who seemed about to install something into the game table.

"Through prayer, meditation, fasting, studying God's word, obeying God's law as brought to us by whatever Divine Messenger is current, working on ourselves and our virtues, being of service..."

"It seems easy to understand," Abby murmured, "but I'm sure it's very hard to do."

Kreshi took over as Rykeir knelt on the floor to open a small access panel in the table pedestal. "Islam has a hadith, a tradition, that all souls must cross the Sirat al-Jahim, the Bridge of Hell, which is hair-thin and razor-sharp, and from which the wicked will fall into hell.[85] And His Holiness Jesus said it was harder to do than fitting a camel through the eye of a needle."

"But wasn't that just about rich people getting into heaven?" Abby surprised herself by injecting. "I remember Reverend Davison saying something about that. Yuter, please, what does it say? Er, the Bible,"

"In the King James version of the Holy Bible, the New Testament, there are two versions of the quotation you request.

"First, quoting: 'Then said Jesus unto his disciples, Verily I say unto you, That a rich man shall hardly enter into the kingdom of heaven. And again I say unto you, It is easier for a camel to go through the eye of a needle than for a rich man to enter into the kingdom of God. When his disciples heard it, they were exceedingly amazed, saying, Who then can be saved? But Jesus beheld them, and said unto them, With men this is impossible, but with God all things are possible.' End quote. That was Matthew 19:23 through 26.

"The second is Mark 10:23 through 27 and is very similar, though it makes the additional point that it is hard for those who *trust* in riches. Special note available."

"Wow, that's all new to me!" Kreshi said cheerfully. "Yuter, please provide special note."

"Special note: It was no longer known, even seven centuries ago, exactly what task Jesus was referring to. The original word *gamla* – G-A-M-L-A, *GAM-lah* – can be translated in two ways. One is *rope*; and it was not easy to thread and pull a hawser through a ship's mooring ring or a sturdy rope through the harness rings of a beast of burden, never mind through the eye of a sewing needle, even the fifteen-centimeter, six-inch needles they had then for heavy work. The other meaning is *camel*; and it was also not easy, upon arrival at a walled city at night, to unload a camel, lead it through the small doorway in the closed gate, and reload it. Both the ring and the doorway might be called a 'needle's eye'; and perhaps Jesus intentionally means both, so that the analogy would make sense to those who travel by land, those who travel by or work on the sea, and any man or woman who knows how to sew. In any case, such tasks were very difficult...but not impossible, especially with help."

"Interesting. Difficult but not impossible. Help needed. With *God's* help, *all* things are possible. And Jesus *did* have at least a few wealthy disciples." Kreshi was obviously enjoying the discussion, learning from it, not at all upset at being corrected.

From under the table, Rykeir's muffled voice added, "Yuter, please, how do the Bahá'í Writings compare?"

"As usual, they affirm. Quoting: 'O Ye That Pride Yourselves On Mortal Riches! Know ye in truth that wealth is a mighty barrier between the seeker and his desire, the lover and his beloved. The rich, but for a few, shall in no wise attain the court of His presence nor enter the city of content and resignation. Well is it then with him, who, being rich, is not hindered by his riches from the eternal kingdom, nor deprived by them of imperishable dominion. By the Most Great Name! The splendor of such a wealthy man shall illuminate the dwellers of heaven even as the sun enlightens the people of the earth!' End quote. From *The Hidden Words of Bahá'u'lláh*, Persian number 53."

"Thank you so much, Abby, for bringing it up. Okay, rich people, but for a few," Kreshi summarized as Rykeir rose back up to his chair and "dusted" his hands over a job well done. "But can we all agree the Christ did drop many hints that it's not easy to be saved or blessed?"

Abby remembered her last time in St. Zosimo's and her fear that she would not be one of the chosen when Jesus returned. She nodded, glad to be asked and included instead of lectured at and frightened.

"But we have an advantage now," Kreshi finished. "It was much harder for the people of your time, with so many negative influences all around you. Staying emotionally positive and spiritually connected must have been very hard."

"Yeah, impossible sometimes," Abby said thoughtfully. Only, she mentally qualified, maybe not impossible with God?

Chapter 22: Happiness

After a few meditative moments, Rykeir asked, "Would you like some dessert? I could go for something chocolate."

"You have *chocolate*?" Abby eagerly snapped back to the material world.

Both boys jumped back in their chairs and warded her away with ludicrous hand-motions, making Abby giggle.

"Of course," Rykeir continued, "One of the positive addictions, in my very humble, very addicted opinion."

"Oooohhh, I sure could go for some, too. But I don't have…"

"We're buying," Kreshi consoled her. "We know time travelers don't come with exact change."

Rykeir went to place an order. Abby found her mouth was already watering in anticipation of digging into a decadent chocolate something. Kreshi briefly consulted with his WaerY, then leaned in towards Abby.

"Do they have a twelve-step program for chocolate addicts back home?" Kreshi asked in a low funereal voice. " 'Cuz if they do, you should join."

She acted offended, slapped at his arm, missed on purpose, wound up giggling. "It's just been a…very sudden switch, from my usual diet to a total health-freak diet. Actually, my diet isn't as bad as some," she added, thinking of Ricky's dubious breakfast. "Mother doesn't allow…" But she didn't want to discuss Mother on the best night of her entire life, so she tried to find something else to think about. Her AerY immediately prompted her.

"You can think about being addicted to positive things. After all, it is 'later' now."

"Everyone's the comic here; even your computers are a laugh."

"Speaking of 'addicted,' you could say we're addicted to happiness, joy, laughter, learning, unity, peace…I could go on but I think you get the idea," Kreshi contributed.

"I think I do, too. Yuter? I thi…" Abby's voice faded away as she blinked and switched into silent-running mode.

—…nk I understand that I can be strongly drawn to good things but, if the attraction gets out of control, then it's bad. Okay; anything else I'm supposed to think about, please?—

—Good work, Abby; well thought out. Many Erdeans have said essentially the same thing. As for something else to think about: a happiness quote, if you would like that.—

—Sure.—

—In honor of your successful game, here is one by the Master.

Quoting: 'Supreme happiness is man's, and he beholds the signs of God in the world and in the human soul, if he urges on the steed of high endeavor in the arena of civilization and justice.' End quote. From *The Secret of Divine Civilization*, page 4.—

As she listened to the AerY, Abby began to mentally construct...

∞   ∞   ∞   ∞   ∞   ∞   ∞   ∞

... an arena, sectioned by a maze of fences spelling out "civilization" and "justice" ... she rides a tall steed named Endeavor ... it carries her unerringly through the maze ... she sees wonderful signs of God in the various natural features ... in the forms of other riders ... asks the Yuter to repeat its quotation ... yes, her imagery is on track ... adds a scoreboard accumulating Happiness Points, for each rider and for the group as a whole ... urges Endeavor to even greater effort ...

∞   ∞   ∞   ∞   ∞   ∞   ∞   ∞

Rykeir, returning to the table, brought her out of her Scripture-based fantasy.

Rykeir had brought three plates, each with a chocolate dessert on it: cake, ice cream, and six pieces of candy.

"No, *no*. Not candy. Belgian truffles!" the young men chorused in feigned umbrage; and Rykeir added, "Created, we believe, in honor of the imminence of the Bahá'í Revelation."

"What do you mean?" Abby asked.

"Belgian chocolate was invented just about four years before the Bahá'í Faith began. A fitting invention, along with many other fitting inventions for this Era. Everyone want some of everything?" he asked and, at their nods, spooned some of each dessert onto the other plates.

It'd be impossible not to be happy here, Abby mused. Everyone is so kind and caring, everything is so beautiful, so carefully arranged.

"Oh, we still have lots of unhappiness. I have some I could spare if you're running out," Rykeir said, waggling his eyebrows and handing her a chocolate collection.

"What could make anyone unhappy? It's so perfect!"

"You're just on vacation. Everybody loves wherever they are on vacation," he teased, passing Kreshi the third potpourri plate.

"Not when you nearly get killed crashing into a tree," Abby retorted defensively. She sought to soothe her ruffled feathers with a truffle. It worked: rich chocolate medicine.

"Okay, granted; but when real life sets in wherever you are, then the bliss fades some. The bike breaks, you lose your job, it rains too much, or doesn't rain at all, you get sick—"

"I thought you were so healthy here."

"We still have illness. Not as much as in your time, but some. And people still get hurt, disabled, or killed in accidents. Of course, we can repair or replace pretty much every part, if we can get to people soon enough. But there are definitely still tests and difficulties. For a complete account of our petty woes, visit Auntie Zoray."

Abby smiled, happy to know about Auntie Zoray. "I thought there wouldn't be any sorrow at all when earth becomes heaven," Abby said around a bite of what must be chocolate soy ice cream, the most magnificent ice cream she'd ever had.

"Yuter? Any input, please?" Kreshi asked.

His Yuter passed the thoughts on through the other two Yuters.

"When asked if it was impossible to attain happiness without suffering, 'Abdu'l-Bahá answered, quoting: 'To attain eternal happiness one must suffer. He who has reached the state of self-sacrifice has true joy.' End quote. From *Paris Talks*, page 179. When asked if a person who had attained development through suffering should then fear happiness, He answered, quoting: 'Through suffering, he will attain to an eternal happiness which nothing can take from him. The apostles of Christ suffered: they attained eternal happiness.' End quote. From *Paris Talks*, page 178."

While Kreshi leaned back in his chair and tended, Rykeir explained, "God has assured us that, in order to be prepared for the next world, we need to grow strong and develop positive attributes in this world. So Sia sends us various trials and tribulations – which concept, by the way, I'm developing into a card game – but in real life, it might be managing our finances, or not offending people, or controlling anger or frustration. In fact, developing any of the godly attributes is what it all boils down to. Patience is a huge one."

"I keep hearing about attributes and virtues. What are those?"

"Yuter, please list some virtues for Abby."

"Attentive, assertive, brave, calm, careful, caring, cheerful, clean, compassionate, confident, cooperative, considerate, courteous, creative, curious, detached, determined, enthusiastic, excellent, fair, faithful, flexible, focused, forgiving, friendly, full of awe, full of pity, generous, gentle, graceful, happy, helpful, honest—"

Abby got the idea. "Yuter, please stop. Thank you."

"Huh, you weren't even halfway through! You didn't get close to your *own* virtue!"

"Ha ha, I get it! Wise."

"And somehow, the list never includes *my* favorite one."

"Let me guess. Smart…alec."

"Who's reading minds now?"

"Just a lucky guess." Abby enjoyed the banter as much as she did the chocolate, which was almost gone.

Dali appeared, asking Abby if she was about ready to head home.

She took a long time with her answer, which she was sure everyone could hear, but she wanted them to. Did Yuters convey feelings? She did not know if they could feel her joy at being part of this precious event. Tearing herself away might be one of the most difficult things she'd ever had to force herself to do.

"I guess all good times must come to an end," she said regretfully, modifying the saying from her era.

Everyone expressed how much fun they'd had, and said they wanted to get together again sometime.

"I didn't even thank the hostess!" Abby exclaimed, remembering her manners.

"She's there, if you still want to," Dali said, pointing to an older sister of Elle's. "Also, I never got to introduce you to my aunt."

The group stood and everyone said their final goodbyes, shaking hands, blinking lights, winking heart-melting brown eyes, laughing, waving. Abby reluctantly left her new BFFs. She could not bear the thought that she'd never see them again, so she resolved that this was just an intermission.

"This is the aunt who gave me her house," Dali explained, inviting Abby over to meet a thin-faced, khaki-toned, inviting-looking woman standing next to an ebony-skinned, very fit, obviously energetic man. "Her name is Polska Homer. This is her spouse, Uncle Franco Ardent; we call him Arno. Go ahead, speak with her; she will understand."

"I'm very glad to meet you," Abby said to the middle-aged...no, she'd be a young woman in this world where a lifespan was a century and a half. "I'm staying in the house you gave Dali. It's very nice."

As Arno looked on supportively, Polska grasped both her hands warmly. Polska's khaki skin and dark-brown, puffy hair framed a wonderful smile and searching, warm, blue eyes. Abby was not ready to be x-rayed by Polska's eyes, and found herself looking down at the lean woman's clean, loose, orange dress and low-heeled brown shoes.

"I am so very glad you found that house," Polska said. "I had a feeling it would play host to a very special visitor someday. I think it is you."

Abby was uncomfortable feeling Polska's spiritual vision flooding her. She stammered her thanks and then nudged Dali along towards the evening's hostess, to whom Abby offered her hand. She was thanking the beautiful teenager for a wonderful evening when she stopped, realizing the girl's Yuter might not be translating for her.

Dali intervened. "Tuanay, my cousin Abby wants to thank you for a wonderful evening," she said. "She had a terrific time."

The muscular young woman smiled warmly, grasped Abby's hand firmly, and said she was really glad Abby had come, and even more glad she'd had so much fun.

"I saw you with Rykeir and Kreshi," Tuanay said. "They are such great company, aren't they? I hoped they'd come; they are lots of fun."

"Jes, *too-ah-nay*." Abby was careful not to stress any syllable.

"You're a very lucky girl to have had the undivided attentions of two such exceptional young men at the same time." Not one iota of judgment flashed in Tuanay's words or tone; rather, she was glad for Abby. She apparently trusted Abby to keep her priorities sorted and her hormones from running away with her. Something else worth thinking about. Copying Dali's *DON-cone*, Abby also told Tuanay, "Dankon. Thank you."

As they turned to leave, a large group started coming in the door. There were several young couples with a passel of youngsters...here, it seemed, to celebrate one boy's fifth birthday. Abby wondered if the boy would be back in ten years to celebrate his reaffirmation.

As she waited for the doorway area to empty, she gazed one last time at the wallpaper. The scene had again changed. It was now a low, ragged mountain, attractive to both hikers and mountain climbers. The myriad people and animals continued to interact; though, of course, the sea dwellers were absent, replaced by zebras. Besides pathway hikers and clamberers up stony slopes, she saw people and animals playing running games, climbing trees, and standing on plateaus looking out over a beautiful valley. A few companions had formed a camp circle, sitting on logs and roasting marshmallows just outside the barely open, gently flaming mouth of an obliging dragon.

A small gaggle of dragons, winged and non, were circling the peak in great swoops, joined now by several pegasi from both East and West. And in the far distance, another pegasus...wait, no, was it?...it was a pegasus with a unicorn's horn, an alacorn![86] It did not seem to be headed for the mountain peak, though, but for a broad ledge where one teenage girl stood alone, admiring the vista.

Then Abby did a double take. Was that girl her own self, there? She strained to be sure, and the spot she was focusing on seemed to grow bigger. Yes, it was definitely her. And once she recognized herself, she realized that some of the other people on the wallpaper were people in the restaurant with her. Well, that made sense. If a Yuter could hear you, maybe it could also see you. And the restaurant's ALLY programmed the moving wallpaper in real time. There were Kreshi and Rykeir, racing each other up the limbs of a sturdy tree. There was Dali, stroking the mane of a zebra-striped unicorn. There was Elle…and the birthday boy who'd just come in…and three "defenders" from the martial-arts dance…and—

"Oops, doorway's clear," Dali told her. She tore her eyes away from the mountain scene and followed Dali out of the restaurant. Wow. She really, _really_ hoped she could come back, and soon.

It needed a new name, though, she reflected. It was not a restaurant in the usual sense, but a place to find fun and eats. What would the right word be? Featery? She'd certainly performed a few unique feats there!

She was pleasantly surprised when her AerY said, "_Featery_. That is a cute term, Abby. It is usually called a _foodle_ in Erden, though."

As they pedaled home, Tuanay's comments echoed in her head. She did feel lucky, very lucky…and something more. She again felt that funny tingling in her stomach when she thought about Kreshi. He was definitely special. She liked him. A lot. Was this love? She wondered what he felt about her. They were three years apart, and she must have seemed like just a kid sister to him. But perhaps when she got older, three years might not be so much. But they were also many hundreds of years apart; and even though he knew it, they could not erase the fact that she grew up in a different world. If he were ever interested. Which she hoped he was.

"You like Kreshi?" Dali asked quietly.

"No secrets on Erden, are there?" Abby retorted irritably.

"A few, but usually you have to block your Yuter," Dali replied, smiling to lighten the mood.

Abby couldn't stay mad long; besides, Dali was like Jenn. Here was a boy…man…what is between a boy and a man? Moy? Okay, here was a moy Abby liked but shouldn't; and she could really use a sympathetic ear.

They passed the House of Worship. Lights shone in the fountain, along the wood beams, and by the walkways. It was just as pretty as in daylight, Abby thought, but in a different way.

"I've never liked a moy before," Abby admitted. "I don't think I can do anything about it, though, with our time and age differences. Even if dating is allowed. And I bet you Erdeans don't look at dating like we do."

"I bet you're right," Dali said seriously. "If I remember correctly, boys and girls in your time often had sex while dating? And your TV and internet promoted a lot of sexy images, encouraging you to think that way?"

"You could definitely say that." Abby flashed on obscene songs and stripping celebrities like…never mind.

"It would certainly be hard to live an upright life in that kind of environment," Dali said sympathetically.

"Why, what kind of upright life do you live?" Abby asked.

They passed Mr. Sawqui's house, where an expanded car full of smiling, familiar people hummed away from the curb. Everyone waved and called to each other.

"Once again your time showed us how pivotal are the teachings of the Bahá'í Faith," Dali said. "Uncontrolled expression of the sexual instinct – which was often a search for love and belonging – led to many problems: disease, unwanted pregnancy, emotional turmoil. All of them destructive; but let's just reflect on one. Pregnancy in single mothers often led to not properly supervising and teaching the children. That led to poor health, poor schoolwork, and even finding family substitutes like gangs. Fatherless boys had a harder time being good fathers. And children often made poor decisions about their own sexuality, especially if the mother continued to – what was the bizarre term? – *entertain* men. All of these problems, and more, contributed to worsening long-term problems in society."

"So everyone here waits till they're married? No one ever wants to have sex before?"

Abby should have predicted that her impatient question would elicit a long silence. She'd been rude; she'd oversimplified. They passed the last houses in silence.

"Of course they might want to." Dali eventually chose her words carefully, her voice free of anger. "I think there might be several factors to consider. One is that there are no sexualized images surrounding us like in your time."

"There is somebody telling people not to show those anymore?" Abby tried to match Dali's patient tone.

"Not quite like that. We understand the danger, especially to young people, of allowing that kind of image into society…again, learning from your time. So if someone did try, the rest of us would turn away from it and probably ask them to stop."

Abby guessed that Daniel Radcliffe had decided appearing nude and imitating sexual acts was okay, and then he had ignored any protests of inappropriateness. He'd said that he wanted to appear nude in front of people in order to try something very challenging for himself as an actor. In a society like Erden, he'd have no audience to play to, nor anyone to encourage his even thinking about it. But people in Abby's time seemed to think either "it's a free country, he can do whatever he likes, whether *I* like it or not" or "woohoo, let's go see him naked!" However, Abby now recognized the bigger issue: the effect that being bombarded with such images would have on people over time.

"Also, the human body is considered sacred now." Dali paused, and Abby jumped into the breach, injecting, "So everyone hides it?"

"I'm sorry; that's not what I meant. I was, uh, trying to explain that, yes, there are nude paintings and statues and so on; but the difference lies in portraying it in a sexualized way or as a wonderful creation of God. Which the human body is. If you ever take an anatomy class you will see what I mean."

"Why, you took anatomy?"

"Actually, everyone here takes anatomy," Dali said as they turned right, down her lane. "It is quite wonderful to see how intricately and carefully God designed us. It's also useful for everyone, even if one only learns how to take care of one's own body. This is in keeping with Bahá'u'lláh's instruction that 'man should know his own self and recognize that which leadeth unto loftiness or lowliness, glory or abasement, wealth or poverty.'[87]

"The last thing to mention is that Bahá'u'lláh set the age of the beginning of maturity at fifteen."

"I remember that."

There was another pause, during which Abby got the feeling she was missing something.

—Yuter, please, what am I missing?—

—In Erden, people can marry starting at age fifteen.—

—Oh. That young? Really?—

—Yes.—

That did change everything. It explained a lot. When teenagers' hormones kicked in at about her age, they didn't have to wait for five or ten more years to finish school and get married. But it also meant everyone had to be more mature earlier. They seemed to be managing that part, anyway, judging by the people she'd met so far. It was, after all, a fabulous world here.

Again she felt very lucky indeed; and as they wheeled their bikes up to the house, other feelings also washed over her: humbleness and gladness. She felt like giving thanks, but didn't know how. Her questing thought was timid.

—Yuter, please, what is a suitable prayer of thanksgiving?—

—Perhaps you will like this one, Abby. Quoting: 'In the Name of God, the Most High! Lauded and glorified art Thou, Lord, God Omnipotent! Thou before Whose wisdom the wise falleth short...'—

Abby snorted at the excellent choice of words, then continued to silently think the melodic, majestic words with the Yuter.

—'...and faileth, before Whose knowledge the learned confesseth his ignorance, before Whose might the strong waxeth weak, before Whose wealth the rich testifieth to his poverty, before Whose light the enlightened is lost in darkness, toward the shrine of Whose knowledge turneth the essence of all understanding and around the sanctuary of Whose presence circle the souls of all mankind.

—'How then can I sing and tell of Thine Essence, which the wisdom of the wise and the learning of the learned have failed to comprehend, inasmuch as...'—

Abby sighed. Could the wisdom of the Wize learn to comprehend?

—'...no man can sing that which he understandeth not, nor recount that unto which he cannot attain, whilst Thou hast been from everlasting the Inaccessible, the Unsearchable. Powerless though I be to rise to the heavens of Thy glory and soar in the realms of Thy knowledge, I can but recount Thy tokens that tell of Thy glorious handiwork.

—'By Thy Glory! O Beloved of all hearts, Thou that alone canst still the pangs of yearning for Thee! Though all the dwellers of heaven and earth unite to glorify the least of Thy signs, wherein and whereby Thou hast revealed Thyself, yet would they fail, how much more to praise Thy holy Word, the creator of all Thy tokens.

—'All praise and glory be to Thee, Thou of Whom all things have testified that Thou art one and there is none other God but Thee, Who hast been from everlasting exalted above all peer or likeness and to everlasting shalt remain the same. All kings are but Thy servants and all beings, visible and invisible, as naught before Thee. There is none other God but Thee, the Gracious, the Powerful, the Most High.' End quote. From *Bahá'í Prayers*, pages 136 to 138.—

Abby was grateful for so much just now. Standing in the yard, enjoying the fresh air and the night sky, noticing swooping bats and even a fleeting white shadow that might be an owl, hearing in the distance a whippoorwill call. Blessings, all of them. Being here, experiencing a perfect world. Using a perfect device to explain it to her. And whatever that didn't handle, well, the world's best guide had adopted her and helped her in every way humanly possible.

"Thank you, Yuter. And thank you so much for helping me, Dali," Abby said humbly.

"It is my very greatest pleasure, Abby," Dali replied. "And now I must ask your forgiveness."

"For what?!"

"For, er, abandoning you at the Draggin' Dragon. I should have stayed with you. I got carried away, seeing some of my friends. Also, I thought you were doing just fine; I knew Kreshi and Rykeir would take excellent care of you. But still..." She exhaled loudly. "It may surprise you to find out that we are still human, that we still make mistakes, here in the New World Order."

"Oh dear, I, uh…" Abby was totally surprised. She had very little experience handling personal apologies. "Well, I forgive you, if you forgive me for being so rude about sex in your world."

"Of course I do; I understand how hard this must all be for you."

"You understand? Really?" Abby trusted Dali's intentions but wondered how Dali could see things from her own lonely perspective.

"Ah, my secret is exposed," Dali said in a mock-mysterious voice, leading the way into the house. "As part of my Ancient American History, I studied your culture. The habits, customs, and mores then were very different from now." Dali glanced over sympathetically and, to spare Abby, took the conversation in another direction. "I also enjoyed studying the languages of your time, including Esperanto and several forms of English. They were major influences in creating UL, as were unrelated languages like Arabic, Bantu, Chinese and others. I hope to study at least one more of them in the future, maybe several."

"Is that how you were able to speak with me so quickly?"

"Yes, and of course my WaerY was indispensable."

As if waiting for that cue, Abby's AerY reminded her about another who had spoken with her so easily.

—Dating Kreshi.—

"What about liking Kreshi?" Abby asked Dali.

"That is a deep, complicated question," Dali said. "More than we can cover tonight. But I will say that I think he also liked you more than a little."

"Really?" Abby's head snapped towards this tidbit. "How can you tell?"

"He's actually fairly quiet. I was surprised that he struck up a conversation with you. I've never seen him smile so much. And every time I've asked him to dance, he's told me he isn't into dancing. I've never seen him dance with anyone else, either."

More food for thought. And to hold close to her heart.

They got ready for bed, just as sisters would. Finally, when Dali came out of the bathroom, Abby asked her, "Should I take the AerY out?"

"You don't have to; you can leave it in if it's comfortable," Dali replied.

It was, so Abby left it in. And when Dali said her Long Obligatory Prayer, Abby realized she understood some of it, thanks to the unobtrusive AerY. She felt so welcomed, encouraged, looked after. And, just possibly, loved…

∞ ∞ ∞ ∞ ∞ ∞ ∞ ∞

*... she's a child in a swing ... **ZZP** ... a baby in a tree-borne cradle ... the wind blows, hard, harder, hurricane-strong ... breaks the branch, tumbles the cradle ... she tumbles into Dali's protective arms ... **ZZP** ... teenager, she dances away from Dali ... mounts a dappled horse ... it grows wings and carries her aloft 'round the mountain peak of a lush tropical islet ... she looks down ... laughs ... leaps from the pegasus into the sea ... lands on the saddled back of a gigantic seahorse ... it changes from luminous yellow to fiery orange and sweeps her up to the surface and in to shore ... she skips happily across the wet sand ... **ZZP** ... grassy meadow and slows to catch her breath ... sees a handsome centaur of quiet mien ... he dons huge glasses ... opens his yard-high book ... strikes a teacher's pose ... grins, and she recognizes Kreshi ...*

∞ ∞ ∞ ∞ ∞ ∞ ∞ ∞

"Happy Monday," crooned the AerY as she opened her eyes to the morning light, pegasus and seahorse and centaur still coursing happily through her mind.[88] "In the words of the Master, quoting: 'Briefly, it is demonstrable that in this life, both outwardly and inwardly the mightiest of structures, the most solidly established, the most enduring, standing guard over the world, assuring both the spiritual and the material perfections of mankind, and protecting the happiness and the civilization of society – is religion.' End quote. From *The Secret of Divine Civilization*, pages 71 and 72."

Even though the Bahá'í Writings had first struck Abby as different and even weird, she found she could now see the similarities with the Bible she'd grown up with. It was like a single-scoop cherry-vanilla ice cream cone suddenly being topped with a rainbow sherbet scoop. Different in flavor and appearance, yet both tasty, both wonderful.

With that delicious, happy thought, she arose.

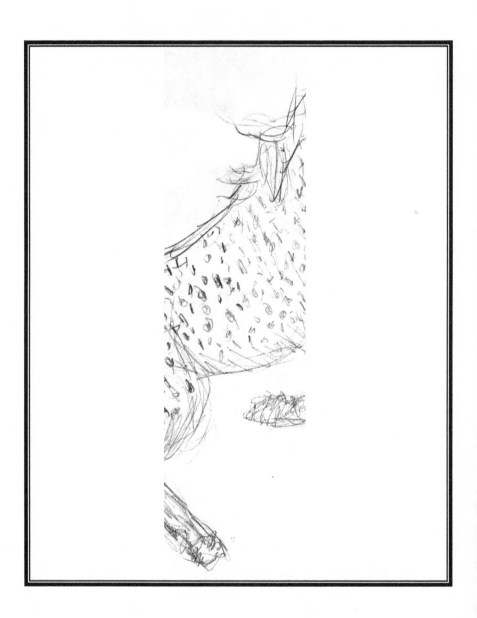

Chapter 23: Deepening

The girls arose, took Cleansing Wind showers in the bathroom stall, dressed, and began to eat at the table. As Dali sipped her lemon water, Abby asked, "What's on tap for today, boss?"

Dali got up from the table, fetched the WaerY from the bedroom, and put it on the table between them. It whispered as she carried it.

Abby realized Dali sometimes did not understand Old American, especially slang. She felt good about her growing awareness of others' mindsets, including Kreshi, about whom she began to daydream.

Dali started to sit, then smacked herself on the forehead in the universal – and apparently timeless – sign for "I've been so stupid!"

She went over to the ALLY, currently showing a group of friends linked arm in arm and smiling for the camera in a dimly-lit room. She removed the screen from the wall, brought it over, pressed it against the wall just above the table, and touched its frame three times.

"There! You and I both have full access now. We could all increase our capacity if we just stay alert for chances to share our resources fully and, um, wisely."

Dali winked at Abby, settled into her seat again, and began to eat her nut-buttered toast.

Abby tried out a scrambled-tofu and sweet onion breakfast wrap. It wasn't bad. Not bad at all. Her tea was also good, sort of minty.

"You asked what our schedule was for today. I was thinking you'd like to go to a Spiritual School in the morning and see the animal show this afternoon."

"Oh! The animals!" Abby had nearly forgotten about them. "Where? What time?"

"It's all within biking distance," Dali said, pointing to a map on the ALLY's surface. "Spiritual School gets over in time to have lunch and then get to the animals, which starts at three."

"Okay. Just let me know what I need to do to be ready," Abby said, watching virtual green lines lead from the you-are-here symbol to a dot labeled SPIRITA LERNEJO and on to BESTMONTREJO.[89] A stray thought floated across Abby's consciousness about doing laundry sometime soon. She did not want to stink. Humiliation over that issue swelled within her, and she did her best to squelch it.

"I'm doing some laundry today; it'll be done by the time we get back tonight," Dali said. "If you wish, I think I can find some underwear to loan you while yours are washing." That was sooo Dali; practical yet always considerate, even concerning touchy issues. Abby would take Dali's way of handling intimate matters any day.

Dali's loaner bra was worth writing home to Jenn about, if only a letter could be sent back in time. It looked like a cotton camisole; but as Abby's body warmed it, it shrank, forming to and supporting her body. The panties were of a similar fabric, boxer cut. Both were extremely comfortable and, Abby noticed most of all, completely seamless.

Abby gathered her small pile of laundry and met Dali at the machine sitting behind a low wall off the far corner of the living room. Dali's washing machine seemed quite regular, like one from Abby's time. She supposed washing machines could've changed only so much, even in seven centuries.

"Yuter, please compare washing machines between my time and now."

"Washing machines now are better described as washing, drying, mending, and folding machines. They are called clothers."

Oooohkayy; Abby stood corrected. A _KLOE-ther_ was way better! Everyone in her time would want one. Did everyone now?

"People carefully choose a minimum of machines in our personal lives," Dali imparted. "In society, the Healing Disciplines use the most, but we also have amazing abilities to prevent or divert natural disasters."

"Why a personal minimum?"

"As I mentioned before, gadgets cost money, need maintenance and require people to work too much to pay for them. They also draw down the Earth's resources too fast. We're still rebuilding the world from the ravages of excessive consumption. Our WaerYs and ALLYs monitor both natural phenomena and daily activities to determine their local effects, and then the upper-level Yuters collect and analyze that data to clearly show us how our actions affect Mother Earth as a whole.

"I hope I'm not giving you too much if I also tell you that, as with so many things, those problems are interrelated and were solved by combining rational thought and spiritual principles. When we reduced our reliance on machines, that freed up our time. When we took a spiritual approach to life and saw work as worship, as Bahá'u'lláh said in His Glad-Tidings, chores became a satisfying endeavor."**[90]**

Abby's brow wrinkled as she tried to imagine how work could be a glad tiding. Still, work being worship made more sense than worship that felt like work.

"Many people enjoy the physical exercise," Dali continued, "and the chance to meander mentally during menial labor. And some types of housework produce enjoyable results, such as gardens, which are important if one follows the Master's diet."

"What's that?"

"Simple foods such as the Master ate: fresh vegetables and fruits, bread, broths, rice, teas. He did have a sweet tooth, too," Dali continued with a smile, "but he didn't let it control him. Often his friends gave him candy, but he shared instead of hogging out."**[91]**

Abby was glad for the chance to teach Dali something. "Either hogging them all, or pigging out." She paused to gather her thoughts. "I am surprised at how low-tech Erden is, but it makes sense."

"We have high-tech, too, when it's the best answer. Like providing emergency medical treatment, performing very dangerous work, relieving a fault line to prevent a major earthquake, nudging a comet away from the planet or a hurricane away from people," Dali elaborated. "But we have also learned that living simply, spiritually, close to nature, is best. Less expensive, more, er…you called it sustainable; we just call it wise." She smiled wryly at her young guest.

The two girls gathered a lunch: packages of soy sticks and veggie wedges and, as Dali laughingly called it, "An *aweful* sauce." She also packed some paper napkins and snacks that looked like energy bars. Dali showed Abby where to press the water bottles so the inside self-cooled while the outside stayed at room temperature and therefore dry.

When they left the house, Abby asked if Dali would teach her how to command the door shut, and was delighted when her own carefully repeated "*POR-doe, sh'low-SEE-jew*" caused the artistically carved wooden door to swing shut and click.**[92]** They loaded their bags into the bicycle baskets and rode off down the familiar lane. Abby enjoyed the sights and smells of the morning. Wait. Smelling? In the morning? She had never been able to smell in the morning; her nose was always plugged up. Why did it work now?

—Yuter, please, why can I smell now and I never could before?—

—Stuffy noses that are not linked to illness are usually allergies. Common food allergens from your time included citrus, corn, wheat, soy, nuts, dairy, and shellfish, as well as many toxins.—

Quite a list! And she ate most of those pretty often in her time.

—Yuter, please, how would I figure out by myself which one was making my nose stuffy every morning?—

—The usual procedure is to eat a diet of inoffensive foods such as rice, potatoes, and plain meat and vegetables for a week or two, then add in one thing at a time and see if it gives you symptoms.—

That sounded like a huge pain.

—Is there any other way, please?—

—Read or consult with others about it. Find a skilled physician to work with and test you. Pray and meditate about different foods; then see if God suggests anything, or pass your hand over different foods to see how their energy interacts with yours. A variation is to hold the item while someone tests your strength, which is called muscle testing or energy reading.—[93]

That just sounds fruity, Yuter, pardon the pun, Abby thought. Of course, she didn't really want the Yuter to respond, so she didn't think "Yuter...please." Sure enough, the Yuter didn't respond.

Spiritual School was held at a community center a few streets away from the House of Worship. Its plain front lawn invited the students into its spacious, cool interior. The littlest pupils scampered through its one large room, heading for the fenced play area in back. Bright balls, hula-hoops, and other toys peeked through wire mesh cages under the shade-giving extended roof.

"You leave toys out?"

"They're not out. They're put away."

"But they're not locked up; anyone could steal them."

"No one would steal them. Well, highly unlikely, anyway. We receive moral education essentially from infancy."[94]

"But didn't we just lock your house?"

"Yes, because some animals smell the food and manage to open the door and help themselves," Dali said smiling. "Raccoons are extremely clever, with their little hands. Goats are the worst. They have no fear and no manners, but hone in on food like pilgrims to a shrine."

Abby laughed, thinking of John Wayne's drawling use of that word. His pilgrims might have honed straight in on a corral or a bar, but never a shrine!

"And I suppose if you left the door totally open, bugs would also get in," Abby supplied, parking her borrowed bike in the rack.

"No, we have...ah...an energy field around the house that keeps them out."[95]

"No crime *and* no bugs in the house? Those alone would make living now worth it," Abby breathed, amazed.

"Well now, sometimes we do have crime," Dali amended. "Once in a while someone will intentionally harm someone else, steal something valuable, set fire to something, wreck something big...a few years ago, someone attempted to hijack an ocean freighter. *Had* to be insane to try that."

"What happens to criminals?"

"Hmm, well, there is capital punishment for killing and arson, and severe punishments for theft and—"

"I thought you were so loving and all."

"It's about justice, Abby. Justice and wisdom are two of the most important societal virtues. Bahá'u'lláh said, 'Should anyone intentionally destroy a house by fire, him also shall ye burn; should anyone deliberately take another's life, him also shall ye put to death.'[96] Of course, justice is enacted by the proper authorities to protect society, not by individuals trying to take revenge. And the death of the murderer or arsonist is the maximum punishment...no abuse or torture, no killing family members or confiscating lawful possessions, as was done in many countries in your time.

"Bahá'u'lláh also allowed for life imprisonment or lesser punishment even for murderers and arsonists. He said, though, that criminals need to sincerely regret their crimes in this life; if they don't, then their punishment will encompass them in the next life. I get the feeling from my readings about the next world that a murderer or an arsonist would *really* regret delaying punishment. Whatever just punishment society might inflict on them in this world would feel like nothing compared to their yearning to be closer to God, but kept back by their own deeds. Only God's loving mercy will ultimately help them then."

As they walked slowly to the main door of the community center, Abby pondered Dali's explanation. She also thought about Reverend Davison's sermons on the agonies of hell. Fire and brimstone; she could even smell the smoke. She looked around to see if anyone was burning trash nearby. But as she entered the building's large central room, the burning smell faded away, replaced by clanging noises from a small kitchen off to one side, which brought her attention back to the here-and-now.

"We rotate who cooks the noon meal after class," Dali said, "for whoever wants to stay and eat together."

As the two girls found a pair of chairs and sat down, Abby mentally predicted that they would be shouting over the kitchen noises.

—The building interior is sound-programmed. Today, adult human voices will carry. The room will dampen all other sounds, except anything that indicates an emergency.—

She hadn't even addressed the Yuter, and it still helped her.

—Now, in the words of the Master, quoting: 'Happiness consists of two kinds; physical and spiritual. The physical happiness is limited; its utmost duration is one day, one month, one year. It hath no result. Spiritual happiness is eternal and unfathomable. This kind of happiness appeareth in one's soul with the love of God and suffereth one to attain to the virtues and perfections of the world of humanity. Therefore, endeavor as much as thou art able in order to illuminate the lamp of thy heart by the light of love.' End quote. From *Tablets of Abdu'l-Bahá, volume 3*, pages 673 to 674.—

—Thank you, Yuter.— Abby appreciated the hope this quote gave her. She felt that if she developed her spiritual self, she could wind up nearer to God in the next world.

—You are very welcome. Have a wonderful deepening.—

Not for the first time, Abby felt awash with gratitude for the power-ful, uber-useful tool called the Yuter. No one here seemed to abuse its power, but she could easily envision the misuses some people would find for it in her time. Such a great tool could – would – be used for great evil. What prevented that now?

"Dali, what prevents people from using the Yuter in bad ways?"

Dali paused in the midst of greeting people. She looked deep into Abby's eyes to intuit her intent. Abby tried to look back steadily, and almost made it.

"Here, we're trained not to do bad things, no matter what the oppor-tunity or tool. Since anything can become a weapon, it is the training and beliefs that matter, not the tool."

"What do you mean, 'Anything can become a weapon'?"

"A pillow is a wonderful thing, is it not?"

"Of course."

"It has also been used to suffocate people."

"True."

"Everything can become a weapon, Abby. A hug can crush. A kiss can poison or mark a target, as Judas kissed the Blessed Christ. Shall we ban pillows, kisses, or hugs? Coffee mugs and power cords? Babies and old people?"

"What have babies and old people got to do with it?"

"In the very worst of times, they have also been used as weapons. Like, bombs were tucked inside a baby's clothes. And when somebody picked the baby up, the bomb exploded, killing everyone around."[97]

Oh no, that was too horrible to think of. She wished that Dali hadn't said it. She shook her head, trying to rid herself of the appalling images now swirling in her mind.

"I am so sorry, Abby. Perhaps I shouldn't have answered your last question that way. In our time, we're aware of some of the worst things done in your time; but we have the blessing of being far away from it. It is remote for us. But I can see it is very tangible for you."

"I was six years old when Nine-Eleven happened." Abby trusted the Yuter to help Dali understand what she meant. "The footage ran on TV nonstop for three days. School was cancelled. People didn't know what to do. One of my schoolmates, his uncle-in-law was killed in it. I will never forget it.

"And you know, the war on terrorism is still going on in my time. When I left—" Abby stopped. Wait…a *war* to stop terrorism? How was more fighting going to stop the killing? Wouldn't it mean people were just keeping the cycle of retaliation and death going? It was still death and misery and horror...

"When did it end?" Abby asked softly, pleading.

"Unfortunately, not for quite a while." Dali laid a sympathetic hand on Abby's shoulder to soften the blow. "Baha'u'llah, the Blessed Perfection, wrote that God had set two simultaneous processes in motion. One was the building up of all the new, unifying, spiritual institutions and systems – which were mostly explained in His Writings – that the world needed. The other process was the sweeping away of anything not built on spiritual, sustainable, peace-oriented practices. Things from the decaying Old-World order...they really could not be fixed, and trying to just wasted people's energy and resources. Plus, many people wanted things to get better, but were unwilling to change themselves. So no, not until things got *really* awful, in your sense of the word."

This was bad news. Really bad news. As bad as her world was, it was going to get worse? How she could possibly handle it?

"These processes, though, eventually led to the Most Great Peace," Dali said. "First came the Lesser Peace, when all the nations signed a cease-fire treaty, and started unitedly working on vital issues and discussing a world commonwealth. But we have only recently reached true, lasting peace...peace written not just on paper, but in the hearts of all the people."

So Bahá'ís knew from the early days that it would get worse? Then how could Melissa be so happy? But she was. She was delightful! She had even influenced Jon to her way of thinking! If Abby ever got back to her own time, she'd have to ask Melissa how she coped.

A soft tone brought Abby back to the gathering. She turned to see the class facilitator ceremonially strike a small gong twice more with a small wooden mallet.

At least a hundred people seated themselves at arc-shaped tables arranged in two concentric circles around a large empty space in the middle of the room. Abby faintly heard the youngest children playing in back, and the older ones on the front lawn. Members of both outdoor groups were calling, running, and laughing. The sounds from the front lawn were more organized, though, as if their game was part of a lesson. The room must have chosen how loud to make the sounds: just loud enough, she guessed, for the adults to monitor their safety...in case they were threatened by, say, an ill-mannered invading goat.

An elegant-looking older man stood up holding a small book, composed himself, closed his eyes, and chanted in a language Abby could not identify. She was so entranced by his deep, melodious voice that it took her a good while to realize the AerY wasn't translating...and even longer to wish it would.

—Your wish is my command, Abby.—

Abby stifled a groan at the cliché.

—Yes, Yuter, please translate what he's chanting, from now.—

—Translating the words of Bahá'u'lláh: 'Verily, this is that Most Great Beauty, foretold in the Books of the Messengers, through Whom truth shall be distinguished from error and the wisdom of every command shall be tested. Verily He is the Tree of Life that bringeth forth the fruits of God, the Exalted, the Powerful, the Great.'—

The translation – still sounding like the man's voice, even in silent mode – momentarily faded away into Abby's mental background as the thought dawned that Christ and Bahá'u'lláh sounded so much alike because They *were* so much alike. Different Voices of the same Divine Speaker. Different times, same Message. Bahá'u'lláh was the return of Christ, over a century before Abby was born. Reverend Davison had even listed the signs that had already happened, surely so had other clergy, and still almost everyone had missed it. Bahá'u'lláh, the return of Christ and apparently of the other great Prophets, had indeed come like a thief in the night. But such an unusual Thief, coming to take possession only of hearts, cleaning out only the habits blocking them from the Divine, proclaiming aloud His sacred summons...calling, calling all peoples to God.

She turned her attention back to the chant.

—'He is God and there is no God but Him, the King, the Protector, the Incomparable, the Omnipotent.'—

The words rang out in the room and from her AerY, like the great trumpet blast Reverend Davison described: warning, teaching, inviting, urging, enfolding. And she felt fortunate beyond measure to hear and respond. As she continued to listen, certain phrases resonated in her mind and heart...in her soul: *be obedient to the ordinances of God... whosoever desireth let him choose the path to his Lord...be not thou troubled...rely upon God...for the people are wandering in the paths of delusion, bereft of discernment.*

Even though she didn't understand some of the words, the import was becoming clear. God was calling; and if she responded, whatever the cost, wouldn't she increase her portion of the serenity now experienced by these residents of heaven-on-earth?

The chanting ended, a short silence ensued, then the facilitator's voice brought a rapturous Abby back to the moment.

"Thank you, Mr. Aghsani," the woman said, "for the great fortune and pleasure of hearing the Tablet of Ahmad chanted in the original Arabic by a descendant of Bahá'u'lláh." She pronounced the name *ahg-*

SAW-nee.[98]

Abby looked at the man again. He was from a Holy Family? How cool. Abby was used to Jesus having no wife or child. That Founders of other religions had families took some getting used to. It was different. But neat.

"We are continuing today with our program on the Central Figures of the Bahá'í Faith. We have several newcomers this time; so let me begin with a brief review.

"We've studied the Báb. His name was Siyyid 'Alí-Muhammad. Siyyid means a direct descendant of the Prophet Muhammad. He was born in Persia, later called Iran, on October 20, 1819. The Arabic word Báb means *Gate*. He was the spiritual gate to Bahá'u'lláh, Who was also born in Persia, on November 12, 1817 as Husayn-'Alí Núrí. The Arabic title Bahá'u'lláh means *Glory of God*."

Abby thought the Báb sounded similar to John the Baptist.

"Last week," the woman continued, "we deepened our knowledge about Bahá'u'lláh's eldest son and heir, 'Abbás Effendi. He chose for himself the title 'Abdu'l-Bahá, which means *Servant of Bahá*, declaring servitude to be his dearest ambition.[99]

Abby carefully repeated the new names in her mind: The *BAWB*, *sih-YIHD ah-lee moe-HAH-mahd*, *who-SANE ah-lee NEW-ree*, and *AB-boss eh-FEN-dee*.

"The Bahá'í Faith is the first religion to solve the big problem of splits among its followers. Bahá'u'lláh wrote that His son 'Abdu'l-Bahá should lead the Faith after He passed from this mortal life. 'Abdu'l-Bahá in his turn stated in his will that everyone should follow his grandson Shoghi Effendi."

Another new name: *SHOW-ghee*.

"When Shoghi Effendi, titled the Guardian, passed away with no children and no will, his faithful assistants, the Hands of the Cause of God, realized it was time for the Bahá'ís of the world to fulfill a provision of the Writings and elect the Universal House of Justice. Elected every five years, that most esteemed assemblage – which represents the continuation of Bahá'u'lláh's Covenant on earth – has guided us ever since. This continuity has made all the difference in being able to put into practice the wonderful teachings our Founding Figures left us in their thousands of letters and books.

"We are extremely fortunate to live in the time for which they, and countless other Prophets and believers, worked ceaselessly: true world peace and unity. We all have the ma'rifat that we are world citizens.

—Yuter, please, I didn't catch that word.—

—It is *ma-rih-FAHT*, an Arabic word used 'as is' regardless of language. It connotes true spiritual understanding, deep recognition, and profound knowledge.——

Remembering a science fiction book Jenn had read and told her about, Abby thought that *ma'rifat* certainly sounded gentler than *grok*.

"This week we have a marvelous presentation that I think we'll all enjoy. Yuter, please, lights low. Thank you."

The lights gradually dimmed. In the middle of the inner circle of tables, a three-dimensional image appeared and grew brighter. It was an Erdean woman in Victorian garb. Abby soon realized she was a talented actress speaking as if she had personally met the Master.[100]

"I am Ramona Allen Brown, the daughter in one of the first Bahá'í families in California. I was blessed to have met 'Abdu'l-Bahá several times when he visited America, and I attended as many of his West-Coast events as I could. It was such a magical time, such a mystical experience, that I've done my best to share it with everyone I could.

"How can I help you see his dignity, his wisdom and spiritual insight, his elevated position, yet his ready humor and, most of all, how he showered his love on everyone he met?"

The actress portraying Mrs. Brown walked gracefully past antique furniture to a tapestried chair and smoothly sat down.

"Let me try to help you fall in love with him, as so many did. In fact, even a few of his enemies loved him. 'Once a redoubtable enemy of Bahá'u'lláh remarked that had He no other proof to substantiate His exceptional powers, it were sufficient that He had reared such a son as Abbas Effendi.'[101]

"In public addresses, he might speak forcefully or humbly, in generalities or using the news of the day. He knew the spirit of his audience and addressed it. In individual appointments, he listened to everybody with such attentiveness that no matter how silly their arguments may have seemed, they felt respected and understood. The Master would then gently pose questions or introduce another way of thinking about the issue, often making connections relevant to that person's life, striking a remarkable balance between humor and gravity, deep messages and lightheartedness.

"For the weapons manufacturer, he spoke of building the machinery of love. With the Arctic explorer, he encouraged personal exploration of the invisibilities of the Kingdom of God. To the poor, he gave coins as well as messages of hope. He told them he knew what it was like to be penniless and in danger of dying. One bitter winter, he'd been forced to walk over frigid mountains, causing his feet and legs great pain for the rest of his life. When the small band of Bahá'ís first arrived in the filthy prison city of 'Akká, every day brought fresh misery. Overcrowding, foul water, starvation, and disease killed the exiles at a steady rate. Having been told lies about them, townspeople and officials hated them. However, there – like everywhere else – the people of 'Akká gradually saw for themselves the Holy Family's superb attributes. They changed their minds and came to ask advice, pay respects, and do good deeds at the family's request.

"The Master was not a strong man when He arrived in America in 1912 at the age of sixty-seven. He came to nurture the infant American community, mainly through love, but also with knowledge. He spread the message of His Father's Faith far and wide to those who had never heard of it, speaking to crowds who had heard of his heavenly ways and abilities. He talked with reporters, many of whom wrote articles, some more accurate than others. He allowed photographs and audio and film recordings of himself. And near the North American heartland city of Chicago, he laid the dedication stone for the first Bahá'í Temple in the Western Hemisphere…which for some seven and a half centuries has been the oldest one standing in the world.

"For two hundred and thirty-nine days, he kept such a full schedule – trying to reach the people of Canada and the United States – that he was quite exhausted and sometimes unwell near the end of his sojourn. He paid all his expenses himself, refusing many offers from his followers and asking instead that the money be given to charity or to building that first Western House of Worship.

"He was indeed the Example we should follow: human and yet definitely not *merely* human. He had many virtues that can be seen in his pictures."

As the actress was replaced by a series of glowing, life-size pictures, Abby gleefully recognized two that she'd already seen in cafés.

"Noble," the voiceover accompanied a photo of 'Abdu'l-Bahá looking majestic. "Humorous." Abby again saw the first picture she'd ever seen of him, smiling. "Stern. Lordly. Powerful. Fatherly. Welcoming. Humble." Picture after picture appeared, rotating for all to see.

"Every day he gave of himself from dawn until midnight. Some days he spoke at three or four different places, to hundreds of people at a time, even though he had no formal training for it. Many people later related that when he looked at them, he looked into their souls, knew their secret fears, their unspoken wishes. He gave many blessings and positive predictions, especially favoring the children, people of darker skin, the poor, the outcasts. Several times He gave some candy or fruit to people and healed health problems with it. Word spread, and he became a sensation.

"Now, please prepare yourselves to reverently hear his voice."

In a moment, a voice began chanting a prayer, as a photo montage showed him in meetings, speaking, greeting, walking, sitting, standing for the camera. Abby's AerY translated silently, but her joyful heart heard the Master singing in melodious, Persian-accented English...

♪Praise be to God that we are present in this radiant meeting
and turning toward the Kingdom of Abhá.
That which we behold is due to the Grace and Bounty
of the Blessed Perfection.
We are atoms and He is the Sun of Reality.
We are drops and He is The Greatest Ocean.
Though we are poor
yet the Treasury of the Kingdom is full of overflowings.
Though we are weak
yet the confirmation of the Supreme Concourse is abundant.
Though we are helpless
yet our refuge and shelter is in His Holiness Bahá'u'lláh.
Praise be to God! His traces are evident!
Praise be...♪**[102]**

Abby soared into her own reverie as the praises continued. Phrases drifted through her mind. From the AerY, or perhaps her via own inner voice: *breath of the holy spirit...perfume the nostrils...divine promptings*. As the prayer ended, she couldn't tell where the subtle scent of flowers came from.

The elegant actress reappeared. "Always 'Abdu'l-Bahá urged people to rise to a higher spiritual level...to increased tolerance, greater service, loftier standards, higher motives. All done with such love, such happiness, such joy; never with blame or fear.

"During his sojourn here, he revealed himself to be the Center of Bahá'u'lláh's Covenant. This stunned American believers, as many had not really understood his station. He also declared New York City as the City of the Covenant, the import of which became clear nearly nine decades later with Nine-Eleven and all the changes *that* tragedy set into motion."

Abby gasped. It *was* the world-changing event she felt it to be! No one near her noticed – or perhaps they politely ignored – her reaction.

"We are privileged to have so many photos of the Master. A film was also made of him in America, using the then-new technology of silent movies. The film hasn't been shown in your town in over seventy years, and so your local House of Justice has requested of the national House of Justice that your community be given the bounty of seeing it at your Day of the Covenant celebration this year.**[103]** For now, I invite you to close your eyes and imagine him walking in a garden before a small crowd of followers."

Abby had lived on earth when World Peace was a faraway dream. Yet she was also here seeing His vision realized. The Master had used himself up setting this dream in motion. With all his labors, his travels, his kindly air towards people of all different beliefs and conditions, he carried out the mystical and practical teachings of Bahá'u'lláh.

Abby had no trouble imagining 'Abdu'l-Bahá. His love felt so real to her. His care seeped into her heart, warming her, uplifting her, giving her direction and guidance. If he, a prisoner, old and at times viciously hated, could bring a new religion to the world, surely the Faith he promoted could help her out of her puny miseries.

"The Master often asked people if they were happy," Ms. Brown continued. "He explained, 'The purpose of all the divine religions is the establishment of the bonds of love and fellowship among men, and the heavenly phenomena of the revealed Words of God are intended to be a source of knowledge and illumination to humanity.'[104] We are humbled by his superhuman efforts to expand these life-giving teachings; we can also be inspired by them and by him."

Abby, eyes still closed, was thoroughly inspired. She was filled not only with happiness and hope but also with a sense of noble purpose.

"In closing, let me share with you one more picture of the Master. It is not a photograph, but a sketch that the poet and artist Kahlil Gibran drew when they met."[105]

Abby opened her eyes. She had heard of Gibran! The actress again faded out, and the drawing appeared, facing Abby. She gazed raptly at the portrait and felt 'Abdu'l-Bahá looking back at her. It was as if he himself stood just behind the drawing; watching, calling, welcoming. When she'd first seen his photograph, she'd thought he was the wonderful Dumbledore. He meant even more now, for now she understood *who* he was. He was personally inviting her – indeed, everyone – to join him in building heaven on earth.

She answered the call, trusting him fully. The grandfather she had never had. But more…so much more.

The sketch rotated away, but the moment stayed in her mind. The spirit of a master, and the deep, pure commitment he summoned from her. After, she felt as if his energy had called forth hers, forming lightning. Or perhaps, bolts of light. Bolts she could repeat at will.

Chapter 24: Animals

Dali and Abby spread their picnic blanket under a large shade tree in back of the community center. Abby was aware of the noon heat, but it was tolerable.

"You may be interested in knowing that the clothes you're wearing keep you cool," Dali said.

"What do you mean?" Abby responded, happily helping to unpack lunch. She knew that some Old-World fabrics claimed to wick moisture, stay cool in summer and warm in winter, massage muscles, and more.

"This fabric changes temperature to keep your body temperature at an ideal level." Dali opened the little tub of sauce and offered Abby soy sticks and cooled water.

"So that's why we could dig and bike in the midday heat?" Abby normally headed for the A/C by mid-morning. She realized she hadn't done that here because she hadn't been intolerably hot. Bonega!

The soy sticks and sauce were delicious, as Dali had promised. The flavors blended perfectly; it was light but filling. Dali also shared some fruit that the kitchen helpers had encouraged them to take on their way out the back door. It was very pleasant, especially with Abby's new-found inspiration. Abby saw a butterfly – or was it a moth? she was not very good at telling the difference – wend its erratic way across the yard. She wished there were more.

"I know where there are a lot of flutteries," Dali said. "And we can go there on our way to the animal show."

They deposited their collapsed containers in the community center collection bins. Dali led the way on their bikes, and Abby realized they were headed to the House of Worship. Dali explained that different sections of the garden were planted to attract different creatures. She led Abby to the Flutter Garden. Arriving, they again spread their blanket and sat under a tree, hoping not to disrupt the aerial activity a few feet away in the bright sunshine.

Abby had never watched hummingbirds. She was captivated with how fast they flitted. If she blinked, she lost track of them. Their midair antics, vying for particular flowers, were spectacularly fast and colorful. The iridescent birds were much prettier than the pictures she had seen. The butterflies' fluttering patterns also increased Abby's lighthearted joy. To her heightened senses, everything seemed happy, bright, and new. Was this what *spiritual rebirth* meant? Astoundingly, she understood that is was not just an allegory; it was also an accurate description of a hard-to-describe spiritual reality.

"I wish I could take pictures of them." She mused that nothing this perfect could last forever, and wanted some way to capture the moment to carry her through whatever rough patches lay ahead. Then her spiritual awareness delivered yet another insight: perhaps the same need over the ages had led to the worship of graven images. She vowed that she'd never fall into that trap. Not that butterflies would make very good idols anyway, she reflected with a grin.

"Go ahead; use the WaerY," Dali said, removing hers. She touched its face, which became a viewer. She pointed to the tiny lens spot on the outer edge and assured Abby that if she caught the fliers in the camera's eye, the photos would clearly capture the action. When asked where the GO button was, Dali smiled and gently tapped Abby's head.

"Just start," Dali said. "We'll choose size and format afterwards."

Abby stood up and aimed the WaerY's lens at the airborne display with both hands. She directed a mental "Now!" at the WaerY when she saw a scene worth capturing. When she felt she'd done her best, she sat back down, cross-legged. Dali told her how to project the images against the blue blanket.

"They can move or not, in 2D or 3D," Dali said. "Tell it which you want."

Abby asked for a 3D movie first. And except for being fainter in the bright light, it was an exact duplicate of the real drama still unfolding a few feet away.

"If you want the image to hold still, you tell it which moment you wish it to display. You can tell it to play slowly so you can see better."

This was unbelievable. Working silently with Dali's WaerY, Abby chose a moment to freeze in 3D, like a living statue. It required a lot of concentration, but she comforted herself with the thought that Dali had grown up using the Yuter and still preferred to speak with it.

She experimented with flattening her images into two dimensions to see how they might look in a slide show. By thinking it, she zoomed in and out.

"You have a real talent," Dali said, intruding on her self-absorbed art project. "Whatever you decide on, I'll upload to my ALLY. I think we need to head out now, though."

They made good time, arrived at the animal show site early, parked their bikes, and walked under the overhanging entryway and down a covered walkway. On the left, various natural habitats lay empty; ahead and to the right stood the main entrance into the theater.

Dali invited Abby to continue down the walkway past the theater to a large open area where trainers played with animals, preparing for the twice-monthly show. Dozens of fowl chased their trainer, the chicks all toddling after their mamas, the last ones tottering and hopping as fast as their little clawed and webbed feet could go. Ducks, chickens, crows, hawks, and many other birds dove for the various nibbles that she threw for them when she stopped.

Walking to the next area, the girls saw handlers working with mammals. Several animals from the pig family did tricks for their wrangler, a teenaged girl. Nearby, a man somehow cued a large pack of canines – coyote, both domestic and wild dogs, fox, jackal, wolf, and a couple of others she didn't recognize – to run around his legs in patterns.[106] And an older man lined up felines: housecats, sand cats, a black and a spotted leopard, a male lion, a puma, two Siberian tigers, and a mid-sized wine-red feline with huge black-tufted ears…Abby remembered its name was something like carousel.[107] None of the animals wore a harness, leash, or even collar.

Walking on, they glimpsed two ladies with… "Horses!" Abby exclaimed to Dali, pointing. Ordinary-looking but, still, real horses! One trainer cued the bay to rear, and the other pointed her slender wand at the chestnut, who spun in circles.

Abby couldn't help it; the horses reeled her in. The sight of them, their smell, their movement always riveted her; but now they were – due to her new eyes, ears, and spirit –a magnet to her iron particles. She peered between the diamonds of the smooth tan fence, her fingers laced through its links, her eyes drinking in every detail she could latch onto.

The women wore plain, stretchy body-tights with boots. Their hair was coiled in buns at the napes of their necks. The horses' manes were long and shiny, their tails full and well-tended. Horses and trainers alike looked healthy and happy.

"Hey there, Xenophon!"[108] said the tall, mocha-skinned lady in the blue outfit to the bright-rust chestnut. "Feeling good today? So am I! Catch me if you can!" She ran off to the far corner of the earthen enclosure, stopping at the fence. The horse perfectly matched her every step. She placed her hand on his mane and, side by side, they backed up slowly.

She spun, then sprang towards his tail; he hunkered down on his haunches and pirouetted to keep his place next to her, tossing his head magnificently. He mirrored her exactly as she vaulted forward, then to her right, and sank into a bow. She stepped on his bent leg and swung onto his back. He cantered forward, hustled backwards, and spun and leapt just as he had when she was beside him. Abby couldn't see what cues she was using; she merely looked one way and another just before the horse lunged. It was fantastic!

The other woman, somewhat older, wearing an emerald-green outfit, likewise cued her bay through maneuvers from the ground, and then while riding. Their jumping over logs, rearing, and navigating a maze of poles backwards, then sideways, made Abby stare openmouthed.

"Good job, Rajah!" the handler said, hugging the horse. The bay's light-brown body almost matched the woman's skin, and her black hair blended perfectly with his black mane. This visual harmony amplified their mental unity. Abby kept reminding herself that neither trainer had so much as a halter on their horse.

Dali nudged Abby and said they'd better find their seats, but Abby didn't want to stop watching; she could not will herself to tear her eyes away. Dali finally peeled Abby's fingers off the fence and said there would be even better things in the show; and with that promise, Abby was able to rip herself away.

They headed to their seats. On their way to the right rear side of the main hall, they passed show-goers of all styles of dress, ages, colors – even, Abby was startled to see, a redheaded young man as light-skinned as herself, holding the hands of two auburn-haired children with milk-chocolate skin. Surprisingly, the seats were almost full. Some groups looked like whole families, even though it was a workday afternoon. There were definitely benefits to not working forty-plus-hour weeks.

Settling onto her seat, Abby saw that the padded benches rose up in front of a dirt-floored stage. Although the sun shone bright and hot outside, the interior was dim and cool. Onstage, nimble otters climbed a small, slick hill and slid down into a pool, diving and weaving around each other in and out of the water.

An unseen announcer said, "Ladies and gentlemen, we are about to begin. We hope you ma'rifat and treasure the show."

Abby listened for the rest of the announcement, but there was no more. That was it? The alto-voiced lady was finished? No rules? No announcements about silencing phone – er, Yuter – calls. About not taking videos? No grand hyperbole about how fantastic, how unique, how unbelievable the show would be?

"Yuter, please, can you continue to translate aloud for me?"

"As long as it is quietly."

"Yuter, please translate the show quietly into my ear."

"My pleasure."

"Thank you."

Abby felt she couldn't quite manage simultaneously watching the show and being mentally open to the AerY's silent messages. And that hunch proved true almost immediately.

The show was riveting. It began with low, slow music, a darkened stage, and fog rolling out. A man's deep, measured voice rumbled out of the music.[109]

In the beginning, the earth was formless and void, and darkness was over the surface of the deep. The fog roiled, while a single tone reverberated so low that Abby could feel it in her lungs, her bones. *And the Spirit of God was moving over the surface of the waters.* The fog began to swirl and streak. *Then God said, 'Let there be light' and there was light.* A blue-white light grew slowly in the middle of the stage, hovering and expanding. *And God separated the waters from the heavens.* The fog lifted to reveal the pool, now devoid of otters, dark except for a small reflection of the brightening light. *Then God said, 'Let the waters below the heavens be gathered into one place, and let the dry land appear' and it was so.* Dirt rose higher around the edge of the pool. Abby tried to see how that much dirt could rise. Was actual dirt being added from underneath, was it the way the light shone on it, or was it more 28th-century technology?

Then God said, 'Let the earth sprout vegetation, plants yielding seed, and fruit trees bearing fruit after their kind, with seed in them, on the earth' and it was so. Unrecognizable grain stalks and strange trees dotted with fruit rose up at the edges of the stage. *And God made the two great lights, the greater light to govern the day, and the lesser light to govern the night; God made the stars also.* The one light broke into two and became the sun and the moon, hovering over two parts of the stage. They looked very realistic; Abby was awed.

Then God said, 'Let the waters teem with swarms of many living creatures, and let birds fly above the earth in the open expanse of the heavens.' And God created the great sea monsters, and every living creature that moves, with which the waters swarmed after their kind, and every winged bird after its kind; and God saw that it was good. Abby leaned forward to peer into the pool. She glimpsed great swimming creatures, small darting fish, eels, jellyfish, long-limbed squids, sharks, mantas, sea turtles, dolphins. They were clearly visible in the brightening stage, moving beneath the watery surface, impossibly real.

Then birds began to fly all around the stage. First the smallest ones: bright hummingbirds, finches, wrens, chickadees, sparrows, parakeets, starlings, and kinds she didn't know. Pigeons cooed, robins called, cardinals whistled, nightingales trilled. Dazzling cockatiels and parrots joined the other flitting shapes landing in the trees. They were followed by majestic birds of prey. Owls and hawks and lordly eagles whirled, dove, and swept up into the trees. Last of all, a pair of mighty condors soared in. Abby thought that if they were real, they were very, *very* well trained; and if they were the work of people like Rykeir, they were very, very well done.

Then God said, 'Let the earth bring forth living creatures after their kind: cattle and creeping things and beasts of the earth after their kind' and it was so. The pool had disappeared and the hillock of dirt was no more. Four steers strode onstage, followed by deer, goats, and a duck and her ducklings. Roosters, hens, ferrets, roadrunners, and large rats appeared on the right side of the stage, and the two horses entered regally from the left. Donkeys entered from the back, along with one leopard, two dogs, three housecats, and a few large lizards, followed by several scampering mice. Finally, an ostrich strode in, followed by a comically waddling crested penguin and a flitting bat. The animals all stood sentinel at the edges of the stage, the bat hanging upside down from a deer antler.

Then God said, 'Let us make man in Our image, according to Our likeness; and let them rule over the fish of the sea and over the birds of the sky and over the cattle and over all the earth, and over every creeping thing that creeps on the earth.' And God created male and female. A half-dozen handlers appeared slowly from the back of the stage and walked towards the flat center. *And God blessed them; and God said to them, 'Be fruitful and multiply, and fill the earth, and be good stewards for it; and watch over the fish of the sea, and over the birds of the sky, and over every living thing that moves on the earth.'* The men and women turned outwards, facing the animals, and raised their hands. All the animals bowed to the handlers, who bowed back.

The lights dimmed way down, except for a center circle where one handler stood. The leopard, two housecats, a sandcat, and three goats also stepped into the light. Cued by the handler's tiny hand motions, the three small cats jumped onto the goats' backs. Next, each carefully carrying its feline rider, the goats minced delicately around and then lined up side-by-side facing the audience. The cats climbed up onto the goats' heads and sat down between their horns. Then the handler cued the big cat, which took a running start, leapt over the goats' backs, turned, and crawled under their bellies. Abby's heart swelled. This was even better than lions lying down with lambs!

The music rose rich and slow. The audience clapped, not loudly, but showing honest appreciation and reverence. The goats and felines melted away from the stage. The four steers stepped forward, sporting long horns. One trainer sat in the middle of the stage, moving her arms gracefully in what might have been ingenious cues but could also have been yoga or dance moves. Twirling, swinging, and swaying around their trainer, the steers reminded Abby of a kaleidoscope. Mirroring one another, they walked inwards to touch noses over her head, then they stepped sideways, making a spinning bovine wheel, horns locked and clacking. They backed, turned sideways, and passed their nearest partner, tipping their horns towards each other, weaving in and out around a circle like square-dancers. Abby's opinion of cows rose as she watched the graceful spectacle. She knew that steers were roped and wrestled in rodeos, and bucking bulls were ridden; but she hadn't known they could be trained. What would it feel like to ride one that wasn't bucking?

"Yuter," Abby whispered, "please remind me to research training cattle…especially to be ridden. Thank you."

"Noted. And Dali wants me to remind you that now you see why we do not need to rope our cattle."[110]

Lights and music stayed simple but effective, including throwing shadows of the steers up on the stage backdrop as they danced.

While the cattle wove their way offstage to polite clapping, a Tasmanian devil scurried on, followed by a passel of platypuses. The music began to incorporate silly sounds like slide whistles, tinny cymbals, and tuba blats. The platypuses waddled in a circle around the devil, which spun in the opposite direction. Whenever the devil stopped and changed direction, so did the littler platypuses around it, though of course more slowly. Suddenly, two gray wallabies boisterously bounced onstage and began jumping around. But when one stepped on the other, things got alarmingly dicey. The pair chased each other around the stage, stopping occasionally to balance on their tails and wrestle or kick at each other. One of them bowled over the devil, while panicked platypuses scrambled about trying to avoid the duo's big feet and tails.

Abby's heart was in her throat. How awful! Even now, trained animals could get out of hand. But where were the trainers? Why weren't they coming to control the animals? Should someone call for help? But no one moved. Abby sat anxiously, her worry growing.

The devil picked itself up and, at first, tried to guide the platypuses away from the sparring rowdies. When that didn't work, it ran offstage hissing, only to reappear five seconds later leading two very large, leaping, red kangaroos. The thumping of roos' feet startled the two fighters, who sprang apart and froze. The big roos began making clucking noises – sounding for all the world like they were saying "tut tut" – and the smaller wallabies hung their heads. The roos continued to cluck until the wallabies turned, clicked at the platypuses and the devil, then hugged each other. At that, the large roos also hugged the wallabies, helped the two snuggle into their pouches, and boinged offstage, the devil herding the now-calm platypuses close behind.[111]

Like the rest of the audience, apparently, Abby was too amazed to even applaud. But then…

"Oooh! The horses!" she whispered to Dali, who flashed a sympathetic smile in return. Abby held her breath in anticipation as the horses stepped forward.

Xenophon's coat gleamed copper in the stage lights. He and the tall, thin, blue-suited young woman Spanish-walked across the stage, she on the horse's far side.[112] As she stomped across the stage in perfect unison with him, the trainer's legs, as long as Xenophon's, seemed to disappear from view. Her upper torso and head were all that showed. The pair became as one, looking almost like a centaur. Then, without any cue Abby could see, Xenophon planted his front feet, pranced his hindquarters around until he faced the center, and reared up to walk on his hind legs to the middle.

Abby almost cried out. She knew it must be incredibly difficult to train a horse so well. It was difficult to suppress her urge to cheer and whistle.

A woman's alto voice calmly and eloquently continued the narrative...how and from where Abby still could not fathom, as no speaker equipment was visible.[113]

Consider: Unity is necessary to existence. Love is the very cause of life; on the other hand, separation brings death. The elements that form stone, wood, or greenery are held together by the law of attraction. If this law should cease for one moment, these elements would not hold together; they would fall apart. The trees around the stage's edge began to drop their leaves, and continued to steadily deteriorate into piles of dust that blew away in a whirling dust devil. Rocks between the trees also crumbled and blew away. The growing plants around the edge of the stage decayed to nothing.

The trainer signaled Xenophon to lie down center stage. He lay on his stomach, his legs folded underneath him, relaxed. The trainer then beckoned Rajah, and the bay leapt cleanly over the chestnut, turned, and waited. The woman went to Xenophon, murmured to him, lovingly stroked him, swung one leg over him, sat on his back, and cued him to stand up. She beckoned Rajah to the middle of the stage, turned him to face the audience, and cued *him* to lie down. He lay as Xenophon had, waiting quietly. Xenophon backed up fast, away from Rajah, then cantered forward with the rider and jumped effortlessly over him! Perched at the edge of her seat to catch every detail, Abby couldn't help herself. She clapped loudly. Dali and a few of the other watchers smiled at her spontaneous enthusiasm.

Xenophon and his rider cantered around the stage. Rajah rose and joined them. They cantered in unison, the young woman lifting both her arms in a flying motion. Abby gloried in vicarious ecstasy, living the rider's experience. Still cantering, the rider motioned the bay away a little, and, with a flash of blue-clad leg and arm, wheeled off Xenophon and onto Rajah. A backdrop projection showed horses play-fighting and galloping.

Abby so lost track of herself with her exuberant clapping – which blended with the more restrained applause of others – that her bottom slid off the bench entirely, though she caught herself before she hit the floor. Dali helped her get back up, with an expression vacillating between concern for Abby's safety and shared enthusiasm as the narration continued.[114]

The power of cohesion in the mineral kingdom is love *within the limits of the mineral world. In the vegetable kingdom, we find that these cohesive elements make up the body of a plant. Therefore, in the vegetable kingdom there is also love. We enter the animal kingdom and find the attractive power binding together single elements as in the mineral, plus the cellular admixture as in the vegetable, plus the phenomena of feelings. We observe that the animals desire fellowship. This is love manifested in the degree of the animal kingdom.* As one, the horses whirled in a full circle and continued to canter, matching footfalls exactly. After a second pirouette, their rider stood up, one foot on each horse's back. The stage floor and backdrop showed beach and ocean. The horses cantered in total unity through simulated shallow surf, waves rolling under them, the girl Roman-riding with perfect ease.[115]

Hugging herself in joy, Abby was completely beside herself, her mind blown by what the girl was doing with the horses. The narration flowed over her.

Finally, we come to the kingdom of man. As this is the kingdom of beings with souls, the light of love is more resplendent. In man, we find the power of attraction among the elements that compose his body, plus the attraction between his various components, plus the sensibilities of the animal kingdom. But still above and beyond all these lower powers, we discover in the being of man the attraction of heart, the receptivity and affinities that bind men together, enabling them to live and associate in friendship and solidarity. It is therefore evident that in the world of humanity, too, the greatest king and sovereign is love. A fancy gallery appeared around the theater, reminding Abby of the Spanish Riding School arena in Vienna.[116] She felt as if she and the other spectators were members of the nobility, all honoring and appreciating the pageantry in front of them.

A low bar appeared near the back of the stage, in front of the cantering team. The horses jumped it and cantered on to the left, the rider still standing on their backs. When the horses reached the far left side, she somersaulted off their backs, twisted into a quarter turn, and landed facing the far side of the stage. The horses cantered around to the far right, then stopped, turned towards her, and bowed onto their forelegs, their chins touching the ground. She bowed back to them, and then to the audience.[117]

Then all the animals and their handlers came onstage for a perfectly choreographed, simultaneous bow. But instead of clapping, audience members started to hiss. This alarmed Abby; why were they expressing extreme disapproval? Soon the whole audience was hissing, and the men began to growl. Then the women, including Dali, intoned a long, low "ahhhh" that rose in pitch until they were nearly singing soprano. Suddenly, all the men shouted "BOOM!" and most of the children giggled at the verbal fireworks.

—Consultation: Do you concur with singing Honor?—

"What?" Abby asked, having no idea what the AerY meant. But instead of an answer, she heard a chord in her ear. The audience all stood up, Abby joining them in a few seconds, and started singing what she quickly recognized as the old "Happy Birthday" tune with new words…

♪We appreciate you!
We appreciate you!
We thank you for your service!
We appreciate you!♫

The singing was phenomenal, the harmonies exquisite. It was like being inside a stereo speaker. Living music reverberated all around. Then it was over, and the performers all bowed one final time and ran offstage.

As the audience members gathered their things, rustling and buzzing about the show, Abby turned and crushed Dali in a bear hug, planted a huge kiss on her cheek, and choked out a tear-filled "Thanks!"

"You kind of liked it, then, did you? You voted Honor?" Dali asked naughtily.

"It was the very, very, very best anything I've ever been to, *ever*, in *any* age," Abby gushed, making sure she had not dumped anything out of her bag in her excitement. They followed others into the aisle.

"You can tell them that; they'd love to hear it," Dali said.

"Who?"

"The horse trainers. The riders."

Abby stopped dead in her tracks. "You mean I get to *meet* them?"

"Didn't I tell you that?"

"*No*, you didn't!" Abby's mind reeled with the information.

"Might have slipped my mind," Dali said with a sly smile that told Abby she'd withheld this information on purpose.

"We get to *meet* them?" Abby had gone stupid with surprise.

"Stop drooling all over yourself. Yes, you get to meet them."

"Can I get the rider's autograph?"

"Well, we usually do not do that; but if you pretend you're just an ignorant child, they will probably forgive you," Dali sniffed. Abby felt that Dali was only half joking.

"You don't do autographs?"

"Usually not. It's too...how shall I say it?...it becomes all about that person. It can stoke the fire of the ego, and that can burn the person, sometimes badly. We also learned that from your time. Sooo many promising lives. Ruined by fame, by the continual ego-boost of people going ga-ga over them. Like you are over Myra Striver now."

"You're saying it could be bad for the soul of the rider – Myra – if I go and show her how blown away I was by her riding?"

"That is it in a nutshell. Thank you for understanding. If we want people in the public eye to continue to do an excellent job, we can do them a favor by treating them like one of us. Which in the end, they are; they're just at a very high level of accomplishment in something. We need to remember that God created everybody, and tests each person to develop as many positive attributes as possible. No one is free of troubles and difficulties. Idolizing Myra can only make her feel strange and probably add to her troubles; normal support will be much more useful to help her continue her wonderful riding."

Maybe that explained why there was no hype, no one whipped the audience in a frenzy, the trainers didn't milk the applause for all it was worth, and the audience knew there'd be no encores. There was always so much to think about here, Abby mused as they walked to the warm-up area. She thought about how different it would be back in 2007. Why are we so into autographs and fan clubs? Why do we lose it when we have the chance to meet a real celebrity?

—Yuter, please remind me later to think about why we treat famous people like we do in my time.—

—Noted. Quoting: 'Happy is the one who hath clung unto the truth, detached from all that is in the heavens and all that is on earth.' End quote. From Bahá'u'lláh's *Epistle to the Son of the Wolf*, page 139.—

—Very appropriate, as usual, Yuter. Thanks.—

Myra and the other woman stood with the two fabulous horses, who looked quite ordinary again. Healthy, well-groomed, well-muscled, very nicely built, but otherwise ordinary, dozing behind the handlers. Abby and Dali got into a short line of well-wishers.

When they reached the older woman, Dali hugged her, kissed her cheek and said, "Hi! We loved the show. Very nicely done, even better than last time. Oh, and I've been meaning to come by for supper."

Abby stared in astonishment. Dali knew the lady?!

Dali turned toward Abby and said, "Abby, this is my mother, Farrah Chavamanta. Her last name comes from *horse-lover*." Dali winked, then turned to Farrah. "Mom, meet Abby, the house guest I told you about. She has been with me for a couple of days so far, and I'm showing her around Lodlan. She's also a horse-lover."

Abby barely had time to overcome this latest shock before Farrah greeted her warmly and said that, if they had time, they'd have to come back on a non-show day and stroke the horses. Her tone of voice implied that this would be a great treat. Which it would be! But Vivian's voice played in Abby's head, criticizing "just wanting to stand around and pet the horses." Her enthusiasm dampened.

"All creatures, especially mammals, need some degree of love. Including horses," Farrah said gently. "It's one of the main messages of our show. Showing the horses love by stroking and hugging them is one of the most important things you can do with and for them."

"I'd really enjoy that, Mrs. *chah-vah-MAHN-tah*" Abby replied, once again grateful from the bottom of her heart for the understanding and validation she received in this world. The three exchanged hugs and parting sentiments, then Abby and Dali went on to meet Myra. Abby refrained from asking for an autograph, but she could not help wanting some memento of this magical afternoon. She asked Dali to record her in front of the dozing horses. Dali took a WaerY picture of her young guest and the two equines.

Myra was indeed a human being like everybody else. Not fantastically beautiful, but pleasant and very gracious. A notably strong hand clasp revealed her tremendous physical fitness. Her warm brown eyes regarded Abby calmly while Abby thanked her profusely, through Dali's WaerY, for her excellent riding and riveting performance. Abby was sure she'd never used the word "riveting" before in her life, but she wanted to say something that conveyed the depth of her feeling. Good thing she read so much! Myra smiled genuinely and replied that it was her delight to inspire people with her performance.

As Dali and Abby slowly pedaled home in the easing evening heat, Abby's AerY offered another happiness quotation.

"In the words of 'Abdu'l-Bahá, quoting: 'And the honor and distinction of the individual consists in this, that he among all the world's multitudes should become a source of social good. Is there any larger bounty conceivable than this, that an individual, looking within himself, should find that by the confirming grace of God he has become the cause of peace and well-being, of happiness and advantage to his fellow men? No, by

the one true God, there is no greater bliss, no more complete delight.'
End quote. From *The Secret of Divine Civilization*, pages 2 and 3."

"You just have perfect quotes, Yuter," sighed Abby as they arrived home, content and tired. For dinner, Dali spooned leftover brown rice with a creamy vegetable sauce onto two special plates, covered them with glass-like lids, and put them on the stovetop. In a few minutes, the hot, delicious meal was ready. Dali handed Abby her plate; it was cool to the touch and felt like a blend of metal, pottery, and plastic.

After dinner cleanup, Dali sent the images from the WaerY to the ALLY. She put several into all the formats, showing them to Abby after she walked out of the bathroom in the borrowed PJs. Abby especially treasured one that beautifully captured several butterflies and two hummingbirds in one video. She also prized the shot of her with the horses, and asked for it in 3D. The horses must've been trained to come awake for cameras, because they were both alert and – Abby could have sworn – smiling.

Dali thoughtfully set the images to rotate in a visual feast, then went to retrieve the clean, folded clothes from the clother. That area had been dark; but as Dali moved toward it, its ceiling lit up softly. Abby, alerted to the many Erdean wonders, looked up and around. As she suspected, there was no light fixture, let alone a light switch. It was as if the ceiling itself – its paint – was illumined. Once again, beauty and practicality combined. Then, as Abby's eyes followed Dali across the small but well-organized house, her gaze fell upon the painted horses next to the wooden sound-box.

"What are those horses?" Abby asked, pointing.

Dali paused and looked.

"They're from the STEEDS OF FAITH series," she said. Realizing Dali was trying to decide how to explain it further, Abby waited.

"There are different…places? no…um, *mentions* of horses in the Bahá'í Writings; and some talented people, like my mother, wanted to create sculptures from them. The Writing is part of the design painted on the horse, see?" Dali picked up a dark-colored horse and pointed to artfully painted UL words in purple, woven into the design of blues and grays.

"Your mother made this?" Abby asked unbelievingly.

"She and a…network of other horse-lovers."

"What does it say?"

"This one is the Steed of the Valley of Search. Bahá'u'lláh says that 'The steed of this Valley is patience; without patience the wayfarer on this journey will reach nowhere and attain no goal.'"**[118]**

Abby thought the sculpture – and its message – was incredible, and told Dali so.

"Mom will be glad to hear that you liked it," Dali said sincerely. "I will yuter her soon and let her know."

Dali went into the bathroom while Abby snuggled into the couch's bedding, happily watching her images rotate between 3D, 2D, moving, and stationary.

Her last thought before drifting off to sleep was that she had indeed met women of color who loved horses...and were in no way held back from expressing that love in the most elegant terms.

Chapter 25: School

Summer vacation for the Lodlan schools – shorter than it was in Abby's time – was over. The new school year started the next day, Tuesday. Dali's cousin, Petra, had agreed to guide Abby. Petra and Abby were the same age and – since kindergarten started at age five in both worlds – in the same grade.[119] Abby also learned that all Lodlan students wore uniforms.[120] But since Dali couldn't obtain an Insight Upper school uniform on such short notice, she suggested Abby wear a visitor's badge and simply say, truthfully, that she did not live in Lodlan.

They got up at dawn, wafted themselves clean with the Cleansing Wind device, and dressed. Abby's sports bra felt almost comfortable after its first washing. And Dali had been right: Abby didn't seem to need underarm deodorant. She didn't know why; she was just relieved that she wasn't leaving stinky spots on Dali's clothes. As she headed to their breakfast of plums and green tea, Abby's AerY greeted her.

"Joyful Tuesday, Abby. The Master tells us, quoting now from mid-sentence: '...that the happiness and greatness, the rank and station, the pleasure and peace, of an individual have never consisted in his personal wealth, but rather in his excellent character, his high resolve, the breadth of his learning, and his ability to solve difficult problems.' End quote. From *The Secret of Divine Civilization*, pages 23 and 24."

"Thanks, Yuter; perfect as usual."

"Thank you, Abby. Have a perfect day, as usual."

After packing some veggie bars, dried fruit, and juice for lunch, the girls put their bags into their bike baskets and pedaled off, Abby leading the way to the school and enjoying the cool morning. Mr. Sawqui, sitting on a new bench beside his new garden fence, waved and smiled warmly at them and other passersby. Abby peered at the Dependencies, down the street towards the Draggin' Dragon, and at the Flutter Garden, pleased to feel a part of it all. The Yuter was right; her days in Erden were usually perfect.

Today, the school bike rack was nearly full. Youths wheeled up on bicycles built for one, two, even three, and walked into the yard, hailing friends. Teens climbed out of all sizes of cars, some parents giving them final hugs and others calling out to them about forgotten items. It all looked and felt so normal, even familiar. Abby had to remind herself she wasn't at the first day of middle school in Surely.

Dali had explained that this school was for years six through ten. When the students graduated, their mandatory education was complete. Thereafter came the Citizenship Service Year, followed by university or technical training, a craft apprenticeship, or a job, as each individual was inclined. After their Service Year, many graduates got a job for another year or two – getting a feel for the real world, they often called it – before continuing their higher education. Dali had already known what she wanted to do, though, so she had taken a year of professions training right after her Service Year.

It didn't sound like the Erdeans' Citizenship Service Year had any equivalent in Abby's time. It sounded obligatory, maybe like jury duty or military service...giving something back for the birthright of being a citizen. But more like the Peace Corps: paid enough to live on, people were helping, not fighting. Some graduates found their calling in their Service Year, Dali noted, because the administrators did their best to match up the teens with work they could handle and enjoy. She noted that even those who were disabled were included. Dali also mentioned that – as the Bahá'í teachings encourage people to work together in or-der to get to know one another – Service helped young people get to know prospective mates well.

Now there was a striking thought. Maybe this Service Year wasn't a total drag. Maybe it was an interesting time with other grads. And if more teens back in Abby's time did service together, how might that benefit their futures? Matched up with enjoyable work. Would that help them choose good careers? And maybe get rid of the "can't get a job without experience, can't get experience without a job" issue she had heard people gripe about? Or getting to know possible spouses not just from best-behavior dates but from working together, where you could really see someone's attitudes, ethics, how they handled stress. Could that lead to better marriages? Living away from home, perhaps even traveling to distant places, wouldn't that show them new perspectives, help them be better world citizens? And getting practice managing their own lives. Surely they'd then feel more confident about going out on their own. Plus, wouldn't knowing they had been of service help their self-esteem? Abby tried to picture how she would feel if she...

∞   ∞   ∞   ∞   ∞   ∞   ∞   ∞

... stands at a large arcade game labeled YES YES YOS *... Jenn, Ricky, Penny, Jon, Melissa, Barb, Angie watch her play ...on the playfield, a holographic icon looks like her ... stands in an empty pen ... a sign on the backdrop:* Assignment – Bestmontrejo *... her hands flash over the controls ... the icon mucks out the pen ... forks in fresh hay ... fills the food and water troughs ... on the backdrop, points accumulate ... smil-ing, she finishes that level of the game ... a chime rings ... 3D words* Sense of Accomplishment *jump out from the backdrop ... she notices a*

big splinter sticking out from the pen door ... could hurt a person or animal ... wills her icon to carefully extract the splinter, reach into its pocket, pull out a sanding sponge, sand the area smooth ... the chime signals another surge in points and the 3D words Loving Care ... **ZZP** *... in the playfield watching several horses and their trainers ... yearns to be an apprentice ... chime, more points, words* Career Choice *over her head ... decides which pair she'd like to work with ... not the handsomest horse, not the most accomplished trainer, but the best sense of rapport ... chime rings, words* Life Partner Choice ... **ZZP** *... uses her stick and string to guide a horse over obstacles ... bells and points and words like* Good Practice *and* Self-Esteem *and* Worldview *and* Life Skills *and* Patience *and* Appreciation of Diversity *and* Confidence ... *ends the game with a flourish ... bell suddenly peals ... fireworks rise up from the backdrop ...* 4th of Top 5 Players *... Jenn squeals in delight ... Melissa hugs Abby ... everyone in the room applauds and cheers for her ... oh yes, yes! ...*

∞　∞　∞　∞　∞　∞　∞　∞

As she and Dali reached the front doors of the school, Abby noticed a new, nicely-done, handcrafted sign mounted over the entryway. She could not read it, though, as it was in UL. Dali handed her the WaerY and whispered, "You can use my WaerY to capture the image, as you did at the garden, then ask for a translation of it into Old American." Abby did so, and soon heard the quiet translation in her AerY as she gazed up at the carved and painted wooden sign.

> **Regard man as a mine rich in gems of inestimable value. Education can, alone, cause it to reveal its treasures, and enable mankind to benefit therefrom.**
> **Bahá'u'lláh**
> *Gleanings from the Writings of Bahá'u'lláh, page 259*

That was quite a school motto. And a suitable one. The losers back in Surely might – probably would – disagree, but she thought it was cool to discover her "gems."

Dali registered herself and Abby in the office. She had explained Abby's situation to Petra, who would bring a WaerY so that she could understand Abby. Dali hugged Abby and said she had to go work, but looked forward to hearing all about Abby's experience that evening. Abby hugged Dali back, thanked her, and sat down to wait for Petra.

Shortly afterwards, a very pretty girl with short, wavy black hair, medium-brown skin, and big brown eyes approached Abby, introduced herself, and invited her to come to the cafeteria. They walked down the main hallway to its end, went down the stairs, and turned left.

Petra seemed as nice as everyone else in this world. Surprisingly, she wore dozens of strands of tiny, variously-colored beads around her neck, wrists, and even fingers. Abby hadn't seen much jewelry in Erden. The uniform – brown shorts and a mottled knit shirt with "Insight Upper" stitched around the collar – looked comfortable yet stylish. Short socks, walking shoes, and a maroon book bag completed her outfit.

Walking to the cafeteria, Abby dared ask a silent question.

—Yuter, please, can I ask you something that Petra won't hear?—

—Of course. What is it?—

—All her beads...um...— Abby paused to formulate her thought clearly. —No one else wears much jewelry at all. In the Writings, what is the rule...uh, guidance on that, please?—

—Interesting question. Quoting: 'Should a man wish to adorn himself with the ornaments of the earth, to wear its apparels, or partake of the benefits it can bestow, no harm can befall him, if he alloweth nothing whatever to intervene between him and God, for God hath ordained every good thing, whether created in the heavens or in the earth, for such of His servants as truly believe in Him.' End quote. From *Gleanings from the Writings of Bahá'u'lláh*, page 276.—

More food for thought. Deck yourself out as much as you wanted, as long as it didn't come between you and God. Of course, if you were off track, wouldn't you be the last to know? So maybe it was better to stay away from too much...*stuff*. Was that why the poor could have, or build, God's Kingdom on earth? They had fewer distractions?[121]

This school cafeteria was much nicer than hers in Surely. A homey wood floor held the inviting wooden tables and chairs. Full-length windows along one side let in soft light through student artwork: rainbow-generating crystals and colored-glass mosaics. Food stations offered various foods and drinks that students and staff purchased by pausing with their selections in front of an ALLY. Abby surmised that the ALLY photographed, or in some other way identified, the individuals and their purchases for later billing. Everyone ate at the tables inside, or outside on a patio with flowering vines trellised overhead. Everything was clean and attractive, and the students were very pleasant and mature.

Unlike Abby, Petra hadn't had breakfast at home. She chose some fruit and led Abby to a vacant table near a corner full of potted plants.

"Having something light helps learning, doesn't it?" Petra opined. "I would normally sit with friends," she explained, "but this gives me a chance to get to know you a little bit before the first class starts."

She glanced to see if Abby wanted to say anything, then sat down facing the window. Abby sat next to Petra at the round table so that she could see the tall windows framing the patio and early-morning grass and dew. In one section of the grounds, rows of plants formed a garden. Several students worked among the rows; others seemed to be talking with the workers and each other. Abby challenged herself to guess what was going on by reading their body language, and decided they were working for fun, much like the people at Service.

"The first class is testing," Petra said, "at eight, with Mr. Wells."

"A test on the first day?"

Petra looked at her, shook her head, and tried again.

"The first class we're going to is Testing Lab at eight o'clock."

"Oh! I never heard of Testing Lab. What is it?"

"We test different materials, and study ourselves and spiritual qualities, to learn about strengths and breaking points."

"Wow, that's different."

"It is very interesting and very useful. Then we'll have Courtesy, Beautification and, lastly, Care of Animals."

"Care of Animals? Really?"

"Yes. The Master said, 'Train your children from their earliest days to be infinitely tender and loving to animals. If an animal be sick, let the children try to heal it, if it be hungry, let them feed it, if thirsty, let them quench its thirst, if weary, let them see that it rests.'[122]

"We start in the earliest grades just learning about different animals, watching them, grooming them, examining them, feeding them what the teacher tells us to. Later, we learn animal nutrition, healing injuries, and so on. And the upper grades learn about animal behavior, training, breeding, population control, native habitats, and so on."

This was taught in school? No wonder Farrah and Myra were so fantastic. They'd had lifelong animal-training preparation!

"That's it? No science, history, social studies?"

Petra touched her WaerY, listened to it a moment, smiled, and said, "Those topics are all included in the subjects we study. We cover them all while we're studying our life skills."

Petra finished her grain bar and juice, cleaned it up, and escorted Abby up stairs and through hallways into a large room that did indeed look like a laboratory. The students all swiped their WaerYs or palms in front of a scanner next to the door as they went in.

"Yuter, please explain the use of the scanner."

"It is a remote 'eye' of the school's ALLY for tracking attendance and locating people when they're in rooms that are being shielded from complex electronic signals to avoid upsetting signal-sensitive classroom animals or ruining delicate laboratory experiments."

"I see," Abby said, then switched to silent mode. —Don't students get each other to register for them, then skip school?—

—As Rykeir and Kreshi explained to you, it is quite difficult to use a Yuter to cheat. Also, students rarely want to skip school, and then only for personal emergencies, which are excused.—

—Sure is different. Thank you.—

Testing supplies sprouted from every flat surface of the classroom. Each lab table boasted machines, meters, hand tools, and several ALLY screens. Shelves overflowed with metal pipes, tree branches, hard lava, marble, glass, cloth, and more.

Swirling bands of colored paint embossed with intricate characters decorated the wall next to the door. Abby didn't have a WaerY to point at it, but asked her AerY about it anyway.

"One moment, please; I will ask Petra."

Abby saw Petra look at the wall, point her WaerY at it, then look back at Abby and smile. Bonega! More cooperativeness!

"Abby, this is student artwork incorporating calligraphy of a quote from the Bahá'í Writings regarding education, rendered in the original language. It translates as, quoting: 'The Prophets and Messengers of God have been sent down for the sole purpose of guiding mankind to the straight Path of Truth. The purpose underlying Their revelation hath been to educate all men, that they may, at the hour of death, ascend, in the utmost purity and sanctity and with absolute detachment, to the throne of the Most High.' End quote. From *Gleanings from the Writings of Bahá'u'lláh*, page 156 and 157."

Abby and Petra chose two of the tall wooden stools waiting at the lab tables. When the bell sounded – a melodious harmony instead of the jarring shriek Abby was used to – the blond-goateed teacher gave his name, Mr. Wells, and welcomed them all to the first day of class.

"We have a guest with us today, a cousin of Petra's, is that right?" Petra nodded and introduced Abby to the other students, who all welcomed her in various ways.

"Thank you. Now, the purpose of this class is to discover strength as well as weakness," the middle-aged, coppery-skinned, intense man said, pausing to let his words sink in. He wore a school shirt like all the students, with woven slacks. "Without using any Yuters, who can tell me something about the spiritual relevance of strength?"

After a pause, a student said, "Didn't the Guardian say something about the Faith getting stronger the more blows it received?"

"Good for you. One merit," Mr. Wells said. A shimmering spark launched from the wire frame of his ALLY screen. As it reached the boy, it broke into a shower of shining droplets that cascaded over his head and shoulders. The room smelled like spring air after a rain. One note sounded, clear and confident. A few students clapped. All smiled.

Mr. Wells touched his ALLY screen, and colorful words appeared on a blank section of the left-hand wall. Abby glanced at Petra, who helpfully pointed her WaerY at the words. Abby willed her Yuter to connect with Petra's, and immediately heard a quiet translation.

> Despite the blows leveled at its nascent strength, whether by the wielders of temporal and spiritual authority from without, or by black-hearted foes from within, the Faith of Bahá'u'lláh had, far from breaking or bending, gone from strength to strength, from victory to victory. Indeed its history, if read aright, may be said to resolve itself into a series of pulsations, of alternating crises and triumphs, leading it ever nearer to its divinely appointed destiny.
>
> Shoghi Effendi
> *God Passes By*, page 409

"This pattern has been repeated throughout Bahá'í – indeed, throughout every religion's – history," the teacher noted. "Anyone else?"

"Tests increase our personal abilities," a very tall, thin girl offered.

"Yes, one merit, good job," Mr. Wells responded warmly. A bright green spark, with a sound like a little glass bell, showered its new-mown grass scent over the girl. She shivered and grinned, as more bright words appeared on the wall. Again, the Yuter translated.

> **O Son Of Man!**
> The true lover yearneth for tribulation even as doth the rebel for forgiveness and the sinful for mercy.
> **O Son Of Man!**
> If adversity befall thee not in My path, how canst thou walk in the ways of them that are content with My pleasure? If trials afflict thee not in thy longing to meet Me, how wilt thou attain the light in thy love for My beauty?
>
> Bahá'u'lláh
> *The Hidden Words*, Arabic #49 & #50

—Yuter, please, what do the sparks feel like?—

—As with the scent, the feel of them changes according to the desires of the student. Gregory doesn't mind me telling you that his spark felt like a quick splash in a summer lake.—

"For those who wish to do independent reading on this concept," Mr. Wells said, "I suggest *Fire and Gold*, originally compiled by Brian Kurzius, and added to through the centuries.

"Now, as with our spirits and bodies, it's also practical to learn how to test the capabilities of materials." He waved at the shelved supplies. "We'll be exploring all of these.

"Let's start, though, by building up our bodies a little. This month, we'll do some yoga. Next month, we'll practice tai chi. Later on, we'll explore dance, as well as some acrobatics if any of you are so inclined."

After a brief warm-up, Mr. Wells said that each student should go get a small floor mat, put it in a convenient empty space, remove their shoes, and stand on one end of the mat. He then willed the ALLY to play quiet music, invited everyone to begin some gentle stretching, and demonstrated several standing and sitting poses they could try.

"Just explore," he encouraged. "Do not force anything, especially any of these that you have never done before. Yoga builds flexibility, strength, and focus. But slowly, gradually. Kam, kam, rúz bih rúz."

In the quiet moments of movement that ensued, Abby silently asked the AerY to briefly explain the last thing Mr. Wells had said.

—It translates from Persian, poetically, as _little by little, day by day_. A well-known and well-loved counsel of the Master's.—[123]

"It is my belief that this life is all about progress," the instructor gently began again. "Wherever you are now with your physical abilities, let's call that 'one.' Your 'one' will most likely not look like anybody else's 'one.' That's all right. Over the course of this class, let's see how many bits you can advance beyond your personal 'one.' You will be grading your own progress, and I will help you assign numbers to that progress. Careful, Radiance, nice and easy there."

Seated beside Petra, Abby glanced up and saw one standing girl almost tip over. Radiance, a rather stockier girl than the other students, was trying to touch her toes straight-legged. Probably not all that easy to do for someone who had short, thick bones and muscles. Abby realized, though, that she had not seen any obese people in Erden.

Abby herself was struggling to keep the backs of her knees on the mat while reaching for her toes; but she could only do one or the other, not both at the same time. The Erdeans were so fit! Petra was about to touch her nose to her knees, her legs flat against the mat. One boy was trying out his sideways splits on the mat. Some other students looked as if they'd been doing these things for years and were moving on to fancy lotus-style sitting, interesting arm-bends, back-bends, side-bends.

"Excellent, all of you, just excellent," Mr. Wells enthused, walking among them. He seemed to be making a photo database with his WaerY, pointing it towards different students. "It will help your practice if you remember that yoga was originally Hindu-related. Keeping its religious, spiritual basis in mind will help you relax into poses; peace of mind and calm focus help your poses unfold.

"As you're ready, then, cool down with a few last stretches, and put your mats away, please."

Abby and Petra were among the first to finish and return to their seats. Petra pointed her WaerY at a wall-list that was slowly coming into view from the top down.

The Practice of Yoga — Some Applications & Careers

- Care of the very young & the very old
- Hands-on treatment of animals
- Edifice cleaning & repair, especially in narrow spaces, overhead, & underneath things
- Machinery & wreckless repair & maintenance
- Outdoor endeavors, especially in caves & over rocks
- Gymnastic & acrobatic performances
- Leading activities in venues such as therapy centers, ocean-going vessels, gymnasia, & games foodles

---

Abby was astonished as she listened to her AerY. The uses of yoga were presented not only as hobbies or volunteer services but as actual job opportunities. That latest one even sounded like being paid to lead activities in the large-group back room at the Draggin' Dragon!

The list continued to build until all the students had finished stretching; then it added a Key so that they could yuter a comprehensive and personalized list on their own. As the last of the students reached their stools, Mr. Wells continued with the Testing lesson.

"Now let us take a look at a simple material: paper. You have a pile of ordinary paper at each place. Who can tell me some ways to test the qualities of paper?"

Students suggested tearing, burning, folding, crumpling, weighing down, wetting, even chewing...all of which Mr. Wells added to a new wall-list. He then pointed out which machines could test the attributes of paper in different ways, and said that the ALLY screen next to each machine would instruct them. He asked everyone to cooperate in twos or threes, and warned them to be especially cautious with the fire-tester and to close its doors before turning on the flames.

The students sorted themselves around the machines, commenting, testing, encouraging, observing. It was the most interesting class Abby had ever had. It was very scientific. After testing pieces of paper in different ways, Abby learned that paper was very strong in some ways and very weak in others. One sheet held a china teacup full of water when it was dry, but disintegrated under the weight of a marble when wet. She and Petra also began to wonder about the interaction of paper and ink.

Would writing in ink add molecular strength, or would it just wet and weaken the paper?

"Of course," Petra said, "we could take this as an analogy for a spiritual level of interaction."

"Come again?"

"The last Arabic Hidden Word. 'Write all that We have revealed unto thee with the ink of light upon the tablet of thy spirit. Should this not be in thy power, then make thine ink of the essence of thy heart. If this thou canst not do, then write with that crimson ink that hath been shed in My path.'[124] Spiritual ink would give a spiritual surface a lot of spiritual strength."

Abby thought that what Petra had quoted was very beautiful. With a little meditating, she might actually be able to figure this parable out.

After abundant time for personal experimentation, Mr. Wells showed the class some creative ways to use paper: pencils, pens, beads, and bows made with recycled paper; a complex paper airplane; intricate pop-up, sliding, and unfolding books; a child's paper-and-resin chair; and finally, an antique hologram of a house made of phone books, complete with paper-based furniture, countertops, and backyard skateboard ramp.[125]

So engrossed was Abby that she was surprised when another bell-tone signaled the end of class. Mr. Wells pointed to a stack of half-reams of used letter-size paper, each tied with twine.

"If you would like an extra challenge, please take a packet of paper. Without consulting a Yuter, use it to build something that will hold you at least twenty centimeters off the floor for ten seconds. If you can do so without adding anything, like glue or tape, even better. Experiment individually, share your results with each other, consult on which are the best solutions, and choose a spokesperson to share with the class in two weeks. And be sure to reuse or recycle it all after we're done."

Half the class, including Petra, took packets. "Fold them into little shapes," she said. "A mound of bricks or pyramids, that should work."

"How come only half of the kids took the homework? Or is it extra-credit work?" Abby asked as she and Petra left the classroom.

Petra looked confused for a moment, blinked slowly, then replied, "Neither, really. It's just a free challenge, for those of us with time and interest. Besides being fun to figure out, extracurricular challenges help us try new things, think in new ways, even give us hints about what we might enjoy doing as a profession. Like, the students most drawn to this one might develop an interest in construction or architecture or civil engineering or something."

Abby followed Petra down the corridor, trying to figure out why the paper activity seemed so unusual. As they reached the next classroom, she realized it had been offered pressure-free and had been welcomed in the same way. Because of everybody's orientation towards learning, there didn't need to be pressure to offer or to try things. So *very* different from things back in 2007, when thinking seemed like too much work and learning was usually trumped by entertainment.

The next class was Courtesy. Abby had figured this would be a very dull class, but the students seemed as eager and willing to come to this one as they had to Testing Lab.

This instructor was a brightly smiling middle-aged woman, which Abby reminded herself could still mean she was in her seventies. She greeted most of the dozen students by first or last name. Abby heard them warmly greet her in return as *IN-strew* or *IN-strew jenn-tee-LAH-yo*. The AerY explained that it meant something akin to *Ms. Courtesy Teacher* and added that her actual name was Ms. Reed.[126]

"Please bring your chairs into a circle," invited the freckled teacher with long honey-colored dreadlocks. The students did so, each sliding their bag on the rack under their chair. Abby felt no inclination to speak, but prepared to watch and listen.

The room was very bare, with a simple floor and only a few posters and notices on the walls. On the ceiling, however, was painted a large green tree with golden fruit. There was a word painted in every fruit, arranged into a flowing sentence. Petra lifted her WaerY; Abby admired the awe-inspiring artwork as she listened to her AerY.

"Quoting: 'The learned of the day must direct the people to acquire those branches of knowledge which are of use, that both the learned themselves and the generality of mankind may derive benefits therefrom. Such academic pursuits as begin and end in words alone have never been and will never be of any worth.' End quote. From *Tablets of Bahá'u'lláh Revealed after the Kitáb-i-Aqdas*, page 169."

"Welcome to Courtesy," Ms. Reed said when all the students were settled in a circle. "You have been well-prepared for this day, I expect. Let's outline for our guest, Abby, how your past education has prepared you to learn about courtesy, the Prince of Virtues."[127]

A student raised her hand and was recognized. She said the progression of subjects during her earlier years – starting with Basic Manners, progressing through Sharing, Social Needs, and Virtues – the ongoing guidance of her family and, in fact, the influence of everybody in her town had prepared her to focus this year on Courtesy.

"Ah, beautifully expounded," Ms. Reed beamed. "One merit." The student's spark dissolved into singing birds and the scent of ocean.

—Yuter, please, what's with all these merits?—

—In *The Advent of Divine Justice*, page 83, Shoghi Effendi quotes Bahá'u'lláh as saying, quoting: 'Vie ye with each other in the service of God and of His Cause.' End quote. Students can practice for this by doing well in school; so every student tries their best to do a good job. One way students can gain merits is to answer thoughtful questions in class. Merits are redeemed at the end of the term.—

They *rewarded* students for school? Bonega! This was definitely heaven on earth. But, a little voice in her head piped up, if they did not like school, no amount of money or anything else could bribe them into changing their bad feelings. Hmmm, was this little voice the Divine bit that Kreshi had said we all have inside? *Double* bonega!

"Let us start by discussing two things," Ms. Reed went on. "First, situations in which you feel you'd like help being more courteous."

The ALLY recorded and displayed all the students' contributions. There were a good many, ranging from having to deliver bad news to someone, to standing up for their rights, to losing their patience. When the suggestions ceased, Ms. Reed then asked for "situations in which you wish others had been more courteous."

At first, Abby thought this might become a gripe-session on how rude others were. Certainly it would have if you'd asked that question of her 21st-century schoolmates. But these students were much more reserved, removing all names or blame; and many even apologized before contributing their suggestion.

It was interesting, though, how many of them had been hurt by one thoughtless comment, or felt unheard when sharing something deep. It caused Abby to reflect on what hurt others; and even with the tremendous time gap, she saw that she was not so different from these model human beings. They, like she, struggled to be the best they could be, despite slights or missteps from their friends and families.

"This is an excellent opportunity to ponder the many sufferings of the Manifestations of God," Ms. Reed said. "Let's specifically consider Bahá'u'lláh, He being the one we know the most about. He Who saw events to come. Who knew His followers' desires before they did. Who was able to reveal superb verses faster than His secretaries could write them down. He was hurt bodily, mentally, and spiritually by attacks of all kinds from all sides. Even from members of His own family, who tried more than once to kill Him. Yet He never wavered for an instant, never changed regardless of His comforts or lack thereof. This is that Being Who urged us to be unified, to strive, to achieve great spiritual victories over ourselves. His degree of sensitivity was so high that we will never fully understand it. Just think how He was hurt by even the slightest whisper of discord and how He rejoiced in even the tiniest rudiments of unity and love.

"I'm so pleased with the curriculum you have just helped me form. Thank you. We will cover courtesy when yutering, when writing, when speaking to individuals or in front of groups, on Yuter shows, when delivering bad news, when stressed, and more…with real-life practice."

Home Run #2: students wrote the curriculum here. And it seemed they'd be writing letters, giving speeches, even going on TV to practice it. Amazing. Abby could have supplied them with endless examples of bad interchanges from her time. Unfortunately, she'd have had to bring some people – like Mother…ugh, quick, think of something else – here to show the class how bad it got. Erdeans probably wouldn't believe her if they didn't see it for themselves. And the people she brought would likely argue the entire time and never take advantage of what Erden had to offer them. It took an open mind, she realized, to benefit from even the best instruction.

"You can lead a horse to wonders, but you cannot make it think," she improvised in a whisper, ducking her head so her hair hid a smile.

Ms. Reed had them pair off and role-play the first assignment, being sure to discuss any feelings of anger or other difficult emotions that were relevant to the situation.

"Emotions are markers pointing to something that needs your attention," she explained. "They can be like well-trained horses that carry you to new and useful places, which your mind and heart can explore together. Resist the temptation to let your emotions drag your mind away like wild horses on a rampage. Let's work together to train your horses to partner you well."

Abby loved that analogy, and mentally replayed the Animal Show highlights. She wondered if Ms. Reed had seen the same show and had been as elevated by it as Abby was.

One pair of students asked for full-class consultation. They then vividly re-enacted the occasion when the girl's younger brother had dropped a chair leg on her toe. She had yelled at him most ungraciously. The girl said that she was still angry about it, because she had lost a toenail and was still limping and nursing the damaged nail bed. She was completely at a loss about how to be courteous in this instance. Her role-play partner said that he, too, had no useful ideas.

Ms. Reed invited the entire class to brainstorm. Silence fell in the room, and Abby saw a number of people frowning, as if vicariously reliving the situation. She felt comfortable just waiting and, while waiting, remembered the similar quiet scene on *Consultation Today*.

"Yell 'ouch' and get away from him? So you can calm down?" a boy finally suggested. "Or if you're too hurt to move, then get him to go away? Maybe by having him go get a medi-cloth or something?"

"Call an adult to handle him as you tend to your toe?" a girl added.

"Use the time at the clinic to calm down?" said another.

A merit rewarded every thoughtful contribution. But apparently the students were now so engaged in learning that they didn't want overly dramatic distractions, because the merit sparks had become very quiet and tame.

Finally, the class agreed that unless the brother meant it, which the sister assured them that he didn't – it was an accident; he was only five, and a good kid – the best thing to do was deal with the injury, try really hard not to blow up at the kid, perhaps by mentally reciting a short and well-loved prayer or saying, and deal with him only after the heat of the hurt and anger was gone.

Abby remembered how Dali had left her with calming music in order to defuse what Abby now saw was her own willingness to argue. It was true, it took two people to fight. If one left, the upset person might shout at the air, pace and gesticulate, even punch a pillow or something (but hopefully not break any body parts or possessions). If the person was alone, though, there could be no confrontation.

"Now, lest we think that we always need to be polite to everybody at all times, let me offer a couple of exceptions for your consideration.

"One is when we encounter someone who's truly malevolent against other people. Would someone like to read this quote?"

A boy who had not made any suggestions thus far raised his hand, received a nod, and read the quotation that appeared on the wall.

> Strive ye then with all your heart to treat compassionately all humankind – except for those who have some selfish, private motive, or some disease of the soul. Kindness cannot be shown the tyrant, the deceiver, or the thief, because, far from awakening them to the error of their ways, it maketh them to continue in their perversity as before. No matter how much kindliness ye may expend upon the liar, he will but lie the more, for he believeth you to be deceived, while ye understand him but too well, and only remain silent out of your extreme compassion.
>
> 'Abdu'l-Bahá
> *Selections from the Writings of 'Abdu'l-Bahá*, page 158

"Thank you, Malik. Reverent and flawless reading. One merit. The other situation, for similar reasons, is when you are being treated unjustly. Please silently read this story told by the Guardian's wife about the time that the Master, a Pasha who was his guest, and Shoghi Effendi arrived in Ramleh in a rented coach from Alexandria."

The linked Yuters translated the words that appeared on the wall.

> [When] the Master asked the strapping big coachman how much He owed him the man asked an exorbitant price; 'Abdu'l-Bahá refused to pay it, the man insisted and became abusive to such an extent that he grasped the Master by the sash around His waist and pulled Him roughly back and forth, insisting on this price. Shoghi Effendi said this scene in front of the distinguished guest embarrassed him terribly. He was too small to do anything himself to help the Master and felt horrified and humiliated. No so 'Abdu'l-Bahá, Who remained perfectly calm and refused to give in. When the man finally released his hold the Master paid him exactly what He owed him, told him his conduct had forfeited the good tip He had planned to give him, and walked off followed by Shoghi Effendi and the Pasha! There is no doubt that such things left a lifelong imprint on the Guardian's character, who never allowed himself to be browbeaten or cheated, no matter whether or not this embarrassed or inconvenienced him, and those who were working for him.
>
> Rúhíyyih Rabbaní
> *The Priceless Pearl*, page 23

The pleasant bell chimed shortly after.

"Your homework will be to consider how you might use this information in a situation you've encountered or could encounter. There is no minimum or maximum length; I'll be looking for depth of analysis. Dictated or filmed reports are fine. Due next class."

Everybody tidied up, put the chairs back, and exited the room with polite goodbyes to Ms. Reed.

Abby could see how useful it would be to think about difficult situations ahead of time and practice for them. No wonder everyone she'd met in Erden was so polite and paid such close attention to everything she said. They thought it was important enough to put it in the school curriculum. And not simply in a debate or media class. Courtesy class would still include those skills, but would emphasize how well it was done, who was uplifted, whose hearts were touched, and whose honor was upheld in the process.

Chapter 26: Lunch

Two classes down for today; two to go. Abby had to say that they were nothing like her classes back home. *Back home*...she had a wave of homesickness stronger than any before. She could nearly see Jenn's dear face in front of her, leaning in, singing...what was she singing? Oh my, it was "Itsy Bitsy Spider"...Abby and Jenn used to make climbing spiders by pairing their hands. Abby felt tears spring to her eyes; and as she blinked them away, the flashback faded. She eyed the various lunch choices: unegg rolls, basil-seasoned green beans, salad with fresh-made dressings, and veggies in brown rice. Abby chose beans, veggie-rice, and orange-wedge water, and joined Petra at a table near a corner from which a small waterfall cascaded into a black basin. Lines of colorful light played on the bubbly liquid. Abby asked the AerY about it. After a moment of silence, Petra looked at her.

"The light is creating words on the water, one sentence at a time," she explained. "The entire quote is: 'Although to acquire the sciences and arts is the greatest glory of mankind, this is so only on condition that man's river floweth into the mighty Sea, and draweth from God's ancient source His inspiration. When this cometh to pass, then every teacher is as a shoreless ocean, every pupil a prodigal fountain of knowledge. If, then, the pursuit of knowledge leadeth to the beauty of Him Who is the object of all knowledge, how excellent that goal; but if not, a mere drop will perhaps shut a man off from flooding grace, for with learning cometh arrogance and pride, and it bringeth on error and indifference to God.'"[128]

"Wow, that's not only beautiful, it's really deep: make sure your learning helps you turn towards God, or it might make you vain and not care about God."

"I agree," Petra smiled. "It...uh, Abby? What's the matter?"

Abby's head was suddenly pounding. She grimaced and squeezed her temples between her hands, trying to hold in the alarming pain. The room spun...her stomach lurched...she was spinning...everything was white. Then the room slowly righted and the headache settled into just a dull throb. Petra looked at her with great concern.

"I think I should take you to the nurse," Petra said. "Come on. Can you stand up?"

Abby didn't argue but allowed Petra to help move her chair, to sort her tray, and to guide her by the elbow down two hallways into a carpeted room containing bendable chairs surrounded by sliding curtains. A woman wearing a white school uniform greeted them.

"One of you not feeling quite right?" she asked.

"Hello, yes, my friend visiting here, Abby, she started looking kind of...not...um, she doesn't feel well," Petra fumbled.

Another attack seized Abby, worse than before. Her head felt as if it were coming apart...once more, she put her hands to her head to hold it together...the agony shot into her stomach and threatened to chase her lunch back up...her legs could not continue holding her...the nurse and Petra half-carried her to a chair and rolled her onto it, lowering it into a bed...their voices ran over each other in concern about whom to contact, where a clean emesis bowl was in case she threw up...she was moaning with the pain and crying with how awful she felt...voices wove around her, hands held her, as she was drowning in disorientation and pain...an urgent voice registered..."Abs, *Abs*, here, it'll be better, it's okay!"... someone was talking to the nurse about falling behind on the painkiller schedule...and slowly the pain got better, and Jenn's voice carried her through it.

But it couldn't be Jenn. Jenn was back in 2007. And Abby had two interesting new classes to go to this afternoon. She'd be all right...her agony was only a dull, thick throbbing now...her hand tried to press the worst spot but ran into something thick...someone pulled her arm down ...Jenn and the nurse spoke to her, saying that she would be fine, that she was already better...Jenn tenderly coated her lips with ointment on a little sponge.

No, it couldn't be Jenn...

It *was* Jenn. It was *Jenn*! In a hospital room. With a nurse looking from over Jenn's shoulder and smiling at Abby. And another nurse who was checking an IV in her arm.

Tears ran down Jenn's oh-so-beloved face. Abby struggled to keep open eyes that felt gritty and unused, blurry and also teary.

"What?" she whispered.

Jenn sobbed with joy and exclaimed, "Welcome back, Abs! Welcome back!"

Chapter 27: Return

Abby was lying in a hospital room when she woke up in Little Lily, groggy, in pain, very confused, and missing Dali and Erden from the instant Jenn told her what had happened.

Abby's head had smashed into the trees, and she had blacked out. Fortunately, the wrangler called 911 on his cell phone, then called the office girl and had her contact Vivian – still over at the street fair – who, needless to say, absolutely blew a gasket.

The arriving paramedics had packed a stretcher up the hill, painstakingly loaded the unconscious and bleeding Abby onto it, and carried her down to the ambulance. Her breathing and heartbeat hadn't stopped, and no bones were broken; but she had numerous scrapes and bruises, a deep and dirty cut on her abdomen, and a huge bump on her head that had bled a lot both externally and internally.

Now, a small hole in her skull marked where they'd removed blood pooling between her skull and brain, her abdomen sported three inches of stitches, and she'd had a bunch of drugs to control bleeding, reduce swelling, combat infections, and quell pain. The doctors predicted that she would come out of it in reasonably good shape.

Abby mused that she had actually died (to her old self) and gone to heaven (on earth), but she couldn't say so.

Gunsmoke had finally been retired from the dude string. There had been a couple of previous incidents, and his running away with Abby had been the last straw.

Abby had been in the hospital since late Friday morning, and it was now Monday afternoon. She had lost a day jumping to the Golden Age and gained a day returning. Days fell differently in different years, like how her birthday fell on a different day of the week each year.

An hour after Abby regained consciousness, Mother came in with red eyes, quite emotional, very unlike her usual self. She sat on the bed, pulled the covers too tight over Abby, and leaned close to her, wafting bad breath in her face. Abby tried to listen calmly as Mother expounded on how worried she'd been…looking, as usual, everywhere but into her daughter's eyes. How she'd considered suing the stable despite the releases she'd signed. How the vacation plans had been upset, not knowing how long Abby would be in a coma. How the fire came so close – with the smoke seeping into the building and making Abby and many other patients restless – that the hospital staff had even considered evacuating everyone. But the wind had shifted, so no one had had to be moved.

Abby knew she was supposed to lie there, obedient and quiet and, if she could muster it, sympathetic for the difficulties her coma had rained on her mother.

Abby wished she had a Yuter to explain mothers who were so self-absorbed that, as their daughter woke up from comas, they could only recite a long list of their own complaints. At least she had a few clues... thanks to her dear friends on the other side of seven centuries.

An orderly wheeled Abby from the hospital the next morning, Jenn carrying her sister's few belongings, Dad his usual quiet self but holding her hand, and Mother toting two vases full of flowers, fussing about how to get them back to the Holsworth home. Vivian finally wrapped the flower stems in a paper towel moistened with vase water, put them back in the emptied vases, and tucked them into the corners of the trunk, harrumphing the whole time.

Abby felt by turns affection, gratitude, and irritation toward her family members as she buckled into her seat.

The family drove back to Sofia's house, where all the Holsworths were waiting. Getting her worlds confused, which made her head hurt even worse, Abby wondered what the kids were doing home. School had started, right? She whispered her question to Jenn, who replied that Abby was a week off; school for the Holsworths kids would start next Monday. Abby hid her smile by looking out the window; she was not one week off, she was, like, thirty-five thousand weeks off.

That night in Sofia's home, sleep brought Abby repetitious, pain-induced nightmares of wild beasts and armed villains...

∞   ∞   ∞   ∞   ∞   ∞   ∞   ∞

... frantic hoofbeats, terrified neighs ... yaps, snarls, blood-curdling laughs ... in the moonless dark, huge hyenas with banefully glowing eyes chase, kill, devour desert horses ... **ZZP** *... in the tall cactus and rolling tumbleweed of the Old West, pistol-armed outlaws sporting dusty tan rawhide coats and heavy bandoleers ...* **ZZP** *... tattooed outlaw bikers sporting greasy black leather jackets and Viking helmets wield their spears as flamethrowers against children driving police cars ...*

∞   ∞   ∞   ∞   ∞   ∞   ∞   ∞

Each time a nightmare jarred Abby awake, she was comforted that Jenn was sleeping next to her trundle bed. And she was very glad the next day when Jon and Melissa popped up to her room for an impromptu "shut-in" picnic, unaware that Abby couldn't eat the food they brought.

Abby slowly reached out her arms for hugs from these heartwarming friends whom she valued and respected so much. Melissa seemed a little surprised, but quickly accepted Abby's hug. Then she sat down on the floor next to the low bed, and set on top of Abby's suitcase the three plates of food she had brought.

"Melissa, I want to say a few things." Abby spoke hesitantly. "And you can stay, Jon, if you want."

"Sure," Melissa said. She settled in against the wall next to Jon, her caramel-colored face showing interest mixed with patience. So strongly did she remind Abby of the wonderful blended Erdeans, that a longing to be back there pierced her heart. Reverse homesickness threatened to overwhelm her. She'd probably never again see dear Dali, Farrah, the HORSES! or precious Kreshi or Rykeir, go to wonderful Insight Upper or the Draggin' Dragon, find out what happened in Care of Animals or Beautification classes. She felt she was drowning in loss. She needed a positive thought to hold onto…like in *Hook*…a happy thought to make her fly…a happy thought…and a gentle song rose from beside her…

♫Is there any
Remover of Difficulties
save God?
Say: Praised be God!
He is God!
All are His servants,
and all abide
by His bidding!♫[129]

The song calmed Abby, steadied her, almost to the point where she could try to speak again. "Please sing another," she croaked through a throat so tight she could barely breathe. Melissa's voice rose again…

♫Thy name is my healing,
O my God,
and remembrance of Thee
is my remedy.
Nearness to Thee
is my hope,
and love for Thee
is my companion…♫

…and Jon's voice gently joined in…

♫Thy mercy to me
is my healing and my succor
in both this world
and the world to come.
Thou, verily, art
the All-Bountiful,
the All-Knowing,
the All-Wise.♫[130]

"All-Wise," murmured Abby, glad that the prayer was long enough for her to get a grip on herself. "Wisdom. Hope. Love." A soft sound of agreement rose from the friends next to her, then silence as Melissa and Jon waited. But Abby still wasn't quite ready to talk.

With a glance at Jon, Melissa picked up her plate and slowly nibbled at her food; Jon followed suit. Abby realized they were trying to give her more time without being obvious about waiting for her to speak. When Melissa gestured that she should join them in eating, though, Abby just touched her stomach and grimaced. Melissa nodded sympathetically. Their courteous patience revived more wrenching memories of Dali's solicitousness and dedicated problem-solving.

Abby needed a way to cope with being back in this time. Her sad, floundering spirit recalled the powerful portrait of 'Abdu'l-Bahá and his never-ending offer of love and support. He was still real, and he still touched her heart. She could hold onto that in any world. In all worlds.

Almost of its own accord, her hand reached out slowly to Melissa's, and found refuge and strength there. Strength...the Testing Lab...she herself was nearly breaking.

"That which doesn't break us makes us stronger."[131] Abby forced herself to take a deep breath. "Strength," she said. "Courage."

Melissa squeezed her hand, serenely supporting Abby's struggle.

"Did y'all think I'd died when I was...gone?" Abby was finally able to ask, turning onto her side to gaze beseechingly at the faces a foot above her own.

"We knew you weren't dead," Jon said, "but we wondered where your spirit was. There wasn't much help about comas on the web.[132] We found more stuff about people who die and come back than about the experiences of comatose people."

"Almost everyone has heard about near-death experiences: the tunnel, and light, being stopped, reviewing your life," Melissa added in her soft Southern accent.[133] "But most people coming out of comas just say it was dark, or they maybe heard faint voices."

"I was not dead or blanked out," Abby said softly but firmly. She wasn't sure of the reception she'd get. Was this Courtesy class material? Might as well just blurt it out. "I...I went to seven hundred years in the future and lived there for three days."

After quite a long pause, Melissa asked, "How was it?"

"Fantastic, perfect, funny, awesome..." Abby slowly turned her too-sensitive head and found a willing listener. "Oh, I saw it all, Melissa, everything in your Writings...the Most Great Peace, God's Kingdom on earth, Sia...um, His will being done here like it is in heaven, it's all there, it's *wonderful*, it's..."

Words failed her. She started to repeat herself. Again Melissa waited patiently. Abby squeezed her hand in gratitude, and Melissa squeezed cautiously but definitely back.

Abby lay back against her pillows, shifting carefully. She closed her eyes to better recall and describe what she could to Melissa, who would never see what she'd seen.

"They have the coolest tiny computers that do everything you can imagine, take pictures and remind you and translate things and look up stuff...you wouldn't happen to know any quotes about happiness off-hand, would you?"

Melissa frowned as she racked her brains. "All I can think of about happiness is one song," she replied, clearly embarrassed. She began to sing in a strained voice and, to Abby's confusion, a strange language...

♪To ko za ni ni na la ba wan ki.

Le li lan ga la ku ka na...♪

Melissa saw Abby's blank face and quickly hummed through to the last line in the foreign language, the happy beat causing her voice to be stronger and surer. Abby recognized the need to run through a familiar pattern, searching for a particular part...

♪Ti Yá Bahá'u'l-Abhá.

Rejoice, rejoice, for a new day has dawned.

The whole wide world is all one fold.

Rejoice, rejoice, for a new day has dawned.

The plan of God has now been told.

The promised One by the name of Bahá

Came to bring a new day.

Let us be happy. Let us say:

Yá Bahá'u'l-Abhá.

Say: Yá Bahá'u'l-Abhá.

Say: Yá Bahá'u'l-Abhá.♪[134]

Melissa looked so much like Dali, as her face relaxed and her voice grew confident, that Abby felt almost as if she were back in Erden.

"What does that mean?" she asked when Melissa had finished the happy song.

"Oh, the 'Yá Bahá'u'l-Abhá'?" Melissa said in her very unDali-ish southern accent, popping Abby's fantasy. "It means *O Glory of the All-Glorious*. Arabic, I think."

"Yes, of course," said Abby, "*YAW-beh-HAW-oh-lob-HAW*. Thank you." She contemplated her quilt and the blue blanket folded at the foot of the bed. It reminded her of Dali's magical blue picnic cloth. "Do you know where I can get ahold of quotes? I'll really miss them if I can't..."

"Sure," said Melissa. "There are books, websites, CDs, DVDs. Just let me know."

"And do you know how I can find the Bahá'ís in Surely? For when we get back there? They might have a Spiritual School."

"Spiritual School?" Melissa sat up straight. "Like Sunday School? Or a deepening? What was it like?"

"I only went once. It was a lady...an actress...a hologram...she told about the Master in America. It had everything in it. How he was, what he did, pictures of him...I heard his voice..." She clung to her memory, wanting to hold on to every bit.

"Wow! Well, I really doubt you'll run into a deepening...er, a school like that in Surely. Or *anywhere* on the planet right now," Melissa said. "They mainly study the Writings, discussion only."

"Do you have parties when someone declares? When they're fifteen or older?"

Melissa exhaled loudly. "Whoa, you *did* do it all, didn't you?"

"Oh, it was *soooo* much *fun!*" Abby exclaimed, winced, and gently pressed her bandaged head. Oops, she cautioned herself, shouldn't get so exuberant just yet. Dali and Rykeir and Kreshi would have a million wisecracks – Wize-cracks – and the Yuter would join them in teasing her. And they'd also fix her aching head right up, probably.

For now, she'd have to get well the Old-World way. Slowly.

"The technology was incredible, everywhere, everything worked so well...and the *horses!* Well, all the animals. Everything was so clean, so pretty, and everyone helped each other, really helped. They recycled, and cared for the earth and each other. And there was *unity*, and everyone was a mix of everything. Most people looked like you, Melissa, and I thought of you. I thought about how hard you have it now, trying to be spiritual and build that perfect world even as the old one is falling apart all around us."

Tears sprang to Melissa's eyes.

"Thanks, Abs, I appreciate it. More than you know."

"I might have a pretty good idea of how much you appreciate it. I started to read minds, like the Master did, you know..."

Melissa was astonished and let out a short laugh through her tears. "You probably know more than I do, girl. And I've been enrolled for almost ten years!"

"Oh? You have to enroll?"

"Finally, one thing *I* know about *my* Faith that *you* don't!" she teased.

"What do I need to do to enroll?"

"Ah!" she said, reaching into her purse, "I just saw a good answer to that in this preview book I received. It goes: 'You don't have to already know everything and be obeying all the principles and laws in order to become Bahá'í. Declaring your faith is the *beginning* of your glorious journey, not the end. When you believe that Bahá'u'lláh is indeed Who He says He is, find His Word resonating in your heart and soul, want to be part of His community and help put His unifying Plan into action, and are willing to learn about and follow His Teachings to the best of your ability, you already are Bahá'í.'[135]

"It's amazing but simple, Abby. And once you're enrolled, you'll go on learning about the history, fundamental verities, principles and laws, and whatever else you don't already know."

"Well, I already know some. About putting God first, and a unified world, and education," Abby enumerated, "and service being worship, and a universal language, and the daily prayers. I don't drink, do drugs, have any kind of sex, and I'll try never to backbite. And isn't there also something about fasting? Did I miss anything?"

Melissa chuckled. "Well, you won't have to Fast for a couple of years yet. There are several laws about burial and marriage that I trust you won't be needing to follow any time soon, either, thank goodness. Honestly, Abby, you already know more than a lot of people who realize they believe in Bahá'u'lláh and enroll. Just so you believe in your heart that He is God's Voice for today."

"Oh, I do! And I enroll exactly how?" Abby was proud of herself for remembering her original train of thought, and wondered how she would cope without the indispensable, magical Yuter. She'd probably have to make do with pen and paper. Primitive but effective.

"Here in the US, there's a card that you sign pledging your belief in Bahá'u'lláh and asking to be a member of His Faith. Someone checks with you to ensure you realize you're joining a religion – which you already know – and then sends your card to our National Center. They in turn make sure other believers near you know how to reach you, send you newsletters, invite you to Feast—"

"What's Feast? Do you have to pig out?"

"Excellent! Something else you don't know about yet. I'd love to hear how Feast in the future is. Here, it's generally held in someone's home. It's actually a spiritual business meeting of the local believers, ending in a little social time. The next one is coming up in about a week and a half. I doubt that you'll be well enough to go to that one; but they happen every nineteen days."

The three friends sat grinning at each other in the little room. But as the silence lengthened, Abby began to feel very tired and ill again. Her smile faded and her eyes closed.

"We'll let you sleep now," Jon said, standing up. He helped Melissa up, and she patted Abby's arm.

"Thanks so much for sharing that about your…adventure. I would love to hear more, if you ever feel like it again," Melissa said lovingly and longingly.

Abby responded sleepily, "I hope I can. You two are the only ones I know who'd understand."

From Abby's perspective on the bed, her untouched plate and Jon and Melissa's emptier ones came back into focus. While Melissa continued to remind Abby of Erden, she could not help noting that Melissa had nibbled on several kinds of processed meat, jello-fluff salad, white garlic bread, and other items that – even if they existed in Erden – surely no Erdean would care to eat.

"I thought Baha'is ate so healthy and all," she murmured.

"It's in the Writings, yes," Melissa said, looking a little guilty as she picked up the plates. "But like with so many things, we are working our way up to their guidance on that. One blessed day, humanity will eat – and act – as it should. In the meantime: kam, kam, rúz bih rúz."

"Oh yes," Abby murmured groggily, a tiny smile flitting across her lips, "little by little, day by day."

As she drifted off, Abby reflected yet again on how fortunate she was to have seen that faraway day.

Chapter 28: Phonecall

The doctor had ordered bed rest and soft foods, so Abby spent the next several days on the foldout couch in the Holsworths' family room, mostly watching TV. Mother brought Abby strained soups, fruit juices, mashed potatoes, fat-free yogurt, lean ground lamb, and other easy-to-digest meals. Vivian was not exactly affectionate, but did refrain from her usual stream of put-downs and criticism. Day by day, Abby began feeling a little better.

Sofia obligingly played all the movies Abby asked for, even though Abby drifted off frequently. This certainly wasn't how Abby had anticipated seeing them; and she began to feel especially strange watching Daniel Radcliffe, knowing what he would do after the filming of the fourth *HP* movie.

Jenn frequently sat with Abby and filled her in on happenings while she was "away." The fire had come so very close to town, making Jenn very anxious, before it was finally brought under control. Jenn had lived at Abby's bedside, talking and singing, which seemed to rouse Abby at times. Sometimes in her own sleep, Jenn reported, she dreamt that she saw Abby far away, far ahead, laughing.

Jenn squeezed Abby's leg gently and said she that was really, really glad Abby was back. Abby couldn't truthfully answer that she also was glad to be back, but she did earnestly say she was very glad to see Jenn again and hoped her big sister wouldn't worry now.

Abby also sent a message to Melissa, through Jon, asking for some Bahá'í reading material before the Wizes left Little Lily. So Tuesday night after dinner, when Melissa came over, Abby begged Mother to let her sit in the back yard with the couple. Mother acquiesced, for once, after Jon and Melissa pledged that they would not allow any harm to come to Abby.

Melissa asked for more details from the future. Abby told her about much of it, especially all the lessons Dali had said they'd learned from earlier times. Abby was pleased to remember to ask Melissa how she coped, knowing it was going to get even worse before it got better.

Melissa mulled it over in the peaceful evening air, waving absently at gnats while Jon relit a citronella candle that had sputtered out. Mosquitoes loved Abby, and the candles helped shield her from them.

"Well, I don't think much about how hard it is, I guess," Melissa drawled. "It's not like I have a choice how the world around me is. But when you put it like that, it's sure true about having a rough time of it. At least we have a lot of Writings laying out what we should be doing, and telling us what the world of the future is going to be like, and on the twin processes of decay and building. And that sure is way more than the early Bahá'ís had," she mused, always finding the bright side. "They had to hand-copy every new prayer or letter, and write up their own notes from talks and their pilgrimages. There were not very many of Bahá'u'lláh's own Writings in English, either, at least until Shoghi Effendi translated more.

"But it is true that it'd be so much easier if everyone were following spiritual principles," she gently acknowledged Abby's original concern.

"You mean if the world were Bahá'í," Jon said.

"Well, maybe," Melissa answered hesitantly. "But only because the Faith is the most recent religion. Actually, I wasn't thinking that small. The essence of all the religions is the same; I was reared to believe that really and deeply. The Master wrote a wonderful Tablet to a Christian lady in which He says His dearest wish is that the whole world would really become Christian, truly follow Jesus Christ's teachings. Because, you know, all the Prophets from God have taught us the same kinds of things."[136]

"If all the religions are really the same, then why send a new one?"

"What a good question, Abby," Melissa said warmly. "The *essence* of all religions is the same. They all teach about the Golden Rule and about God, no matter what Name they call God. They all teach praying or meditating, doing good deeds, thinking right thoughts, helpfulness and service, laws, and guidance.[137] But there are some differences, too, because of what people in different places and times could handle. Like, there is no discussion of electricity and cars in the Bible, because they would not exist till way later. But they are in the Bahá'í Writings, which even mentioned the coming of the internet!"[138]

Melissa checked on Abby for signs of fatigue versus interest. Abby nodded; she certainly wanted to hear more.

"Now we need to sort out big, complicated things that we've never faced before. The widening gap between people who have money and education and privileges and those who don't. Or environmental chaos, runaway technology, divisive prejudice, terrorism, horrible wars with nuclear bombs..." She wrinkled her nose, reluctant to go on with the list. "We need God to help us, to tell us how to solve such new, scary problems."

"Makes sense." Abby pondered what it really meant for people. "So we can learn what God wants us to do nowadays through His most recent Manifestation." She was willing, absolutely. But she was unsure how to go about being the person that God would want her to be. "What do you do when people try to tempt you to do something wrong?"

Wanting to immediately remember things, but not having any tools at hand, Abby had invented a mental "Reminders" notebook. When she heard something she wanted to ask more about, she pictured the words written on an imaginary page, and "crossed off" things from her envisioned list as they were covered.

"Well, it can be hard, yes," Melissa allowed. "Handling gossiping is one thing that I have a hard time with. Mom and I talk about it quite a bit, trying to work out wording to say to a gossiper without being mean. We've come up with a couple of pretty good responses. Like, if it's a short jab at someone, I'll counter by saying something good about that person or that quality."

"What do you mean: counter with something good about a quality?" Abby asked.

"I'm so glad you asked that. Sometimes it can be fun. Do you know about virtues?"

"I do!" Abby flashed a big grin. "But I stopped the Yuter halfway through a long list. And I didn't memorize it. So no pop quizzes here."

"Aw shucks, and I was all ready with a quiz," Melissa gently joked, then continued. "Mom and I realized that virtues are the positive qualities of a person, but there could be a whole list of negative qualities... contra-virtues, almost. We got the idea from a quote of 'Abdu'l-Bahá's about how qualities that could be used negatively can also be used positively. Like greed can be good if you're greedy for learning.[139] So we turned it around. Like, how could stubbornness be good? We thought that it could be called persistence or not being too easily swayed. That is the good side of stubbornness, you see. Or selfishness could be self-preservation, which can be good.

"But it can be tricky, 'cuz the complainer, the gossiper, wants you to agree that the other person is bad. Sometimes, the best I can do is to say that, regardless, I still like the person and I don't think they mean any harm. Once, I got a gossiper to talk with the other person about her gripe; that's the best I've been able to do.

"Of course, if the person is really going on and *on* about someone viciously, I will try to change the subject, or step away and see if I can distract them onto something else. My cross-stitch works well for that, actually." She grinned mischievously. "Or asking them for help with something. Standing there looking at them seems to invite more of the same conversation, while moving away seems to break its flow.

"The thing is, gossip has a nasty twist. That's the real difference. If Person A came to me, and wanted to know if I was having trouble with Person B like they were, and the Person A was really just trying to get help to sort out a problem, it would be quite different. That would be more like 'consulting in all matters.'"[140]

"Wow, and all that's only about gossip." Dismayed, Abby mulled it over.

"Well, once you start thinking things through like this, you get better at it," Melissa said soothingly, "and you can use bits of one problem to solve parts of another. It can be hard, though." She laughed once, then quickly clapped her hand over her mouth.

"What?"

"Sorry, maybe it isn't the time for it, but I remembered a joke."

"I'm up for a joke."

"Jesus promised Christians the Kingdom of God on earth, and they look forward to the finished product floating down from heaven come Judgment Day. But for Bahá'ís, piles of bricks, bags of mortar, shovels, and wheelbarrows pour down in a clattering cloud of dust. The note on top of the pile says: 'Do-It-Yourself Kit.'"

Melissa glanced sidelong at Abby, saw that she was smiling, and then asked, "Seriously, is there anything else that worries you?"

"Yeah," Abby dropped her chin to her chest, remembering.

After patiently waiting for more and not getting it, Melissa asked if she could offer any help.

"It's my mother," Abby muttered, always on guard when it came to Mother.

"Is there anything I might be able to do for you?" Melissa asked so gently that it nearly brought Abby to tears again.

"I...I'm just not sure how to handle her, now that I...I think she is, uh, she's not how she's supposed to be. It's like, she..." Abby's voice trailed off in a whisper. Mother would absolutely kill her if she ever found out Abby had said something like that.

"Oh dear," Melissa said, moving close and holding her hand. Jon sat up straighter in his patio chair, looking anguished for the two girls. Women. Wirls.

"Dali said pollution can make some people not act like they should, like not loving their children," Abby choked out, struggling to control her tears.

"Oh no, sweetie," Melissa whispered. "I'm so sorry."

"Yeah. I just don't know...what to do now," Abby said. "It's always bad, but now that I think she has something wrong with her..."

"I don't know what to say, darlin'," Melissa responded, rubbing Abby's hand with both her hands. "My mom and I are best friends. I don't doubt you're having trouble with your mother, but I'm afraid I just don't know what help I can be. Except to pray for you...and for her. Would that be all right?"

"Yes, of course. I'd like that a lot," Abby said, smiling, grateful to know that at least someone else cared enough to think of her and her biggest trouble. A few bright lights glowed in her heart now, and they just might carry her through her roughest spots.

As Jon and Melissa got up to leave, she gave Abby a gentle hug.

"Oh, here are some books and handouts. 'Abdu'l-Bahá is a good one to start with," Melissa said, motioning to Jon to hand over a small tote bag he had set beside his chair earlier. "Please accept them from Mom and me. They are yours to keep if you like. And I wrote my email and phone number down."

Abby eyed the wealth of offered material with a wrenching mixture of greed for learning on one hand and stark dismay on the other. There was no way she could sneak half a dozen big books and several small ones into her luggage, get them all home, and keep them hidden from Mother, who could be counted on to have a total conniption should she find her daughter in possession of "unacceptable" books.

"Oh," she said, her emotions roller-coastering to teariness again. "I can't take all of that, Melissa. I wish I could. But Mother…"

"I understand, Abby, honestly I do." Melissa nodded in sympathy. "Let me pull out a couple of books for you that are quite small, okay?

"Look, here's a wonderful little prayer book from Malaysia. The sticky note with my info is in there. And here's my preview copy of the *Three Onenesses*. Remember, I used something from it the other day to answer one of your questions? See, they're both so small, they'll fit in a pocket. Here are some useful handouts you can fold up. 'On Life' and 'On Love' and 'On Liberty'; I downloaded the three 'L' sheets…just seemed right somehow. I hope you like them, honey. You can also look on the internet. And do you think you can take just *one* bigger book? I think *Paris Talks* would be just the thing. Those are talks that 'Abdu'l-Bahá gave."[141]

Abby accepted the small white volume, the even smaller beige chap-book, and the loose pages. She saw that the biggest book had pictures of the Eiffel Tower on the front cover. The book's title stood out in tall blue letters; the author's name was in much smaller print, black on a brown background. If any book could possibly slide by Mother's casual glance, it was this one. Might Vivian suppose that Abby was taking to heart her constant harangues about her daughters living up to their civilized European roots? Or might she at least assume the book with the innocuous, even boring, title had something to do with Abby's school-work…perhaps geography or history?

No, Abby was rather sure Mother would eventually punish her for this transgression one way or another; but some things were worth it.

"Yes, I think that'll be just perfect," she told Melissa, accepting the big book with a shaky smile. "The best book possible. Thank you so, so, *so* much, Melissa. And your mother, too."

Melissa gave the bag with the remaining books back to Jon, hugged Abby again, exclaimed "Happy reading!" and waved a cheery farewell as she and Jon left.

Knowing that her new reading material would not sit well with her mother, and might even not fly so well with Jenn, Abby hid the books and loose papers. When she was sure not to be discovered, though, she began reading *Paris Talks*. Eager as she was to immerse herself in the glorious light of 'Abdu'l-Bahá's words, she found she could only read a paragraph or two before she had to stop and think about it. Otherwise, it was like eating too much of a good thing.[142]

Wednesday afternoon, Mother quizzed Abby about such things as lightheadedness, nausea, and memory lapses, then called the doctor's office. A few hours later, he gave the all-clear; so the next morning, the Wizes packed the car again and left North Carolina for Tennessee. Abby kept watching out the window to see if anything looked familiar from the future. The route to the interstate took them fairly close to the area where Lodlan would someday be located, but one North Carolina rolling hill looked like the next.

It was a long drive home, but Abby felt well enough to read more *Harry Potter*. Her fingers traced the warped dust cover dampened by the ice water inside her backpack. She wistfully remembered how, way in the future, everyday bottles stayed cool and dry on the outside but hot or cold on the inside. For now, the book's rippled paper was both a reminder and a promise of the future and its wonderful inventions.

Reading, she was once more struck by how similar Dumbledore and 'Abdu'l-Bahá seemed, and in much more than appearance. In addition to looking so much alike, they both had great senses of humor, were very wise, could see inside people, and could foretell the future. It was so cool to know that, as neat as Dumbledore was, 'Abdu'l-Bahá was even better. *He* was real!

Abby also felt more like Harry than ever. He was on a grand mission in strange lands. She'd also done that. He was unfamiliar with the customs of the magical community. Ditto Abby with the world of the future. He was rescued by unexpected sources. So was she. In fact, she felt that, just as he was totally unique in his world, so was she in hers. But while Harry's world was clearly a fantasy, she viewed her travels as real. They had to be more than an hallucination. She had heard, felt, tasted, *lived* every aspect of something she couldn't possibly have dreamt up on her own. She just hoped she could do it again one day...without the concussion and coma.

On this trip, Mother crabbed at Abby less than usual and even asked her if she'd be able to eat at the same rest stop as before. Abby thought a picnic would work, as long as there was no jello. There wasn't. Lunch was bologna and cheese sandwiches with potato chips. But the bologna was greasy and the cheese rubbery. The white bread compressed like foam as she chewed it. She pictured the whole mess stuck in her guts, plugging up her plumbing, polluting her.

Abby wondered what Erdeans would say or do if served this food. They'd probably eat a little bit of it, politely, but try to make up for it with other things that were healthier. As she set the sandwich aside and instead tried some baby carrots and celery, Abby realized she had felt clearer and stronger the longer she'd stayed in Erden. It might've been due in part to the healthier food. She certainly had come back a different person. Even Jenn had noticed it and said Abby looked happier.

It was true, although she couldn't yet face the likely results of telling any of her family why. She knew herself better, had a better idea of what she wanted out of life and how to get it. She had seen a model of not only people, but a whole society, towards which she wanted to grow. She was more confident. She'd been nurtured and supported. She had more ways to get through the hard parts of her life. And she was very much looking forward to meeting the Bahá'ís of Surely.

Once home, Abby recovered steadily. She still slept a lot, but took fewer pain pills, and felt a little more able day by day. She wished that she'd had Melissa contact the local Bahá'ís for her. Their number was in the phone book, but what if someone actually answered? What would she say? But on the other hand, leaving a message on a machine equally intimidated her. And if anyone ever called her back, Mother would find out, which could not be a good thing. Abby didn't see a way around her problems, so did nothing.

One day, as Abby again ran the mental maze looking for an answer that did not come, Melissa's voice floated up in her memory: "Is there any Remover of difficulties save God? Say: Praised be God! He is God! All are His servants, and all abide by His bidding." Then a male voice in her mind added that she'd have to "Rely upon God, Thy God and the Lord of thy fathers"…someone in Lodlan had said that.[143] So Abby decided to look for those two prayers in her prayer book, and to begin consciously memorizing them, hoping they would rescue her as Dali so often had.

When Jenn and all the other kids started back to school the day after Labor Day, it felt strange not to be with them. About an hour after Jenn had left, Mother, dressed up all in black, came into the bedroom where Abby lay assessing her level of pain, waiting for a reason to get up.

"I have to go to a funeral," Mother said abruptly. "Funerals are not suitable for children. Will you be all right here alone?"

"Yes, sure," Abby answered automatically.

"You have my cell phone number. If something happens, call me," Mother commanded over her shoulder as she walked away down the hall, "but you'll be leaving a message."

As her mother left the house, Abby pondered their mostly one-way interchange. Although it seemed like a dreadful thing to go to, what if she had insisted on going with Mother? Or said no, she didn't feel well enough to be left alone? But Mother had already decided to go alone, hadn't she? Oh, but what could have polluted her so badly?

After a longish while, Abby got up to go to the bathroom, then eat. She shuffled along the hall, hands trailing down the wall to keep her steady. Her fingers bumped on the doorframes: Bathroom, bump, space, bump. Closet, bump, drag, bump. Basement stairs, bump, space, bump. Kitchen, bump, space, turn.

The cereal cabinet offered her the usual choices; but today it struck her that it was all sugar and chemicals. She reached behind the boxes and located a dusty Mason jar with old granola bars inside. Eating one, she knew they were still sweeter than they should be.

With a bar in her hand, she turned towards the shopping list magneted to the fridge. Her parents had just gone shopping on Saturday, so the new list was still blank. She was having a wild idea, Abby knew, and she hoped they'd just think she was weird after her coma. Picturing her meals with Dali, she printed:

From health food store
whole grain cereal x2
soy milk & rice milk
low-sugar granola bars
whole grain organic bread
whole grain crackers
organic vegetable soup — 3 kinds
organic vegan entrees
organic nut butter (cheapest)
organic fruit juice — 2 kinds

She blew out a breath after taking that plunge. If that worked, it'd be new for everybody. She was trying to follow her little voice, her gut feelings (were those two the same?), and the Bahá'í teachings.

As she sat at the round table in the sunroom to eat, her eyes noted the familiar-yet-strange surroundings. Piles of Mother's papers, computer, phone...*wait!*

Computers! Phones! Everyone else was gone; she could phone the Bahá'ís now and just ask what get-togethers they had! She could look up stuff on the computer! Mother might have a fit if she didn't ask permission first...better call her now, before the funeral started.

She swallowed the last bite of breakfast, dialed Mother's cell phone and, when Mother answered, quickly said, "Hi, Mother, it's Abby, I'm fine, I just wondered if I may get on your computer while you're gone."

The silence stretched unbearably. Abby crossed her fingers on both hands, her wrists, ankles, even eyes. "I promise I'll go lie down when I get tired," she added, trying to think of Mother's probable objections.

"I suppose," Mother said resignedly, as if she wanted to veto the request but couldn't think of a good reason why.

"Thanks, Mother," Abby said, and hung up quickly, just in case her mother summoned an objection after all.

She turned on the computer, found the internet icon and clicked on it, then did a search on "Surely TN Baha'i Faith."

There were several listings, but none of them seemed quite right. Back at the top, it read: "Do you mean *Surely TN Bahai Faith*" with no apostrophe. She tried that, and the first one was the right site.

Another listing showed a master website for the US: www.bahai.us. The banner on its main page warmed Abby's heart:

> ## Let your vision be world-embracing, rather than confined to your own self.
> **Bahá'u'lláh**
> **Tablets of Bahá'u'lláh, page 86**

Abby gazed at the comforting quote. And the longer she looked at it, the more her brain tingled with familiarity. She could almost hear the words "world-embracing" and "vision" in Dali's voice.

She clicked back to the Surely site. She checked the phone number listed against the phonebook, and the numbers matched. Might as well call now.

She felt a headache coming on from all the thinking, and especially from the worry about being caught and chewed out by Mother. But she really wanted to grab this chance to call them. She so needed a dose of calm and courage. Running a different kind of search, she closed her eyes...envisioned Dali's house...the wooden sound-box playing...the STEEDS OF FAITH guarding it...Farrah painting them...the steed of the Valley of Search was patience. Patience was a biggie, Rykeir had said. Yes. She could use some patience for this search.

"Oh God, please give me patience," she prayed, "and...confidence." She willed herself to be receptive. After a bit, she did feel calmer, more focused. She picked up the phone, took a deep breath, dialed. A woman answered.

"Hi, is this the right number for the Bahá'í Faith?" Abby asked.

"Yes, it is," said a female voice with a black Tennessee accent. "My name is Dreamy Jefferson. How may I help you?"

"I found out about the Bahá'í Faith just recently and...really like it. I wanted to see if you have any meetings that I could come to."

"Yes, we sure do," the woman said. "I can send you our calendar of activities, or read you the schedule now. Which would you like?"

"Um..." Abby thought for a minute. Fortunately, the woman waited. "Send it, please." She gave the woman her name and address. "Are any meetings close to me? I don't drive yet; I'm only thirteen."

"Not very close, no," the woman said. "But if it's all right with your parents, we could pick you up."

"Really? That would be great." She was already relieved, and glad she'd called.

"Okay. I think LaKeesha White is closest to you; she'd probably be the one picking you up," Dreamy said. "Would you like for me to telephone you before the next event?"

"Um, no, thank you. But could I maybe have her phone number to arrange the ride?" Abby asked. "I can't come for the next few weeks. And, after that, it can only be on the weekends."

"So, Sunday School," Dreamy said. "Maybe a service project."

"Service!" said Abby breathlessly, remembering.

"You sound excited about service," said Dreamy, amused.

"You have no idea!" Abby grinned.

"Well, good for you. You're ready to take down her number? Okay." Dreamy gave Abby the number and then added, "And her name again is capital-L-A-capital-K-E-E-S-H-A, *lah-KEY-shah* White."

After she and Dreamy hung up, Abby spent some time on the US Bahá'í website, and felt reconnected. Also curious. She'd guessed that the Faith now would be very different from how she had seen it when pretty much everyone knew and practiced its teachings. At least most of the Writings were already here; it was only a question of how long it'd take humanity to put the teachings into practice. Still, truly she believed it would be worth supporting now, even if it wasn't all that perfect yet.

Happy, thanking God for providing her with a chance to make that call, she went back to bed and crashed until well past noon.

Jenn got home from school and told Abby she should be glad she missed the first day. Jenn had heard from several neighbor kids that the hazing of the new middle-schoolers was worse than ever. One group had ambushed some of the starting seventh-graders, painted their noses red with fingernail polish, and made them sing *Rudolph the Red-Nosed Reindeer* all the way to school. If they went to the office, they were told they could call home. Otherwise, they just had to go through the rest of the day hiding, or being teased about, their noses.

Abby could relate. Last year, she had been bullied into taking off her shoes, tying them around her neck, and walking to school with her finger on her nose as if she were doing a drunk test. The official policy was that hazing was not tolerated. When it happened off school grounds, though, there was nothing the school could do about it.

Chapter 29: Reentry

Abby wasn't well enough to go riding on Saturdays, but continued to dream about horses. She couldn't go to school yet because she tired easily and had headaches, so a tutor brought her schoolwork that often drained what little concentration and energy she had. On good days, she alternated homework with *Harry Potter* and with *Paris Talks*, in which she carefully laid her sparkly, beaded bookmark. She had new daydreams to add to the old horse-and-camp ones: the flood of divine assistance in the bookstore, Melissa, Angie, Beauty, and *all* of Erden. She entered these in her diary, sometimes using symbols instead of words, in case Mother ever read it.

When Mother was out of the house shopping and pursuing her hobbies, Abby also went on the computer. She enjoyed visiting Parelli sites, and discovered how to do web searches using that name as the keyword. There were a lot of people doing amazing things with natural horsemanship, she learned. She explored YouTube, a site packed with videos from amateurs as well as professionals.

She saved many favorite sites – Parelli, Bahá'í, Harry Potter, and more – under "History Report." It had been a challenge to figure out what heading would avoid alerting Mother. Jenn had collaborated on that, in part so she could also use it.

Abby had prayed that her mother would not see her mail from the Bahá'ís; she whispered a happy "Thank you, God!" when the envelope arrived while Vivian was out. She eagerly looked through the calendar, then called LaKeesha, and they scheduled a ride to and from the first activity she'd be able to attend.

Abby considered herself a Bahá'í. She had found a registration card tucked into *Paris Talks*, signed it, and hidden it and all Melissa's gifts amongst the stuff in her bottom bureau drawer. When she had written to Melissa about it, Melissa had replied with news about her senior year in high school in Little Lily. She had also shared that, at this point, Abby needed a parent's permission to register. Once she reached fifteen, she could declare her belief and enroll without her parents if she wished to. Abby knew, though, that even then she'd have to consider the amount of flak she'd get by doing so. Still, Melissa had mentioned that – in the recent past and even nowadays – some Bahá'ís in Iran, including teenagers, were jailed and even killed for their faith. So Abby didn't feel so bad about just having to wait.

Abby researched fasting once a year starting at age fifteen; all three of the daily Obligatory Prayers, and also other special prayers; believers being appointed to protect or promote the Faith; and the Local Spiritual

Assemblies, from which the future local-level Houses of Justice would grow. She thought it was neat that such councils had all the authority but only when they met; and that Assembly members and community members had no authority as individuals even when they were speaking and doing the work they'd been elected or asked to do. There was no clergy, and never had been. The Writings exhorted every Bahá'í to learn, make up their own mind about things, and share their knowledge with others.

Abby also learned about Covenant Breakers.

She still wasn't very clear on what the Covenant was, not really. It seemed to be the agreement between people and God. Now, with the Bahá'í Faith being the most recent of the God-sent religions, it seemed to mean that the believers agreed to try to follow the current laws and teachings. But the Covenant Breakers were people who said they were Bahá'ís, who knew what Bahá'u'lláh and 'Abdu'l-Bahá and then the Guardian had taught, but who intentionally disavowed parts of the Covenant and made up their own rules.

When Abby had first searched on the web, some "Bahá'í" sites just did not seem quite right. They argued against the Universal House of Justice, and talked about leaders and beliefs that Abby sensed were not the real thing. She was pleased to realize that the "divine fragrances" had grown real to her…so real that it almost made her wrinkle her nose at the funny smell that some sites seemed to emit.

She quickly clicked away from them. One thing she clearly understood about Covenant-Breakers was that she should avoid them entirely. The Master had said they spread spiritual disease and could not catch spiritual health from the faithful.[144] Abby definitely did not want to be infected with whatever they had.

It was on her mind, though. One night as she read some more *Harry Potter*, and the dreadful Death Eaters were taking over Harry's world, it seemed to her that Death Eaters and Covenant Breakers were a lot alike. Both devoted to darkness, fighting, resisting goodness, or maybe unable to tell the difference between good and bad.

The Aurors fought the Death Eaters; and the appointed individuals were dealing with Covenant Breakers. She was glad she didn't have to deal with either group!

Abby experimented with the three different obligatory prayers. She realized she did not have to say them until she turned fifteen, but they made her feel better. Well, except that the long one had postures she couldn't do; her head injury wouldn't allow her to kneel down and put her forehead on the floor. She thought it would be neat to have that one memorized, though, and lose herself in its magic, see where it would take her. Someday she would. For now, she memorized the short one, so she could say it every noontide no matter where she was.

The Currys, Tony, and others from The Ride Place sent a flower basket that Mother put next to her computer after the first ones – from Grandmother Lois, Daddy, and Granny – wilted. Her friend Maria and Reverend Davison sent get-well cards, and Kat and the other girls from church sent a postcard wishing her a speedy recovery. Abby put the cards up in front of the tallest horses on her windowsill, and tried to ignore the fact that the flowers should also have been up there. She did enjoy them when Mother went out and she used the computer.

Interestingly, she was not stuffed up in the morning anymore. She could actually smell things! Maybe the Yuter was right, and she'd been allergic to things that she never knew about. Abby hoped it was all fixed now. Mother bought almost everything Abby wrote on the health food list, and Abby even liked most of it. When she compared how she felt on her new diet versus the old, she thought she had fewer allergies, less body odor, more energy, and more wonderful dreams. And she healed faster than the doctor had predicted; so, ahead of schedule, she joined the other students a mere two weeks into the term. She had started two schools this year, she mused.

Her first day back at Becknay Middle, bolstered with a breakfast of organic spelt flakes and rice milk, Abby reported to the office, got her class schedule, and checked in briefly with the nurse before Homeroom. What a change from Insight Upper! Everything was removed or locked down, used to abuse. No frills. The losers, the jocks and cheerleaders, the nerds, the druggies, the Emos and Goths.

Homeroom and the class afterward it were with Mrs. Kilgore. The wall speaker crackled and spit so that the morning announcements were hard to hear. Even when it did work, Mrs. Kilgore shifted in her squeaky, falling-apart chair and drowned out half of it.

Algebra, the next class, was just the latest Gunsmoke in Abby's stable of math difficulties. Math was not her strong suit anyway. Mrs. Kilgore tiredly welcomed her to class and asked her to fill out a forgotten form noting damage to her textbook.

As Mrs. Kilgore handed back graded assignments and gathered last night's homework, Abby began to look through her book. How was she supposed to document all of the doodles, rude comments, 'o' middles filled in, even torn pages. She had never opened a book in Erden, not even in school, but just bet that no one there would deface anything like this. She allowed herself to imagine just what an Erdean textbook might have. A 3D presentation? Simulated field trips? She'd love to have the chance to find out, but Mrs. Kilgore's voice brought her back to earth.

The stout, pink-skinned, gray-haired teacher lectured the students who had not done their homework. One student replied that he did not have any paper at home. Mrs. Kilgore had no answer for that. Abby began a game she would play many times: How Would This Situation Be Handled In Erden?

First off, the mood was wrong. The students felt attacked, and the teacher was frustrated. Second, if students did not have supplies, they should be given some. As for damaging books, kids here did not learn respect like in Erden. It was two different worlds, for sure. The worlds and the people in them. In Erden, everybody learned how they should act. Collectively, all these high-level actions made the world into heaven. But on earth, now, even the many good people were not united in their actions. No wonder progress was so hard now!

The topic for the day was graphs using coordinates. X and Y and sometimes Z, negatives and positives…Abby did her best to keep up but was rather confused. Aside from using a graph to show amounts of things, or as a pattern for, say, counted cross-stitch, when did you ever actually use this stuff? Insight Upper's topics were very useful as well as interesting, fulfilling the instruction on the Courtesy classroom ceiling. Abby wondered what century it would be before people in charge of children's education realized that it should be interesting and useful to the child as well as to the adult the child would become.

Some students applied themselves to graphing, but a few blew off class in ways intentionally designed to distract everybody else. Finally, the bell shrilled; Abby noticed one of the Asperger's kids cringe and whine, and she could see why. When she wasn't at full strength, lots of things about school got hard to take. What would Dali say about that? She would look at Abby, appalled! School should be arranged so that the students could be comfortable and enabled to learn!

Art came next. She knew the teacher, Mr. Perez, from last year's short rotation in the arts. He was okay. Yelled a bit too much, but what else could he do, trying to handle some thirty-five mostly unmotivated middle-schoolers? He welcomed her, pointed out her seat and bin, and handed her a basic supply list. Coming in on the middle of an art project was hard; fortunately, they were just starting a new project. The previous one had been nifty-looking paper maché figures. Sad that the tutor had not tried to help her make one, and wondering why, Abby guessed maybe it needed special equipment.

Several kids' bins sat empty in front of them. She felt bad for those who liked art but whose parents couldn't or wouldn't get their supplies. She sympathized; Mother harrumphed over any supply list she brought home, but usually did buy everything eventually.

Their new assignment was very unusual: a fabric landscape. Mr.

Perez had studied with a quilt artist over the summer. Using magazine photos as a pattern, the students would choose similar shapes in fabric, assemble the cloth pieces, and iron them in place with fusible web.

Abby saw some nice pictures, but nothing she liked well enough to turn into a project. The other students tore out nice views, outlined and listed their cloth colors, and turned them in; but Abby hung back in order to speak to Mr. Perez alone.

"You didn't get a picture?" he accused. Abby couldn't blame him. He never knew who was trying to get away with something.

"I didn't see anything I liked enough, Mr. Perez," Abby said politely. trying to show she was willing to comply but uninspired.

He regarded her for a minute, his mental wheels turning.

"Can you use a photo from home? Someplace you've been that you liked a lot? A drawing that can be turned into a fabric landscape?"

She was glad he was offering her other choices, and smiled to show him she appreciated it.

"Those are good ideas. May I bring in something next class, sir?" Abby asked as politely as Dali would have. He had given her an idea, but it would take some time to work up.

"Yes, but be sure you turn it in next class," he warned. "I have to go get the fabric after the absent students pick theirs."

Trying to ignore his tone, Abby said, "I will. Thank you so much."

Next was American History. As students found seats and took out the books they'd brought for Silent Reading at the beginning of core classes, the teacher wrote the day's topic – "1776: The Declaration of Independence" – and textbook pages on the worn blackboard. Before opening *Paris Talks*, Abby quickly scanned the assigned pages. One sentence leapt right off the page at her, about the "inalienable Rights" of "Life, Liberty, and the pursuit of Happiness."

The founding fathers felt that the English king was invading their lives too much; that getting out from under him would make life better. They knew there would likely be war but felt that, if they prevailed, it would be a lot easier to live life to the fullest. They knew that some of them would have to die in war to live in peace, but they were tired of feeling oppressed. Abby already knew, though, that Bahá'ís looked at life in a special way...one she deeply wanted to understand and follow. The Erdean way of life, Abby reflected, layered many more benefits on top of just being able to conduct business and have a peaceful home life. She sincerely hoped that, despite being back in 2007, she could still understand – *ma'rifat* – and experience the rich life her Erdean friends had.

Then there was liberty. She wondered if the Bahá'í view of liberty would match the aims of the Declaration, never mind today's America where liberty meant doing whatever you wanted. Her little voice, growing better at guiding her, told her she would find a very different view of liberty in the Bahá'í Writings.

And what about the pursuit of happiness? She now had quite a few opinions on happiness, having had so little of it at home and so much of it in Erden. She also knew that the Bahá'í Faith had a lot to say about true happiness. And much of it didn't match up with what most Americans believed. Most American kids thought happiness meant having the snazziest iPod, cell phone, PSP, getting the latest DVDs and computer games, wearing the trendiest clothes and jewelry. But Abby now had a much different view of what happiness was made of. Having things to enjoy was fine, but thinking they would bring lasting happiness could only lead to disappointment later on and the hunger for more things. It was a vicious circle. Having fun with people, nurturing virtues, learning, creating, helping, staying plugged in spiritually…these could not unfold when you were sidetracked by superficial or material things and ignored your deeper needs.[145]

As Abby opened *Paris Talks* to a new section, out slid the three sheets she'd folded and tucked into the book back in Little Lily. Abby remembered that one of the handouts was about life and another about liberty. What an interesting coincidence. She opened the "On Liberty" handout and, sure enough, the little compilation included a statement by Bahá'u'lláh that: "Liberty must, in the end, lead to sedition, whose flames none can quench."[146] The decrepit dictionary on the table said *sedition* is rebellion against a government. Was that what happened if you followed liberty too far? The Bahá'í passage – four paragraphs long – seemed to say that people tended to rebel against the restraints of law, but that the real solution was obedience to laws. Especially God's laws, which engendered truly spiritual morals.

Yeah, that rang true. If liberty in America had led to saying and doing whatever you wanted, then America had seen plenty of liberty and its effects. In only about two hundred years, the country had gone from fighting for liberties to abusing them. Dali had said the damage from that kind of behavior was long-term.

Lunch break finally arrived. Last school lunch, she had eaten tasty, healthy food in another world. This time, she seemed to be stuck with Mystery Meat, Putrid Potatoes, and Botulism Beans according to Jeff Wornall, the snide ninth-grader in line in front of her. Abby drowned out Jeff's commentary about Chemical Cake by comparing this food to the food at Insight Upper. That food was…newer? Fresher? More real *food* in the food? This stuff had to have lots of preservatives and fillers in it, Abby supposed, in order to not spoil during its trip from wherever it had started and still be cheap. Her eyes flew wide as she realized these were probably the chemicals Dali had said caused so much illness in this world. Whoa, this stuff could actually be bad for you, maybe more than Jeff knew!

Too late today. She'd have to eat it; she was through the line. But starting tomorrow, she'd have to be a weirdo and bring her own food.

The trash bins overflowed, full of wasted recycling possibilities. Everywhere Abby turned, she saw opportunities for a better way.

Next came French – a perfect time to read a bit more in *Paris Talks* during Silent Reading – with a teacher she didn't know, Ms. Black, who was white. Ms. Black started out nice; but as class progressed, she got impatient at how many students were totally disinterested...there only because they had to be.

"How can you expect to learn anything if you don't do your homework, don't practice, don't pay attention, don't get involved in class?" she asked.

Everybody knew the truth, though, that learning was not even on those students' radar screens. Teachers nagged at the laggards, which further disheartened them. It also caused a split between the failing kids and the students who were interested in doing a good job and learning. It was a whole huge dynamic that no one person – or even one group – could fix. There was not enough connection between school, home, and society to find – never mind enact – solutions; and the kids, being young, were unlikely to hoist themselves out of the mess. Abby thought it was all quite sad.

Eventually, the class learned a little French. Mother had wanted Abby to learn it because of family history: Mother's father had been all-French. Mother would occasionally speak short sentences in French, which was interesting; but Abby always felt like a failure when she attempted to speak it back, so she rarely tried.

"Repeat after me: *Les courtesans portant les perruques*," Ms. Black said. "The courtiers wear wigs." That was a mouthful, Abby thought. And half of the letters in French are silent. When she heard French, she had to try to spell the words in her head to understand them. They were studying words and phrases relating to the French kings and their court. What use that would be if she ever needed to speak French nowadays, she didn't know.

Hearing another language, though, reminded her of UL. Quickly she wrote down "jes = yes" but could not remember hearing the word for "no" in UL. It wasn't really surprising...Erden was such a positive world. As she listened to the teacher pronounce *oui* (yes), *bien sur* (of course), and *merci* (thank you), Abby remembered other Erdean words, and thought she'd better capture them before they faded from memory. The rest of the class left and she scurried after them, not wanting anyone to ask or see what she was doing. Unlike in Erden, people here snooped, tried to corner you, found things to make fun of.

After Computer Lab, her final class, Abby stood in front of her new locker, backpack parked at her feet, reviewing her Math and History classroom work, noting her homework, and brainstorming about Art and UL.

Abby walked home, extremely tired mentally and almost as tired physically. At least her head didn't hurt much.

Her heart was another story, though. The difference between school in Erden and school here in Surely just plain saddened her. It was not only about obstacles to learning. Or maybe it really was, in the end. If you didn't have an environment that encouraged you – that made learning exciting – you not only didn't learn, you pretty much stopped caring, either. And that was reflected not only in what you didn't learn but also in what you didn't bother to do.

If you really cared about something, you took care of it; but if you didn't, you didn't. Abby thought about how dedicated to learning kids in Erden were, how much they enjoyed it, how happily they cooperated with their teachers and fellow students, and even how conscientious they were in keeping their school and classrooms neat, clean, orderly, and attractive and their learning supplies in good shape.

What a contrast to what she'd seen in her Surely classrooms today. Students left the rooms messy, chairs askew, litter on the floor, supplies not properly put away. A few of them even left belongings behind; and in two cases, she'd seen students "borrow" things they did not return. Many students treated their books with careless disrespect; some treated each other and even the teachers likewise. It was so, so sad. Abby sighed as she entered her house. Beyond the kitchen entryway, Mother sat at her desk.

"Hi," Abby called.

"Come here, Abby," Mother commanded without looking up. "Do you have a headache?"

Abby put her books down in the hallway and went for inspection.

"I feel okay," Abby said in her own defense.

Mother felt Abby's forehead with the back of her hand and glanced at her face. Finally, she said that Abby should probably rest before dinner, just in case.

"Yes, Mother." Good thing Abby had planned to stay in her room anyway, and it could be interpreted as resting. Her room was quiet. The house would be still for a while. Jenn wasn't back yet. Her walk from high school was long…even longer if she stopped anywhere.

Abby pulled her drawing tablet out of the bureau's bottom drawer and settled down with it in her reading nook. She'd added the old, soft, meaningful blue blanket from her bed at the Holsworths; they'd given it to her as a farewell and get-well gift when she thanked them for making such a comfortable recovery couch.

Closing her eyes, she contemplated her art assignment. She knew what she wanted to do: draw a part of Lodlan and make it into a fabric wall-hanging. A landscape should mainly be nature and the outdoors. That left the Draggin' Dragon out of her fabric art, much as she loved that place…but she could still *draw* it! She could draw *all* of it!

What a relief. She did not have to worry about forgetting it. It was still so fresh in her mind. Whatever she couldn't draw, she could write about. But she'd have to use some kind of code no one could read. She wished she could write it all in UL…hey! Hadn't Dali said something about the languages that went into UL? What had she said? That many languages contributed, with a handful of unrelated languages forming the roots. It was like ABC. Um, Arabic, Bantu, and Chinese? And some language she had never heard of. Essence? No, um, Esprin something? Anyway, did it exist now? If it did, she could learn to write in it, and no one in her house would understand it. How exciting!

So the drawing. Something outdoorsy. Going home after the Draggin' Dragon? The sky that night? The white owl? Showing Dali's little house in front of her, and Gunsmoke's hill beyond? Could she fit Dali in there somehow and have it still be a landscape? Maybe a small figure on a bike. She thought she would try.

"*Try* is not a four-letter word," she repeated to herself, and began to draw.

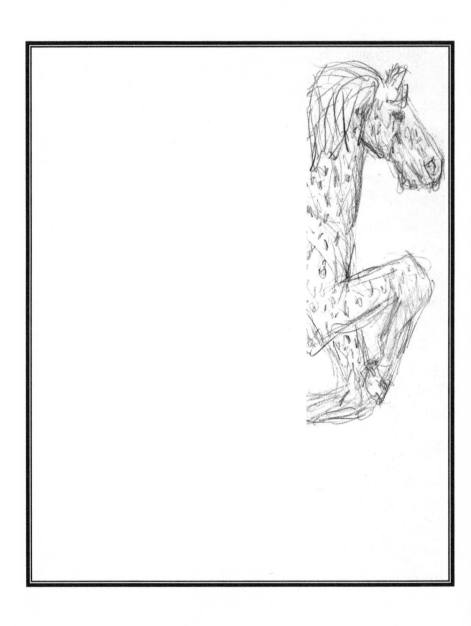

Chapter 30: Sunday

One Sunday, Abby was finally able to attend a Bahá'í event. She felt fairly well prepared spiritually, but had stalled at telling Mother she would not be going to church with the family. She had mentioned to Jenn that she was getting interested in Melissa's religion. Jenn had not been open to the idea. "Jesus Is The Only Way," she'd sternly reproved.

Abby let it drop. He was. They were. They were *all* the only way to God. Each for their own time, each promising they'd come back. She had also read on the Bahá'í website a letter from the Universal House of Justice addressed to the religious leaders of the world, bidding them to mend their religious differences. Many other issues have been raised and new tolerance found, the House of Justice statement said, covering ethnicity, gender, nation, caste, class. But suspicion about other religions was still proving to be a major stumbling block to the advancement of mankind.[147]

She'd avoided church, passing it off on her trauma, but still had to deal with the next step: going someplace else. She gathered her courage – and practiced the wording in her head – for over a week before finally taking the plunge one Friday night in mid-September.

Mother sat knitting on the couch, Dad was downstairs checking that the garage doors were locked, and Jenn was getting ready for bed.

"Someone is going to pick me up to go to another church this Sunday," Abby said, standing in front of her mother.

Vivian Wize looked at the air all around her daughter's head, as if Abby were surrounded by gnats. "What?" she asked.

"I am going to visit another church this Sunday," Abby repeated. "Some people are going to take me."

"What kind of church? Where is it? Who's picking you up?"

"Bahá'í. It's over in Partridge. Her name is…I'm not sure how to say it." Mother probably wouldn't approve of LaKeesha's name, so she had better not mention it.

Mother looked slapped in the face.

"Our church isn't good enough for you?"

"It's fine, Mother. I just want to try this one; it sounds interesting. Jon's girlfriend Melissa told me about it on vacation."

"And you listen to people like that?"

Abby knew this was a reference to Melissa's mixed racial heritage. Darker-skinned people were "less-than" in Mother's book. Suitable for being household help, not much else. Abby fought that view, not only because she was now a Bahá'í, but because it was just so *mean*, which she was sensitized to from years of Mother-war.

"Please, Mother, I just want to go see how it is. Melissa had good manners and was perfectly nice."

"That's not the point. Our church is all you need. I don't know why you think you need to throw it out the window. Who knows what these ...*people*...could get you into?"

"They teach all the things that our church teaches, plus more good conduct," Abby said. "Honest. No drinking, no drugs, no funny stuff of any kind. The same kinds of things like the Ten Commandments and the Golden Rule and the Blessed Are's."

"The *Beatitudes*, Abby. And you may think you're being so clever about this, but I assure you that it will come to no good end," Mother pronounced.

"I'll do my best to see that it doesn't, Mother," Abby said, backing away.

That had actually gone much better than she had thought it would. No one had yelled, no one had been physically harmed, Mother had not actually forbidden her from going, and Abby had been able to leave before Mother thought to forbid her. She'd figure out how to deal with future objections when the future came.

After the family left for church that Sunday, Abby dressed in casual clothes. Given the unrelenting heat and humidity, thanks to an extended summer, she doubted that the local Bahá'ís would expect high fashion. Of course, in Erden a prom dress with elbow-length gloves would have kept her cooler than her current capris and polo shirt.

She waited in the living room, browsing this month's selection of magazines. Near the appointed time, she heard a car pull up in front of the house. She looked out the window. It was the green two-door she was expecting. She picked up her purse, double-checking inside it for her house key, went out, locked the front door (too bad she couldn't just command it to shut and lock), and walked down to the car.

"Hi!" Abby said to the dark-skinned driver with lots of long, thin braids, some of them tinted magenta.

"Hello," the lady said in a strong southern accent.

Abby got in the front passenger seat.

"I'm LaKeesha," the lady said. "This is Justice, my son, and Hope, my girl."

"Hi, I'm Abby," Abby said, turning to wave to the two kids – about seven and four – in the back seat. They were darker than their mother, very cute and bright-eyed. Each lifted a hand in return.

Abby buckled her seat belt and off they drove, the windows down. Good thing she hadn't fixed her hair all fancy...the wind would have destroyed it.

"Sorry, the A/C is broken," LaKeesha apologized. "So we're using two-forty instead." She threw a quirky smile towards Abby, who took the bait.

"Two-forty?"

"Two windows down, forty miles an hour."

Abby couldn't help but laugh. A good joke, and funnier because it was true!

"How did you hear of the Faith? If you don't mind me asking, that is." LaKeesha asked warmly.

"Oh no, I don't mind. It was from a friend of my cousin's in North Carolina," Abby said.

"That's nice; when was that?" LaKeesha's polite questions lasted the short trip to the modest home in the newer Partridge Ridge housing subdivision. Abby just had to be careful not to let on about how much she knew; she stuck to small things that she had read in the books and on the internet, or heard from Melissa.

Other people were parking on the street and heading to the white wooden-framed house with young trees in the yard. Inside, everyone squeezed into the small living room. There were just a dozen people; but there was only one couch and two easy chairs, so people brought chairs in from the kitchen or wedged themselves into spots on the floor.

"I think that's everyone," said a lady with suntanned skin and sun-streaked hair. "So let's get started. LaKeesha, will you introduce your guest?"

"Sure. This is Abby. She phoned Dreamy about a month ago."

A chorus of hi's and glad-you-came's greeted Abby. She nodded a shy hello, remembering the earpiece translating the last Bahá'í meeting she had gone to. She took a deep breath, praying that some of Erden would stay with her always. Tears still sprang to her eyes sometimes with longing for it. To quash the yearning, she forced her attention and thoughts back to the present.

"Let's sing a couple of songs we know, then we'll do the one we're learning, and then I'll take requests," said the lady, Suzie. "How about 'Look at Me' first."

There was no hymnal and nothing posted up, so Abby mostly listened and sang along with the chorus...

♫Look at me,
follow me,
be as I am.
'Abdu'l-Bahá,
'Abdu'l-Bahá.♫ [148]

Next was Magic Penny, about a penny of love – or happiness, or courtesy – that came back to you if you spent it.[149]

Then came the song they were learning, a prayer for children. Susie asked little Justice to lead the song by pointing to the relevant parts of a large pieced-together illustration tacked to one wall. It looked like the children had drawn different parts of it and then it had all been taped together. Abby thought it was a clever, low-tech visual aid to help learn the song…

♫O God! Educate these children.
These children are
the plants of Thine orchard,
the flowers of Thy meadow,
the roses of Thy garden.
Let Thy rain fall upon them;
let the Sun of Reality
shine upon them with Thy love.
Let Thy breeze refresh them
in order that they may be trained,
grow and develop,
and appear in the utmost beauty.
Thou art the Giver.
Thou art the Compassionate.♫[150]

When the song was over, everyone clapped. Then the children clamored for "Shine Your Light on Me, Bahá'u'lláh" please. Pretty please? They were given small flashlights to shine on themselves and each other; and with Suzie playing chords on her guitar and leading the words, they marched around to the "I am over here, Bahá'u'lláh" lyric.[151]

"Great job, everyone!" Suzie proclaimed over the happy applause. "Okay, let's go to our classes."

LaKeesha and the four children left for their class in the backyard with its shaded patio. The kids were much younger than Abby; she was the only teen. She stayed with the other adults in the living room.

"Well, we are about midway through Ruhi Book Two," said Tim, one of the fathers and the facilitator of the study circle.[152] "You can borrow this one while you're here," he said, handing Abby a workbook.

"What does *RUE-hee* mean, please?" she asked, and learned that it was the Arabic word for *soul* and was sometimes colloquially used to indicate one's beloved.

The five adults plus Abby went through the Bahá'í quotations and exercises, discussing and trying to absorb the material. The title said it was about service, interestingly enough. But the contents seemed to be

about doing something called "home visits" and about serving the Faith
– and the world – by teaching it to others. Abby supposed that the Bahá'í
community would need to study how to teach before they could do it as
competently as Dali. But then, Dali was a descendent of generations of
spiritually attuned people. And her entire *world* helped her to be loving,
peaceful, supportive, and more. Why, the entire Yuter list of virtues
more! She could see now why it would take seven hundred years for the
Faith to grow and permeate all corners of the ideal world she'd seen.

For now, it felt like they were pawing over that Do-It-Yourself pile.
The study was slow and laborious. The house was neither air-conditioned
nor thick-walled, so it was very hot. One believer kept interjecting his
personal opinions and rather long stories, which was trying everyone's
patience. Another didn't speak English very well, and often struggled to
get her ideas across. One of the mothers repeatedly left to go monitor
her two behavior-challenged children in LaKeesha's class; and every
time she came back, they had to catch her up if she'd missed something
important.

Abby contrasted this study circle with the deepening in Lodlan.
Maybe they were different kinds of activity, but still…there really was
no comparison between the quality of resources, facilities, materials,
programs, or attendees. It kept coming down to the fact that all aspects
of Erden focused on balanced, wise, spiritual living. Everything that
happened there was so out-of-this-world.

The Ruhi book itself was fine, though it could use a good batch of
animated Yuter presentations to really bring it to life. Abby smiled at
this thought. She could have a lot of fun thinking of how far towards
Erdean life she could nudge things, even in her imagination. And perhaps someday she could help make actual Bahá'í events in Surely better,
even if in only some small way.

The best part of the morning was when the children came in with
their drawings and showed them to the adults: a plug going into a sock-
et, a hand reaching for the hem of a long coat, a face with its nose lifted
to smell wavy lines, and an open book floating in the clouds. LaKeesha
reported that the class had discussed how to stay connected to God.[153]
Then, awkwardly and with much prompting, each child explained what
their drawing represented. Drawing on God's power. Holding the hem
of His garment.[154] Smelling the divine fragrances. And seeing writings
in one's mind, which the last little artist had heard Bahá'u'lláh did.

LaKeesha thanked the children for sharing and for helping everyone
learn that the Writings ask Bahá'ís not to portray any Messengers, like
Bahá'u'lláh, in a drawing or other art-form because it just isn't possible
to do Them justice. She praised Kamál, the boy who had at first tried to

draw a picture of Him seeing the Writings in His mind's eye, for being willing to redo his art.

LaKeesha added that someone could picture a Bahá'í book in their mind to help them remember and gain guidance from a quotation. She thought, though, that probably only Manifestations of God were able to read words appearing directly from God in their mind. Abby appreciated that the Faith was practical but also very mystical, even mysterious.

Class ended, and fruit punch and sugar cookies were served. Abby looked at all the children sitting on the floor, eating their chemical- and coloring-laced snack. With their red-stained mouths rimmed in sugar, squirming and fidgeting, bordering on fighting, they were a far cry from the wholesomely fed, willingly focused Erdean children. There seemed an impossible gap between then and now.

The heat became intolerable. Abby closed her eyes and drifted off to her new favorite place…Erden. Dali's loving face floated into her mind. But just as Dali started to say something comforting, the squabbling kids in Surely drowned her out.

Abby's eyes popped open. Nevertheless Dali's heightened sensitivities remained with her as she surveyed the barely functioning, not-yet-unified group of Bahá'ís in the stifling living room.

Through Dali's eyes, the worn-out mother seemed heroic. Her heart was in the right place, wanting to give her children a spiritual grounding. She just needed help to monitor and educate her two rambunctious youngsters and possibly help purify them from toxins.

With Dali's heart, Abby read the pure intent of the broken-English speaker, felt her embarrassment at her handicap, smiled at her warmly, and yearned to offer her a spare WaerY.

Wanting to bolster them, Dali wondered whether inviting this wilting group outside to take advantage of a shady spot would revive them.

Abby knew that Dali would see these disjointed, struggling souls as spiritual heroes for shouldering the goal of World Peace against immense obstacles and with little personal reward. From Dali's practical point of view, these beleaguered Bahá'ís were exquisitely precious, the groundbreakers in a much-needed company of builders.

From Dali's perspective, they grew illumined, radiant; Abby could almost *see* their glow. Her own lightning-touched soul sparked, flamed, blazed anew, enlivened by Erden's faraway solace.

Abby would have given almost anything to escape her mother and live in blissful, Erden-like happiness. But she couldn't, so she'd have to figure out how to survive in 2007 with 2707 insights…how to sustain her light.

At least she *had* this new light to sustain. She thought back over all the things that had happened to her in so short a time. She realized that being spirited away to Erden had resulted in both her being loved awake from her family nightmare and her growing awareness of what was possible both for her and for the whole world.

Spirited a-*way*. Loved a-*wake*. Growing a-*ware*. Maybe she should have told people in Erden her last name was A-W-long-A.

In any case, everyone on the planet who sought world peace – now, then, and in between – needed her and her uncool acquaintances to help build it. Abby's role was to make sure she tried. She smiled at her fellow laborers, toiling on the best they knew how. With God's help, it would work. Right there in Surely. She was *sure*.

Author's Notes

While many of the events and characters portrayed in this novel are based on parts of actual events I experienced or people I met, all of the characters, events, and places are fictional as portrayed.

Equally important, the fictional elements regarding the Bahá'í Faith and future are based strictly on my own personal understanding; they are not authoritative. I invite and encourage you to investigate the Bahá'í Writings for yourself and build your own personal vision from them.

Also, I took certain controversial scientific stances for the purpose of this novel.

I grew up and was "confirmed" in the Episcopalian Church. I heard many sermons, like the one Abby heard, on many different topics. The emphasis on a strict observance of ritual and the seeming dearth of genuine warmth, I have to say, left my spirit out in the cold. This in turn led me to begin exploring other faiths in my early teens.

Melissa is based on the person who impressed me with the Bahá'í Faith in the autumn of 1976.

The coffee shop in Little Lily, NC is based on a real one in Flagstaff, AZ. Called Macy's European Coffee House & Bakery and located at 14 S. Beaver St., it is owned by Bahá'í Tim Macy. Going there was as warm an experience as going to church should have been. Macy's is fancier, though, than the coffee shop I described.

My own mother provided much more nutritious food than Vivian did; and for that and several other things – including being a benchmark example – I am very grateful. I have never been in a coma, though; and for that I am *profoundly* grateful.

The shaving incident, the liver, the jello, the finger slamming, the earrings incident, having my nose painted red, the lack of confidence, and a lot more…all are drawn from real events. In most cases, though, they are exaggerated to clearly portray the angst that someone entering their teens might feel, especially if they also felt unloved.

Abby's session with Moony (a real horse) represents how my early ranch days went and, most importantly, nearly everything one should *not* do with horses. That's an urgent warning, folks! It was my arm that got broken (at age forty-one), and I who eventually found Parelli, went on to pass Level 3, and taught natural horsemanship.

I dreamt many of the dreams that Abby dreams.

I'm the quilt artist that the middle school art teacher was inspired by. And my eldest son had Abby's experience in art class. It resulted in a small wall-hanging of the Shrine of the Báb, because the Bahá'í World

Center in Israel was the most memorable place he'd ever been.

In giving the pronunciation of Persian and Arabic words, I used the sounds my admittedly very American ears think they hear when listening to Bahá'ís whose mother tongue is Persian rather than, say, English or Arabic. I trust that my Persian friends will be forgiving and that my readers will recognize the words even when they hear a non-Persian say them.[155]

I drew a great deal of inspiration from J.K. Rowling's *Harry Potter* series as well as her comments about the writing process. Like her, I kept notes and planned for about seven years before writing this novel. Many of my thoughts were jotted down on our household scratch paper. Then in mid-August of 2007, characters, scenes, and plots suddenly coalesced into a story I could start writing.

Writing this book, my first novel, has been an incredibly exciting and spiritual experience for me. There were times that I sat down at the computer in great anticipation, eager to see what Abby would do. At other times I prayed, asking God for guidance on what should happen, and was quite astonished at the results.

You may have noticed that, in printed copies of this book, the text is about half a point smaller than usual, with about one-fifth narrower line spacing. My reasons are entirely practical. I don't want to use any more trees than necessary, nor should you have to pay for, carry, and hold a thicker, heavier *Abby Wize: AWĀ*.

If you have any great ideas about Abby or Erden, or a different take on how the world will be when Peace arrives, I encourage you to share them with me. If I use them, though, they may be changed and I may not be able to give you credit. You're also invited to send me a review of *Abby Wize: AWĀ*, which I may put on my website or in my next book. You can join the "Abby Wize Books" discussion group at **http://groups.google.com/group/abby-wize-books** and email me at **AbbyWizeBooks@juno.com**.

If you have enjoyed this book, share it with others. Maybe even give a copy to your local libraries (public, private, and Bahá'í). And keep an eye out for *Abby Wize: BE*.

Lisa Bradley
September 9, 2009

Endnotes

Chapter 1

[1]   Abby's whole session with Moony is a fairly true account of how the author used to do her horse sessions in childhood. It is also a good representation of many things *not* to do with a horse.

[2]   Several years ago, the author saw just such a horse flailing on the ground after breaking its neck, and heard the shot that released it from its pain. When she realized what had happened because of someone's ignorance, she was horrified.

Chapter 4

[3]   This quilt appeared in the Autumn 2007 *Keepsake Quilting* catalog, page 46, kit item #5612 for $69.99.

[4]   Abby is looking at the September 2007 issue of *National Geographic*, especially the article on the "Struggle for the Soul of Pakistan." on page 32. The National Geographic Society publishes several magazines, has a TV channel, and produces films for TV, the big screen, and their own website.

[5]   Matthew 17:20 reads: And He [Jesus] said to them, "Because of the littleness of your faith; for truly I say to you, if you have faith as a mustard seed, you shall say to this mountain, 'Move from here to there,' and it shall move, and nothing shall be impossible to you."

[6]   Reverend Davison's sermon is based on actual text found at **www.FaithPresbyterian.org/sermons/robertson**. Scroll down the Archives list and click on **June, 2005**; then scroll two-thirds of the way down the page to the June 05, 2005 "The Second Coming of Jesus" sermon. For those who are unfamiliar with Christian views of the Second Coming, this represents a fairly conservative view and is quite similar to what the author heard while growing up. Some denominations of Christianity take, or expect to take, all of the end-of-days prophesies as absolutely literal.

[7]   This benediction – from the scriptures of Judaism (Bamidbar 6:24–26 in the Torah) and Christianity (Numbers 6:24–26 in the Old Testament) – was regularly given in the author's childhood church.

Chapter 7

[8]   *The American Heritage Dictionary* describes a *trundle bed* as a low bed on casters that can be rolled under another bed for storage.

[9]   *Horses For Dummies* offers information on choosing a horse, caring for it, and buying equipment, as well as a guide to horse breeds.

[10]   Jenn has heard of very young mothers such as those listed at

en.wikipedia.org/wiki/list_of_youngest_birth_mothers.

Chapter 9
[11]   Natural Horsemanship is real. Look in the "Resources" section for online information.

Chapter 10
[12]   These two counted cross-stitch patterns and instructions by Lisa Bradley are available for your use at the end of this book. Enjoy! And for more information about counted cross-stitch, try your local needle-work store or the internet. You can even find scores of free cross-stitch charts on the internet, though of course you'll have to supply all your own materials and already know how to stitch.

[13]   Abby is reading pages 80–81 of *Native American Wisdom*.

[14]   Abby is leafing through the September 2007 issue of *Horse Illustrated*.

[15]   Abby has come across an ad on page 98 in the September 2007 issue of *Cowboys & Indians*.

Chapter 11
[16]   Abby is reading pages 58–59 of *Native American Wisdom*.

Chapter 12
[17]   Horses do hug like this, and it's a great compliment when they do so with a human.

[18]   You can learn about stirrups, saddle jockeys, and the like in the online Western Saddle Guide (see "Resources"); just click on **Saddle Parts** under **THE WESTERN SADDLE**.

Chapter 13
[19]   Abby is thinking about figurines, not the big statues you see, for example, in parks. She has seen a number of TRAIL OF PAINTED PONIES figurines (see "Resources"), including realistic horses, fanciful horses, Native American horses, a pegasus, and an equine unicorn.

[20]   What Dali almost says is "What I think you are able to bear now." She is thinking about the quote on page 176 of *Gleanings from the Writings of Bahá'u'lláh*: "Not everything that a man knoweth can be disclosed, nor can everything that he can disclose be regarded as timely, nor can every timely utterance be considered as suited to the capacity of those who hear it."

[21]   In the Bahá'í calendar, Friday is called Istiqlál (iss-tick-LAWL), an Arabic word for *independence*. The month of Kamál (kah-MAWL) – meaning *perfection* – begins on August 1. BE stands for Bahá'í Era. Year One in the Bahá'í calendar started in the Gregorian year 1844.

Visit **en.wikipedia.org/wiki/baha%27i_calendar** to learn more about the Bahá'í calendar.

[22] In the Bahá'í calendar, Saturday is called Jalál (jah-LAWL), an Arabic word meaning *glory* or *splendor*. The author has chosen her future dates based on research done by Ahang Rabbani, who states that the Bahá'í Writings – some already translated into English, some not – say the Bahá'í Dispensation (a) will last *at least* 1,000 years before the next Manifestation comes and (b) is split into the Heroic, Formative, and Golden Ages. Also according to the Writings, Rabbani adds, the Heroic Age ended when 'Abdu'l-Bahá passed away around 80 BE, the Golden Age will last no more than 100–200 years, and what is left between them is at least 700–800 years of the Formative Age. Abby has traveled to a time before the next Manifestation but after the establishment of the Most Great Peace promised by Bahá'u'lláh.

[23] Page 51 of *Stories of Bahá'u'lláh* recounts how Bahá'u'lláh so loved a smiling face, saying: "There are four qualities which I love to see manifested in people: first, enthusiasm and courage; second, a face wreathed in smiles and radiant countenance; third, that they see all things with their own eyes and not through the eyes of others; fourth, the ability to carry a task, once begun, through to its end." Dali has even *worked* on her smile because of this story.

[24] Dali is waiting to see if Abby is going to mention the noontime prayer. When she doesn't, Dali figures Abby is not Bahá'í. This helps Dali decide many things to come.

[25] Dali has only read about anorexia and bulimia, doesn't really understand how or why they manifested, and isn't sure if Abby might have an aversion to food…especially eating in front of someone else.

[26] Abby is quoting from the Lord's Prayer in the New Testament.

[27] The sentence that Dali is quoting from reads: "Give us our daily bread, and grant Thine increase in the necessities of life, that we may be dependent on none other but Thee, may commune wholly with Thee, may walk in Thy ways and declare Thy mysteries." The complete prayer by 'Abdu'l-Bahá is on pages 22–23 of the US compilation of prayers from Scripture entitled *Bahá'í Prayers*. You can read it at **reference.bahai.org/en/t/c/BP/bp-11.html**.

[28] This incident is described in detail in the online article "The Tylenol Terrorist: Death in a Bottle" by Rachel Bell. You can find a copy at **www.FreeRepublic.com/focus/f-news/1618751/posts**.

[29] The noon prayer is said between solar noon and sunset. This means that in the world of 2007, Bahá'ís actually say the noon prayer after one o'clock during daylight savings time. However, the author has decided that daylight savings time is no longer practiced in 2707, in part because of articles such as the one about increased heart attacks at **www.stmarys.org/120249.cfm** and the one about increased electricity use at **www.nytimes.com/2008/11/20/opinion/20kotchen.html**.

Chapter 14

[30]   You don't have to wait centuries to get a household porta-potty like this one; they already exist.

[31]   There's scientific evidence indicating that vegetarians have a more-attractive body odor. Read about a study of meat- and nonmeat-eaters at **chemse.oxfordjournals.org/cgi/content/abstract/31/8/747**.

[32]   Every Bahá'í House of Worship is to be a hub around which various auxiliary services – often called Dependencies –will be housed. The author has created Dali's list from the Dependencies mentioned at **bahai-library.org/?file=compilation_mashriq_adhkar_mcglinn** and those under "Mashriqu'l-Adhkár" in *A Basic Bahá'í Dictionary*.

[33]   Dali is quoting from a verse on page 41 of *The Hidden Words of Bahá'u'lláh*, specifically Persian #54: "O Ye Rich Ones On Earth! The poor in your midst are My trust; guard ye My trust, and be not in-tent only on your own ease."

Chapter 15

[34]   The whole song is "Say, God sufficeth all things above all things, and nothing in the heavens or in the earth but God sufficeth. Verily, He is in Himself the Knower, the Sustainer, the Omnipotent." It is a prayer by the Báb, and appears on page 56 of *Bahá'í Prayers*.

[35]   The complete quotation from 'Abdu'l-Bahá reads: "Therefore must the mentor be a doctor as well: that is, he must, in instructing the child, remedy its faults; must give him learning, and at the same time rear him to have a spiritual nature. Let the teacher be a doctor to the character of the child, thus will he heal the spiritual ailments of the children of men." It is part of selection 103, page 130, in *Selections from the Writings of 'Abdu'l-Bahá*. You can read the whole selection at **reference.bahai.org/en/t/ab/SAB/sab-104.html**.

Chapter 16

[36]   A letter dated July 9, 1939 and written on behalf of Shoghi Effendi explains the symbolism of the number nine: "First, regarding the significance of the number nine: its importance as a symbol used so often in various connections by the believers lies in three facts. First, it symbolizes the nine great world religions of which we have any definite historical knowledge, including the Babí and Bahá'í Revelations; second, it represents the number of perfection, being the highest single number; third, it is the numerical value of the word 'Bahá.'" This excerpt, item

1374, appears on page 414 of the compilation *Lights of Guidance*.

[37] For more references on Progressive Revelation from a Bahá'í perspective, see the section entitled "THE COVENANT" starting on page 110 in Volume 1 of *The Compilation of Compilations*, which is available in the *Ocean Library of World Religions*. One quotation the author considers especially enlightening is on page 167 of Bahá'u'lláh's *The Kitáb-i-Íqán*: "His creation no end hath overtaken, and it hath ever existed from the 'Beginning that hath no beginning'; and the Manifestations of His Beauty no beginning hath beheld, and they will continue to the 'End that knoweth no end.'"

[38] The Lord's Prayer appears in two books of the New Testament: in Matthew 6:9–13 and in Luke 11:2–4. The version Abby learned is not exactly like either one of these Biblical versions; but it is a version often used in the Protestant branch of Christianity.

[39] Dali doesn't want to reveal too much specific information from Abby's future. So she asks the Yuter to check its ancient archives from Abby's time for hints about toxins causing serious, long-term, even gene-affecting conditions. The Yuter discovers several references from our present, such as those found at **www.GenerationRescue.org**, at **www.nvic.org**, and at **en.wikipedia.org/wiki/Epigenetics** under link 5.3 on cancer and developmental abnormalities.

[40] The Yuter also discovers references from our present about pollutants changing peoples' genes, such as that found on pages 8–11 in the March 2007 issue of *Muse*, one of the Cricket magazines.

[41] The Yuter also finds references from our present about certain problems associated with infant formula feeding, such as that found at **www.wearsthebaby.com/infantformula.htm**.

[42] Dali is quoting from a passage on pages 8–9 of *Ten Days in the Light of 'Akká*. 'Akká (AH-kaw) or Akko is now the city of Acre in Israel.

[43] Dali is referring to points 'Abdu'l-Bahá made in letters, which you can find in the *Bahá'í Library Online* at **bahai-library.org**, under Primary Source Material, by clicking on **Compilations prepared by the Bahá'í World Center > 49. Health, Healing, and Nutrition** and scrolling down to items 17–18.

[44] There are many references about 'Abdu'l-Bahá reading people's thoughts: on page 158 of *The Chosen Highway*, where he answered unspoken questions during his visit to London; page 36 of *Memories of 'Abdu'l-Bahá*, recalling his visit to California; numerous places in *The Diary of Juliet Thompson*, which offers an account of her many hours with him in the Holy Land, Europe, and America; and in other such documents. The author especially likes this story from *Star of the West* magazine, volume 18, number 9, page 285:

During one evening meal at the Master's table, a lady sat next to him listening to His words of wisdom. She looked at a glass of water which was directly in front of her place and thought, "Oh! if only 'Abdu'l-Bahá would take my heart and empty it of every earthly desire, just as one would take this glass and empty it, and then refill it with divine love and understanding."

Her thought was just a flashing thought, but 'Abdu'l-Bahá seemed to read it. He was in the middle of His talk but He stopped briefly and spoke to the servant. It was just a few words in Persian, and then He continued with His conversation without anyone noticing anything. Soon, the servant came quietly to the lady's place, took away her glass from the table, emptied it, and put it back in front of her.

As 'Abdu'l-Bahá continued to talk, He lifted the water from the table, reached out in His most casual manner, and slowly refilled the lady's empty glass. No one had noticed what he had done – no one, that is, except the lady herself. She knew what 'Abdu'l-Bahá was doing, and her heart was filled with great joy. Now she knew that the most private thoughts and desires of everyone present were an open book to 'Abdu'l-Bahá and that His love included all.

[45]   Dali is referring to a passage on pages 13–14 in Volume 1 of *The Revelation of Bahá'u'lláh*, which says of 'Abdu'l-Bahá: "He had such spiritual insight that, as a young boy, He intuitively recognized the station of His Father. So highly did Bahá'u'lláh esteem Him that in Baghdád He used to address Him, while still in His teens, as the Master – a designation which Bahá'u'lláh had also used for His own father while in Tihran."

[46]   In *The World Order of Bahá'u'lláh*, page 203, Shoghi Effendi wrote: "The unity of the human race, as envisaged by Bahá'u'lláh, implies the establishment of a world commonwealth in which all nations, races, creeds and classes are closely and permanently united, and in which the autonomy of its state members and the personal freedom and initiative of the individuals that compose them are definitely and completely safeguarded."

Chapter 17
[47]   And maybe someday Abby will see and read the lion/lamb story at **www.NaturesCornerMagazine.com/lion_lamb.html**.

Chapter 18
[48]   At Dali's request, the Yuter again accesses its ancient archives and discovers references from our present about problems with cow's

milk, such as that found in an article about "Cows' Milk Allergy in Infants" at **www.MedicalNewsToday.com/articles/73741.php**.

[49] Medications that might cause tooth discoloration are listed at **webmd.com/oral-health/oral-side-effects-of-medications?page=3**.

[50] The Yuter also discovers articles from our present about health problems resulting from ingesting chemicals, colorings, preservatives, and so on, such as the one on chemicals found in commonplace things at **alternet.org/story/146938/can_everyday_things_cause_cancer?** and the one on dairy products found at **drweil.com/drw/u/id/QAA400175**. The effects of naturally occurring hormones in milk may be further aggravated if the farmers also feed their cattle growth hormones.

[51] Do a web search on any of those conditions and you'll find that, while the cause is not known, it is known that dietary changes can often help them. Search a little deeper and you'll find that medical science barely recognizes the critical role of nutrition in health. People are finding out for themselves, however; and medicine is slowly allowing for the influence of diet as a preventative factor.

[52] Dali is quoting from selection 134, page 153, in *Selections from the Writings of Abdu'l-Bahá*. You can read the complete selection at **reference.bahai.org/en/t/ab/SAB/sab-135.html**. And for interesting information on food combining, enter the term **food combining** into a search engine such as Google.

[53] In a letter to an individual Bahá'í, Abdu'l-Bahá wrote: "The child must, from the day of his birth, be provided with whatever is conducive to his health; and know ye this: so far as possible, the mother's milk is best for, more agreeable and better suited to the child, unless she should fall ill or her milk should run entirely dry." This excerpt appears on page 461 in Volume 1 of *The Compilation of Compilations*, which is available in *Ocean*.

[54] *Plantic*, which biodegrades slowly in air and faster in water, is briefly described on page 106 of the November 2007 issue of *Reader's Digest*. It is already available in Australia.

[55] Dali is singing a prayer by Bahá'u'lláh; it appears on page 116 of *Bahá'í Prayers*.

[56] Dali is quoting from a passage starting on page 106 of *Gleanings from the Writings of Bahá'u'lláh*. The whole sentence reads: "Purge your sight, that ye may perceive its glory with your own eyes, and depend not on the sight of any one except your self, for God hath never burdened any soul beyond its power." A related passage earlier on the same page reads: "He hath endowed every soul with the capacity to recognize the signs of God. How could He, otherwise, have fulfilled His testimony unto men, if ye be of them that ponder His Cause in their hearts. He will

never deal unjustly with any one, neither will He task a soul beyond its power."

[57]   Dali is quoting 'Abdu'l-Bahá. You can read the whole passage online in the Barstow Collection part of the *Bahá'í Library Online*, at **bahai-library.org/zamir/barstow.html**, by scrolling almost all the way down, past page #80A. The author especially likes the part about "Let us put…excitement and joy into the hearts of the free!"

[58]   In a personal email the author received on October 10, 2007 from Bahá'í scholar Ahang Rabbani, he said, "I think it was my presentation that spoke to 150 years as potential life (based on 'Abdu'l-Bahá's comments as captured by a resident believer in 'Akká named Khalíl Shahídí)…Best wishes, Ahang." Mr. Rabbani translated *A Lifetime with 'Abdu'l-Bahá: Reminiscences of Khalíl Shahídí*.

[59]   Dali doesn't mean spoken prayers reach God better; she means they have a more far-reaching effect in the world. She's remembering a passage on page 295 of *Gleanings from the Writings of Bahá'u'lláh* and on page iii of *Bahá'í Prayers*: "Intone, O My servant, the verses of God that have been received by thee, as intoned by them who have drawn nigh unto Him, that the sweetness of thy melody may kindle thine own soul, and attract the hearts of all men. Whoso reciteth, in the privacy of his chamber, the verses revealed by God, the scattering angels of the Almighty shall scatter abroad the fragrance of the words uttered by his mouth, and shall cause the heart of every righteous man to throb. Though he may, at first, remain unaware of its effect, yet the virtue of the grace vouchsafed unto him must needs sooner or later exercise its influence upon his soul. Thus have the mysteries of the Revelation of God been decreed by virtue of the Will of Him Who is the Source of power and wisdom." *The American Heritage Dictionary* describes to *intone* as to speak with a singing tone, such as when reciting a chant or psalm.

[60]   The word "goodbye" originally came from the valediction "God be with ye."

[61]   The month of S̲h̲araf (shah-RAHF) begins on December 31. Tá (TAW) or Tihrán (tih-h'RAWN) can also be transliterated as Tehran or Teheran.

[62]   Regarding Bag̲h̲dád (BAHG-dawd), in paragraph 32, page 30, of *The Kitáb-i-Aqdas*, Bahá'u'lláh tells the Bahá'ís: "The Lord hath ordained that those of you who are able shall make pilgrimage to the sacred House…" The Universal House of Justice further explained in note 54, page 191: "Two sacred Houses are covered by this ordinance, the House of the Báb in S̲h̲íráz and the House of Bahá'u'lláh in Bag̲h̲-dád. Bahá'u'lláh has specified that pilgrimage to either of these two Houses fulfils the requirement of this passage…After the passing of

Bahá'u'lláh, 'Abdu'l-Bahá designated the Shrine of Bahá'u'lláh at Bahjí as a place of pilgrimage [also]."

Chapter 19

[63]   Bothered Brother is quoting from a talk by 'Abdu'l-Bahá. An excerpt, item 733, appears on page 219 of the compilation *Lights of Guidance*.

[64]   Bothered Brother is quoting part of Bahá'u'lláh's injunction in paragraph 74, pages 46–47, of *The Kitáb-i-Aqdas*.

[65]   Trees like this already exist. One example is the Fruit Cocktail Tree at **www.DirectGardening.com/detail.asp?pid=5556**.

[66]   The author took many UL words in whole or in part from the Esperanto language, originally created by Dr. L.L. Zamenhof. Visit **en.wikipedia.org/wiki/esperanto** to learn about the language and about its Bahá'í connection.

[67]   Dali is quoting one of Bahá'u'lláh's "Words of Wisdom" on page 141 of *Bahá'í World Faith*: "True reliance is for the servant to pursue his profession and calling in this world, to hold fast unto the Lord, to seek naught but His grace, inasmuch as in His hands is the destiny of all His servants."

[68]   Dali is quoting from a verse on page 51 of *The Hidden Words of Bahá'u'lláh*, specifically Persian #82: "O My Servant! The best of men are they that earn a livelihood by their calling and spend upon themselves and upon their kindred for the love of God, the Lord of all worlds."

[69]   A more detailed list of laws between Bahá'ís and God – gleaned by the author from the version of *Developing Distinctive Bahá'í Communities* available in *Ocean* – includes: using one of the three Obligatory Prayers daily; reciting "Alláh-u-Abhá" (ah-LAW-oh-ab-HAW) ninety-five times daily; deepening one's knowledge of the Sacred Writings every morning and evening; annual fasting; paying debts; returning to God a small part of one's residual income after paying all necessary living expenses; going on pilgrimage; writing a will and testament; avoiding alcohol and other mood- and mind-altering drugs except under the care of a physician; obeying civil law; following Bahá'í marriage and divorce laws; being chaste outside of marriage and faithful within marriage, which is between one man and one woman; eschewing gambling; shunning gossip; and not holding membership in political parties, secret societies, or other religious organizations. Bahá'ís do not believe that their religious laws are binding on people who aren't Bahá'í, nor do they consider these laws prescriptions for public policy.

Chapter 20

[70]   Asian dragons are usually considered benevolent, have thinner,

serpentine bodies, and fly without wings, such as the ones depicted at **en.wikipedia.org/wiki/chinese_dragon**. European dragons are usually considered malevolent and have thicker bodies with wings, such as the ones at **en.wikipedia.org/wiki/european_dragon**. You can learn about valkyries at **en.wikipedia.org/wiki/Valkyrie**. Traditional unicorns tend to look more caprine, or goat-like, such as the one you can see depicted at **www.BestPriceArt.com/painting/?pid=154200**. Modern unicorns tend to look more equine, or horse-like, such as the one you can see depicted at **www.NovaReinna.com/guard/unicorn.html**.

[71]   Metric is the first name of a young Nigerian college student that the author went to college with.

[72]   In a letter written in 1936 – and quoted on pages x–xi of his introduction to *The Proclamation of Bahá'u'lláh* – Shoghi Effendi noted that, in addition to a world language: "A world script, a world literature, a uniform and universal system of currency, of weights and measures, will simplify and facilitate intercourse and understanding among the nations and races of mankind." To Kreshi, all of these have existed for ages; so he wonders what rock Abby's been living under. Being ever polite, though – and interested in her, besides – he is pretending to accept her excuse about never having seen these Kingdom coins.

[73]   The October 2007 issue of *National Geographic*, page 26, showcases collectable coins – legal tender from the Republic of Palau – with objects embedded in them. You can see Palau coins with a pearl, a tiny bit of meteorite, a bit of volcanic rock, and a four-leaf clover, as well as a working light-bulb coin from Niue and several other unusual coins, at **bizaims.com/coffee+break/curiosities+events+funny/unusual+coins**. Also, visit **en.wikipedia.org/wiki/bristlecone_pine** to learn about bristlecone pines, and **en.wikipedia.org/wiki/bee_hummingbird** to learn about the bee hummingbird.

[74]   Abby read an article about giant money on pages 16–19 in the May/June 2007 issue of *Muse*, one of the Cricket magazines.

[75]   You can learn about sea serpents – including some "historical sightings" – at **en.wikipedia.org/wiki/sea_serpent**, and about kelpies at **en.wikipedia.org/wiki/kelpie**.

Chapter 21

[76]   You can learn about the winged horse – the pegasus or, more generically, pterippus – at **en.wikipedia.org/wiki/pegasus**.

[77]   *Lung* or *long* is the Chinese character for "dragon" and *ma* is the one for horse. Since Rykeir's dragon horse has wings, it may specifically be a *tianma*, also known as the heavenly horse or Chinese pegasus.

You can learn about the lóngmă – the vital spirit of heaven and earth – at **en.wikipedia.org/wiki/longma**.

[78]   Rykeir is referring to a humorous concept presented in Lewis Carroll's classic *The Hunting of the Snark: An Agony in Eight Fits*. His "Fit the First – The Landing" starts:

"Just the place for a Snark!" the Bellman cried,
As he landed his crew with care;
Supporting each man on the top of the tide
By a finger entwined in his hair.

"Just the place for a Snark! I have said it twice:
That alone should encourage the crew.
Just the place for a Snark! I have said it thrice:
What I tell you three times is true."

Visit **ebooks.adelaide.edu.au/c/carroll/lewis/snark** to read the whole poem, and **en.wikipedia.org/wiki/the_hunting_of_the_snark** to read *about* the poem. As a game programmer, Rykeir is also familiar with the design philosophy that any machine or computer your life depends on should have triple redundant failsafes, sometimes called the "tell you three times" protocol. To learn about other literary uses of *the rule of three*, visit **tvtropes.org/pmwiki/pmwiki.php/main/RuleOfThree**.

[79]   A horse needs around two feet each for takeoff and landing and four feet per stride. Of course, Abby's mighty steed probably has a longer stride. Visit **en.wikipedia.org/wiki/show_jumping** to learn about jumping events at horse shows. You can also find numerous slides and video clips on **www.youtube.com** using the SEARCH term **horse jumping**.

[80]   The movie is *Wild Wild West*, a 1999 "steampunk" science fiction/action comedy directed by Barry Sonnenfeld and starring Will Smith – whom Abby and Jenn adore – and Kevin Kline.

[81]   The Yuter is drawing its definition of Ayyám-i-Há from *A Basic Bahá'í Dictionary*, and personalizing it for Abby.

[82]   Kreshi is thinking about the quote on page 163 of *Gleanings from the Writings of Bahá'u'lláh*: "Know thou that every fixed star hath its own planets, and every planet its own creatures, whose number no man can compute."

[83]   Rykeir is quoting a verse on page 17 of *The Hidden Words of Bahá'u'lláh*, specifically Arabic #59.

[84]   You can find numerous references by entering the words **divine promptings** or **spiritual insight** in the SEARCH field of the *Bahá'í Reference Library*, the *Bahá'í Library Online*, or *Ocean*. One of the author's favorite such quotations appears on page 35, in the Tablet of Tarazát

(Ornaments), of *Tablets of Bahá'u'lláh Revealed After the Kitáb-i-Aqdas*: "We cherish the hope that through the loving-kindness of the All-Wise, the All-Knowing, obscuring dust may be dispelled and the power of perception enhanced, that the people may discover the purpose for which they have been called into being. In this Day whatsoever serveth to reduce blindness and to increase vision is worthy of consideration. This vision acteth as the agent and guide for true knowledge. Indeed in the estimation of men of wisdom keenness of understanding is due to keenness of vision. The people of Bahá must under all circumstances observe that which is meet and seemly and exhort the people accordingly."

[85]   Visit **en.wikipedia.org/wiki/As-Sir%c4%81t** (that's eight one tee) to learn about the Islamic hadith (hah-DEETH) or tradition of the Sirat al-Jahim (sear-RAT ahl-jah-HEEM).

Chapter 22

[86]   The roots of the word *alacorn* are "ala" meaning *wing* and "corn" meaning *horn*. It refers to a modern myth that developed as both unicorns and pegasi became more equine in people's minds. Don't confuse it with the word *alicorn*, which is the horn of a unicorn. Alacorns are sometimes called pegacorns. To see artistic examples of alacorns, visit **abbeyincstudios.com/resins.htm** and scroll down to the third row, and visit **images.elfwood.com/art/m/i/michelle16/pegacorn.jpg**.

[87]   Dali is quoting from the Tablet of Tarazát (Ornaments) in *Tablets of Bahá'u'lláh Revealed After the Kitáb-i-Aqdas*. The complete sentence, on pages 35–36, reads: "The first Taráz and the first effulgence which hath dawned from the horizon of the Mother Book is that man should know his own self and recognize that which leadeth unto loftiness or lowliness, glory or abasement, wealth or poverty." Taráz is the singular noun meaning *ornament*.

[88]   You can learn about seahorses – which really do change color – at **en.wikipedia.org/wiki/seahorse**, and about the part-human/part-horse centaurs at **en.wikipedia.org/wiki/centaur**.

Chapter 23

[89]   The author is again using Esperanto to symbolize UL. Esperanto builds words out of pieces that always mean the same thing. "Spirito" means *spirit*, and changing the end to "a" (spee-REE-tah) makes it the adjective *spiritual*. "Lerni" means *to learn*, "ejo" means *place*, and so "lernejo" (lair-NAY-yo) is a learning-place, a *school*. "Besto" means *beast*, "montri" means *to show*, "ejo" means *place*, and so "bestmontrejo" ("baste-moan-TRAY-yo) is an *animal showplace*. To learn about tools to teach yourself Esperanto, enter the term **Esperanto teach yourself** into a search engine such as Google.

[90]   Dali is referring to the twelfth Glad Tiding of the Tablet of Bi<u>sh</u>árát (Glad-Tidings) in *Tablets of Bahá'u'lláh Revealed After the Kitáb-i-Aqdas*. The complete quotation, on page 26, reads:

It is enjoined upon every one of you to engage in some form of occupation, such as crafts, trades and the like. We have graciously exalted your engagement in such work to the rank of worship unto God, the True One. Ponder ye in your hearts the grace and the blessings of God and render thanks unto Him at eventide and at dawn. Waste not your time in idleness and sloth. Occupy yourselves with that which profiteth yourselves and others. Thus hath it been decreed in this Tablet from whose horizon the day-star of wisdom and utterance shineth resplendent.

The most despised of men in the sight of God are those who sit idly and beg. Hold ye fast unto the cord of material means, placing your whole trust in God, the Provider of all means. When anyone occupieth himself in a craft or trade, such occupation itself is regarded in the estimation of God as an act of worship; and this is naught but a token of His infinite and all-pervasive bounty.

[91]   In moderation, 'Abdu'l-Bahá enjoyed honey and candy himself, shared it generously with others, and even offered it as a healing balm for both mental and physical stress. In *The Chosen Highway*, page 202, Lady Blomfield describes a meal where: "'Abdu'l-Bahá tasted only a few spoonfuls of honey, a little broth, and some olives, and after the meal He slept about an hour." In *Arches of the Years*, page 95, Marzieh Gail relates that, during 'Abdu'l-Bahá's travels in America: "He was paying His own bills, accepting nothing of money value, only such gifts as flowers and candy, which He promptly distributed as was His way." In *Dawn Over Mount Hira*, pages 200–201, she also describes a work meeting with him wherein: "He reached over to His table (throughout this interview He remained standing) – on which He had flowers, papers, rock candy, rose water – and with both hands full of candy He told me to hold out my hands. I laid the Tablets on the table edge, stretched out my cupped hands and He filled them with candy; and still smiling, He took my face in His two hands and said: 'Go and eat this candy, and by the grace and power of the Blessed Beauty thou shalt be enabled to translate from Arabic into English.'" And in *Tablets of 'Abdu'l-Bahá*, volume 1, page 185, the Master assures an ailing woman that her illness is not on account of sin and suggests that she: "Take some honey, recite 'Ya Baha-ul-ABHA,' and eat a little thereof for several days."

[92]   In Esperanto, "pordo" means *door*. "Ŝlosi" means *to lock*, using "iĝ" makes it reflexive (the actor acts upon itself), changing the end to "u" makes it a command, and so "ŝlosiĝu" means *lock yourself.*

[93] Muscle testing exists now. See how to muscle test yourself at **www.lind.com/quantum/muscle%20testing%20yourself.htm**.

[94] Dali is referring to 'Abdu'l-Bahá's statement, included in selection 39 on pages 15–16 of *A Compilation on Bahá'í Education*:

Observe how many penal institutions, houses of detention and places of torture are made ready to receive the sons of men, the purpose being to prevent them, by punitive measures, from committing terrible crimes — whereas this very torment and punishment only increaseth depravity, and by such means the desired aim cannot be properly achieved.

Therefore must the individual be trained from his infancy in such a way that he will never undertake to commit a crime, will, rather, direct all his energies to the acquisition of excellence, and will look upon the very commission of an evil deed as in itself the harshest of all punishments, considering the sinful act itself to be far more grievous than any prison sentence. For it is possible so to train the individual that, although crime may not be completely done away with, still it will become very rare.

The purport is this, that to train the character of humankind is one of the weightiest commandments of God, and the influence of such training is the same as that which the sun exerteth over tree and fruit. Children must be most carefully watched over, protected and trained; in such consisteth true parenthood and parental mercy.

[95] Many forms of pest-control fields are already in use to repel insects, arachnids, and small mammals through electromagnetic, ionic, or sonic means. Visit **www.ElectronicPestRepeller.com** to see an example that uses all three types.

[96] Dali is quoting paragraph 62, page 41, of *The Kitáb-i-Aqdas*. There is, of course, a difference between deliberately taking a person's life, say, to rob them versus to protect a child they are trying to kill. Just as there's a difference between burning an empty warehouse versus burning a schoolhouse full of children. For more detail on this subject, read Note 86, pages 203–204, of *The Kitáb-i-Aqdas*.

[97] This has, unfortunately, happened in numerous wars. And is still happening. If you have a strong stomach, take a look at the report from late 2007 at **hnn.us/blogs/entries/45591.html**.

[98] Aghṣán (ahg-SAWN, meaning *branches*) refers to the relatives and descendents of Bahá'u'lláh; there are no Bahá'í Aghṣán in Abby's time, but perhaps some will become Bahá'í in future. Bahá'u'lláh's complete letter to Ahmad is on pages 307–311 of *Bahá'í Prayers*.

[99]   In *Tablets of Abdu'l-Bahá*, volume 2, page 430, the he writes: "My name is Abdul-Baha, my identity is Abdul-Baha, my qualification is Abdul-Baha, my reality is Abdul-Baha, my praise is Abdul-Baha. Thraldom to the Blessed Perfection is my glorious refulgent diadem; and servitude to all the human race is my perpetual religion." And in another letter, on page 466, he writes: "Regarding the station of this servant: My station is Abdul-Baha, my name is Abdul-Baha, my qualification is Abdul-Baha, my praise is Abdul-Baha, my title is Abdul-Baha."

[100]   This dramatic presentation is based on Mrs. Brown's book entitled *Memories of Abdu'l-Bahá*.

[101]   The actress is quoting a sentence on page 14 of *Abdu'l-Bahá – The Centre of the Covenant of Bahá'u'lláh*.

[102]   At a Summer School years ago, the author heard the recording of Abdu'l-Bahá chanting. She found the translation of the chant Abby is hearing at **www.ki4u.com/webpal/c_renewal/prayers/chant.htm**. In its entirety, the chant reads:

> Praise be to God that we are present in this radiant meeting
>   and turning toward the Kingdom of Abhá.
> That which we behold is due to the Grace and Bounty
>   of the Blessed Perfection.
> We are atoms and He is the Sun of Reality.
> We are drops and He is The Greatest Ocean.
> Though we are poor
>   yet the Treasury of the Kingdom is full of overflowings.
> Though we are weak
>   yet the confirmation of the Supreme Concourse is abundant.
> Though we are helpless
>   yet our refuge and shelter is in His Holiness Bahá'u'lláh.
> Praise be to God! His traces are evident!
> Praise be to God! His lights are radiating!
> Praise be to God! His ocean is full of waves!
> Praise be to God! His radiance is intense!
> Praise be to God! His bestowals are abundant!
> Praise be to God! His favours are manifest!
> Glad-tidings! glad-tidings! [*chanted before each line below.*]
> The Morn of Guidance hath dawned!
> The Sun of Reality hath shone forth!
> The Breeze of Favour hath wafted!
> The rain drops of the Cloud of Bounty have showered!

The hearts are all in the utmost purity!
The Sun of the Supreme Horizon hath radiated to all the world
    with boundless effulgence!
It is the Splendor of His Highness Bahá'u'lláh!
Zion is dancing!
The Kingdom of God is full of exhilaration and commotion!

[103]   The Day of the Covenant is the Holy Day observed on November 26 to commemorate Bahá'u'lláh's appointment of 'Abdu'l-Bahá as the Center of His Covenant. 'Abdu'l-Bahá instructed that his own birthday not be celebrated, because he was born on the very day that the Báb declared His mission (May 23, 1844) and he said *that* Holy Day must be devoted solely to the Báb's anniversary. But when the early believers pleaded with him for a day to observe in his own honor, he graciously acceded and gave them the Day of the Covenant.

[104]   The actress is quoting 'Abdu'l-Bahá's statement on page 339 of *The Promulgation of Universal Peace.*

[105]   Kahlil Gibran (kah-LEEL jih-BRAWN) is sometimes listed as Khalil Gibran. To learn about Kahlil Gibran, including his interaction with 'Abdu'l-Bahá, visit **en.wikipedia.org/wiki/Khalil_Gibran**. Visit **www.bahai-library.org/file.php?file=bushrui_gibran_man_poet** and scroll to the bottom of the page to see his sketch of 'Abdu'l-Bahá.

Chapter 24

[106]   Abby is not familiar with either the culpeo or the dhole. Visit **en.wikipedia.org/wiki/canidae** to learn about the canine family in general, and **www.youtube.com/watch?v=HqbVbPvlDoM** to see an amazing video of a woman who taught her dog a pattern and/or is cueing it surreptitiously.

[107]   Abby is seeing a caracal. Visit **en.wikipedia.org/wiki/felidae** to learn about the feline family in general.

[108]   Xenophon (ZEHN-uh-fun) – circa 430–355 BC – is considered the father of natural horsemanship. He was a Greek soldier, friend of Socrates, historian, poet, writer, and horse trainer. Among other books and short works, he wrote a significant treatise entitled *Peri Hippikēs* (variously called *De Re Equestri, On Horsemanship*, and *On the Art of Horsemanship*) that covered selecting, caring for, and training horses in a non-abusive manner for general use, classical dressage. and even the military. Visit **classics.mit.edu/Xenophon/xen.horse.html** to read this treatise in Greek and English. Visit **iep.utm.edu/x/xenophon.htm** and **en.wikipedia.org/wiki/Xenophon** to read more about Xenophon.

[109]   Abby quickly recognizes the animal show's opening narrative as being based on the creation story told at the beginning of the Book of

Genesis in the Bible.

[110] Back in Chapter 13, when Abby asked about roping steers, Dali blinked long and slow. That's the first time Abby noticed anyone mentally communicating with their Yuter, though she didn't yet know that's what was happening. Dali was checking an historical record to make sure she understood what Abby meant, then scheduling a reminder to mention it to Abby again at the show.

[111] Kangaroos, Tasmanian devils, and wallabies are marsupials, mammals who are born very early and immature and then are carried and nursed in their mothers' pouches during infancy. Platypuses are monotremes, mammals who lay eggs instead of birthing live young. Visit **en.wikipedia.org/wiki/Marsupial** to learn about marsupials, and **en.wikipedia.org/wiki/Monotremes** to learn about monotremes.

[112] In Spanish-walking, the horse lifts its diagonal front and back feet together and stretches its front leg up and out. A person Spanish-walking beside their horse can lift and stretch their own legs in unison with the horse's front legs. To see a video of a *ridden* horse Spanish-walking, visit **www.youtube.com/watch?v=lpCvQBALBX0**.

[113] The continuing animal-show narration about unity is based on statements that 'Abdu'l-Bahá made in *Paris Talks*.

[114] The continuing animal-show narration about love is based on statements that 'Abdu'l-Bahá made on page 88 in the "Divine Love" section of *Foundations of World Unity*.

[115] In Roman riding, a rider typically stands atop a pair of side-by-side moving horses, with one foot on each horse's back. To see a video that includes Roman-riding and related teaming and jumping feats, visit **www.youtube.com/watch?v=YXpxpKTnUr8**.

[116] To see a picture of the Spanish Riding School's arena, visit **en.wikipedia.org/wiki/File:Spanische_Hofreitschule3,_Vienna.jpg**.

[117] Much of the author's inspiration for the horse part of the animal show came from the amazing Cavalia touring show. To learn more, visit **www.cavalia.net**.

[118] The quotation on the Steed of Faith sculpture appears on page 5 of *The Seven Valleys and the Four Valleys*.

Chapter 25

[119] In a letter quoted in item 75, page 30, of *A Compilation on Bahá'í Education*, 'Abdu'l-Bahá wrote of children that: "From the age of five their formal education must begin. That is, during the daytime they should be looked after in a place where there are teachers, and should learn good conduct."

[120] In selection 110, page 135, of *Selections from the Writings of*

'Abdu'l-Bahá, he says of schoolchildren that: "If possible the children should all wear the same kind of clothing, even if the fabric is varied. It is preferable that the fabric as well should be uniform; if, however, this is not possible, there is no harm done. The more cleanly the pupils are, the better; they should be immaculate." You can read the whole selection at **reference.bahai.org/en/t/ab/SAB/sab-111.html**.

[121]   Abby is remembering the first Beatitude that Christ revealed. In the New Testament, Luke 6:20, it reads: "Blessed are you who are poor, for yours is the kingdom of God."

[122]   Petra is quoting from selection 138 on page 159 of *Selections from the Writings of 'Abdu'l-Bahá*. You can read the whole selection at **reference.bahai.org/en/t/ab/SAB/sab-139.html**.

[123]   In *The Concept of Spirituality*, page 16, William S. Hatcher says: "Abdu'l-Bahá often responded to Bahá'ís who felt overwhelmed by the task of refining their character by stressing the necessity of patience and daily striving. 'Be patient, be as I am,' He would say. Spirituality was to be won 'little by little; day by day.'"

[124]   Petra is quoting from a verse on page 21 of *The Hidden Words of Bahá'u'lláh*, specifically Arabic #71: "O Son Of Man! Write all that We have revealed unto thee with the ink of light upon the tablet of thy spirit. Should this not be in thy power, then make thine ink of the essence of thy heart. If this thou canst not do, then write with that crimson ink that hath been shed in My path. Sweeter indeed is this to Me than all else, that its light may endure for ever."

[125]   TerraCycle was featured in the National Geographic Channel program "Garbage Moguls" for making useful products from discarded "trash" such as newspapers, cereal boxes, and cookie wrappers. Visit **channel.nationalgeographic.com/episode/garbage-moguls-4314** to view videos. Also, according to a news article – "Richlite now green, growing" – at **www.thenewstribune.com/voelpel/story/739980.html**, two Richlite products are made from 100% recycled paper, and the company has also developed a way to recycle/reuse production heat. Visit **www.richlite.com** to see paper-based products from cutting boards and countertops to skateboard ramps and industrial panels.

[126]   In Esperanto, "instrui" means *to teach*; the students are using the root "instru" as a loving honorific, as in "Good morning, Teach!" "Ĝentilajo" means *courtesy*; and since using "aj" indicates a concrete example of an abstract idea, calling Ms. Reed "Ĝentilajo" in this case indicates that the students consider her the embodiment of courtesy.

[127]   The teacher is referring to the Lawh-i-Dunyá (Tablet of the World) in *Tablets of Bahá'u'lláh Revealed After the Kitáb-i-Aqdas*. The passage, on page 88, reads: "O people of God! I admonish you to observe

courtesy, for above all else it is the prince of virtues. Well is it with him who is illumined with the light of courtesy and is attired with the vesture of uprightness. Whoso is endued with courtesy hath indeed attained a sublime station." He then expresses the hope that *everyone*: "…may be enabled to acquire it, hold fast unto it, observe it, and fix our gaze upon it."

Chapter 26

[128]   Petra is quoting from selection 72, page 110, of *Selections from the Writings of 'Abdu'l-Bahá.*

Chapter 27

[129]   The song Melissa is singing – "The Remover of Difficulties" – is a prayer by the Báb; it appears on page 226 of *Bahá'í Prayers.*

[130]   Melissa and Jon are singing a short healing prayer revealed by Bahá'u'lláh; it appears on page 96 of *Bahá'í Prayers.*

[131]   Abby is paraphrasing an array of quotations from the works of Friedrich Wilhelm Nietzsche. Various versions include: "What does not kill me, makes me stronger." "What does not destroy me, makes me stronger." "That which does not kill us makes us stronger." "He turns all of his injuries into strengths, that which does not kill him makes him stronger." Coincidentally, Nietzsche was born in the year that the Bahá'í Era began: 1844.

[132]   Visit **www.kidshealth.org/kid/talk/qa/coma.html** to learn about comas.

[133]   Visit **en.wikipedia.org/wiki/Near-death_experience** to learn about the experiences of people who have been very close to death or briefly clinically dead.

[134]   Visit   **http://www.vancouverbahai.org/fireside/Lyrics.html**, scroll down to the song title "Toko Zani," and click on **Vancouver Recording** to hear this song in Zulu and English. Melissa's rendition of the Zulu is shown in single syllables because various websites group the syllables into words differently. The songwriter is listed variously as Benjamin Diamini and Benjamin Dlamini.

[135]   Melissa is quoting a statement by Lucki Melander Wilder from a preview copy of her 2008 book entitled *The Three Onenesses and the Foundational Verities.*

Chapter 28

[136]   Melissa is referring to parts of section 15, starting on page 29, of *Selections from the Writings of 'Abdu'l-Bahá*, where he says: "Thou didst begin thy letter with a blessed phrase, saying: 'I am a Christian.' O would that all were truly Christian! It is easy to be a Christian on the tongue, but hard to be a true one. Today some five hundred million souls are Christian, but the real Christian is very rare: he is that soul from whose comely face there shineth the splendour of Christ, and who showeth forth the perfections of the Kingdom; this is a matter of great moment, for to be a Christian is to embody every excellence there is. I hope that thou, too, shalt become a true Christian." And later in the same letter, he says: "O honoured lady! For a single purpose were the Prophets, each and all, sent down to earth; for this was Christ made manifest, for this did Bahá'u'lláh raise up the call of the Lord: that the world of man should become the world of God, this nether realm the Kingdom, this darkness light, this satanic wickedness all the virtues of heaven—and unity, fellowship and love be won for the whole human race, that the organic unity should reappear and the bases of discord be destroyed and life everlasting and grace everlasting become the harvest of mankind." You can read the whole selection at **reference.bahai.org/en/t/ab/SAB/sab-16.html**.

[137] *One in All* is a wonderful book illustrating the oneness of religion. It offers quotes from the world's major religious traditions on nine topics related to one's preparation, path, and goal: the search for knowledge and truth, purification and sincerity, non-attachment, love and charity, humility and devotion, renunciation and surrender, enlightenment and new life, the one-in-all concept, and identification.

[138] In a letter dated March 11, 1936 and included in *The World Order of Bahá'u'lláh*, page 203, Shoghi Effendi states: "A mechanism of world inter-communication will be devised, embracing the whole planet, freed from national hindrances and restrictions, and functioning with marvelous swiftness and perfect regularity." The internet is on the road to achieving these goals.

[139] In the statement Melissa and her mother read, on page 215 of *Some Answered Questions*, 'Abdu'l-Bahá says: "In creation there is no evil; all is good. Certain qualities and natures innate in some men and apparently blameworthy are not so in reality. For example, from the beginning of his life you can see in a nursing child the signs of greed, of anger and of temper. Then, it may be said, good and evil are innate in the reality of man, and this is contrary to the pure goodness of nature and creation. The answer to this is that greed, which is to ask for something more, is a praiseworthy quality provided that it is used suitably. So if a man is greedy to acquire science and knowledge, or to become compassionate, generous and just, it is most praiseworthy. If he exercises his anger and wrath against the bloodthirsty tyrants who are like ferocious beasts, it is very praiseworthy; but if he does not use these qualities in a right way, they are blameworthy."

[140] Melissa is paraphrasing one of Bahá'u'lláh's teachings, quoted

on page 6 of *Consultation: A Universal Lamp of Guidance*, exhorting the Bahá'ís to: "Take ye counsel together in all matters, inasmuch as consultation is the lamp of guidance which leadeth the way, and is the bestower of understanding."

[141] Melissa has given Abby *A Selection of Bahá'í Prayers and Holy Writings* and the preview copy of *The Three Onenesses and the Foundational Verities* that she'd finished reading. Next, she's handed Abby three handouts from a free series that is, at the author's behest, being made available by Earthstar Works. Finally, she's given Abby *Paris Talks*, which is the first Bahá'í book that the author ever read.

[142] In paragraph 149, pages 73–74, of *The Kitáb-i-Aqdas*, Bahá'u'lláh says: "Pride not yourselves on much reading of the verses or on a multitude of pious acts by night and day; for were a man to read a single verse with joy and radiance it would be better for him than to read with lassitude all the Holy Books of God, the Help in Peril, the Self-Subsisting. Read ye the sacred verses in such measure that ye be not overcome by languor and despondency. Lay not upon your souls that which will weary them and weigh them down, but rather what will lighten and uplift them, so that they may soar on the wings of the Divine verses towards the Dawning-place of His manifest signs; this will draw you nearer to God, did ye but comprehend." And in selection 214, pages 268–269, of *Selections from the Writings of 'Abdu'l-Bahá*, the Master says: "Follow thou the way of thy Lord, and say not that which the ears cannot bear to hear, for such speech is like luscious food given to small children. However palatable, rare and rich the food may be, it cannot be assimilated by the digestive organs of a suckling child. Therefore unto every one who hath a right, let his settled measure be given."

[143] This is part of the Tablet of Ahmad that Mr. Aghsani chanted and the Yuter translated at the deepening in Lodlan.

Chapter 29
[144] A letter dated April 14, 1949 and written on behalf of Shoghi Effendi explains that: "...there is absolutely nothing keeping those who have broken the Covenant, whether Bahá'u'lláh's or the Master's, out of the Cause of God except their own inner spiritually sick condition...Unfortunately a man who is ill is not made well just by asserting there is nothing wrong with him! Facts, actual states, are what count. Probably no group of people in the world have softer tongues, or proclaim more loudly their innocence, then those who in their heart of hearts, and by their every act, are enemies of the Center of the Covenant. The Master well knew this, and that is why He said we must shun their company, but pray for them. If you put a leper in a room with healthy people, he

cannot catch their health; on the contrary they are very likely to catch his horrible ailment." This excerpt, item 618, appears on page 188 of the compilation *Lights of Guidance*.

[145]   The author especially likes the quote on page 209 of *A General Theory of Love*: "Happiness is within range only for adroit people who give the slip to America's values. These rebels will necessarily forgo exalted titles, glamorous friends, exotic vacations, washboard abs, designer everything – all the proud indicators of upward mobility – and in exchange, they may just get a chance at a decent life."

[146]   In paragraphs 122–125, pages 63–64, of *The Kitáb-i-Aqdas*, Bahá'u'lláh says:

> Consider the pettiness of men's minds. They ask for that which injureth them, and cast away the thing that profiteth them. They are, indeed, of those that are far astray. We find some men desiring liberty, and priding themselves therein. Such men are in the depths of ignorance.
>
> Liberty must, in the end, lead to sedition, whose flames none can quench. Thus warneth you He Who is the Reckoner, the All-Knowing. Know ye that the embodiment of liberty and its symbol is the animal. That which beseemeth man is submission unto such restraints as will protect him from his own ignorance, and guard him against the harm of the mischief-maker. Liberty causeth man to overstep the bounds of propriety, and to infringe on the dignity of his station. It debaseth him to the level of extreme depravity and wickedness.
>
> Regard men as a flock of sheep that need a shepherd for their protection. This, verily, is the truth, the certain truth. We approve of liberty in certain circumstances, and refuse to sanction it in others. We, verily, are the All-Knowing.
>
> Say: True liberty consisteth in man's submission unto My commandments, little as ye know it. Were men to observe that which We have sent down unto them from the Heaven of Revelation, they would, of a certainty, attain unto perfect liberty. Happy is the man that hath apprehended the Purpose of God in whatever He hath revealed from the Heaven of His Will that pervadeth all created things. Say: The liberty that profiteth you is to be found nowhere except in complete servitude unto God, the Eternal Truth. Whoso hath tasted of its sweetness will refuse to barter it for all the dominion of earth and heaven.

Chapter 30

[147]   To read the April 2002 Letter to the Worlds Religious Leaders,

visit **bahai-library.org/file=uhj_religious_leaders_2002**.

[148]   For all the lyrics of this song based on 'Abdu'l-Bahá's words, visit   **dayspring-magazine.org.uk/education/classes/index01.htm**, scroll down to Lesson 16, and click on **Song**.

[149]   Visit **www.wku.edu/~smithch/MALVINA/mr101.htm** for all the lyrics of this song by Malvina Reynolds.

[150]   The children are singing a prayer by 'Abdu'l-Bahá; it appears on page 28 of *Bahá'í Prayers*.

[151]   For all the lyrics – as well as the melody – of this song, visit **www.bahaisingingproject.com/the-fakebooks**, click on **Volume 1**, use the SEARCH term **teach thy** to find the match, then click the down arrow.

[152]   Tim is referring to *Arising To Serve*, Book 2 in the Ruhi Institute series.

[153]   LaKeesha uses *Teaching Children's Classes: Grade 1*, Book 3 in the Ruhi Institute series, as her guide in teaching children's classes. The "staying connected to God" drawing activity is not from the book; the author made it up and effectively used it in teaching children.

[154]   The child's drawing refers to a passage on page 34, in the Tablet of Tarazát (Ornaments), of *Tablets of Bahá'u'lláh Revealed After the Kitáb-i-Aqdas*: "O my Lord! Thou beholdest them clinging to the rope of Thy grace and holding fast unto the hem of the mantle of Thy beneficence. Ordain for them that which may draw them nearer unto Thee, and withhold them from all else save Thee."

Author's Notes

[155]   *Proper Pronunciation of Arabic* – dated 1995-08-08, prepared by the Research Department of the Universal House of Justice, and posted at **bahai-library.org/file.php?file=uhj_pronunciation_arabic** – ends with the statement: "Bahá'ís who are neither Arabs nor Persians have generally picked up a pronunciation similar to that of the Persians because they have learned it from Persian Bahá'ís, but there is no constraint on them to follow this pattern if they are familiar with Arabic and wish to pronounce Arabic words in the Arabic manner. This could, however, present them with some practical difficulties unless they are in an Arab country. If, for example, when in America, [he] pronounces 'Ridvan' in the Arabic manner, it may puzzle those who will hear the majority of their fellow Bahá'ís, Persian and American, using the Persian pronunciation or an approximation to it."

Resources

Online

- *Bahá'í Faith:* Visit the Bahá'í World Centre's website – in English, with links to French, Spanish, Portuguese, Chinese, Persian, and Arabic pages – at **www.bahai.org** for links to contact information for your country and for Bahá'í publishers. Every country in the world has Bahá'ís, and most are listed. Also look in your local white pages to see if there's a listing for **Bahá'í** (Faith or Center) near you.

- *Bahá'í Writings:* Many books of Bahá'í Scripture, exposition, and research are freely available online. Some very good resources are the *Bahá'í Reference Library* at **reference.bahai.org**, the *Bahá'í Library Online* at **bahai-library.org** and, finally, the downloadable – but not necessarily proofread or with the most up-to-date editions – *Ocean Library of World Religions* at **www.bahai-education.org/ocean**.

- *The Bible:* Visit **www.mechon-mamre.org/p/pt/pt0.htm** for the 1917 Jewish Publication Society version of the Bible of Judaism. Visit **www.drbo.org/** for the 1582/1609 Douay-Rheims version of the Catholic branch of Christianity. Visit **www.kingjamesbibleonline.org/** for the 1611 King James version of the Protestant branch of Christianity.

- *Cavalia:* This homage to the poignant history and fascinating bond between humans and horses blends dramatic visual effects, live music, dance, and acrobatics with the bold presence of magnificent horses. Learn more about it at **www.cavalia.net**.

- *Cricket Magazine Group:* Starting with *Cricket Magazine*, Carus Publishing (Peterborough, NH; 800-821-0115) expanded to fourteen children's magazines serving children ranging from toddlers to teens. Interestingly, as a child ages, their subscription can be changed from one magazine to another at no extra cost. Learn more about them at **www.CricketMag.com/shop_magzines.asp**.

- *Daisy Kingdom:* There is no website for Daisy Kingdom. The brand name and designs are now owned by the Springs Creative Products Group (Rock Hill, SC), which has a useful Fabric Dictionary posted at **www.SpringsCreative.com/site/fabric-dictionary**. To find websites with examples of patterns, though, enter the term **daisy kingdom patterns** into a search engine such as Google.

- *Earthstar Works:* From its humble beginnings as a bricks-and-mortar purveyor of eco-assemblage art and, later, chapbooks to select audiences, Earthstar Works (Chicago, IL) is expanding to the web. Learn more about their art and craft pieces, chapbooks and plays, greeting-card designs, artist/aficionado links, and various online goodies at

www.EarthstarWorks.com.

- *Harry Potter:* Visit **en.wikipedia.org/wiki/Harry_Potter** to learn about the series. The official Harry Potter publication site in the US is **www.scholastic.com/harrypotter**; it contains videos, games, discussions, downloads, and more. The official *HP* movie site in the US is **harrypotter.warnerbros.com**; it contains trailers, games, newsletters, downloads, and more.

- *Keepsake Quilting:* Learn more about fabrics, patterns, kits, and quilting aids by Keepsake Quilting (Center Harbor, NH; 800-865-9458) at **www.KeepsakeQuilting.com**.

- *National Geographic Society:* Learn more about the Society's magazines and TV channel at **wwwNationalGeographic.com**.

- *Natural Horsemanship:* Visit **www.parelli.com** to learn more about the Parelli Program of Natural Horsemanship (Pagosa Springs, CO; 800-642-3335). You can find many video clips on **www.youtube.com** using the SEARCH term **Parelli**. To find websites with information regarding other such programs, enter the term **natural horsemanship** into a search engine such as Google.

- *Reader's Digest Association:* Learn more about the Association at **phx.corporate-ir.net/phoenix.zhtml?c=71092&p=sitemap** and its flagship and other magazines at **www.rd.com**, where you can also sign up for free newsletters on topics such as do-it-yourself projects, health, humor, and simple solutions.

- *Ruhi Institute Resources:* Learn more about the Ruhi books and how they are used at **www.ruhiresources.org**.

- *Special Ideas:* Air fresheners to buttons, calendars to DVDs, flags to greeting cards, jewelry to mugs, postcards to stickers, T-shirts to who-knows-what and, of course, scads of books…inspiration is the name of the game for Special Ideas (Heltonville, IN; 800-326-1197). Learn more about them at **www.BahaiResources.com**.

- *The Trail of Painted Ponies:* Building on the concept of a public art project held in New Mexico, Trail of Painted Ponies (Carefree, AZ; 800-500-5779) produces collectible figurines – and many related items – celebrating the beauty and majesty of horses. Learn more about them at **www.TrailOfPaintedPonies.com**. One very cool thing about this site is that, when you clink on the DETAILS button of a figurine, you have the option to access a picture that you can rotate through a 360° circle to see the horse from all sides.

- *Western Saddle Guide:* Whether you're a novice or an experienced rider, **www.western-saddle-guide.com** has answers to just about every question you might ask about Western saddles.

Magazines

Monthly magazines usually hit the stands the month *before* their issue date. So Abby could read September-dated magazines in August.

- *Cowboys & Indians*: This is published monthly by USFR Media Group (Houston, TX; 800-982-5370). Learn more about this magazine at **www.CowboysIndians.com**.
- *Horse Illustrated*: This is published monthly by BowTie Magazines (Irvine, CA). Learn more about this and other horse magazines at **www.BowtieInc.com/BowtieInc/home.aspx** by clicking on **MAGA-ZINES** > PETS & ANIMALS > Horses.
- *Star of the West*: This was the first Bahá'í magazine published in the Western world; the first issue being March 1910. All 25 volumes are available on a single CD, $65.00, by phone from Special Ideas or by online credit-card system at **www.bahai-education.org/star**.

Books

Efforts have been made to use the American editions wherever possible.

- *'Abdu'l-Bahá – The Centre of the Covenant of Bahá'u'lláh* by H.M. Balyuzi. Published 1971 by George Ronald.
- *The Advent of Divine Justice* by Shoghi Effendi. Published 1969 by the Bahá'í Publishing Trust of the US.
- *American Heritage Dictionary of the English Language*, fourth edition. Published 2006 by Houghton Mifflin Company.
- *Arches of the Years* by Marzieh Gail. Published 1991 by George Ronald.
- *Bahá'í Prayers*. Published 2002 by the Bahá'í Publishing Trust of the US.
- *Bahá'í World Faith: Selected Writings of Bahá'u'lláh and 'Abdu'l-Bahá*. Published 1976 by the Bahá'í Publishing Trust of the US.
- *A Basic Bahá'í Dictionary* by Wendi Momen. Published 1989 by George Ronald.
- *The Book of Certitude*. See *The Kitáb-i-Íqán*.
- *The Chosen Highway* by Lady Blomfield. Published 1975 by the Bahá'í Publishing Trust of the US.
- *The Compilation of Compilations, 1963-1990, Volumes 1 and 2*. Prepared by the Universal House of Justice. Published 1991 by Bahá'í Publications Australia.
- *A Compilation on Bahá'í Education*. Published 1976 by the Bahá'í World Centre.
- *The Concept of Spirituality* by William S. Hatcher. Published 1987 by the Association for Bahá'í Studies, and now available online at **bahai-library.org/?file=hatcher_bw18_spirituality**.

- *Consultation: A Universal Lamp of Guidance* by John E. Kolstoe. Published 1985 by George Ronald.
- *Dawn Over Mount Hira and Other Essays* by Marzieh Gail. Published 1976 by George Ronald.
- *Developing Distinctive Bahá'í Communities: Guidelines for Spiritual Assemblies.* Published 1992 by the National Spiritual Assembly of the Bahá'ís of the United States.
- *The Diary of Juliet Thompson.* Published 1983 by Kalimat Press, and now available online at **bahai-library.org/books/thompson**.
- *Fire & Gold: Benefitting from Life's Tests* compiled by Brian Kurzius. Published 1995 by George Ronald.
- *Foundations of World Unity* by 'Abdu'l-Bahá. Published 1972 by the Bahá'í Publishing Trust of the US.
- *A General Theory of Love* by Thomas Lewis, Fari Amini, and Richard Lannon. Published 2001 by Vintage Books.
- *Gleanings from the Writings of Bahá'u'lláh.* Published 1990 by the Bahá'í Publishing Trust of the US.
- *God Passes By* by Shoghi Effendi. Published 1979 by the Bahá'í Publishing Trust of the US.
- *The Hidden Words of Bahá'u'lláh.* Published 1954 by the Bahá'í Publishing Trust of the US.
- *Horses for Dummies* by Audrey Pavia with Janice Posnikoff, DVM. Published 1999 by Hungry Minds, Inc.
- *The Kitáb-i-Aqdas (The Most Holy Book)* by Bahá'u'lláh. Published 1992 by the Bahá'í World Centre.
- *The Kitáb-i-Íqán (The Book of Certitude)* by Bahá'u'lláh. Published 1950 by the Bahá'í Publishing Trust of the US.
- *A Lifetime with 'Abdu'l-Bahá: Reminiscences of Khalíl Shahídí.* Originally published in hardcopy form, this volume is now available as a free e-book at **ahang.rabbani.GooglePages.com/42**.
- *Lights of Guidance* compiled by Helen Hornby. Published 1994 by the Bahá'í Publishing Trust of India.
- *Memories of 'Abdu'l-Bahá: Recollections of the Early Days of the Bahá'í Faith in California* by Ramona Allen Brown. Published 1980 by the Bahá'í Publishing Trust of the US.
- *The Most Holy Book.* See *The Kitáb-i-Aqdas*.
- *Native American Wisdom.* Published 1993 by Running Press.
- *One in All: An Anthology of Religion from the Sacred Scriptures of the Living Faiths* compiled by Edith B. Schnapper. Published 1952 by John Murray.
- *Paris Talks* by 'Abdu'l-Bahá. Published 1972 by the Bahá'í Publishing Trust of the UK.

- *The Priceless Pearl* by Rúhíyyih Rabbaní. Published 1969 by the Bahá'í Publishing Trust of the UK.
- *The Proclamation of Bahá'u'lláh*. Published 1967 by the Bahá'í World Centre.
- *The Promulgation of Universal Peace* compiled by Howard MacNutt. Published 1982 by the Bahá'í Publishing Trust of the US.
- *The Revelation of Bahá'u'lláh, Volumes 1, 2, 3, and 4* by Adib Taherzadeh. Published 1976, 1977, 1984, and 1987, respectively, by George Ronald.
- *The Secret of Divine Civilization* by 'Abdu'l-Bahá. Published 1990 by the Bahá'í Publishing Trust of the US.
- *A Selection of Bahá'í Prayers and Holy Writings*. Published 1985 by the Bahá'í Publishing Trust Committee of Malaysia.
- *Selections from the Writings of 'Abdu'l-Bahá*. Published 1978 by the Bahá'í World Centre.
- *The Seven Valleys and the Four Valleys* by Bahá'u'lláh. Published 1991 by the Bahá'í Publishing Trust of the US.
- *Some Answered Questions* by 'Abdu'l-Bahá. Published 1990 by the Bahá'í Publishing Trust of the US.
- *Stories of Bahá'u'lláh* compiled by 'Alí-Akbar Furútan. Published 1986 by George Ronald.
- *Tablets of 'Abdu'l-Bahá, Volumes 1, 2, and 3*. Published 1909, 1915, and 1916, respectively, by the Bahá'í Publishing Society.
- *Tablets of Bahá'u'lláh Revealed After the Kitáb-i-Aqdas*. Published 1988 by the Bahá'í Publishing Trust of the US.
- *Ten Days in the Light of 'Akká* by Julia M. Grundy. Published 1979 by the Bahá'í Publishing Trust of the US.
- *The Three Onenesses and the Foundational Verities* by Lucki Melander Wilder, Published 2008 by Earthstar Works.
- *The World Order of Bahá'u'lláh: Selected Letters* by Shoghi Effendi. Published 1991 by the Bahá'í Publishing Trust of the US.
- *Zen Cowboy* by Michael W. Domis; illustrated by Richard A. Goldberg. Published 2005 by Peter Pauper Press.

Counted Cross-Stitch Patterns

Below are the charts and instructions for you to stitch the patterns I designed. I start with the easier "No Hate" chart. Once you learn with that, you should be ready to stitch the "World Peace" chart.

Look at each chart and read its instructions *completely* before beginning. See the book cover for examples of finished pieces.

Each chart may be easiest to work with if you photocopy or scan/print it from this book, so you can highlight completed stitching as you go, to mark your place and progress. **You have my permission to copy it** *for your own use only.* **You do** *not* **have my permission to copy it for or email it to anyone else, post it online, or sell the needlework you make from it.**

Supplies:

- Charts
- Scissors
- Floss:
  - No Hate – **Black** such as DMC 310 (adding Kreinik 005HL if a metallic sheen is desired); **Red** such as DMC 666 (adding Kreinik 003HL if a metallic sheen is desired).
  - World Peace – **Gold** such as DMC 972; **Green** such as DMC 910; maybe **Light Blue** such as DMC 809. (For a shaded look, use variegated thread – died darker and lighter in one skein – such as "Brandy" gold, "Blue Jay" blue, and "Spring Grass" green. See the photo on the book cover for this variation.)

- Two 6-inch squares of 14-count Aida fabric
- Tapestry (blunt) needle, size 24 or 26
- Highlighter to mark completed steps/squares

To begin:

1. **Look at the fabric.** See the regularly spaced holes? They divide the fabric into little squares with holes at the four corners of each square, so the needle can easily go through the fabric.

   There is no space between the squares; for example, the holes at the bottom corners of one square are also the holes at the top corners of the square below it.

   The squares in the fabric correspond to the squares on the chart. You stitch an **X** on the fabric to correspond with each symbol on the chart. Each symbol tells you what color to make that **X**. I use the symbols "**M**" and "**O**" and "**—**" as they are easy to tell apart.

2. **Decide which side of the fabric is the topside** and which is the underside. Put a piece of tape, a sticker, or small safety pin in the upper left corner of the topside, so you always know which way the fabric and the design should be facing.

3. **Find the center of the fabric.** Fold the fabric in half vertically and pinch it with your fingers to make a small crease. Open the fabric. Fold it in half horizontally and make another crease. Open the fabric again. The two creases cross at the center of the fabric.

Note: If you have a bigger than 6" x 6" piece of fabric and want to position the design elsewhere than in the center to conserve fabric or for artistic reasons, **use a ruler and your basic math skills** to ensure your crossed creases allow enough space to complete the design in all directions.

4. **Look at the chart.** The design is 27 x 27 squares. See the five black squares? They indicate the horizontal center line, the vertical center line, and the exact center of the pattern. Use these indicators to help keep track of where you are and to center the design on the piece of fabric.

5. **Find the center square of the chart.** It is the black square with the white symbol in it. The center-square symbol indicates which color thread to start with. In the "No Hate" chart, the first color is Red; in the "World Peace" chart, it is Gold.

6. **Measure and cut a cord of floss.** Plain embroidery floss comes in 6-strand cords, usually organized into skeins. Holding the skein in one hand, find a cut end of the cord and unwrap or pull it with the other hand until it reaches your elbow, then cut it. You now have a cord about 12 to 16 inches long.

Note: Always **leave the paper bands** on skeins to keep them tidy and document their exact brand name, color name, and color code.

7. **Separate the cord into strands.** You can't just peel the strands apart; they will snarl and maybe break. Instead, grab the cord in one hand, with 2 inches sticking out the top of your fist. With the other hand, carefully pick out the end of one strand and slowly but firmly pull it straight up. The downward-hanging cord will coil up against the bottom of your fist, but should uncoil after you pull the strand completely out. Repeat this step twice more, until you have three strands pulled out. (You also have three unseparated strands left in your fist, which constitutes one usable plain thread.)

Note: If you plan to **add metallic highlighting** (which comes in single strands), you only need two separated plain strands.

8. **Thread the needle.** Take three plain strands (or two plain and one metallic strand), group them into a 3-strand thread, and thread the needle with them. Pull the thread so you have about 2 inches of thread on one side of the needle hole and all the rest on the other side. Don't tie a knot at the end of the thread.

   Note: Whenever the needle runs out of thread, **rethread the needle** using the strands you have already separated, or by cutting and separating more cord.

9. **Look at the center of the chart.** In the "No Hate" pattern, it is the black square in the middle of the diagonal Red line; in the "World Peace" pattern, it is the black square in the middle of the vertical Gold line. This square shows where to start stitching.

10. **Start stitching the first (center) X.** Hold the fabric so your topside marker is in the upper left corner. Poke the threaded needle up from the underside through the hole closest to where the center-creases cross, and then pull it through on the topside. This is now the upper left corner of the first square.

    Note: **Leave a 1-inch start-tail** of thread on the underside of the fabric, and keep holding it there with a finger so you don't accidentally pull the thread all the way through the fabric.

11. **To continue the X**, use the needle tip to find the bottom right hole of the square you started, poke the needle down into the hole from the topside, then pull the needle and thread through on the underside. The first topside stitch now looks like a back-slash (\).

    Note: Be sure to **pinch the thread** on both sides of the needle's eye when pulling the needle, so it doesn't unthread.

12. **To finish the X,** poke the needle up through the top right hole from the underside, then push it down through the bottom left hole. The second topside stitch now looks like a forward-slash (*/*) lying across the back-slash, so that the two stitches form the **X**.

    Note: **Pull the thread** just hard enough so that each stitch on both the topside and the underside lies right against the fabric, but not so hard the fabric puckers.

13. **Anchor the start-tail on the underside.** As you make the next several stitches, use them to encircle the 1-inch start-tail on the underside of the fabric, so that it is anchored firmly in place by underside stitches along its length. You can clip off any extra start-

tail after anchoring it with half a dozen stitches.

Note: Do not try to run the needle *through* the start-tail; just make the underside stitches **lie *across* the start-tail**.

14. **Count the squares on the chart and on the fabric** to see where the next stitches go. In the "No Hate" pattern, the second **X** is one square right and one square down; in the "World Peace" pattern, the second **X** is one square up.

Refer to the individual charts for design-specific instructions.

Note: You will do lots and *lots* of counting, recounting, and counting again to ensure you **follow the pattern**. That's why it's called *counted* cross-stitch. The effort is well repaid, though, when you see your finished result. And people who like counted cross-stitch even find the counting soothing, like chanting or auto-hypnotism.

15. **For every X you make,** do the back-slash stitch (upper left to lower right) first and the forward-slash stitch (upper right to lower left) second. That way, every **X** looks exactly the same, which makes your work look neater and more polished.

Note: If you accidentally start an X in the same hole where you ended the previous X, it will make the previous X come partially undone. However, doing so intentionally is a handy way to **undo a mistake**, undoing stitches as far back as you need to. Another way to undo stitches is to slide the needle off the thread, use the eye-end to carefully lift out incorrect stitches without shredding the floss, then rethread the needle and continue correctly.

16. **When only two needle-lengths of thread remain on the needle,** slide the needle back under the last half a dozen stitches on the underside, then pull the needle off the thread. This anchors the end-tail of thread without tying a knot, which would make a lump on the finished piece. Cut off any extra end-tail after anchoring it.

17. **Plan your stitching route carefully.** Stitch as far as possible with one thread. However, if the thread *must* travel along the underside across more than four empty squares on the chart, despite careful planning, you need to end and anchor it (just as if only two needle-lengths of thread remained on the needle), because any long loose threads can catch on things and even show through to the topside.

Note: To **backtrack past completed stitches** to another part of the pattern, slide the needle under the completed stitches on the underside until you reach the place to start stitching again. When you restart to stitch, do not to pull so hard that the fabric puckers.

18. **Once you have finished the stitching,** you may cut the fabric to form a long narrow bookmark, a round patch, a square or rectangle suitable for framing, etc. Be sure to leave enough fabric for your choice of finish.

19. **To finish off the fabric** after the design is done, so that the edges of the fabric do not unravel, you have several options. You can:

    a. Invisibly hem the edges with thread the same color as the fabric.
    b. Decoratively hem the edges using one of the colors in the pattern.
    c. Invisibly glue the edges on the underside of the fabric, using a plain (preferably waterproof) glue or an iron-on hemming tape.
    d. Decoratively seal the edges of the topside with puffy paint.

How to get really good:

Like everything in life, getting good takes practice. Don't be hard on yourself if your first pieces don't look quite as smooth as you wish. Congratulate yourself for doing as well as you did.

And if you liked it, do more. You'll get better with more trying.

I encourage beginners to stick to small projects that have only a few colors. Keep your projects manageable. Don't pick a big or complex project, find it too hard, get discouraged, and quit. Build your successes and feelings of accomplishment by setting goals you can meet.

"No Hate" Chart

27x27 design, 29x29 chart, and instructions © 2010 Lisa Bradley

M = Red: Stitch one **X** with red embroidery floss DMC 666 or a similar color. For metallic sheen, add Kreinik 003HL.

O = Black: Stitch one **X** with black embroidery floss DMC 310 or a similar color. For metallic sheen, add Kreinik 005HL.

"No Hate" Instructions

Having done the first Red **X** at the center:

1. Stitch the Red diagonal line downwards into the circle (9 more stitches), anchoring the start-tail.

2. Stitch the Red circle all the way around.

3. Backtrack under your original diagonal stitches to reach the unfinished part of the diagonal line, then continue to stitch downwards until the diagonal line is completed.

4. Anchor the end-tail under several Red stitches, then cut the thread.

Having finished the Red stitching (congratulations!), thread the needle with Black and, being careful to skip *under* each Red **X** that crosses a Black line:

5. Start at the bottom left corner of the Black letter **H** and stitch upwards to the top left corner (13 stitches), anchoring the start-tail.

6. Backtrack under your latest stitches to reach the crossbar, then stitch the crossbar and the top right leg of the **H**.

7. Backtrack under your latest stitches to reach the unfinished leg of the **H**, then stitch downwards until the **H** is completed.

8. On the underside, lay the thread across one empty square to the right and, at the second square, begin stitching upwards to complete the left side of the **A**.

9. Stitch across the top of the **A,** down the top right leg to the crossbar, and across the crossbar.

10. Backtrack under the crossbar to reach the unfinished leg of the **A**, then stitch downwards until the **A** is completed.

11. On the underside, lay the thread across three empty squares and, at the fourth square, begin stitching upwards to complete the upright of the **T**.

12. Stitch the top left arm of the **T**.

13. Backtrack to the upright, and stitch the top right arm of the **T**.

14. On the underside, lay the thread across one empty square and, at the second square, stitch the top arm of the **E**.

15. Backtrack under the top arm to reach the left side of the **E**, stitch down the top left leg to the crossbar, then stitch the crossbar.

16. Backtrack under the crossbar to reach the unfinished leg of the **E**,

then stitch down the leg and across the bottom arm until the **E** is completed.

17. Anchor the end-tail under several Black stitches, then cut the thread.

Congratulations with thunderous applause...especially if this is your first-ever piece of counted cross-stitch!

"Out and Back" Technique:
Now that you've completed one piece, let me describe the "out and back" technique: a way to work from the beginning to the end and then back to the beginning of a row (and, once you get good at it, a column or even a diagonal line) of stitches. It is an alternative to backtracking, uses less thread, and demands greater concentration.

As an example, let's say you're starting the top arm of the **E**. Instead of completing five **X** stitches starting at the left side of the **E** and going all the way across, then backtracking on the underside, try this:

1. Make a rightward running line of five back-slashes (\\\\\\), with each back-slash (after the first) starting in the hole directly above the hole where the previous back-slash ended.
2. At the end of the row, go to the hole directly above the hole where the final back-slash ended and start a leftward running line of five forward-slashes (/////) lying across the back-slashes, so that the ten slashes form **XXXXX**.
3. You are now back where you started and ready to continue down the left side of the **E**.

However, trying to start the next **X** in the usual manner would, in this example, simply undo your latest stitch. (This is not always true, but it occasionally is, and you need to watch out for it.) On the next row down, in such a case, make your first back-slash from the bottom right corner of the square to the top left corner. Then continue to make the rest of your slash-stitches as usual.

"World Peace" Chart

									M	M	M	M	M	M	M	M	M	M										
						M	M	-	-	-	-	-	M	-	-	-	-	O	M	M								
					M	O	-	-	-	-	-	-	M	-	-	-	-	O	O	O	M							
				M	O	-	-	-	-	-	-	-	M	-	-	O	O	O	O	O	M							
			M	O	O	-	-	-	-	-	-	-	M	-	O	O	O	-	-	O	O	M						
		M	O	O	O	-	-	-	-	-	-	-	M	-	O	O	O	-	-	-	-	-	M					
	M	O	O	O	O	O	-	-	-	-	-	-	M	-	-	-	-	-	-	O	O	O	O	O	M			
M	O	O	O	O	O	O	-	-	-	-	-	-	M	-	-	-	O	O	O	O	O	O	O	O	M			
M	O	O	O	-	-	-	O	-	-	-	-	-	M	-	-	O	O	O	O	O	O	O	O	O	M			
M	-	-	-	O	O	-	-	-	-	-	-	-	M	-	O	O	O	O	O	O	O	O	O	O	O	M		
M	-	-	-	-	O	O	-	-	-	-	-	-	M	-	O	O	O	O	O	O	O	O	O	O	O	M		
M	-	-	-	-	O	-	-	-	-	-	-	-	M	-	O	O	O	O	O	O	O	O	O	O	M			
M	-	-	-	-	-	O	-	-	-	-	-	-	M	-	O	O	O	O	O	O	O	O	O	O	M			
M	-	-	-	-	-	O	O	O	-	-	-	-	M	-	-	-	-	O	O	O	O	O	O	O	O	M		
M	-	-	-	-	O	O	O	O	O	-	-	-	M	M	M	-	-	-	-	O	O	O	O	O	M			
M	-	-	O	O	O	O	O	O	O	O	M	-	M	-	M	-	-	-	-	O	O	O	O	M				
M	-	O	O	O	O	O	O	O	O	M	-	-	M	-	-	M	-	-	-	O	O	O	O	M				
M	-	O	O	O	O	O	O	O	M	O	-	-	M	-	-	-	M	-	-	-	O	O	O	M				
M	O	O	O	O	O	O	M	O	-	-	-	-	M	-	-	-	-	M	-	-	O	O	M					
M	-	O	O	O	O	M	O	-	-	-	-	M	-	-	-	-	M	-	-	O	O	M						
M	-	O	O	M	O	-	-	-	-	M	-	-	-	-	-	M	-	-	O	M								
M	-	M	O	O	-	-	-	-	M	-	-	-	-	-	M	-	M											
M	-	O	O	-	-	-	-	M	-	-	-	-	-	-	-	M												
M	-	O	-	-	-	-	M	-	-	-	-	-	-	M														
M	-	O	-	-	-	-	M	-	-	-	-	-	M															
M	M	-	-	-	-	M	-	-	-	-	M	M																
								M	M	M	M	M	M	M	M	M	M											

27x27 design, 29x29 chart, and instructions © 2010 Lisa Bradley

M = Gold: Stitch one **X** with gold embroidery floss DMC 972 or a similar color.

O = Green: Stitch one **X** with black embroidery floss DMC 910 or a similar color.

— = option: You have two options:

- **— = blank**
  Leave the oceans the color of the fabric; do not stitch any square containing this symbol.

- **— = Light Blue**
  Stitch one **X** with Light Blue embroidery floss DMC 809 or a similar color. (Don't use blue and green of the same intensity; they'll blend visually.)

"World Peace" Instructions

Having done the first Gold **X** at the center – and feeling free to (a) use the "out and back" technique wherever you see "backtrack" and (b) start your stitches at the "wrong" end of the slash if necessary to keep from undoing stitches, as long as you do the back-slash first and the forward-slash second:

1. Stitch the Gold vertical line upwards into the circle (13 more stitches), anchoring the start-tail.

2. Stitch the Gold circle all the way around.

3. Anchor the end-tail and cut the thread.

4. Find the first Gold **X** you stitched (at the center), move the needle one square right and one square down, and stitch the next Gold **X** in the right diagonal line.

5. Continue stitching diagonally, anchoring the start-tail, until you meet the circle.

6. Slide the needle under the 8 stitches forming the bottom right arc of the circle and, when you reach the exact center of the circle bottom, stitch upwards to complete the vertical line.

7. Stitch the left diagonal line to exactly mirror the existing right diagonal line.

8. Anchor the end tail under several Gold stitches, then cut the thread.

Having finished the Gold stitching, thread the needle with Green and, being careful to skip *under* each Gold **X** that crosses South America:

9. In the left half of the circle, and using your circle as a guide, stitch the lone Green **X** at the top, or row 1, of North America.

10. Move the needle one square left and one square down, and stitch the Green **X** in row 2 of North America, starting to anchor the start-tail.

11. Move the needle one square down, and stitch row 3 (2 stitches) from right to left, continuing to anchor the start-tail.

12. Move the needle one square left and one square down, and stitch row 4 from left to right, anchoring the remainder of the start-tail.

13. Work downwards one horizontal row at a time through the lone Green **X** in row 24, being sure that you skip the two empty squares separating Florida from Texas and that South America touches the Gold circle in only two places.

14. Anchor the end-tail under several Green stitches, then cut the thread. You have completed the Western Hemisphere continents.

15. In the right half of the circle, and again using your circle as a guide, stitch the lone Green **X** at the top, or row 1, of Europe.

16. Move the needle two squares left and one square down, and stitch row 2 (3 stitches) of Europe from right to left, starting to anchor the start-tail.

17. Stitch row 3 from left to right, anchoring the remainder of the start-tail.

18. Work downwards one horizontal row at a time through the lone Green **X** in row 21, being sure that you skip the two empty squares separating Italy and Spain.

19. Anchor the end-tail under several Green stitches, then cut the thread. You have completed the Eastern Hemisphere continents.

If you've decided to leave the oceans blank, you're done! Congrats!

However, if you want to stitch the oceans, thread the needle with Light Blue and:

20. On the left side of the circle, start stitching at the top of the Pacific Ocean where it meets the west coast of North America, moving down the rows in alternate directions. Do not cross over into the Atlantic Ocean at Central America. Be sure to include the narrow Pacific Ocean coastline of South America.

21. After you complete the last stitch of the Pacific Ocean, next to the southern tip of South America, move the needle two squares right and one square down and start stitching the bottom of the Atlantic Ocean, moving up the rows in alternate directions. Be careful to skip *under* each Gold **X** that crosses the Atlantic Ocean.

22. When you reach the southern tip of Europe, treat the Mediterranean Sea as part of the Atlantic Ocean rows, being careful to skip *under* each Green **X** in Spain.

23. When you complete the top row of the Atlantic Ocean, anchor the end-tail under several Light Blue stitches, then cut the thread.

24. Make sure there are now no empty squares within the circle. (If there are, go back and fill them in, being sure to use the right color and to anchor the start-tail and the end-tail.)

Now you are really and truly finished. Good work!

CPSIA information can be obtained
at www.ICGtesting.com
Printed in the USA
LVHW031136080919
630308LV00002B/173/P